W9-BBV-047

Outside There,

Somewhere—!

*
*
*

Outside There,

*

A NOVEL BY LUCILLE KALLEN

*

Somewhere—!

THE MACMILLAN COMPANY, NEW YORK

CARL A. RUDISILL LIBRARY
LENOIR RHYNE COLLEGE

813.54
K120

Copyright © Lucille Kallen 1964. All rights reserved. No part of this book may be reproduced or utilized in any form or by any means, electronic or mechanical, including photocopying, recording or by any information storage and retrieval system, without permission in writing from the Publisher. First Printing. The Macmillan Company, New York. Collier-Macmillan Canada Ltd., Toronto, Ontario. Library of Congress catalog card number: 64–19994. Designed by Jack Meserole. Printed in the United States of America.

Third Printing, 1964

Acknowledgments   48,911

The author wishes to thank the following publishers for permission to quote from:

OH, MEN! OH, WOMEN! by Edward Chodorov
Courtesy of Samuel French, Inc.

JUST ONE OF THOSE THINGS, by Cole Porter
Copyright 1935 by Harms, Inc.
Used by permission.

PAPER DOLL, by Johnny Black
Copyright Edward B. Marks Music Corporation
Used by permission.

YOUNGER THAN SPRINGTIME, by Richard Rodgers and Oscar Hammerstein II
Copyright © 1949 by Richard Rodgers and Oscar Hammerstein II
Williamson Music, Inc., New York, N.Y., owner of publication and allied rights

SUMMERTIME, by George Gershwin
Copyright © by Gershwin Publishing Corporation, New York, N.Y.
Copyright renewed.

Feb., 1965

FOR HERB AND PAUL AND LISE

and for the two people without whom

this book could not have been written:

My Baby-Sitter and My Cleaning Lady

FOREWORD

This book is not really concerned with suburbia, nor with the adventures of a writer, nor with the world of television. It is really concerned with a few of the things Nora should know before she skips out of the doll's house. Like how to laugh.

L. K.

. . . Nora packs up and is going to leave the house and the kids and everything and go out into the world. . . . *"Why,* Nora," says her husband, "why are you blowing?" . . . "I don't even know (she says), I just know that outside there some place— there are people, there are things—that will understand." . . . "I love you," he says . . . "stay home." . . . "No," she says— *"outside there"*—And so it goes. She is yelling *outside there*— and he is saying I love you and stay home—Now . . . Doc—my question is—WHAT is outside there—!

> —EDWARD CHODOROV, describing *A Doll's House,* in *Oh Men, Oh Women!*

I IT WAS OCTOBER in the Westchester Hills—a golden morning full of cornflower-blue sky. The air smelled of apples and grapes. There was a cardinal in the dogwood tree. Through the window I could see my two children leaping exuberantly up the neat suburban road on their rosy-cheeked way to school. My house on the hill was warm and flooded with sunlight. And I was wearing my Maidenform bra.

What more could you ask of life?

Plenty.

First of all, where was Bloomingdale's? Where was Fifty-seventh Street? Where was Fifth Avenue, with its motley horde of minks and broadtails and simple cashmeres? Where were those colorful teeming canyons pulsating with life? Where were those chic little fruit-salad-and-cappuccino lunches with lecherous young men in dim little bistros? Where the hell was my youth? My freedom? For that matter, where was Me?

I had this feeling that I had lost Me somewhere. My mother always said I was careless; I guess she was right. One day I was walking along holding Me firmly by the hand, and the next thing I knew this industrial-law graduate came along with the dark brooding eyes and the yen for a basement workshop, and suddenly there was this typical American split-level house thirty-five miles from the nearest dim little bistro, with two healthy children and two sickly dogwoods, and no Me. I've been looking for myself ever since.

But then, who hasn't? This is the story of our generation. This is the second half of the twentieth century. Loss of identity—every Tom, Dick, and Harry has loss of identity. It's so common you can't even enjoy having it.

But I had had it, right along with everybody else.

✳ 1

And that's why, on that blue and golden morning, with the cardinal in the dogwood tree, I left my comfortable home, my hard-working husband, and my two beautiful and uncorrupted children, and started off, of my own free will and sound of mind and body, down the road that leads to Bedlam, Babel, Sin, Fun, Corruption, and points south.

You could call it a momentary whim only if you would call the eruption of a volcano a sudden attack of hiccups. I mean if you think about it, there must be a lot of elemental things shifting and changing and rumbling deep down inside a crater, long before the lid finally blows off.

Just when those elemental things started shifting around in *my* crater is hard to pinpoint, even for somebody who grew up at a time and in a country where there are maybe two and a half people left somewhere who don't think they know more about psychiatry than Freud ever did. But I'll try.

As a child I was pretty ordinary. I lived in Brooklyn with my father who was a labor lawyer, and my mother who was tied to the house, and my two brothers who were better than I was at just about everything except lying. If I say it myself, I told some of the best lies ever devised between Brooklyn Heights and Coney Island. (It wasn't until the volcano erupted that I realized some people turn this talent into hard cash just by putting the lies down on paper.)

I suppose I had all the usual insecurities and hostilities, and maybe a few extra. My idea of success was to be a boy—possibly because my brothers, Leon and Arthur, were my father's pride and joy, whereas he had to be introduced to me several times before he got it firmly planted in his mind that I was part of the family—and my idea of beauty was a girl in my class called Thea, who was tall and willowy with hair the color of corn on the cob. (I had brown hair and nature decided that five foot two was as tall and willowy as I was ever going to get.)

So you can see that as far as success and/or beauty were con-

✳ 2

cerned, I arranged pretty early in life to give myself goals that were completely impossible of achievement.

I guess that's what I needed to make me happy, though, because I remember being very happy most of the time.

I had the usual adolescent problems. When I was in the chorus of the school production of *The Pirates of Penzance* one of the pirates got personal and made me yell "Mel*vin!*" right in the middle of the Major General's solo, and other cute things like that, other things not so cute, too. But I was very popular with boys, and I could never figure that out, because other girls who were very popular with boys used to tell me the things they had to let the boys get away with in order to remain popular, and I never did those things. When I was an adolescent, that is. To this day I can't imagine what those boys saw in me. *I* wasn't blonde.

However, I got through what they call the formative years in pretty good style. Like all my friends, I went to college and leaned heavily for my emotional security on the fact that President Roosevelt was obviously going to be in the White House for a hundred years and wouldn't let anything nasty happen to us; and I was taken to the theater regularly, and to the jazz joints and other popular places in the Village, and learned to sneer at Lana Turner and worship Katherine Hepburn, and finally got an interesting job in Manhattan and left my mother alternately wailing and faking unconsciousness while I moved my belongings to an apartment on Christopher Street that I shared with three other girls, and fell passionately and eternally in love with a married man whose name escapes me at the moment, and kept an eye out for a likely-looking husband, and found about twelve of them, and ditched them all and went on a cruise with two of the three girls in the apartment, and decided I didn't want to get married, and went to a party, and met Alex, and got married.

Alex had three things which, in combination, proved irresistible. He had those deep-set dark eyes, the ability to sit quietly for long periods of time and just listen (which always

* 3

convinces me that a person knows a lot of things he's not telling you), and an incomprehensible but unshakable determination to capture me that made the Northwest Mounted Police look like quitters.

So after a year or so, David was born.

And a couple of years after that I realized somebody else was going to be born.

And then we left the city.

In all my twenty-eight years I had never—except in the summertime—lived far enough from Times Square to worry about it and I had the cosmopolitan child's fear of and contempt for anything that couldn't be reached by subway.

I had been brought up on the certainty that out there, past the George Washington Bridge, was a vast wasteland composed of something called NATURE, and inhabited by animals and Guy Lombardo fans. No civilized person would think of living there between September and June. A cosmopolitan moving to the suburbs seemed to me like a university graduate re-enrolling in grade school. It didn't make sense.

But Alex had quietly made up his mind about it years ago—not only because the firm he worked for had moved out of the city to one of those industrial parks thirty miles to the north, but because he had a great affinity for grass and none at all for asphalt jungles—and these prejudices of mine were no obstacle to him. Slowly, inch by inch, he got hold of my brain and twisted it, until I found myself thinking things like "every minute of every day, every man, woman and child in this city is breathing poison into his lungs." Or, "with the money we're spending on rent every month, in twenty-five years we could own the Palace at Versailles." Or, "what's going to happen when David gets old enough to play baseball? Everybody knows the Central Park Little League is full of junkies."

And little by little, under Alex's quiet subliminal guidance, this city that I had always loved as simply and naturally as any child loves his home became a threat and a menace and no place to live. He didn't try to sell me suburbia, he simply demolished urbia. And once you turn your back on urbia, what else *is* there? But he didn't win completely. He led me to the water, but he couldn't make me drink. Even as I co-signed the deed to the house, my teeth were clenched. I was through with the city, but I certainly wasn't ready for anything else.

So, with my teeth clenched, we packed the living room rug and the hand-carved chess set and the three thousand books and the crib and the bassinette and the play-pen and the antique English desk and the Danish coffee-pot and David; and in the middle of a monumental September hurricane that tore open the coverings of the moving van so that the rain slashed all over our Italian fruitwood chairs, our little caravan made its way out of the city, past the George Washington Bridge, onward and upward into the unknown. Bravely, with hope in our hearts and David's sticky fingers on our faces, we pushed forward, peering resolutely through a rain-slashed windshield toward the strange new land where, everyone told us, the streets were paved with golden daffodils. The only thing missing was a crescendo of music at the end and the sun breaking through the clouds to form a glorious nimbus around the Statue of Liberty.

The house we moved into was not only not a home; to me, it was not even a house. It was brand new and had no attic, no bay window, no trellises or arbors or curving stairways or gabled bedrooms or any of the things I always thought should come with a house—(in those days I read a lot of English mystery stories)—but after a few weeks of growling I thought, well, what the hell, here we are, and started planting a privet hedge.

The way Alex took that house and that land and made them sit up and listen, there was no question he would be my first choice for someone to be shipwrecked with on a desert island. Rugged and indomitable, like Gary Cooper or somebody, in blue jeans and an old army shirt, he built a sunporch on the outside, a wallfull of bookshelves on the inside; created an outdoor drinking fountain and a log cabin and a sandbox for David; and planted and seeded and moved and raked and dug up whole trees from one place and put them in another and made them grow again. He sprayed and fertilized and weeded and spread peat moss and clipped and trimmed and trained vines to grow up the side of the house, brought home strange-looking bushes and plants and dug and planted and nurtured, and made a vegetable garden in one corner and grew tomatoes. I kept waiting for him to run out of things to do and, out of sheer momentum, go right into somebody else's backyard and start digging, but he never ran out. He would put David in the wheelbarrow and trundle him around with him as he worked. "We're going out to the north forty!" he'd yell to me as they passed the kitchen door. Or he'd come in looking reverent and holding a small, slightly yellow tomato on the palm of his hand and say, incredulously, "Look!"

In the evenings he'd take me by the hand out onto the back steps and make me breathe deeply. "Far as the eye can see," he'd say, looking out over our small plot to the house next door, "it's Bernard land. Clear down to that Ford station-wagon." And he'd grin at me and put his pipe in the corner of his mouth and his arm around me, and look up at the stars, at home and at peace; and I'd think to myself, a happy man is a nice thing to have around.

A happy woman would have been nice to have around too, but you can't have everything.

Actually, in those first years, I had an even bigger thing to adjust to than being removed from my natural habitat. I was a mother, twice. And there's something to that old theory that if you have a pain in your upper left molar all you have to do is cut off your big toe and you'll forget about the toothache. Everything was so full of babies I really didn't have time to appreciate the horror of my geographical situation.

While the kids were still what Lord and Taylor call toddlers, I was in a world of undiluted maternity. Very little existed beyond feeding and training and watching in wonderment as they slowly grew into real honest-to-God children. Of course I cried a lot out of the sheer exhaustion of using physical and emotional muscles I hadn't known existed before, but I don't remember ever worrying about loss of identity. I knew what I was. I was mother earth.

But life has this habit of suddenly one day kicking your whole orientation out from under you. You go along for years with a certain picture of yourself—who you are, what you're there for, and all the rest of it. Then one morning you wake up and it's raining or something and you just can't picture yourself any more. You cling desperately to the old patterns, making occasional French toast for breakfast, getting new books from the children's library, taking trips to the zoo. But now, instead of squeals of delight, the French toast is a big bore to those kids; they'd rather anytime watch TV than cuddle beside you listening to *Mopsy, The Boy Who Wouldn't Get a Haircut,* and they drag around the zoo with all the enthusiasm of a couple of jaded members of the International Set. There are a dozen other places they'd rather be, all of them away from you, and all in all you get the feeling they wish you'd get lost.

As for that virile, passionate, life-loving boy you married, forget it. Time and familiarity have taken their toll. The guy who used to appear at your front door every night because he was wild to see you, now appears there every night because that's where he happens to live. For all you know he might prefer to be somewhere else; there's nothing to indicate he's here by enthusiastic choice. Granted, once in a while, when you're all dressed up for a big night on the town, he'll suddenly look at you with a different look from the one he gives the armchair or the kitchen clock and hand out a kind of self-conscious compliment. But this, on the average, is once every eight months. To be perfectly fair, after so many years of watching you brushing your teeth and carrying out the garbage, you can hardly expect him to get all excited about the nape of your neck—but who's interested in being fair? All you're interested in is somebody

✳ 7

lying prostrate at your feet groaning "I want you! I need you!"—
a possibility that gets dimmer and dimmer as the years roll on.

So there you are. Who are you? Who needs you? You're
just the lady who does the washing and ironing and cooking and
cleaning and yelling.

It's not so much the washing and ironing that get you down.
It's not so much the cooking and the dishes and the vacuum
cleaner and the wet mops and the venetian blinds and the wax-
ing and polishing and scrubbing and the repair men and the
measles and mumps and the shopping and cooking and cleaning
and dishes and venetian blinds and shopping and cooking and
dishes and repair men and chicken pox and flu and cooking and
shopping and scrubbing and dishes and washing and ironing
and cuts and bruises and allergies and venetian blinds and shopping and cooking—it's not *that* so much. It's the goddamn *lone-
liness*.

You don't know what lonely is till you get to keeping house.
I got so lonely for adult companionship I once kept the delivery
man from the grocery standing at the door twenty minutes discussing the world situation, until I discovered that *his* idea of
progress was to drop a few well-placed H-bombs on Russia,
China, India, France, the Vatican, Africa, Cuba, and the New
York Giants, thereby making the world safe for the seven or
eight people who agreed with him.

Contrary to the fairy stories that are circulated, about the
way automation has made housekeeping so easy that women are
playing strip poker all day, the activities mentioned above, plus
a few dozen unmentioned, constitute a good seventy-hour week,
and unfortunately the income of a contract administrator com-
pares somewhat unfavorably with that of a busy house-painter,
so the only help we could afford was a so-called cleaning woman
who came in once a week and gave me a few glorious hours of
freedom which I could have spent lolling about in some expensive country restaurant with a kindred soul, except that I couldn't
afford an expensive country restaurant, there were no kindred

souls in the neighborhood whose cleaning woman came on the same day as mine, and besides I usually had to go to the bank, the doctor, the dentist, the gardening department of Klein's-Westchester, the library, the upholsterer, the garage to have the car fixed, and the drugstore for a prescription.

So, essentially, I was alone five days a week, and if a crisis in contract negotiations out in Denver or Seattle occurred during the week, Alex would spend the entire weekend on long distance, which left me alone for six, or even a round seven days.

Oh, you say, that's not strictly accurate. You did see people from time to time. Right. And the people I saw were my children, my children's teachers, the lady who took in the shirts at the laundry, the checker at the supermarket, the bank teller, the pharmacist, the pediatrician, and assorted salesmen. Nice people, in their way, and they gave me something. They gave me the feeling I was A Mother, A Patient, An Address, A Customer, A Sucker, A Housewife, A Pain in the Neck, and other things of a categorical nature, but they sure as hell didn't give me the feeling I was anybody in particular. Many were the days I looked in the mirror and saw this strange Customer there.

This was my biggest problem. Or maybe my biggest problem was that I had nobody with whom to discuss my biggest problem.

My neighbors had their own seventy-hour weeks to cope with, and most of my girlhood friends had remained happily in Manhattan, in their expensive, cockroach-ridden apartments, skimping on little luxuries here and there so they could send their children to private schools for like thousands of dollars a year. After school they could grab their kids by the hand and, in ten minutes, be down at the Museum of Modern Art or having coffee with other Hunter College alumnae at the nearest Schrafft's, so they didn't really know what I was talking about (over the telephone) when I complained about my lot. Their frame of reference did not include being stuck in a snowbank twelve miles from home on a deserted side road at five P.M. with

※ 9

Dennis the Menace and his female counterpart in the back seat, and other things like that. So them I couldn't talk to.

As for Alex, the nature of my problem being what it was, namely that I didn't like being his unpaid housekeeper, I couldn't very well discuss it with him. I mean, it would always turn out like a slave in the Old South trying to have an intelligent debate on civil rights with the owner of the plantation.

"Mistah boss, suh, how come ah have to stay here all alone an' work twelve hours a day an' I don't get no pay for it, nor no promotions, nor no time off, while on the othah hand you only work *eight* hours a day, an' you gets paid for it, an' you gets time off, an' you gets promotions, an' you also gets to have lunch with other folks. How come?"

"Why because that's the way it is, girl. That's the natural order of things. Ah was born to have privileges and you wasn't."

"How come, boss?"

"Because."

"Oh. Well ahm not so happy with this arrangement, boss."

"Not happy? What do you mean, not happy? What *you* got to worry about? Ah take care of you, don't ah? Ah give you a roof over your head, an' food to eat, an' clothes to wear, don't ah?"

"Yassuh. But it don't seem to even out, somehow."

"Girl, you better fohget those rebellious notions. Ah don't like no troublemakers on mah plantation. Now you just go 'long and be happy like those othah dahkies. See how happy they are? Hear them singin'?"

"That's wailin', boss."

Now that isn't verbatim, of course. Verbatim, Alex would sound like a reasonable and understanding man. He would say things like:

✳ 1 0

"You want to get away from the house? Go ahead. Take Saturday off and go to New York and see some of your friends. I'll stay home with the kids. No problem."

"What about dinner?" I'd say.

"Don't worry about dinner. I'll get dinner."

So I'd go, and by the time I got home there would be stifled sobs coming from David's room and piercing sobs from Sooz's, where they'd been respectively incarcerated, and Alex would be slamming pots and pans around the kitchen with a furious, resentful efficiency. He would have very little to say to me that night or all day Sunday, which he would spend flat on his back with a book, ignoring everybody, with the self-righteous air of one who has already done more than his share.

So you see, for "Take Saturday off, I'll stay home with the kids and get dinner," you really have to read, "Ah was born to have weekends off an' you wasn't."

At the time, though, I didn't consciously make the translation. I told myself he just behaved this way because the kids got on his nerves. Only my subconscious suspected the truth. I don't think even Alex suspected it. In any case he certainly didn't think of himself as one of those old-fashioned tyrants. And he wasn't. He was a *new*-fashioned one. He believed that all women who want to should be free, equal, independent, creative, well-informed, and lead stimulating, interesting lives. Except me. Not me, personally, but me as his wife. And he didn't make this distinction out of malice or selfishness, but simply because he couldn't reconcile his intellectual convictions with his atavistic male impulses. His convictions told him that women are people, but his impulses told him they're not, really. Also, like those Southern gentlemen, he had this deep-rooted conviction that there is only so much freedom in the world, and the more of it our kind get, the less his kind will have, and that's not good for the world.

And, as I say, the reason he could harbor all these conflicting points of view so comfortably, was that he just couldn't admit to having the unfashionable ones. He went blithely along believing he was a totally enlightened fellow.

Well, in spite of all this I was pretty fond of him, because he looked very sexy in almost any shade of blue, he could fix any damn thing that went wrong in the house, he never told anybody we watch *The Untouchables,* he once bought me a black fox muff, he taught the kids how to build a bird-house and how to ice-skate and how to ride a bicycle and how to play a clarinet even though he himself had never played any in-strument in his whole life, not even a kazoo, and was tone-deaf to boot, and besides he stayed with me through nine years and fourteen migraines without complaining *too* much.

So I tried to forget about getting out of the house.

But I couldn't. I was all those things you read about. Rest-less. Discontent. Profoundly disturbed. And gradually I began to get depressed. And then I began smashing little things around the house—a paperweight here, an ashtray there. And then I began not speaking to anybody. And then I got mad.

That's when I found out about the others.

2 IT HAPPENED one day when I was thrash-ing around the supermarket like an eagle trapped in a canary cage. Suddenly I noticed that most of the other women in the super-market were thrashing around too. Taking a sidelong survey, I counted thirty-seven disturbed faces out of a possible fifty. After that I watched closely every time I went to the supermarket, and I came to realize that there were whole *legions* of restless house-wives all across America, smoldering inside as they slammed sullenly up and down those supermarket aisles, gathering in mysterious little groups to mumble tensely about their resent-ments.

Passing by the groups you would hear the angry hissing of certain key words: "Stagnating. . . ." "Stifling. . . ." It was like a hundred million prisoners planning a gigantic, nationwide jail-break.

It was about this time that I noticed newspapers and magazines had discovered a new circulation booster: "What's happening to the American Woman?" Now who's not going to buy a paper or a magazine with a question like *that* on it, in big black type? That question sold papers and magazines like crazy. And pretty soon every self-styled authority with five minutes to spare was jumping on the gravy train with the answer. Psychologists, archeologists, cab drivers, stamp collectors, visiting Egyptian camel drivers—they all had something important to say about the new white man's burden, American Woman. And the titles of the articles were pretty indicative of their detached, objective, mature, intellectual approach to the subject.

"Anti-Servility, The New Neurosis"
"Look Who Thinks They Got Rights!"
"They'll Never Stop at Equality"
"Will the Next Pope Be a Lady?"
"Hadassah Chief Demands Immediate Surrender of West Point!"

And so on. Eventually, of course, some people in Hollywood got in on it, in their own adorable way, and they put out a couple of romantic comedies (those pictures that used to be so good in the old days when Carole Lombard and Melvyn Douglas and all those fellows used to make them, but that nowadays are so full of baloney). These movies were more or less about a typical young middle-class mother of three who is married to an advertising executive, and they live in this typical twenty-room Tudor cottage with a circular driveway and a four-car garage—a typical suburban couple. One day he's trying to think of an advertising slogan for a new product and she comes up with one and he just laughs at her and she gets mad and says she'll show him, and she peddles it to a rival agency. The next thing you know the rival agency offers her a job and she becomes a big career girl overnight, happy as a lark, no problem with the kids or anything; she just scoots off to work every day at the crack of noon in a chauffeured limousine until one day, she comes home wearing one of the five-hundred-dollar creations from her typical suburban wardrobe, and finds hubby sulkily getting ready to go out on a date with a pretty little home-type widow from down the block, and this makes the wife realize what a fool she's been for thinking up a good advertising slogan. She quick gets into a pink organza negligee by Edith Head and when he gets home she throws herself all over him and cries, "Forgive me, forgive me, what a fool I am! I must have been out of my mind! You can make up better slogans than I can, any day of the week! After all, what am I—just a stupid little girl making forty thousand dollars a year. I'm *nothing* without you. There can be no greater joy in the world for me than to lie for the rest of my life at the feet of Fred J. Stipplemeyer! Please stand still so I can grovel!"

After seeing something like this, I couldn't help wondering—again—if there isn't some kind of invisible iron curtain around greater Los Angeles that prevents the truth about the rest of the world from getting through to them. Or is it something more sinister? Propaganda of some sort? Do they think they can get the world to believe that when a wife and mother leaves her home, this is how, and why, it happens? And that her husband's reaction will be so simple and straightforward? And that she will always finally find the answer to everything in his shoelaces, as she crouches there in pink organza?

I couldn't wait to see how they would solve the race problem.

Meanwhile, back at the ranch house, the American woman was busily digesting all these brilliant analyses of her "problem," happy to find herself part of such a national upsurge. Everybody enjoyed being a "topic." Except me. It didn't comfort me at all. As a matter of fact, it did just the opposite. It almost sent me right over to the enemy camp. It seems there's a whole lot of maverick in my blood, and I hate to be part of a crowd. So when the subject of my freedom became very popular, it suddenly became very devaluated as an issue. Trite. Banal. Cliché. All those things. I might even, in sheer rebellion, have become an ardent housewife and champion of the causes of Drudgery and Solitary Confinement, but just when I was getting ready to take that critical step, I made another discovery.

In our immediate neighborhood there were some sixty families, and over the years, with perseverance and a little luck, we found we were compatible with about five per cent of the population, or three out of the sixty families; the Bookmans, the Sands, and the Cardells. One night in late August the Bookmans invited the Sands, the Cardells and us for a barbecue. (All right, we have barbecues.) And after the barbecue Helen Sands and Vera Cardell and I helped Natalie Bookman carry things back into the kitchen, and we sort of lingered there, because the male contingent outside was busy discussing the psychological effects of shelter building, a subject which made Natalie sick, Vera furious, and Helen cry. As for me, it had its pros and cons. On the one hand, there wouldn't be any venetian blinds to clean. But on the other, if my problem was that I couldn't stand being stuck in the *house*—! So we stayed in the kitchen talking about whether movie stars were movie stars because they were beautiful, or whether they were beautiful because they were movie stars.

And somehow we drifted from that subject to the subject we always drifted to; the demoralizing effect of living in a continuum of dirty dishes, dirty clothes, dirty windows, dirty floors, the endless waste of respective abilities and educations, the grinding solitude, and all that. I sat quietly in a little pool of resentment. Everybody has to get in on the act, I thought, bitterly.

But as I listened I began to realize there was less here than met the eye. It started out heroically enough:

"There's something missing," said Vera, who had been with a consumer's information outfit before she got married. "There's definitely something missing in our way of life. A sense of purpose, a goal, or something. I keep wondering what's going to happen to us when the kids are grown up."

"Yeees," said Helen, former private secretary to a top executive of a shipping firm, "I must say I don't look forward to another forty years of dusting the furniture."

"What are you suggesting?" asked Natalie, an ex-industrial researcher, "We should all go back to work?"

"Well," said Vera, "why not?"

"Starting tomorrow!" Helen laughed, "we'll leave the key under the mat so the kids can get in when they come back from kindergarten."

Then the hedging began.

"A lot of women do it," said Vera. "If you could get a good housekeeper. . . Of course that's a major stumbling block right there. . . ."

"The children are still so young," said Helen. "They're always getting sick. How could you have any peace of mind going off to work and leaving a sick child?"

"There would be so many tensions and conflicts," said Natalie. "I keep thinking of . . . what's-her-name . . . Davis. . . ."

"That was another problem entirely," said Vera. "They would've gotten divorced sooner or later even if she hadn't gone back to work."

"And Lila Beech," said Helen. "Of course there's no proof that Warren is a disturbed child because his mother went to work. But still. . . ."

At this point I made a contribution.

"That lady," I said, "whose kid tried to burn down the school this year. Didn't she get the award last year for Most Devoted Mother?"

"Well—" Helen shrugged it off.

Then began the compromising.

"They have some interesting adult courses at the high school this year," said Natalie. "That would be no problem, going at night, when the kids are asleep."

"Except," said Vera, "that by the time the kids are asleep my brain has stopped functioning."

"It's not a bad idea, though," said Helen. "I'd like to brush up on a couple of languages."

I made another contribution.

"Isn't that," I said, "kind of getting all dressed up and having nowhere to go? I mean who are you going to talk French to— the cleaning lady?"

"It's mental stimulation," said Helen, defensively.

"It gets you out of the house," said Natalie, placidly.

"I thought we were talking about a sense of purpose, a goal," said I.

"Somehow," said Vera, sort of agreeing with me, "sitting in a classroom with a bunch of other bored housewives . . ."

"There's always community work," said Helen, "What about all these organizations everybody joins?"

"*That's* what's missing in our life," I said, "endless bickering!"

"Besides," said Vera, "all the committees are full. There's a waiting list."

"Gloria Betz!" said Natalie, laughing. "She's on every committee in the county."

And finally came the withdrawal.

"Maybe we're on the wrong track," said Vera. "Maybe we're too compulsive in this country. We have no talent for leisure. Take the European woman. . . ."

They took the European woman, and from there they went on to European vacations, American tourists, and so on. And that's when it hit me. All this was *talk*. They had no intention of *doing* anything. Laziness, or fear, or insecurity, or maybe just the fact that their dissatisfaction hadn't reached the point of being intolerable, kept them from coming to grips with the problem. In Natalie's case, I thought, it might even be that she was

✷ 17

joining in merely to be sociable; actually solitude suited her temperament. She had a need for monotonous routine; she was shy of new people, new ideas; she didn't like change of any kind. Housewifery was a blessing to her.

Anyway, I realized that these women weren't getting in on the act at all. They weren't crowding me out. They were just talking. They weren't ever going to *do* anything.

The person who *did* something about it . . . *she'd* be the maverick!

It came to me, as they say, in a sudden blinding flash of comprehension. In the final analysis my fellow prisoners were never going to do anything but sit around and act threatening. When H-hour came and it was time to knock out the guard, grab the keys, and make a break for that big stone wall—they'd chicken out!

There'd be nobody out there but me!

After I thought about this a little, it scared the hell out of me. Because, unfortunately, the maverick in me is counterbalanced by a powerful desire to hide in the herd. They take turns, one day maverick, the next day, herd.

On my herd days I worried about all the things *they* worried about; could a woman juggle two jobs and keep everybody happy? *Would* I be depriving the children of their emotional security by not being there to yell at them when they got home from school? *Could* I get a housekeeper who wouldn't spend the whole day watching television or having pains in her back? *Would* Alex desert me for some pretty young thing who'd had a pre-frontal lobotomy and wouldn't give him any trouble?

These were all vital considerations and they worried me to death.

But on my maverick days I knew there was one consideration that was more vital than all the others: "To thine own self be true, and it must follow as the night the day," and so on. If I couldn't be true to mine own self then nothing made any sense

✳ 1 8

and mine own self had to get out of that bloody house once in a while, or die!

Things started coming to a boil in the old volcano when, after I had spent a whole grueling day vacuuming the rugs, washing the bathroom floor, polishing the kitchen linoleum and scrubbing the gas range with Brillo pads, Alex came home and, within one hour, idly dribbled half a ton of pipe tobacco over the rugs, accidentally smeared shoe polish on the bathroom floor, forgot himself and tracked mud from the yard all over the kitchen linoleum, and then decided to make a bacon sandwich at eleven P.M. and splattered bacon grease all over the nice clean gas range.

To put it mildly, I got hysterical.

"What's the big deal?" Alex said calmly, "So it's dirty. Who cares?"

"That's *just it!*" I choked, "just *it!* Who *cares?* Nobody *cares!* If Picasso—Picasso—finished a *painting* . . . and some slob . . . some *slob* came by and . . . and just . . . *sloshed* turpentine all over it—*then* they'd care! *That* they'd care about! Well, my floors . . . my floors are my Picassos . . . my gas range . . . they're the only Picassos I've *got* . . . I don't *paint* . . . I've just got *floors.* But nobody cares if *they're* spoiled—oh no!—they don't *count* . . . nothing I do *counts!* I spend my whole life doing things that don't *matter!*"

"For God's sake!" Alex yelled. "*People* live in this house! People make things *dirty!* Goddamnit!" He turned purple.

I knew he was taking it out on me because his mother used to put newspapers on the floor, but knowing didn't help. I ran out of the house and walked two miles in a drizzle.

The lava was rising in the crater.

I caught a cold and that calmed me down a little. There's something about being sick that takes the sting out of having to stay home alone. There's nowhere you want to be and nobody you want to see anyway. But when I got over the cold the boiling started again, and I said to myself, pulling no punches, if

※ 19

you're worth your salt you'll stop hanging around here being nervous and you'll, by God, *do* something about it.

But I kept worrying about what Natalie and Helen and Vera had said. The children getting sick. Tensions. Conflicts. Alex. And besides, I didn't know exactly what to do. Get a job? What kind of job? What could I supply that was in demand? I had no skills. All I'd done for six carefree years before I got married was work at a place called Prospect Press, a small intellectual-type paperback house that published better science fiction, high-minded mystery stories, anthologies of off-beat short stories, and so on. And there I was something different every other week: reader, receptionist, assistant editor, filler-in, telephone answerer. It was the kind of casual, undefined, undemanding job that never exists when you go looking for it. I'd never find another Prospect Press. One to a customer in one lifetime.

Well, maybe a job wasn't the answer. But if not, then what?

The longer the question went unanswered, the more nervous I got.

Pretty soon Alex began to realize that I wasn't the happy-go-lucky kid I used to be and, while some self-protective device kept him from going to the source of the problem, he did his best, being basically a nice guy, to cheer and divert me.

One dinnertime as I was in the kitchen dishing out meatloaf for David and Sooz to the strains of a seductive tango from the radio, he came up behind me and swept me and my greasy spatula into a silly, slinky dance while the kids watched, bug-eyed.

"What's the matter?" he said to them as he dragged me around, swaying and dipping, "You think only kids are allowed to have fun? Watch *this!*" And he bent me over backwards and nearly broke my ribs.

"Saturday night," he said to me, "I'm taking you to the Persian Room at the Plaza. Dinner, dancing, Lena Horne, everything. Okay?"

"Sure," I said, not believing it for a minute. But we really did go, and he pretended for all he was worth that we were Scott and Zelda and that this was just one glittering link in a chain of golden evenings. Even when the drinks started catching up with him and I could see by his heavy eyes that all he wanted to do was go home and go to sleep, he kept dragging me out on the dance floor, singing along with the music—out of tune, and the wrong lyrics—

"Just one of those nights . . . just me and you and one of those nights . . . a trip to the moon . . . on one of those nights . . . just one of those nights. . ."

He was pretty cute.

But the next day it was clear that he expected this one night of gaiety to have solved all my problems, whatever they were, and when he saw that it hadn't, he retired, wounded and worn out. I hated to let him down like that but I couldn't seem to help feeling the way I felt, and the way I felt was just plain mean.

Finally I completely lost interest in food. Not only mine. Everybody's. The week after the Persian Room we had lamb chops for dinner three nights in a row. The second night Alex passed it off with an attempt at good-natured ribbing: "Mm! What's this? Another new, exotic dish!" But the third night he exploded.

"What the hell is this?" he said. "Lamb chops three nights in a row?"

"Tough!" I said.

He got up and left the dinner table. The kids were watching cartoons on television, which I'd sworn I'd never let them watch. We didn't eat dinner with them except on weekends because Sooz (legally named Susan once upon a time) never stopped talking and David ate as though mankind had never quite made that transition from the jungle.

Alex walked into the living room and turned off the television.

"No!" screamed Sooz.

✳ 21

"Oh *boy!*" David growled, persecuted. "Oh boy! It wasn't even finished! Oh *boy!*"

"Let them watch!" I shouted.

"Go to your rooms!" Alex said, in the special voice that means there'll be no velvet glove on the iron hand tonight!

"That's right," I growled, "pull rank on the enlisted men!" I tore angrily at my lamb chop with a fork.

"Go to your rooms!"

The kids marched upstairs, Sooz racked with fake sobs, David muttering "Oh boy" and probably planning to become a juvenile delinquent.

It was all my fault. I knew it and I didn't even care.

But if nothing else I'm practical. I knew that if I didn't say anything, the tension would build up so that by the time we went to bed Alex would just lie there in the dark with his back to me, not sleeping, and I'd lie there with my back to him, not sleeping, and if there's anything I can't stand it's not sleeping, so I apologized.

"I apologize!" I said, loudly, from the dining room.

He stayed in his chair in the living room pretending to read *Time*.

I went into the living room.

"I didn't know they were lamb chops," I said, "That's the trouble with putting meat in the freezer. It freezes so hard you can't make out what it is until it's all thawed out and then it's too late. I thought it was veal. Honest."

"Why don't you *mark* it!" he muttered. Then he looked up from the magazine. "What's eating you, anyway? For the past three months you've been impossible to live with!"

He always exaggerated. It was six weeks at the most.

I opened my mouth to tell him, and then I shut it again. What was the point of saying "I'm tired of being in this house day and night, I'm tired of being lonely, I'm tired of spending my life doing a lot of things everybody secretly looks down their nose at, no matter how they talk about the importance of being

* 22

a *homemaker*." What was the point of saying all that, when I didn't know what else I could do, or where else I could go? Besides, somewhere deep inside me I suspected that as soon as I said any of this, the real Alex would immediately disappear, and the selfless, understanding, objective, phoney Alex would look out at me from those nice dark eyes, and I'd never really know where I stood with him. (I wasn't thinking this in so many clear-cut, specific thoughts. It was just one of those dark, intuitive things.) So when he persisted, saying "Well? What's bothering you?" I just mumbled, "Nothing."

"*Nothing?*"

"Not really." I plumped the cushions on the sofa. Alex put down his magazine.

"Nothing at *all* is bothering you?"

"Nothing important." I emptied one ashtray into another.

"Nothing *important*? All this is because of something *trivial*?"

"Let's forget it, huh? Let's eat." I gestured unenthusiastically toward the dining-room table.

He gave me a kind of hopeless look and got to his feet, overplaying the weariness a little.

"Well," he said, "when the day comes that something *important* is bothering you, would you please pack a bag and send it to the office, because I think I would have to move out for a while."

So we went back to the dining room and ate cold lamb chops and Alex let the kids come back down and finish watching the cartoons. (Cartoons! I've seen newsreels of national disasters that were more fun.)

And that night I found myself lying in bed not sleeping after all. The situation was grim, not to mention dangerous. How long could I go on making everybody miserable? I had to do something. But what? Get on a banana boat? Take guitar lessons? Join the marchers at the UN? Start an affair with the delivery man?

None of these alternatives really appealed to me, except the

* 23

banana boat. And on a banana boat I couldn't come home every night.

I lay there in the dark, sleepless, wondering.

I wondered how other women got through a crisis like this.

I wondered if any of them *did* get through it.

I wondered what was really bothering Elizabeth Taylor and Judy Garland.

I wondered how come there wasn't a single male movie star I could get excited about since Humphrey Bogart.

I wondered why people are always attracted to ruthlessness.

I wondered about those articles saying that we modern women should be ashamed of ourselves because our grandmothers and great-grandmothers, without any modern conveniences, raised seven children apiece, scrubbed floors, baked bread, ploughed fields, never complained, and didn't need psychiatrists.

Finally, as the misty light of dawn began to show through the cracks in the venetian blinds, the answer to that last one came to me. It was so simple it was startling. The answer was— who *says* they didn't need psychiatrists?

And as a footnote, how come so many of them died at the age of twenty-six?

Finally I fell into a deep, untroubled half-hour sleep, just in time to get up.

When the kids had gone off to the bus stop, I started bothering myself again about this business of getting a job. Should I or shouldn't I, and if I should, *what* should I?

And just then fate dropped in for a cup of coffee, in the person of Vicki Warsaw.

3   IT COULD BE that nothing would ever have happened if it hadn't been for Vicki Warsaw. I had only known her for a month or two when she dropped in for that morning cup of coffee. When I found her, I found a friend, a confidante, a fellow-indignant, an example of heroic womanhood, an ornithologist, a comparison shopper, a reference book, an enthusiast, an innocent, a female who knew more curse words than I did, and a devil-may-care pediatrician.

It happened one night in late June when, as we always did before going to bed, we looked in on the children in their respective rooms.

Sooz was fast asleep, all three feet of her, looking like one of the few things God scatters around the earth every so often to kid us into thinking that life really can be beautiful; but David, instead of being in his usual position outside the covers with one leg and arm hanging over the edge, was sitting up, very flushed and puzzled, his great luminous brown eyes glazed with fever and his magnificent brow wrinkled in an effort to remember what had made him wake up.

We took his temperature, which was about as high as it could go, and immediately called the pediatrician I had contacted about two minutes after crossing the threshold of our new house (I can't settle down anywhere without having a direct line to five or six doctors).

The answering service picked up the phone and told us that Dr. Sundergard was off duty and that Dr. Warsaw was covering him, and gave us Dr. Warsaw's number. We called Dr. Warsaw's number and the answering service picked up the phone and told us Dr. Warsaw was out on a call and would be calling in shortly, so we left our address and phone number and a request

✳ 25

to come immediately, and added the words "temperature one hundred and five."

For the next forty-five minutes we took turns sponging him with alcohol and going to the window to see if Dr. Warsaw's car was coming up the street—whoever Dr. Warsaw was, and whatever his car looked like. Finally, just as Alex announced we'd gotten David down to one hundred and two, I saw a station wagon pull into our driveway.

"He's here!" I breathed, and ran down to the front door, and opened it wide, and there, running up the steps carrying a little black bag and wearing a dirndl skirt and roman sandals and a white peasant blouse and a crown of chestnut-colored hair, was Dr. Warsaw. Vicki.

She grinned at me and panted, "I'm coming, I'm coming!" with a mock life-or-death breathlessness.

"Dr. Warsaw?" I murmured, just to make sure.

"Yeah. You got a cigarette? Where's the boychik?"

"Upstairs." I made a trancelike gesture and, as she scurried up the stairs, I went in search of my cigarettes, feeling strangely exhilarated. There was so little of the unexpected in my routinized life.

She had stopped in the bathroom to wash her hands, so I made it to David's door just behind her.

She flat-footed into the room, grinned at Alex, said "Hi!" to David, then turned to me with eyebrows raised in admiration. "Hey, those eyes!" and then back to David. "So what do you mean dragging an old woman out in the middle of the night!"

David gave her a wry smile. "You're not old."

"You're my friend for life. Stick your tongue out and say ah!"

In order to appreciate David's comment you have to understand that ordinarily everybody who looks as if they've been hanging around for more than seventeen years is, to him, old. Obviously Dr. Warsaw had to be in her thirties, but even I had the fleeting thought that maybe she'd been one of those strange kids who enters medical school at the age of twelve, because she certainly didn't look over thirty, and in this dim light and dressed the way she was, not even old enough to vote liberal, which I could bet my life she would.

I glanced at Alex to see how he was taking this whole person, but I should have known better. Alex's face, when it's taken by surprise, becomes an impenetrable mask, working on the same principle as a turtle disappearing into its shell.

After she'd finished examining David, with lots of talk about the latest Little League score and compliments on various parts of his anatomy, she tousled his hair fondly, and said, "Well, there's nothing wrong with you that a good doctor couldn't cure. Where's my cigarette?"

I gave her one and she wrote out a prescription.

"I hate putting them on medication," she said, "but I think we need a little antibiotic for this one. I'm ordering just enough for a couple of days. I don't know about you, but I'm very tight with money."

I saw a glimmer of admiration cross Alex's mask.

Before she left we knew her husband's name and occupation and the fact that in her eyes he was a living doll and probably the smartest researcher ever born; also that she had three young daughters and a lot of trouble with insects on her rosebushes; that the other night they'd seen a new Italian film that was a knock-out; and that she had a father, mother, brother, sister, and grandmother, all of whom were practising physicians.

Later, just as we were falling asleep, I turned around in bed and said to Alex, "What would Dr. Sundergard do if we told him we decided to switch doctors?" And Alex said, "Cheer."

I snuggled happily into the pillow and found myself wondering when it would be Sooz's turn to come down with something so that I could call Dr. Warsaw again.

I didn't have to wait long. Evidently the wrestling holds that David had been teaching Sooz the last few days had kept them within an inch of each other's noses long enough for the germs to make the trip without even packing a bag. Forty-eight hours after her first visit I was calling Dr. Warsaw again.

This time she stomped up the front steps, growling hello, but taking the edge off it with a grin that showed she knew she was in a lousy mood.

"I'm premenstrual!" she snarled. And after examining Sooz, whose irresistible behind she didn't resist, but bit, she marched into the living room, lit a cigarette, sighed, and said, "Listen, kid, we've got to do something about the institution of marriage. It just doesn't work. This morning I threw a whole set of dishes at the dining room wall. Jesus, what a great feeling! Smash! Smash! The only thing I regret is they cost me thirty-five dollars. I can't stand the thought of replacing them. You know me. Cheap."

Now I knew for sure she was going to be a friend. The first time she had impressed—in fact, dazzled—me with her bounce and vigor, but she seemed too happy. I'm wary of people who seem completely happy. Either they're just putting it on to make you jealous, or, if they really *are* happy, I figure they're just not living in the same world as the rest of us.

Now that Vicki Warsaw had given evidence of a nasty, maladjusted streak, I felt I could really talk to her.

So that morning when she dropped in unexpectedly and while she sat at my kitchen table drinking coffee and smoking and discussing birds, it occurred to me that here was the perfect person to consult about this problem of mine. First of all she was a doctor, which is something I refuse to believe is fallible, and secondly, as a woman, she had beat the rap. She was a perfect example of what I had in mind. She was *never* in the house. She was all the time doing interesting, important work that earned her not only money, but appreciation, admiration, respect, and all those other things that husbands seem to think they should have a monopoly on. I knew that whatever she told me to do, I would do it.

I had a hard time at first getting her attention away from the bird feeder out in the yard, which was directly in her line of vision. The conversation went something like this:

ME: "I think I'm going out of my mind."

VICKI: "It's a bluejay. No, it's a cedar waxwing. . . . No, it's a bluejay."

So I pulled the blind and then she concentrated.

"Vicki," I said, "I have this feeling that I'm just hanging around waiting to get old and die and I think I ought to do something about it, but I'm scared. Do you think maybe it's a vitamin deficiency?"

"Actually," she said, "our problem is we have too many vitamins. We're too healthy altogether. What we need in this country is a little sickness, to dispel that feeling of false security. We don't take nature seriously enough."

"Stop horsing around, Vicki."

"Okay, you're getting older. We're all getting older. So— what do you want to do?"

"I don't know. Something. Something that isn't so—lonely. And endless. I mean—" I gestured around at the kitchen, "this stuff never gets *done*. You know that. It's the same thing, over and over until you're eighty-five. It just goes on and on. It never *culminates*. You never have . . . have . . ."

"An orgasm."

"Yeah. Like that."

"You're right. I couldn't stand it. So what do you want to do?"

"I don't know," I repeated, feebly. "I don't want to take just any old job—you know—typing or something. That doesn't make sense. I want . . ." There was a long pause while we both waited to hear what it was I wanted. Then it came to me. "I want to do something that would make people say, 'Hey, that Ruthie Bernard, she's a smart cookie!' "

"Uh-huh."

There was a shrill chirp from the feeder and Vicki lifted a

* 29

slat of the venetian blind and peeked out. She couldn't help herself.

"Vicki!"

"I'm thinking, I'm thinking!" She dropped the blind, and lit another cigarette. "What did you do before?" She waved a hand over her shoulder, indicating the past.

"Oh—I worked in a sort of office—for a publisher."

There was a gleam of interest in her eyes. "Oh yes? A publisher? What did you do there?"

"Everything. Nothing. I started as a receptionist, then I was a copy reader, then the file clerk left so I took over, then sometimes they let me help edit the short-story books, and I wrote fillers—you know, those things at the bottom of a page—stupid anecdotes and useless information— "There are twenty thousand llamas in South America." It was fun. Once they even gave me an assignment writing a short story to fill up a book that was going to be too skinny."

"You wrote a *story?*"

"Well I didn't really write it. I just sort of told it, on paper. It was something that happened to a girl I knew who lived on Long Island, and after six months of propaganda from this boy she was crazy about—who lived in Queens and wanted to sleep with her—she decided to give in. So she told her mother some lie about where she was going for the weekend, and drove off to Manhattan in this boy's car, only it was a Saturday night and Manhattan was so crowded with cars they couldn't find a place to park, and he got mad, and she got mad, so he just drove her back home and they never saw each other again. It was a kind of sad comedy of errors."

"And what happened? They published it?"

"Sure."

"Then it must have been good!"

"Oh I don't know about that. Nobody said anything one way or another. They just printed it."

Vicki leaned back in the chair and raised an eyebrow.

"For God's sake!" she said, "You're a writer!"

"Don't be ridiculous!"

"Well you wrote, didn't you? And they paid you for it?"

"But that wasn't . . ."

"My friend, you've got it made! Writers don't have to take jobs—they can just sit home and write!"

"But I don't *want* to sit home!" I screamed. "That's the whole problem!"

"No," she said calmly, "that's not the problem. The problem is you don't want to keep house. It's different. If you could work at home and make enough money so you could have full-time help; if you could walk out the front door any time you felt like it, if you had places to go and interesting people to meet with—publishers and God knows what all—it would be a different picture, yes? No?"

"Yes."

"And it isn't, as you said, just any old job. It's absolutely something that would make people think you're a smart cookie."

"Mmm."

"So there you are."

"But you don't understand. I'm not a writer. Dostoevski is a writer. Hemingway is a writer."

"Do you want to get technical or do you want to get out of the house? We're not discussing WRITERS—just 'writers.' If you want to talk about WRITERS I'm not sure we should even include Hemingway. But we're talking about 'writers.' Everybody's a 'writer.' You just sit down and you write."

"Yeah," I said, "that's another thing. All these housewives who write! Every other lady you see squeezing grapefruit at the grocery is a 'writer.' It may not be the oldest profession, but I'll bet it's the most ubiquitous."

"You see the words you use? Of *course* you're a writer. Listen, don't worry about other people. You'll be writing from your own, unique, warped point of view!"

✳ 3 1

"About what? What am I going to write about? I don't know what to write about!"

"Write about *another* friend. You've got more than one friend, haven't you?" she stood up. "I've got a new baby in the hospital. Ten pounds eight ounces. *Oi vay!* Can you imagine carrying that around? I leave you with two words—Go! Write! So long, Feodor."

"Who?"

"Dostoevski!"

After she'd gone I started putting the dirty clothes in the washing machine and thinking about being a writer. My spine tingled with excitement at the possibility, but my head told my spine not to get so excited. All very well for Vicki to say "Go! Write!" It wasn't that simple. Sure I had more than one friend, but how many friends do the kind of things anybody wants to read about? What, for instance, was so fascinating about my friend Deedee's life? Or Carol Sappersmith's? Or Bookie Cramm's? All day long I tried to remember everything I knew about everybody I'd ever known. There wasn't one really good story in the lot.

Then late that afternoon, as I was opening a can of Buitoni tomato sauce, I stopped dead. Tomato sauce. Suddenly I was back in the grocery store around the corner from where I'd once lived in Brooklyn. I could smell the grocery store. And the cigar store next to it. Newspapers and loose-leaf books and licorice whips. Winter afternoons. After school. Roughneck boys. Snowballs. Walking down the street with a pain in the middle of my back where the muscles were all tensed waiting for a snowball to hit. Walking beside Vilma, blonde, elegant, disdainful, and sixteen years old.

Vilma! The Grace Kelly of Morrison Street! Vilma and her crazy family!

The next morning, after David and Sooz had raced each other to the bus stop, I took out some paper and Alex's old typewriter, and started "writing."

※ 3 2

I found myself feeling a lot better. I stopped making lamb chops. I stopped breaking ashtrays. And the pages began to pile up. I watched that little pile of pages growing—four, ten, seventeen, thirty-one! All that paper! All those words! It got to be so enjoyable it was almost a vice. I couldn't wait for morning to come and the kids to leave so I could be alone with the story in the typewriter. It fascinated me. I was dying to know how it would all turn out in the end. It was like one of those books you pick up and can't put down. Not that it was *good*, it was just absorbing.

Then one day it ended. Page seventy-nine. A peculiar number. Too long for a story, too short for anything else. But it was mine and I loved it.

And all this time I told nobody about it, except Vicki. I don't know what instinct made me keep it a secret from Alex. (What do I mean I don't know? Of course I know. Do you tell the warden you're digging a tunnel?)

I called Vicki and told her it was finished and I was going to bring it over for her to read, but she said no, her opinion wasn't worth a damn, I should take it to that publisher.

So I called and made an appointment.

This may sound as though the curtain is about to go up on the success story of Ruth Bernard, lady writer. Sorry. Or, take heart, as the case may be. What I'm trying to tell you about is not so much what happened to me because of writing a story, as what happened to me because of trying to get out of the house. I could just as well have taken a job selling real estate, or decided to become a buyer for Macy's stationery department, or opened my own travel agency; except for the details, the story would be the same. What happens when you walk away from a house and family—not what happens to the house and family but what happens to *you*—is what I'm talking about.

I just thought *somebody* ought to tell the truth about it.

So, I called and made an appointment. It was October. The

✳ 3 3

day of the appointment the sky was cornflower blue and there was a cardinal in the dogwood tree.

And downstairs in the laundry room Sarah May, the alleged cleaning woman from White Plains, was in for the day.

4   I CALLED A TAXI, because the car was in for repairs again, put on my good red suit from The French Shop, and very cleverly avoided giving my face a second glance in the mirror, because I knew from bitter experience that a second glance is never casual—in fact, it's endless. It starts with noticing a slackening of the jawline, proceeds through a microscopic inspection of those cracks and crevices that certain idiots refer to as "laugh lines," and ends with my picking up the telephone for a long conversation with Vicki that starts out, "God Almighty, what am I living for?"

Sometimes Vicki tries to give me that jazz about every period of your life having its own joys; and then, as always happens when I find myself tilting at the windmills of hypocrisy, I get depressed. But most of the time she just says, "Let's face it, Ruthie, there's only one word for being over thirty, and that word is lousy."

Somehow this cheers me up.

But I didn't have time for a phone call this morning, so I ignored the face in the mirror. Instead, I picked up my gloves and marched downstairs to the laundry room to talk to Sarah May. Going down the stairs I cleared my throat several times in anticipation of the speech I was going to make to her, to the effect that the exorbitant sum I was paying her for the day was supposed to be for cleaning my house, not for bringing her own washing to do in my washing machine and then spending the day ironing it. I'd stayed up half the night preparing the speech because I'd known about this situation for weeks now. My neighbor, Gloria Betz, had told me that every Wednesday, five minutes after I left my house, the front door opened and Sarah May dashed out to her car (she has a car, yet!), took an enormous bundle of dirty wash from the back seat and ran back into the house with it. I must admit this started me wondering about Gloria Betz. I mean didn't she have anything better to do than watch my front door all the time? However, I had evidence that she was right about Sarah May. First of all, I began to notice that each Wednesday night the house was just about as dirty as it had been Wednesday morning. Also I found lint in the washing machine which I had diabolically de-linted the night before as a trap.

The point is, was I going to let Sarah May get away with it? My first impulse was yes, let her get away with it. Who wants to start up with those girls? Besides, she might quit, and where was I going to find another girl who had her own car and didn't have to be picked up at the bus stop at an ungodly hour in the morning before I even had a cup of coffee in me?

But as the weeks wore on, I found a hard nervous lump growing in my chest which I figured out was monumental resentment, and I decided that having it out with her was vital to my physical well-being. So I stayed up half the night preparing a speech. First I tried out the blunt attack.

"Sarah May," I would say, "have you been using my washing machine to do your own washing?"

But the answer came back to me clear as a bell.

"No!" she would say. And then where would I be?

So I practised a more oblique approach.

"Sarah May, the other day I took the list of things I left for you to do last week, and I did them. And somehow or other it only took me four hours. Now you were here eight hours, and then you explained to me that you couldn't get most of it done because you didn't have enough time. Now it occurred to me that possibly you're going about it the wrong way and using up your energy where it isn't really needed. How about . . ."

Even *I* could see that by the end of this rambling monologue she'd have gone back to the agency and found another job.

Finally I hit on the perfect gimmick. Out of nowhere I had remembered watching Sooz's kindergarten class on visitor's day, and it struck me that the way that kindergarten teacher had handled an obstreperous little boy was exactly the way to handle Sarah May. I would use child psychology. Make her feel I was on her side. We'd be a team.

"Sarah May, we've got a problem here and I'm going to need your help. We just aren't getting enough done on Wednesdays. There must be something wrong with the way we're going at it. Now I've got a good idea. Why don't you make up a timetable— you know, eight to nine the bathrooms, nine to ten polish the furniture, and so on—and when I get back tonight we'll go over it."

That was the ticket. Tact. Diplomacy. Very shrewd.

I rehearsed the speech very carefully until about three a.m. and now as I walked down to the laundry room I went over it in my mind, while I cleared my throat and tried to assume a gentle but firm expression.

There was Sarah May, holding a mop in one hand and half a Fig Newton in the other. Her humid, dark eyes turned on me with what they call a baleful look. She swallowed a piece of Fig Newton.

I started putting on my gloves, which gave me something to look at while I was talking. Psychology, I said to myself. Diplomacy. Tact. I cleared my throat again.

"Sarah May," I said, "have you been using my washing machine to do your own washing?"

Well, you can't win them all.

To my surprise she didn't come out with a straight "no."

She lowered her eyes and said, "A little."

For a minute or two I tried to figure out how you could use a washing-machine "a little." What did she do? Stop it after a few minutes and take out the clothes half-dirty?

"Well," I said, nervously, "it's not that I begrudge you the washing machine but . . . uh . . . I do think you could get more work done during the day if you didn't spend the time doing your washing." She looked at me sullenly and I added meekly, "Don't you?"

"Yes, Mrs. Bernard," she said, in no uncertain terms.

The taxi horn sounded. Saved by the bell. I rushed up the stairs giving her the usual last-minute routine.

"Don't give Sooz any peanut butter and jelly sandwiches for lunch. There's eggs. And when David gets home make sure he changes into his blue jeans."

I knew perfectly well there was absolutely no sense to this parting speech since she never listened to a word of it and I had to telephone the house every hour anyway, but I knew just as well that saying it was one of my deep-rooted compulsions. You can't fight everything.

On the way out of the house I grabbed the big brown manila envelope from the hall table. It felt heavy, solid, important.

All the way into town on the New York Central I felt life slowly returning to my veins. My senses were sharpening, I felt lighter, more buoyant—even my jawline seemed to be toning up all by itself. By the time we reached One Hundred and Twenty-fifth Street it was as though the house, the supermarket, and Sarah May had never existed. And when I walked off the train into the vaulted shrine of Grand Central I knew, with a sudden stab of joy, that somewhere in this marvelous, dirty, over-crowded city with its darling traffic problems and its gorgeous exhaust fumes, I was going to find me again.

I walked to Fifth Avenue and then up the twelve blocks from Forty-fifth to Fifty-seventh. What a twelve blocks! Saks. De-Pinna's. Mark Cross. Elizabeth Arden. I. Miller. Bonwit Teller. They're right—see America first!

At Fifty-seventh I turned toward the familiar old office building that housed the offices of Prospect Press and its publisher, mild wild Simon Marsh. We called him that because that's what he was—mild and wild. Mild by temperament, he never really found anything worth getting into a stew about, and at the drop of a hat he would abandon the pursuit of the dollar and sit for hours over a glass of tea (he had tea-bags hidden all over the office, on bookshelves, in vases, in drawers of the filing cabinet, like an alcoholic only with tannic acid) discussing large subjects with members of the office staff—the decline of the American theater, or the dangers of menopause, or the real reason for juvenile delinquency. He had an interesting theory about the last one; he was convinced it was directly connected with the disuse of the slingshot.

"There was something about a slingshot," he used to say, "that satisfied a basic need in the young male. The purity of it. The simplicity. Take David and Goliath. Try to imagine that story with a switchblade or a zip-gun instead of a slingshot. You see how the difference in the weapon changes the moral emphasis?"

He'd go on like that for hours. He had, incidentally, two teenagers of his own, earnest young people who, I gathered, felt there was something a little morally lax about their father.

Anyway, that was the mild side. The wild side involved his friends; he had a great many kooks for friends—theater people, a few publishers, a group he had collected over his summers at Martha's Vineyard. They were as brothers and sisters to Simon, and Simon was the kind of man who felt impelled to be his brother's keeper. The tension these "brothers" generated, the complicated situations into which they propelled him, the sudden frantic trips to Westport or Philadelphia or the Midtown Turkish Baths—that was the wild side. One day he spent six hundred dollars yelling over long distance to an independent movie producer stranded in Yokohama, trying to explain why he couldn't afford to cable the producer six hundred dollars.

Nobody called him Mr. Marsh; we all called him Simon. The

office atmosphere was very informal. Well, informal isn't exactly the word. Nutty is more like it.

Going up in the condemned elevator I felt again the warm glow of homecoming that I felt each time I'd come back . . . three times in all, since the day I'd said to Alex, "Okay, take me away from all this." But as I stepped out on the seventh floor and suddenly remembered the reason for my visit, I became shy and very nervous. Glancing down at the big manila envelope in my hand I began to entertain serious doubts as to my sanity.

What kind of self-delusion was this? It would be a miracle if he didn't laugh right in my face. The least embarrassment I could hope for was a thud of silence. By the time I reached the office door I was rigid with anticipated humiliation.

I walked in. The same three cluttered desks at right angles to one another, Isabelle Johns at one of them, looking exhausted as usual, hunched over the telephone clutching a bottle of aspirin, a piece of lank hair over her forehead wearing that bulky beige sweater she'd knitted herself, moaning nasally into the phone, "Lissin, Mar-tin, it's sixty thousand words. Who can use sixty thousand words?"

At the middle desk there was a new typist, with purple lipstick.

At my old desk there was another new face—the fourth exchange since I'd left. The first three had been girls; this was a young man with nervous hands. It was nice to know I wasn't easily replaceable.

They'd built a new showcase along the far wall; six shelves of Prospect Press publications; *The Intellectual Criminal, Mystery and the Orient, Six of the Best* (—what?), *The Freudian Approach to Murder. . . .*

Behind a partition there were voices and a sharp laugh as one of the Regular Contributors emerged, a lackadaisical man in a gray suit with gray hair and gray stubble and a gray pullover, biting on a pipe. "Whatever you say," he murmured, "whatever you say. Just send money."

The nervous young man at my old desk looked up and saw me.

"Yes?" he said, shrilly.

"Oh. I'm here to see . . ."

Isabelle Johns turned and smiled, "Ruthie!" And then Philip Bagley, the editor, with that permanent cleft between his eyebrows from frowning all the time, even when he smiled, came out from behind the partition in his shirt sleeves; and Simon came out of his office, and there was a lot of hugging and cheek-grazing, and Simon told Isabelle to make some tea and took me into his office.

Simon's office was chaotic. None of the pieces of furniture had anything to do with each other, a chair from an English castle stood next to a bridge lamp, and so on. There were manuscripts on everything, a sunlamp on the radiator, a pair of water skis in the corner, an electric pencil sharpener nailed to the back of the door, and on the olive green wall behind his rococo desk, dominating the whole room, was an enormous framed Gauguin print of some of those taupe-colored Tahitian ladies going about their chores, their upper halves clothed only in a tropical breeze.

Simon had a bottomless passion for stressing the difference between the sexes. Those unfettered Tahitian bosoms symbolized for him the Real Woman—a luscious, mute, satin-skinned animal who walked around naked, carrying on her glorious, straight, brainless head, large baskets of groceries, or washing, or possibly men. He was constantly urging every girl he hired to get married and fulfill her anatomical destiny. He loved the sight of girls around the office, but he hated to see them doing anything that wasn't somehow related to their bosoms. Isabelle Johns was his big failure; she was still there, after all these years.

Now, as Simon leaned back in his dusty black leather chair, I noticed his brown hair was getting grayer. His face was sunlamp-tanned, as usual, and he regarded me as always with half-shut eyes, an amused smile, and dirty fingernails which somehow didn't bother me—they were part of Simon, I couldn't imagine him without them, and it gave him a kind of literate quality, or something.

"How come you're looking so good?" Simon said. "What is it, all that country air? Motherhood? How's your sex life?"

"I see you've got a new boy," I said, which is the only way to answer him when he starts off like that.

"Boy!" he said, and sighed profoundly. "I think he's a fagel. I asked him about his sex life and he got very upset, as though I'd accused him of something. This is getting to be a problem, you know it? The fagels are taking over. It's like the last days of the Roman Empire. Decadent. Go to Sardi's East any lunch hour. All they need is a couple of indoor pools; it's the Roman Baths. They're all there—the senators, the publicans, the gladiators. You're lucky you got yourself a man before it's too late. Any day they're going completely out of style. What do you do with yourself all day these days?"

"Well . . ." I said, since he'd given me the opening, "as a matter of fact . . ."

"Cooking, cleaning, darning socks—that's the best thing for a woman, take my word for it. There is a fundamental need in a woman to preserve the hearth and home. If she fights it she becomes neurotic. I see it all around me. Marriages breaking up. You know why I've stayed married for nineteen years? Because my wife likes to cook and take care of the house. She *likes* it. She's happy. . . ."

I tried to relax, since it was obviously going to be some time before Simon would let me tell him about the contents of the envelope.

For a while he talked about his wife who got such a kick out of scraping the caked grease off the oven walls and keeping the toilet bowls spick and span, and I began to feel I was some kind of degenerate, not being home on my knees with a scrub brush. Finally he got back to me.

"You're looking good, kid," he said. "Whatta you been doing with yourself?"

I was still trying to relax, but the harder I tried, the stiffer I got.

"Well . . ." I began, and the telephone rang.

Simon made a gesture of impatience as he picked it up.

"Yeah? Harry? . . . Of course you've got a problem. You always have a problem. What's the problem? . . . Yeah . . . Harry, what kind of an idiot buys an off-Broadway theater? . . . Who told you that? . . . Well take it from me it's *not* on the way in. It's *been* in. It's on the way *out*. You want to do something with your money, try saving the United Nations. . . . I don't have to look at it, I know what it is. . . . All right, I'll look at it. . . . No, five o'clock. I know where it is."

He hung up.

"Harry's problems!" he said. "He needs a tax loss!"

From experience I knew he'd been talking to Harrison Wingate, a television producer, one of the Martha's Vineyard crowd. I also knew that once Simon started on Wingate anecdotes we were good for a two-hour monologue, and since I figured I'd be dead of hypertension by then, I leaped out of my chair and threw the manila envelope on the desk.

"Here," I croaked.

Simon picked up the envelope gingerly.

"What is it?" he asked.

"It's—uh—kind of a—kind of a *long* short story."

"*Kind* of a?" He opened the envelope, took out the manuscript, and riffled through the pages. "It's practically a book!" he said, and looked up at me. "*You* wrote it?"

I was a little annoyed at the incredulity in his voice, but I nodded and quickly took out another cigarette and wasted seven matches trying to light it while Simon glanced at the first page.

Finally I found my voice—or somebody's voice. It didn't sound like mine.

"I thought if you had time you might read it and see if it's any good. And—uh—if you think there's a chance—uh—maybe

✳ 42

you know somebody who could—uh—who publishes—uh—
that kind of thing—and—uh—"

I trailed off, looking at him like a dumb animal waiting to be
kicked.

"Of course I'll read it!" Simon said, and he came and put his
arm around me. "Of course I'll read it."

But already there was that queer little formality that creeps
into things the minute one person suspects another person wants
something from him that he can't possibly give. I suddenly realized I had given Simon the alternatives of having to lie in order
to spare my feelings, which he would hate, or having to tell me
an unpleasant truth, which he would also hate.

I started putting on my gloves and blinked back a couple of
tears that had sprung to my eyes, because I felt that with one
stupid move I had lost Simon as a friend.

That feeling was both naïve and unworthy, I found out later.

"Where are you rushing?" Simon asked. "You didn't finish
your tea."

I mumbled something about having an appointment with
the hairdresser, which was ridiculous because I hate all those
assembly-line heads that come bouncing out of beauty parlors
and I wouldn't let a hairdresser touch me with a ten-foot comb.

Simon walked me to the door, asking about the kids, how
old they were, and were they boys or girls (he couldn't even
remember that!). I said hasty goodbys in the outer office and
rushed out.

I felt foolish. I felt as though I'd come into New York in
a pair of wrinkled pajamas with no makeup on and everybody
was being polite and pretending not to notice.

How could I have given that silly manuscript to Simon?
From what dark corner of conceit had I dredged up the temerity
to pass myself off as a writer? The story was juvenile. It was
amateurish. It was ludicrous. I blushed as I thought of Simon
reading it.

Suddenly I hated Prospect Press. I hated Simon, with his

* 43

dirty fingernails. I hated Vicki for giving me delusions of grandeur. Most of all I hated myself, for being so devoid of grandeur that the smallest self-confidence smacked of delusion.

When I got out to the street I found a drugstore, called home, and inquired what Sooz had had for lunch. Sure. Peanut butter and jelly. I walked slowly back down Fifth Avenue.

And as I walked down that lovely elegant street in the sharp sunny October afternoon, strangely and unaccountably my mood began to change. Like the needle in a barometer, it climbed from the cold depths of desolation, through distress and annoyance, to the more temperate weather of indifference, and on up through complacency and buoyancy to absolute glee.

Maybe the story wasn't so bad after all. Maybe it was even good. Who knew? What the hell! Maybe I'd found a profession!

I started looking at the fabulous clothes in the shop windows as though I could afford them. I picked out six pairs of shoes in I. Miller's window that I was definitely going to buy as soon as I got the nod from Simon.

By the time I reached the Doubleday bookshop I'd gone way beyond mere local success to international fame and fortune. It seemed to me that all those bright shiny book jackets behind Doubleday's plate glass bore my name. All the Shirley Jacksons were really mine. All the Katherine Anne Porters. All the Carson McCullers. All of that seven-hundredth printing of *Catcher in the Rye*. Even those big solid Quentin Reynoldses were really Ruth Bernards. Suddenly I was Somebody. I rose out of a sea of indistinguishable suburban faces like Neptune out of a sea of ocean. The one and only Ruth Bernard!

With tremendous élan I swung into a chic little children's shop and told a French salesgirl I wanted that twenty-dollar organdy pinafore in the window in a size five. It wasn't until she asked for the money that I came to my senses, mumbled that it wasn't chic enough after all, and bolted.

5   I TRIED to stay calm and think about other things until I heard from Simon, but it was like asking Sooz to stay calm and think about other things with a pile of unopened birthday presents in the corner. Even if the odds are the presents will all turn out to be pajamas, you can't expect somebody to sit still until they know for *sure*. Of course nobody was expecting me to do anything, because nobody knew anything about it except Vicki, and she was at a medical convention in Atlantic City.

As days passed with no word I became increasingly fidgety, and one late afternoon while I was making dinner I decided to sip a little sherry just to steady my nerves. A little wasn't enough. I sipped more. Alex came in and found me slicing bananas into the asparagus. His eyebrows went up, amused.

"Hey, there!" he said, spotting the glass and bottle next to the salmon casserole, "hello there! Can you hear me? Am I reaching you?" He turned to the kids, who were sitting at the table eating oddly-shaped grapefruit sections, "Good evening, children, we are coming to you from the kitchen of Ruthie the Lush, the chef who invented cooking with wine—in the chef. What's the occasion, Spookie Ruthie?"

In my vulnerable state I might have told him, if the smell of burning Betty Crocker potatoes hadn't distracted me. (Thank you, Betty Crocker. After all, why get into a discussion about something that might never happen?)

All week I alternated between unwarranted pessimism and unwarranted optimism. A couple of times I found Alex looking at me sideways, due, I suppose, to the fact that every time the phone rang I froze in whatever position I happened to be in, and my face turned chartreuse. By the seventh day I had come to the positive conclusion that Simon hadn't called me because he just couldn't think of any words that would describe how bad my story was.

I decided to laugh it off.

Who cares, I said to myself loftily, as I peeled carrots. So I won't have a profession. I lived this long without one, and it hasn't killed me yet. Anyway, who wants to go through all this agony every time you submit a script? Who needs it? Besides, writing is too much trouble. You have to think too much. Probably get a brain hemorrhage. I'm just as glad it didn't work out. I really am.

And then the phone rang and I nearly fractured a leg rushing to answer it. But it wasn't Simon, it was just Gimbel's upholstery department.

"Stop kidding yourself, Ruthie," I said, my heart pounding.

I stared hard at the telephone. My index finger was in actual pain from the frustrated compulsion to dial Simon's number, but I knew if he really didn't like the story it would be easier for him if I just waited until he mailed it back to me with a tactful little note, which Isabelle Johns would help him compose. And after all, why embarrass him?

On the other hand, why *not* embarrass him? If I suffer, everybody suffers. Besides, since when is he the final authority on writing? He'd probably have turned down *Tom Sawyer*. What does he know, anyway?

Besides, I thought—like every writer who ever lived, maybe he hasn't read it yet!

All morning long I kept lifting the receiver to dial his number and then putting it down again. As I lifted the receiver for the seventh time, the Con Edison man suddenly appeared to read the meter. I was downstairs letting him in through the garage (and wondering if he really *was* the Con Edison man— because, let's face it, any smart thief can say he's the Con Edison man, and even if you ask to see his credentials, which you don't, because it makes you feel like an idiot, but even if you do, how would you know what they're supposed to look like? He could print up any old thing with the words Con Edison on it . . .)— when the telephone rang.

I flew up the stairs.

Now that I think of it, if I really expected bad news, why was I so anxious to hear it?

It was Isabelle Johns. Simon had asked her to call me and see if I could arrange to meet him at Harrison Wingate's office on Friday at two o'clock.

My voice came out about an octave higher than usual.

"What?" I squealed. "What do you mean? Mr. Wingate? What do you mean? Did he read it? Did Simon read it? Who read it?"

As Isabelle started to answer, the Con Edison man called me from below. I couldn't make out what he was saying. I couldn't make out what Isabelle was saying.

"Wait a minute!" I said frantically to Isabelle.

"Shut up!" I shouted to the Con Edison man. Then, horrified, "Please!"

"What did you say?" I asked Isabelle.

Isabelle didn't know anything about anything. She was just told to make this appointment for Friday afternoon. I asked to speak to Simon but she said he'd gone to Philadelphia and wouldn't be back until Friday morning.

"Friday morning!" I whimpered. "That's five thousand seven hundred and sixty minutes away!"

She complimented me on my lightning calculation and asked again about the appointment. I said certainly I'd keep the appointment.

By the time I'd hung up the Con Edison man had slammed out through the garage. I ran out the front door to catch him and apologize, but he was already disappearing into the house across the street. I guess he was a real Con Edison man all right. I wondered if he were mad at me, and might he have done some-

✳ 47

thing spiteful like turning off the gas and electricity. I tried them. They worked.

In a state of intolerable excitement I ran back to the telephone and picked it up to dial Vicki's number, and then I remembered she was in Atlantic City.

I sat there with the telephone buzzing in my hand. There was nobody I could tell. I had a mysterious appointment that might lead to all kinds of fabulous things, and there was nobody I could tell. I was alone with my glorious news in an empty split-level silence. All alone. The children were at school. I wouldn't tell them anyway. Alex was at his office, but I wasn't ready to tell him either. The Con Edison man had gone away mad. There was no one. Something earth-shattering was about to happen to me and I didn't even have a dog I could tell it to.

I hung up and went to the window and looked out across the yard to where my neighbor's stiff little row of evergreens sepa-rated their mortgaged property from my mortgaged property. The big lazy-looking boxer was roaming around his yard nosing the ground for some lost dream.

"Hey, Dempsey," I said, "I think I'm going to be a writer!"

He looked up at me and barked.

"Pretty crazy, huh?"

He gave me a steady, mournful look and went about his business. I turned back into the room, reeling from all the adrenalin I was manufacturing. "It happened! My God, it really happened! I made something happen! They want to see me! I have an appointment!"

And suddenly I realized that if I went into the city on Friday there would be nobody at home to take care of the kids. Sarah May only came on Wednesdays.

I rushed back to the telephone table and opened the little book of private phone numbers to the page marked "baby-sitters." There was a list of seventeen names, but thirteen were crossed out for reasons too depressing to go into.

I dialed Mrs. Delaney's number. No answer. Mrs. Kraus, I

knew from trying to get her for last Saturday night, was on a two-week job for some disgustingly rich people who'd gone on a cruise, leaving their young behind. I called Mrs. Romano.

"Weeelll . . ." she whined, "Fridaaaay. . . . I don't know about Fridaaay . . ."

"Oh," I said, crisply. "Well I have to know definitely, because this is a business appointment."

"Weeelll . . ." she said, "I'll tell you what. . . . I'll let you know . . ."

"When?"

"Weeelll . . . could you call me back tonight? See, my husband's home with a virus, and I don't know if he'll be better by Fridaaaay . . ."

"So how will you know tonight?"

"Well maybe he'll feel better. . . ."

"All right, Mrs. Romano. I'll call you tonight."

I called Mrs. Hildebrand. A cool voice with a phoney British accent came over the wire. I told her the story. The reply was monosyllabic, not to mention noncommittal.

"Oh." There was a long pause. Then, "Mrs. Bernahd . . . I actually haven't been doing any sitting lately. I find it's just too strenuous, you know? My doctah has advised me . . . in fact just the othah day I had to refuse Mrs. Zellin . . . perhaps she told you?" This was so I shouldn't think she had anything against me, personally, just in case she ran short of money some day and decided she was once again strong enough to sit in my living room for a few hours while the kids played outside.

I thanked her (for what?) and hung up.

There was one last chance. I'd saved Mrs. Wettke for last because she was so great that she was always busy and it was practically impossible to get her unless you called a month in advance. This lady was an arch-homemaker. Wherever she went furniture gleamed, floors sparkled, window curtains bounced up fresh and starched, and the smell of thick stews and fresh-baked pies filled the air. She was out of that world that Louisa May Alcott once made you think really existed.

Hesitantly I dialed her number. Miraculously, she answered.

"Mrs. Bernard! How are you?" Her quick, cheerful voice came over the wire, pulsing with unused energy. She was a good sixty-five, this lady, but she made me feel senile. When I first met her I used to question her carefully, thinking she had some secret, like pills or Yoga, or lots of good red wine. But there was no secret, it was just metabolism, which they hand out before you're born and that's it for life.

When I asked her about Friday she said "Just a minute" and went to get her little book. I could here the pages rustling, and I thought of all the desperate women whose freedom depended on having their name in that little book.

"Friday," she said finally, "yes. Good. You have it."

From past innumerable experiences I was so predisposed to disappointment that I automatically said "Oh that's too bad," and then it sank in.

"I *have? Really?* That's *wonderful!* Thank you *very* much!" My gratitude was pathetic.

I arranged the time and hung up, feeling wary. Things were going too smoothly around here. It scared me.

I called Mrs. Romano back and told her it was all right, her husband could stay sick, I'd managed to get someone else.

I ran upstairs and threw open the closet door. What should I wear on Friday? How should I look? Bright, tailored and career-womanish like my namesake in *My Sister Eileen?* But I didn't look like Eileen's sister. Neither did I look like Eileen. I examined my reflection. What was I? No smart, angular career girl, for sure. On the other hand, no baby-doll. And that unruly hair, that rebellious face, that peculiar stance—half social worker, half shady lady—that was certainly no suburban mother. Then what? Didn't I belong to any group? Didn't I have a club? Funny. I'd never had this problem before. I'd always more or less looked like something: a kid, a teen-ager, a college student, a

* 5 0

young working-girl-about-town. But now—what? How would Mr. Wingate know what I was unless I figured it out first?

I took an oyster-beige wool dress off the closet rack and held it up against me. Of course, with no makeup and the baggy blue jeans and purple mules sticking out below it wasn't at its best, but it was the only thing I owned that could really be called "an elegant understatement" like in those Bergdorf ads, and if nothing else it would indicate that I read *The New York Times*.

Okay. I'd wear the oyster beige to Mr. Wingate's office.

I came out of my trance.

Mr. Wingate?

The moving parts of my brain which had got stuck together from the pressure of seven days of anxiety, now came unstuck and began to operate. Mr. Wingate wasn't a publisher. He was in television. What did *he* want with me? Was he going to put my story on television? Impossible. Wingate never did anything but serious dramas that started out in a rocking chair on the front porch of a southern town. Could it be that this meeting had nothing to do with my story? After all, nobody had said anything about the story. For all I knew Simon hadn't even read it. But then what was it all about? What the hell was going on?

My chief concern from then on, was how to keep my curiosity, my feverish speculations, and my adrenalin, from killing me off before Friday.

6 ON FRIDAY my oyster-beige wool walked into Mr. Wingate's office with me inside it, squirming with excitement. Twenty minutes later I was still squirming, but excitement was only half the reason; resentment was the other half. There is something about waiting in somebody's outer office that does something unpleasant to your self-respect and your

composure—I don't care if you're George Sanders. And Harrison Wingate's office was more intimidating than most. Maybe this was because Mr. Wingate was a phenomenon among television producers, being well-known by name, face, and opinion, to the general public. In fact he had managed to get himself so much publicity that he was even better than well-known; he had enemies. So the atmosphere of self-importance in that outer office was pretty thick.

As I sat on a slick leather sofa watching a sharp-faced redheaded secretary doing a lot of busy things at a desk guarding Wingate's sanctum, while a variety of smug little people bustled in and out of various doors, I felt less and less like somebody who had been called in for a business conference and more and more like somebody who was waiting in line for unemployment insurance.

This feeling was strengthened by the fact that I wasn't sure I *had* been called in for a business conference. I still didn't know what this meeting was all about, and I wished fervently that Simon didn't have such a laissez-faire attitude toward punctuality. If only he would show up I could find out what I was in for before I was in for it. But Simon didn't show, the secretary pretended I wasn't there, and Wingate was nowhere to be seen —he was probably in Palm Beach. So I sat there crossing and uncrossing my legs, wringing the life out of my gloves, and deciding that Isabelle Johns had had one of her bad days and got her messages crossed, when Wingate's private door opened, and he appeared in the doorway, ushering out a young man who had a lot of Flatbush Avenue under his Brooks Brothers tailoring, and who looked as though two more minutes of Mr. Wingate was two minutes more than he could take.

This was the first time I had seen Mr. Wingate in the flesh, and therefore the first time I was aware that he was madly in love with himself. He reminded me of a pompous little mathematics genius in my old neighborhood who had been known through four years of high school as "The Creep."

✳ 5 2

"It has a marvelous fulcrum," he was saying to Brooks Brothers, "but you see, the—uh—the substratum alone isn't enough. It has to generate. If it doesn't generate, then we have nothing. Once it generates, we have everything: thesis, antithesis, all that stuff. Drama, Perry, drama. Something . . . incisive. Something . . . definitive."

"You gonna try to get Rex?" asked Brooks Brothers.

"If it works out I will definitely show it to Rex."

"Because, you know, that's what I had in mind . . ."

"I know, I know, but in order to interest Rex the script will have to have a lot more . . . ambience. You know what I mean? I mean, if he looks for anything in a script, its ambience. . . ."

He went on like that for a while, throwing in a few more ambiences, a generic or two, a synthesize, and several catharses, while I looked him over carefully. He was a small man, soft, but dapper, with elegant clothes and a smile that was partly suspicion, partly phoney humility, partly insecurity, and mostly unbearable. A kind of composite Beau Brummel and Uriah Heep.

Finally he sent Brooks Brothers on his way, said to the secretary, "Did you send that wire to the coast?" and without even glancing at me, moved on little cat feet back into his inner office.

Well, I thought, he obviously never heard of me. The whole thing is a mistake; I will arise and go now and wring Isabelle John's neck . . . and then a buzzer sounded and the redhead told me to go in.

Dizzy with uncertainty, anxiety, and no lunch, I crossed to the imposing door and opened it.

Mr. Wingate's office was about as antithetical to Simon's as it could be and still be in the same world; angular, spotless, monochromatic, elegant, simple, expensive, and cold. And Mr. Wingate was posed behind a large sweep of polished desk, murmuring into a telephone, quietly trying to give the impression that it was the President of the United States on the other end, informing him of an urgent crisis in international affairs and telling him that in fifteen minutes there would be a limousine waiting downstairs with the motor running to speed him to the airport to catch the next plane for Ankara.

He gave me a deliberately absentminded smile, motioned me to a chair, and continued his tête-à-tête with the telephone.

"Well I don't see how I can make it," he murmured. "I have an Academy meeting at four, and I'm leaving for London in the morning. No, everything's set with Ingrid, it's just a question of doing it here or there. Well England would be better, it's generic, after all . . ."

In the middle of this the door opened. Simon called "Hello, Harry," loudly from the doorway, walked in, squeezed my arm, and collapsed into one of the frigid elegant chairs, which somehow then began to look a little lived-in and disreputable.

Wingate quickly ended his conversation, stood up, and came around his desk, both arms outstretched in apology.

"So sorry," he said, with one of his terrible smiles, and he began to offer us drinks, cigarettes, ashtrays, lighters, stocks and bonds . . .

Finally Simon's chronic impatience with amenities exploded into words.

"Enough of this lovemaking," he said. "Harry read your story. Tell her, Harry."

Mr. Wingate took a cigarette from an onyx box on his desk, lit it, and leaned against the front of his desk, ankles crossed, arms folded, and head tilted back, smiling loosely at the ceiling. I soon realized he had a habit of smiling off into space like that, sadly, before speaking, as though what he was about to say was so perfect the Gods would surely destroy him.

"I read your story," he said softly, "and I think it's very funny. Very original." He lifted the cigarette to his mouth and inhaled deeply, leaving me dangling. What did sadists do before cigarettes were invented, I wondered? "You write dialogue extremely well." He paused.

"Harry has an idea he wants to talk to you about . . ." Simon said impatiently. Mr. Wingate politely cut him off.

"The thing is this . . ." he began, significantly, and then looked up at the ceiling again and smiled sadly. I thought Simon would burst.

"I have a feeling," Wingate finally intoned, "that this would make a very amusing series."

A series? What did he mean, a series?

"A series?" I said, wittily.

He roamed back around the desk and sat down.

"Yes," he said, "a situation comedy series. For television." And he looked at me with an expression I'd seen before many years ago, on the face of a young man who had succeeded in luring me into his apartment after several drinks. As he put out the overhead light and came slowly toward me with his fingers already curling in anticipation of removing all kinds of clothes, he was wearing just such an expression, as though to say, You hit the jackpot, you lucky girl!

And now I had the same reaction I'd had then. My heart hammered against my ribs like it was trying to beat its way out of my body, and I shrank back in my chair, thinking, you pay for everything.

But Mr. Wingate was not a man to be put off by a little look of terror on a lady's face. He went serenely on.

"Now I might be interested in producing a pilot. But—" He stood up and roamed again. "The thing is this . . ." There it was again, tilted head, sad smile. "Situation comedy writing is a very special technique. There are writers who have a . . . penchant for it, and writers who don't. Whether you have a penchant or not, we don't know. And obviously I couldn't commit myself to a project of this nature unless I had some assurance that the material would eventually emerge as a saleable property." He reached into a drawer and pulled out a pile of manuscript. It was my story. All of a sudden it looked very small and lonely, and I had this ridiculous impulse to grab it away from him and say, it's all right, sweetie, mama's here. But Mr. Wingate was busy riffling it like a deck of cards and saying, "All we have here is a—uh—whimsical idea and some rather amusing dialogue. What we need is someone who can turn it into a television script—in other words, an experienced situation comedy writer."

He swung his eyes in my direction and paused.

I don't know what he expected me to say, unless it was "That leaves me out." I said nothing and tried to look shrewd.

"What I want to ask you, dear, is this . . . would you consider *collaborating?*" He leaned forward suddenly, and in a panic I somehow got all confused about the meaning of that word and blushed violently. I stared at him dumbly, and then at the script, and then at Simon, and then back at him, and made a noncommittal sound. Something like "Mmssggrrmm. . . . "

As I expected, Mr. Wingate wasn't the type to admit that any sound was too subtle for his interpretative powers, so he pretended to have received my message and went on.

"The writer I have in mind is a young man by the name of Norman Spain. He's written a good many successful series. 'Me and Bob,' 'The Fiddlers,' 'Mother Was a Shortstop.' . . . Not exactly Molière, but possibly the best of that genre." He tapped my manuscript delicately with one finger. "This is his kind of material. I know he could get a script out of it. That is, the two of you could. Well! How do you feel about it?"

The major thing I was feeling was stunned. I had been prepared for only two contingencies; "Yes, I want to publish your story," or "Thanks a lot but no thanks." It never entered my mind that what I'd written was yard goods, and that it could be made into drapes, slipcovers or ladies' suits, depending on the manufacturer.

If there's anything Simon can't stand, it's somebody sitting around with their mouth open, so after watching me hopelessly for thirty seconds, he got out of his chair with a lot of noise, and started talking.

"Naturally you can't expect her to make up her mind on the

spot, Harry. Why don't you do this? See when this Norman Spain is available, and then we can get the two of them together and see if they click, see if they talk the same language, see how the chemistry works."

I thought it was very smart of Simon, making it sound all of a sudden as though I were too important to be rushed into just any old project. I was too new in the business to know that "click," "chemistry," and "talk the same language" are rudimentary euphemisms for "in case you change your mind about the whole thing, she should have a little face left."

"Naturally, Simon, naturally," Wingate smirked. "*Cela va sans dire*. But first I would like to get Ruth's reaction to the basic *idea*." He turned more or less to me. "Would you be interested in—uh—exploring the possibilities?"

Evidently I indicated that I would be, because he looked gratified and ten minutes later Simon and I were in a coffee shop around the corner, having tea. (I'd like to see the person who could order coffee when Simon's paying for it.)

"Well?" Simon asked.

"My God!" I said. "Television? I can't write for television! That's a whole profession! I can't even play chess!" I added, irrelevantly.

"Chess," said Simon, "is an intellectual exercise. Where's the comparison?"

"Yes, but . . . television!" I repeated, tremulously. "I wouldn't even know where to start!"

"That's what this other fellow is for . . . this Norman Spain."

"I know what *he's* for. But what am *I* for? I don't understand. If Mr. Wingate wanted the story, why didn't he just buy it and give it to Norman what's-his-name to make into a whatchamacallit?"

"Because Harry likes to discover people. He thinks maybe they'll turn out to be gold mines and he wants to stake a claim. Besides, I told him you wouldn't sell it outright."

"*Why?*"

✳ 5 7

"Because that way you'd get peanuts and this way you'll get royalties."

Royalties! *Royalties! Me!* I shivered.

"But—but, I don't know how to *collaborate*. I never did it before in my life!"

"The point is, do you *want* to?"

"*Want* to? With royalties and everything? It's only . . . I don't understand it. How can it be good for television? I just wrote it between the laundry and the pot roast."

"That's how Harry became a producer."

"Really?" I said, with such surprise in my voice that Simon raised his eyebrows at me.

"Why?" he said. "What did you think?"

"Well, I thought it was more like when he got out of Princeton twenty years ago, he got bored just being a rich kid, so he looked around for some place to go slumming and found television."

"Think again. He was a City College boy and his name wasn't Harrison *or* Wingate. Now, let me tell you what happened, and what's going to happen. Harry tries to avoid talking English because he thinks it's too plebeian, so let me explain. The day you gave me the story to read, Harry dragged me down to some hole-in-the-wall in the Village that he wanted to convert to an off-Broadway theater."

"I remember. I was there when he called."

"That's right. Well, I was carrying your envelope and Harry said what is it and I said it's a funny story about a beautiful Brooklyn girl who can't find a guy to marry her because she lives with a houseful of relatives, and he practically tore it out of my hands. Now what he wants to do is this. After you and this Spain boy turn out the script, he'll produce a pilot film. That means he'll put up the money and run around getting in everybody's way, and call meetings and have lunches and carry on like he's in labor and generally be a pain in the ass. But once the film is in the can, and if it's any good, he'll sell it, because he's a great

* 5 8

salesman. Of course there's no way of knowing if it *will* be any good. That depends on how much Harry interferes. You see, sweetheart, Harry doesn't know beans about comedy. Harry never laughed in his life. Harry wouldn't be caught dead laughing. It's too plebeian. That's one of his words, plebeian. Also symbiotic. You may have noticed he's a word-dropper."

"So if he doesn't know anything about comedy and he thinks my story is funny, it must be pretty bad."

"*He* didn't think your story was funny. Somebody told him it was. One of his assistants. You think he *reads*? Especially humor? Harry considers humor a necessary evil."

"Then why does he bother?"

"Because. Harry is building an empire. He, personally, is going to bring the television industry back to New York. And once it's here, he's going to own it. When Harry dreams, he sees NBC, CBS, ABC, and all the affiliates broadcasting nothing but Harrison Wingate productions twenty-four hours a day. He wants to own television. Today. Tomorrow, the world. So he has to expand, he has to diversify. He can't keep raising the level of television entertainment and get anywhere in this business. Don't make any mistake; Harry's shrewd, he's commercial. Just because he puts on those four-hour dramatic shows doesn't mean he's interested in art. Those are just his status symbols. Some people have three cars. Harry has six playwrights. Anyway, what you have to decide is whether the whole thing is going to be worth it. Professionally, of course, you've got nothing to lose. Personally, that's another story. Personally, you could stand to lose a great deal. You should consider it very carefully."

I looked at him with my eyes full of simple, straightforward confusion, and I saw his expression change as he realized this was not Arlene Francis he was talking to, but just me, Ruthie Bernard, an impetuous *klotz* from suburbia, who had no idea what she'd be letting herself in for.

"What's the matter? Lost you?"

✳ 59

"What do you mean—about standing to lose a great deal personally?"

I had visions of finding out too late that television contracts obliged a neophyte situation comedy writer to grant the network executives certain bedroom liberties, or to take a second mortgage on her home in the event the series was a flop and the sponsors wanted their money back.

Simon explained, shrugging, "You're not a career girl. You're a nice, normal kid. You have a husband, a home, children . . ."

"So?"

"So television isn't something you work at with your left hand while your right hand takes care of the family. It's not like writing a story, a few hours a day sitting at your kitchen table. It's not so easy to do this *and* be a wife and mother. A project like this will turn the whole household upside down. It will probably cause a lot of conflicts and tensions."

There it was again. Conflicts and tensions. For God's sake!

"What," I said elegantly, "about the conflicts and tensions that are being caused by my staying home and being a wife and mother?"

Simon leaned back and looked at me through those half-shut, speculative eyes of his.

"I didn't know you were one of those," he said.

One of what? The human race?

"Really, Simon," I said stiffly, "since when is having a husband and children a major crime? Since when are you supposed to be put out of circulation for it?"

He smiled thinly. "Okay. In any case, it's your decision."

"Well, not yet it isn't. This Norman Spain might not like my chemistry. He might tell Mr. Wingate to go fly a kite."

Simon burst out laughing.

"I guess it's possible," he said, figuring out the tip for the waitress. "I guess there must be a television writer once in a while who turns down easy money. But I wouldn't worry about it. No, the only thing that could happen is that Harry could lose interest. Right now he's hot on this story. He's convinced it could be another 'Lucy' or 'Dusy' or whatever it was. He sees it making nice little piles of residual dollars in the years to come. But if it hangs fire long enough he could get disenchanted, or decide to go off to Africa and get Robert Ruark to do a series on the Swahilis. So my advice is, give it a lot of thought and make a quick decision."

He got up. I grabbed his sleeve. I had to hold onto something solid.

"Wait a minute. Just a minute. . . ."

"What's the matter?"

"Is this real? I mean, does he really mean it? Is it serious?"

"Of course it's serious."

"I . . . How can they run television like this? It's so—I mean, I thought they only hired Big People . . . Big Writers . . . from Hollywood and everything . . ."

Simon smiled.

"Reserve your opinion," he said.

But I barely heard him.

The next thing I was conscious of was a large, bright poster picture of the current Miss Rheingold staring at me from the front of the train car as I waited to be pulled out of Grand Central. I stared back at Miss Rheingold, wondering how it was they always, unerringly, picked the contestant who looked least like a living human being.

Suddenly my mouth felt dry. I got up, went to the front of the car, drew a paper cup from the dispenser, and filled it with water.

Television! Harrison Wingate! Where did I come to all that? Royalties! My God, maybe we could go to Europe! Maybe even Greece!

I drank the water and filled the cup again.

Television! My name up there on the screen! Everybody would see it! Helen, Vera, Natalie, the delivery man . . . everybody!

People pushed by me, going into the car. I filled the cup again.

But how would I know what to write? Jokes? Actors? Rehearsals? How did it work? Who was Norman Spain?

More people pushed by me.

Boy, wait'll Alex hears about this! That reminds me, did I take something out of the freezer for dinner? Well, there's still some pot roast left. . . .

"Lady, do you mind . . . ?" A man with two suitcases. I moved up the aisle, holding the paper cup.

What the hell did Simon mean about tensions and conflicts? What could be so tense and conflicting about making a lot of money and seeing your name on the screen and going to Europe? How could it be anything but terrific? How could Alex do anything but cheer? Or could he? . . .

I reached the end of the aisle and turned around and started back again. Strangely enough there didn't seem to be any seats left. Two minutes ago the car had been empty. What happened? And what was I doing with a cupful of water?

The train started. I staggered. The water spilled a little. People looked at me. I drank the rest of the water, quickly, held onto the back of a seat and swayed, all the way home.

By the time I got home my head was swimming and my feet were swollen.

I hobbled into the house, kicked off my high heels, paid Mrs. Wettke, thanked her profusely as she left, took three aspirin, and herded the kids into the bathroom for their showers. Then I went into the kitchen and started warming up the pot roast and making mashed potatoes.

I would've given about five hundred dollars to be able to run over and tell Vicki all that had happened, but even if I'd been free to go, she wasn't due back from Atlantic City until the next day. The news was choking me. But I wouldn't tell Alex. No. Not until it was signed in blood, and too late for me to back out even if he. . . . Even if he what?

I didn't have too much time to dwell on it. The hours between five and seven P.M. in our house were a combination of a
crowded hamburger joint at lunch-hour operated solely by one
inefficient short-order cook, and a sinking ship in midocean on
which all passengers have panicked.

While I was mashing the potatoes, Sooz came flying into the
kitchen in her bathrobe, dripping wet, because in the middle of
her shower she remembered she had something vital to tell me.

I screamed but she ignored it.

"You know what?" she spluttered breathlessly. "You know
what, Mommy? You know what? (It takes her a while to get
started, like a cold automobile engine in the morning.) "You
know what? The teacher brought in a cage and it had two
mouses in it!"

"Mouses?" I shrieked, indicating that her English was faulty
and she was catching pneumonia, both.

"Mices?" she asked.

"No!"

"Mees?"

"Get back up there this minute!"

Then David came sliding in. He never walks. He sprints,
hops, struts, leaps, careens, tumbles, trips, skates, dances, hobbles
. . . but walking is not one of his accomplishments.

"Hey Mom," he said, "when you die, who gets your money?"

It went on like that until the front door opened and they
both rushed screaming out of the kitchen to greet their father,
not so much out of joy at his arrival as out of a mutual grim
determination to beat each other to the front door, or anywhere
else.

As they clung to Alex' legs and arms, the first thing out of
their treacherous little mouths was the information that I'd gone
to New York and Mrs. Wettke had taken care of them all
afternoon.

"How come?" Alex asked me, disapprovingly. (Having some-

✳ 63

body in just so I could go romping off for a day in New York was not in our budget.)

"Well," I sighed, "I guess you might as well know. Deedee's in the hospital." Deedee was my closest friend and one of the girls I had lived with before I got married.

"What's wrong with her?"

"She had a miscarriage."

"I didn't even know she was pregnant."

"It was very sudden. I mean recent. I mean, I didn't know either—"

"Well, that's a shame."

Alex' voice was full of genuine sympathy. He'd always been fond of Deedee.

"How is she now?"

"Well—you know." I shrugged expressively.

"Mmm—that's rough."

I made a mental note to call Deedee the first chance I got and warn her.

I relaxed a little over the weekend, knowing that nothing much could happen with Wingate in England. Then Monday night when the kids were asleep and Alex was unwinding in the big chair with *Life* magazine and I was stretched out on the couch lost in *Balthazar,* the telephone rang. I answered it casually, half of me still roaming around Alexandria.

"Could I speak with Ruth Bernard, please?"

I stiffened. "Speaking," I said, knowing immediately who it was and wondering how I was going to conduct any kind of intelligent conversation under the circumstances.

"This is Harrison Wingate, dear."

"Oh—yes!" I said, and walked as far out of the living room as the telephone cord would let me.

"I have Norman Spain here with me. We've been discussing your story . . ."

He paused, so I said "Oh!" again, and wondered if a man

✳ 64

with his passion for polysyllables would find me refreshing or intolerable.

"We thought it would be a good idea," he said, "if you and Mr. Spain got together at my office some time this week."

He paused again and I searched frantically for some answer that wouldn't involve any incriminating words for Alex to overhear.

"Uh, all right," I said, finally.

"Fine. How about Thursday at four?"

Thursday. Not Wednesday when Sarah May was coming and I could leave the house legitimately. No, it had to be Thursday. I'd have to get another sitter (if I *could!*) and the kids would squeal on me again, and this time Deedee would have to at least die to justify it.

"I'm afraid I couldn't . . ." I said, moving back to the telephone table.

"I see. What day would be convenient for you?"

I picked up a pipe of Alex' that was lying on the table and clattered it against the ashtray as though I were knocking out ashes.

At the same time I mumbled "Wednesday?" hoping the clatter would cover my voice.

"Wednesday." I heard Mr. Wingate turn away from the phone and confer briefly with somebody, then he was back. "Could you make it at two-thirty?"

"Yes."

"Fine. We'll see you then."

"Yes."

"Goodby."

I heard the click of the receiver as he hung up.

"I'm really not interested," I said into the dead phone. "Thanks anyway," and I hung up.

As I waltzed back to the couch I said airily, "That was the Tony and Julia dance studios. They wanted to give me seventeen free lessons."

✳ 6 5

"Mmm . . ." said Alex, studiously absorbed in a five-page spread on Sophia Loren.

I picked up *Balthazar* again, but even though Durrell is to me what the church is to those of other religious persuasions, I read a whole chapter without seeing a word. In spite of what Simon had said, I felt sure Norman Spain held my future in his hands. He would take one look at me and say Yea or Nay, and that would be the beginning, or the end.

Who could read! I dropped my book.

"Hey," I said to Alex, "if I promise not to give up right away, will you try once more? Teach me to play chess?"

7 ON WEDNESDAY I walked into Wingate's office, this time with much less confusion and much more apprehension, because now I *knew* what I had to lose. There, in the chair I had once occupied, sat a lean, neatly-dressed, sandy-haired, worried-looking man in his middle thirties. His eyes never stayed on one object for more than a second. I had the feeling he was late for something. And I had the feeling he'd been giving people that feeling for the better part of thirty years.

When Wingate introduced us he half-rose from his chair, kind of waved with one hand and muttered "Hi," looking at my chin, then sank back. It was the strangest thing, the way he sat. He sprawled all over the place like someone completely at ease, but there wasn't a relaxed muscle in his whole body. All the time he was lounging there so casually he looked like a runner at the starting line waiting for the gun to go off.

As Wingate made some opening remarks, trying to get us into conversation, I watched Norman Spain out of the corner of my eye. I decided nobody could ever accuse him of having a sunny disposition. Not that he was surly or hostile, he just seemed to be harboring some terrible anxiety. What's he worried about, I wondered? Me? The script? It didn't exactly give me confidence.

Then Wingate asked him to tell me his ideas concerning my story, and he got up and started to talk.

I gathered he couldn't talk without moving, because once he began to talk he wasn't still for a minute. He kept walking around the room emptying ashtrays, moving chairs, opening and closing venetian blinds, brushing invisible specks off his suit, taking out his handkerchief, refolding it, putting it back again.

"This," he said, "is basically Romeo and Juliet. Two *schlemazel* kids trying to get together and a bunch of *nudniks* getting in the way. Look at Romeo and Juliet. She sends him a note: meet me at the tomb. She knocks herself out. He hears she's dead. He goes to the tomb. He sees her lying there. He kills himself. She wakes up. She sees *him* lying there. She stabs herself. It could go on forever: her wound isn't fatal after all, they drag her out of the tomb, they pump the poison out of him, he wakes up and sees she's gone, he runs off to find her, she hears he's alive, she runs back to the tomb, he's gone, she runs after him . . . take away Shakespeare's talent and what have you got? Situation comedy. So far so good. We've got the ingredients."

And he kept talking and walking, walking and talking, extracting a formula out of seeming irrelevancies and showing me how the formula applied to my story, suggesting possible scenes, improvising a joke here and there, and never once changing the saturnine expression on his face. It occurred to me that maybe Norman Spain wore gloom the way other people might wear hauteur or geniality, as a variety of armor. Anyway, it didn't crack, even when I laughed at something he said, or asked a question, or made a comment, or agreed with him, or disagreed with him. So I had absolutely no idea what he thought of me, if anything. His real face was somewhere behind that gloomy visor.

I was wondering if he'd already made up his mind about me

✳ 67

and, if not, how much longer it would take him to find out about the chemistry, when Wingate interrupted.

"Well," he said, "it seems to me the two of you are very much *en rapport*—"

(We *are*?)

"—and it's entirely possible that you'll work out very well as a team. I certainly think it's worth a try. What do you think, Ruth?"

"Oh—I—it's fine with me," I said. But they seemed to be waiting for more, so I added, to Norman Spain, "You're very funny."

"Why not?" he said. "I've had a terrible life."

I laughed.

"You see?" he said to Wingate. "Tell people the truth, they laugh. The truth is so tragic they have to pretend it's a joke. I've got to go to Ischia. Rocks, that's what I want. Sun and rocks."

"If this show is successful," said Wingate blandly, "we'll all go to Ischia."

"*You'll* stay *here*," said Norman. "I don't want a lot of people messing up my rocks."

Wingate smiled tolerantly.

"Well, Ruth?" he said.

Well what? I looked at him blankly.

"Are you ready to go to work?"

"Oh!" I said. "You mean . . . ?" I looked vaguely around the room. Is that all there was to it? I didn't have to prove anything? All I had to do was tell Norman Spain he was funny, and I was *in*? I didn't know what to say. I didn't even know what to think. The trouble with me is I'm never prepared for victory, only for defeat. Here I was with a miracle in my hands and I was all thumbs. Ready to go to work? Alex didn't even know there was a *possibility* yet. And my kids! Who would take care of them? "I—uh—I'd have to—uh—make arrangements," I stammered.

"How soon could you let us know?"

"Oh—a week . . . or two . . . or three." I saw them glance at each other. Ah-ha! I thought, that's it. I just blew the whole deal. But what else could I do? How did I know how long it would take to get a housekeeper? Better than that, how did I know how long it would take me to get up the nerve to tell Alex I was *getting* a housekeeper?

But Wingate treated me to an oily smile and said they would try to be patient, and Norman started buttoning his jacket.

"I have an appointment in ten minutes," he said, darkly, "with the head doctor. I have to be on time. He's paranoid. If I'm five minutes late he thinks I'm rejecting him. It takes me weeks to build up his confidence again." He sighed deeply. "If I'd known what a responsibility he'd turn out to be . . ."

I followed Norman out of the office and down to the street, where I watched him hail a cab, say to the driver, "Take me to the Isle of Wight," and disappear in a mess of midtown traffic.

I went into a drugstore telephone booth and called Simon.

"You're right, as usual," I told him. "Anyway, if there *is* a television writer somewhere who turns down easy money, Norman Spain isn't him. He. It." And I gave him a detailed report.

"Good," said Simon. "That gives you plenty of time to make your decision."

I didn't bother telling him I didn't need any time to make my decision. I'd made it long ago, when I was about three years old. What I had to do now was find out if I could get away with it.

The time had come to tell Alex.

Why the hesitation? Why the clammy hands? Did I really expect Alex to rise up in wrath, intoning "No-wife-a-mine-iz-gunna-wurk!"? Not in a million years. Alex was no Babbitt. He was a New Yorker, he'd read Camus and Kafka, he was psychology-oriented, well-informed, mentally sophisticated. He wouldn't be caught dead saying a woman's place was anywhere in particular. In fact he'd said right out in public in somebody's living room that the concept of motherhood as the end-all of a woman's life is ridiculous. He'd been known to speak admiringly

✳ 69

of the smart female scientist who lived next door to his brother, and of the exceptional business acumen of the lady real-estate agent who sold us our house, and the brilliance of the lady lawyer who was the wife of the head of his firm.

And yet . . . I kept thinking of all those phrases that start "some of my best friends . . ."

I felt, not only with Alex, but in the air all around me, the presence of some subtle schizophrenia. The kind of thing, for instance, that makes democracy such a nervous state of affairs. Everybody gets brought up on Lincoln and Jefferson and "all men are created equal," so when the daughter of a Madison Avenue executive ($50,000 a year) decides to marry a cabdriver ($5,000 a year), what does the executive do? All his instincts are crying out "*My daughter* marry a *cabdriver?*" But all his orientation is telling him he mustn't feel that way. So instead of yelling "Getoutahere!" he keeps saying to himself, "He's equal, he's equal," and gives them his blessing, and promptly has a stroke.

I felt this kind of discrepancy everywhere, and if it *was* everywhere, how did I know it didn't envelop Alex? That's what made me hesitate. That, and Simon's warning tolling in my head: tension, conflict. And all the garbage I'd been reading in the magazines about marital strife as the result of women getting up off their knees.

But the time had come.

I took a tranquilizer and planned how I would wait until after Alex had a good dinner and was in a mellow mood, and then I'd introduce the subject, beginning with generalities and gracefully working around to specifics.

That night he came home with indigestion from eating lasagna for lunch, poked at his dinner, and indicated, by a series of short, incoherent, resentful phrases, that the guys in the office were not giving him the respect and credit due a man of his experience and perception.

Oh well, I had three weeks.

✳ 70

The next night he'd had a great day at the office—all kinds of politics going on, rumors, speculations, a turnover on the executive level, possibilities of a promotion. . . . It was bedtime before I could get a word in. At that it was only because he was brushing his teeth.

"You know," I said quickly, "Deedee told me she decided to go back to work, as soon as she's feeling better."

"Good for her," he said through the toothpaste.

"Ha?"

"I said good for her!"

"You think it's a good idea?"

"Sure! Why not? She's a clever girl with a lot of vitality. Why should she hang around the house?"

"Well, the kids, for one thing."

"The kids don't need her around twenty-four hours a day. I think it's a great idea for a woman to get out of the domestic rut, get interested in something besides the kids did this and the kids did that, and what to make for dinner." He got into bed.

"I wonder if Jerry feels that way."

"Why not? What man wouldn't like to come home at night and have his wife greet him with something besides 'Hit him!'?"

I stopped, halfway into a short piece of blue nylon. "When did I ever say 'hit him'?"

"Well, not in those words," he said, eyeing me with interest.

I sighed audibly. "You're right," I said, getting into bed. "I'm included. I'm in a domestic rut." I switched off the light, waited a second, and said, "Maybe *I* ought to go to work."

"Sure. Why don't you?" He crowded onto my side of the bed.

I switched the light on again. "You mean it?"

"Absolutely!" He switched the light off again. And conversation became intrusive.

(He really meant it! I could tell! It would be smooth sailing from here on. So much for your conflicts and tensions, Simon, a lot you know.)

✳ 7 1

The following night after dinner I turned on television's sixty-eighth tribute to Richard Rodgers. I thought it would be good advance publicity, watching a classy show like that, high-toned, glamorous. It would emphasize the remarkable nature of my achievement. I watched Alex watching the show and waited for an opening.

"Boy," he said, finally, "television gets lousier every day."

What an opening!

"That's too bad," I said promptly. "Because I'm going to be in it."

Alex turned to me and there was a silence while Mary Martin proceeded to wash that man right outa her hair. He frowned as though he hadn't heard me correctly. "In it? What do you mean, in it?"

I didn't know where to start, so I said "Wait a minute," and I ran upstairs, came back with a carbon copy of the manuscript that I'd been hiding in my stocking drawer, and thrust it into his hands. He looked at it as though any minute he was going to sniff it.

"What's this?"

"It's a story. I wrote it."

"All right, don't be funny, what is it?"

"I'm *telling* you. I wrote it."

"Come on, now—"

"Okay. It's a translation of a manuscript written in the fif-teenth century by a red-headed monk. I stole it."

"Will you just tell me—"

"All right, I didn't steal it. I borrowed it."

"Ruth, I'm in no mood—"

"All right. It's something I found in an old bedspring at the Salvation Army Outlet store. I think it's a Maxwell Bodenheim."

"Can't you just tell the plain, simple truth?"

"Okay. You want the truth? The real truth? It's one of Sam Levinson's old routines. He gave it to me just before we broke up."

"Ruth—!"

"I *wrote* it! I *wrote* it!"

He stared at me. "All by yourself?"

I sighed. "Okay. There was this close friend of Henry Miller's . . ."

But he seemed, finally, to be convinced.

He riffled through the pages, reading a sentence here and there, and finally he grinned, a big silly grin.

"How about that!" he said, all self-conscious wonderment. "And they're going to put it on television?"

I sat down, crossed my legs, and tilted my chin, as befits a woman whose husband is finally showing her a little respect.

"Well, it's like this," I said, and told him the whole story.

When I finished he riffled through the pages again, with the air of a man who's just been told that the greasy stuff in his backyard may be oil.

"What do you know!" he said, softly. "When's it going on?"

"On?" I looked blank. "It isn't even written yet. I mean it has to be a script first. And then they have to make a pilot film, and then they have to sell it."

"Oh." (On the other hand, it may just be greasy stuff. But still . . .) "And this guy Norman Spain, he's going to write the script?"

"With me."

"Oh. Both of you."

"We're going to—collaborate." I could see that word would always be ambiguous for me.

"Well, well. How about that." He made a sound like chuckling.

I wanted to make sure he understood all the implications. "So—uh—so I'll be going to work. Every day."

"Yeah. I suppose so," he said, still smiling, and put the script on the coffee table. "When do you start?"

"Well—I—I have to get a housekeeper first. Naturally."

"Yeah," he said, "housekeeper. That's right." He chuckled

✳ 73

again, or whatever it was, to show a joke was coming. "Or we could send the kids away to boarding school."

I went along with it. "West Point. We'll cut Sooz's hair."

He chuckled again. That chuckle was beginning to get on my nerves. I was waiting for him to say some of those enthusiastic things he'd said the other night about Deedee. Like, "Good for you!" or "I think it's a great idea."

"Well," he got up and stretched, "as long as you can find somebody competent to take over the house—"

"Naturally."

He wandered around the room, still smiling faintly. "Well, well, what do you know. An authoress. . . . Housekeepers run about a hundred dollars a week now, don't they?"

"Gloria Betz has one for forty."

"Mmm? . . . Well, I suppose they'll be paying you for this. Of course we don't know how much . . ."

"Enough to pay for a good housekeeper, anyway."

He grinned again, but it seemed to me he was straining just a little.

"Wage earner, huh? Working girl." He patted me on the cheek. "How about that."

"You said that already."

He chuckled. I winced. Something wasn't quite right. He picked up a pipe from an end table and began stuffing tobacco into it.

"Well," he said brightly, "this is what you always wanted. A chance to get out of the house. Now you've got it." He grinned that lopsided grin and began lighting his pipe. "By the way . . . (puff) been meaning to ask you. Did you notice . . . (puff puff) that David stopped . . . (puff) . . . reading lately? (puff puff) Doesn't seem to have much . . . (puff puff) . . . interest in his schoolwork either . . . (puff)."

"So?" I felt chilly, suddenly.

"Maybe you ought to . . . (puff) . . . speak to his teacher . . ."

✳ 74

"There's nothing wrong with him. He's baseball crazy, that's all. All boys his age are baseball crazy."

"Maybe he needs glasses."

"Glasses!"

"Maybe his hearing is defective. He doesn't seem to know what goes on at school. I ask him, 'What did you do today?,' he can't tell me."

"They're *all* like that."

"Well . . . might be a good idea to look into it, anyway. I mean, if you have the time."

My eyes narrowed.

"And Sooz . . ." he began.

"Wait a minute," I said, getting up. "Why all this concern, suddenly? How come the kids are suddenly falling apart today? They were fine yesterday."

"Nobody said they were falling *apart*."

"What do you mean 'if I have the time'? What are you trying to say here? That I'm a rotten mother? That I'm going to skip out and live it up while the kids go to rack and ruin? Is that the message?"

"Who said anything about . . ."

"I know you didn't *say* it. I'm just *decoding*."

"You're a very strange lady, you know that? All I said was—"

"It's not what you *said*. It's what you *mean*. If you don't want me to go to work why don't you just come right out and say so?"

"Don't want you to. . . . ! Who said that? Did I say that?"

"Of course not! That's what I just *said!* Why *don't* you say it!"

"You *want* me to say it?"

"No, *you* want to say it!"

He laughed. "Honey, I know what you're trying to do, but—"

"What *I'm* trying—?"

"Don't use me as an excuse—"

"Excu—?"

 ⁎ 7 5

"I know and *you* know that you feel guilty about leaving the kids."

"I—? *Who? What?*"

"So let's not pretend that *I'm*—"

"No, no! I'm not crazy! 'Housekeepers run a hundred dollars a week'—what was that all about? '*If* I have the time'—what was that?"

"Ruth, don't make a Victorian drama out of it—"

"*Contemporary* Victorian, that's what it is! A whole new thing! A woman can do anything she wants as long as she doesn't do anything she wants! She can go anywhere she likes as long as she stays put!"

Alex threw up his hands. "Don't let me confuse you with facts."

"Forget it!" I said, in my dangerous voice. "Forget it. I won't take the job. Forget it."

I plunked myself down on the sofa, picked up a pamphlet from the Allstate Insurance Company and began to read it furiously.

"Now don't be silly. You did all this work—you got yourself a job—obviously it means a lot to you."

"I said forget it!"

So, like an idiot, he forgot it. He switched the television set to another channel and proceeded to watch a documentary on Puerto Rico.

I kept quiet for about ten minutes, but then I couldn't stand it any longer.

"The only housewife known to man," I muttered, "who was actually offered a job writing for television. And what happens? Nothing. She just goes on making pot roast and washing dishes."

No answer.

"There are women," I said, louder, "who have housekeepers just so they can go to the beauty parlor or sit around gossiping with the neighbors! There are women who have been known to

✳ 76

spend an entire week at Saks Fifth Avenue without even dropping a postcard to the family. Nobody ever accuses *them* of being bad mothers. Because they don't take jobs, see. They don't make it *official*. They don't *say* they want to get out of the house. They're the *sneaky* kind. They pretend that all this roaming around Saks Fifth Avenue is for the Good Of The Family. I mean they're only doing this because it's terribly important that three-year-old Sandra should have a permanently pleated white jersey skirt. And by God they're going to find that skirt if they have to stay at Saks all *year* to do it! *That's motherhood!*"

Alex went over and turned up the volume on the TV set.

"Okay" I said to nobody. "Forget it."

I flounced upstairs and plopped down on the bed in the dark bedroom, cursing Simon because he was always so right.

After a little while I heard the television set go off, and after another while Alex came up, switched on the light, yawning and stretching, and said pleasantly, "I read the story. It's very funny. It should make a good show."

I raised myself slowly on one elbow and stared at him.

"No kidding," he went on, "it's very professional." And he smacked me lightly on my bottom—a sort of intimate version of a pat on the back.

"Too bad I'm not going to have anything to do with it," I said, testing. "Considering your attitude."

"Ruth, will you cut it out? I don't know where you get these ideas. Haven't I always been in favor of women getting out of the house? Come on, let's get some sleep." And he went into the bathroom, humming.

I turned over and stared at the ceiling, troubled, uneasy, suspicious. Was I wrong? Was all that talk about David needing glasses just talk about David needing glasses? Was I too sensitive about this? Did Alex, after all, really mean what he said?

Or did he mean what he was humming there in the bathroom?

"I'm gonna buy a paper doll that I can call my own. . . ."

8   VICKI WARSAW'S living room was fur-
nished in a strangely homogeneous mixture of Early American
and just plain wild enthusiasm. For instance, her fireplace,
which had old New England-type andirons and a bellows and
some kind of Pennsylvania Dutch log basket, also had, hanging
above it, a lovely print of one of those tranquil, oval-faced
Modiglianis, flanked on one side by an abstract mobile and on
the other by a piece of primitive art done in school by her ten-
year-old daughter.

When I walked in Vicki was sitting at the piano wearing
absolutely nothing but a sky-blue smock. I mean no shoes, no
stockings, nothing. She was busy practicing the piano part of a
chamber music quartet, and since the piano part was mostly accompaniment, she was singing what the other instruments were
supposed to be playing, in order to hear the melody. While her
hands were going pom, pom, pom, pom, in the bass, her voice
was going "tiddly-tiddly-tiddly-tiddly-tiddly-tiddly-tiddly-plink-
plink" in the treble. It sounded terrible.

I kicked off my sneakers, curled up in one of the big chairs
by the fireplace, and waited for her to finish so I could tell her
my troubles. It was a gray, windy day; all the kids were at school;
and it was Vicki's day off, which meant another doctor was covering for her and she wouldn't have to run away anywhere or
answer any frantic phone calls about phenobarb or gamma
globulin. A good day for a moody talk.

She hit the final chords: plonk, plonk, plonk, plonk . . .
plonnnk!

"Magnificent!" she exulted, obviously applauding the com-
poser, not herself.

"You're so accomplished," I mumbled.

"Of course!" She curled up in the chair opposite me and lit a cigarette. "Accomplishment is what we're here for. We die without it. So what's happening? What's going on? Did you sign a contract yet?"

"In television," I said wearily, like a veteran (although I'd only heard this the week before from Simon), "it takes five days to make a phone call, two weeks to make an appointment, and twenty-seven years to sign a contract."

"Baloney! So what's happening then?"

I looked down at my feet, where my heart was lying, heavy as a lump of lead.

"I'm not going to do it," I said, "I'm going to forget the whole thing."

"You're serious!" she gasped, meaning I couldn't be.

I nodded, wondering what she was going to do about it. She put her hand over her mouth and stared at me thoughtfully, then got up and took my pulse.

"There's a lot of flu going around," she said. "You got a tickle in your throat? Any diarrhea?"

I pulled my hand away.

"I'm not sick. I just can't do it, that's all."

"Can't do it! Whoever heard of such a thing, can't do it. Every night, all over the world, women over thirty are *praying* for something like this to happen to them. Can't do it!"

"Something's warning me. A little voice. I can't hear what it says but I know it's talking."

"About what?"

"Alex. There's something about his attitude that worries me."

"Why? What does he say?"

"He says, 'How about that.' He says, 'It's a great idea for women to get out of the domestic rut.' He says, he's 'always been in favor of it.'"

"Well, gee," with gentle sarcasm, "that would worry anybody."

"Very funny. But then he says things like, 'David needs

glasses.' I don't know. Maybe he means what he says. Maybe he does. But . . . it's just a feeling I have. It's nothing I can put my finger on. Just a feeling. I get a kind of vibration . . ."

"Ah!" she said, making the diagnosis, "I think what we have here is a typical little tremor; the average wholesome American boy's fear of finding himself married to somebody who can earn her own money. Eventually this gives way to the average wholesome American man's admiration for anybody who *does* earn money. You have nothing to worry about."

"You think so?"

"Don't be a dope, will you? He says he's all for your getting out of the house and going to work. Would a nice, normal, intelligent man say a thing like that if he didn't mean it?"

The question hung in the air for a moment.

"I don't know," I said, anxiously, "about this whole thing, though. I worry about the kids. Will they suffer? Maybe David *does* need glasses. And housekeepers are so expensive. And . . ."

"Ach! Last-minute stage fright. Kids. Housekeepers. Don't give me that nonsense. Listen," she said, giving me a hard look out of her innocent eyes, "when I went into practice I had twenty-three cents, two old brassieres, two babies, and no housekeeper. I couldn't afford a shingle to hang out, so Lenny painted one himself—a two-tone job—the colors ran into each other. When I had to go on calls I got a neighbor to stay with the babies. If I couldn't get a neighbor and it wasn't contagious I took them with me and left them in the patient's living room. I had visiting hours from three to six and between examinations I ran into the kitchen and made beef Stroganoff. And look at my kids today. Gorgeous! So don't tell me you can't work if you want to!"

I looked sheepish. What else can you look in the face of a recital like that? And it was true, about her kids. With all their unconventional upbringing they were the brightest, happiest, most well-adjusted kids in the school.

Vicki saw I was wavering and pressed her advantage.

She said that the only fair and proper criterion for accepting or rejecting the job was the acquiring of a perfect substitute for me in my home. If I could find someone who had the integrity to clean with a vacuum cleaner instead of a dust mop; who would know instinctively whether Sooz really had a stomachache or was just trying to take attention away from her brother; who could make David wear rubber boots when it was raining and pretend to be vitally interested in his unique theories of subtraction; who had enough sense to sprinkle the clothes before ironing them, was gifted enough to make a four-course dinner out of chopped meat and celery stalks, and could sense when Alex would tolerate being confided in and when he wouldn't . . . there was no reason in the world why I shouldn't follow all the other misfits down the road to glory.

I had been growing less and less dubious as she spoke, and by the time she was finished, she'd done what I'd come there for her to do in the first place; she'd convinced me. Then she told me that her housekeeper, by the name of Adelaide, had a cousin who was looking for a job. Vicki had met the cousin because Adelaide had brought her up from the city to be interviewed by a neighbor of Vicki's, a Mrs. Fisher.

"Why didn't Mrs. Fisher take her?" I asked suspiciously.

"Why!" Vicki threw her hands in the air. "Because Mrs. Fisher is mentally unbalanced, that's why!"

She assured me that this cousin of Adelaide's was sweet, pure, loyal, sober, honest, reliable, and practically one of our intellectual giants. If I'd had any sense I would have been less credulous, knowing Vicki. She is such a disciple of the innocent-until-proven-guilty school that she could have met Lady Macbeth and seen nothing but a woman with dishpan hands.

But I was so eager to believe her that I got all excited and made her promise to make Adelaide promise to make her cousin promise to come and see me within the next three days, and I put on my sneakers and ran home in a glow of optimism.

That night, when I was up to my elbows in dishwater (because once, when we'd had a windfall, I'd refused the offer of a dishwasher on the nutty theory that it couldn't do pots and pans anyway, so we spent the money on something else and now I had to keep my mouth shut about dishes), Vicki called up to say that Adelaide's cousin would be up to see me the next day, which was Wednesday.

"Tomorrow! But Sarah May comes tomorrow!"

"So?"

"What'll she think? How can I interview somebody who might be replacing her, right in front of her face?"

"She doesn't have to know what it's all about."

"Are you kidding? She may not know the theory of relativity, she may not even know how to iron clothes, but *this* she'd know! That's all I need, for Sarah May to have something against me. She wouldn't even do the one hour's work she does now."

"Well I can't do anything about it now. Adelaide arranged it, and if she doesn't want to change it she'll just tell me she can't get in touch with her cousin."

So I called Sarah May and told her Mr. Bernard was not well and would be staying home tomorrow and didn't want to be disturbed so she'd better not come, and I'd pay her for it anyway, since it was too late for her to get another day's work. Of course I did this on the upstairs extension, quietly, while Alex was watching the President's press conference on TV, because if he'd heard me there would have been a violent argument as to whether paying Sarah May for nothing was good common sense or despicable cowardice. Of course, he didn't know that I *always* paid her for nothing.

The next morning I got up earlier than usual and went tearing through the house with the vacuum cleaner as if the Board of Health were after me. I vacuumed the floors, the furniture, the sofa pillows, the ashtrays, the venetian blinds, the lamps, the pictures on the wall, the calendar, the clock. . . . By twelve o'clock I was ready to be shipped to a home for the aged. But I had to do it. Because I have this unshakeable conviction that some day a prospective maid will come into the house, see how spotless it is, and be terrified into keeping it that way.

Naturally, Adelaide's cousin arrived just as Sooz—who was, to use the phrase loosely, having lunch—had spilled her entire cup of Ovaltine. Like Gaul, the mess was neatly divided into three parts: the table, the floor, and Sooz's lap. Sooz, who is pretty strange sometimes, was laughing as if it were the funniest thing since the Three Stooges. Instead of throwing a fit, which is my usual reaction, I spoke to her calmly and quietly, as I gently mopped up the three brown pools. Adelaide's cousin was watching and, just in case this ever happened while she was in charge, I wanted to make sure she understood we never throw fits in this house.

Adelaide's cousin proved to be a Jamaican of royal blood. I mean, she must have been. Nobody could be that serene and queenly without having a chieftain somewhere in the background. She was tall and wore a loose, flowing coat which helped the impression. Her head was poised on a long, elegant neck, her shoulders never sagged, her voice was like cool velvet, and her name was Josephine. I ask you. I was so impressed I practically stammered as I asked her if she would care for some lunch. She declined, thank you, and sat regally on a kitchen chair without removing her coat.

I asked her all the usual questions. She was not married, so she had no obligations that might suddenly call her away from me. She had been in her last position four years and had left only because the people had moved to Canada. She showed me a letter of recommendation that was sort of like the inscription on the Lincoln Memorial and said that, if I wished further proof, she would give me the telephone number of the mother of the lady she had worked for, who still resided in Brooklyn.

She cooked, she cleaned, she adored children and had raised six of her own brothers and sisters; she was patently sober, honest, intelligent, conscientious, dignified, mature, and only wanted forty-five dollars a week. I was so excited I could hardly speak, and I decided I would have to do some kind of penance for having any doubts about Vicki's judgement.

When Sooz came back from putting on a clean dress, Josephine gently pulled her over and buttoned up the back, meanwhile launching into a charming Jamaican fairy-tale about a big red button that ran away from a shirt. I insisted she have at least a cup of coffee, and as she drank it, she finally unbent enough to open her coat. Sooz sat next to her, big-eyed and worshiping, and I sent up silent thanks to all the fates. Obviously, my problems were over. This was a gem.

Finally she stood up to go, and I opened my mouth to tell her she was hired, but I never told her. I just stood there, transfixed, with my mouth open, while Sooz whined that she didn't want Josephine to leave, and Josephine smiled down at her and patted her head and said maybe she would be back soon. I pulled myself together before she caught me and tried to smile as I told her that naturally I would have to talk this over with my husband first, but that she had impressed me tremendously and I would call her first thing in the morning. The minute she was out of the house I ran to the phone and called Vicki.

"That cousin of Adelaide's," I shrieked, "she's eight months pregnant!"

Vicki was abashed.

"When I saw her," she said, "she was wearing a big loose coat and she never took it off."

"Yeah," I nodded to myself, thinking of all the women in the country who wore coats like that, "I know. Those big loose coats hide a multitude."

So that took care of Adelaide's cousin.

I was bitterly disappointed. Also I was pretty mad, because I'd done all that vacuuming for nothing.

Well, no use crying over lost Jamaicans. Half a week was gone, Wingate was waiting to hear from me, and I simply had to get a housekeeper. I decided the only way to play this game was according to the law of averages. The more possibilities I lined up, the better my chances. So I dug the classified section of the previous Sunday's *Times* out of the box in the garage where we pile the old newspapers until that special semi-annual day when some organization calls up and says they are having an old-newspaper drive, and I sharpened a red pencil and sat down to pore over the contents of the Domestic Employment Wanted column.

Forty minutes later I had circled one ad.

All the other ad takers wanted things I didn't have, or didn't want things I had. You'd think it would be a fairly simple thing to go through a page full of ads and come up with five or six possibilities, but as I scanned and rescanned that page, it gradually dawned on me that my choice of domestics was severely limited by the fact that, (a) I had a house to keep clean, (b) I had children, (c) I required someone who would be willing to boil an egg, and (d) I needed someone who would spend more than three days out of seven on the job. It seemed that most of these ladies were just looking for a place to rest their weary bones and get a free meal or two.

Oh yes . . . another disadvantage was the fact that I was living, as opposed to dead. There were at least seven husband-hunting opportunists who insisted on a 'motherless home.'

Dispirited, I called the number in the one ad I had circled and was informed by an impatient voice that Mrs. Conway had already taken a position. Of course she had; the Sunday *Times* was already two days old.

I resolved to get up at six o'clock the following Sunday morning and be on the phone by seven. True, there were all those nasty New Yorkers who could get hold of the *Times* as early as eleven P.M. on Saturday and start calling at midnight, and for all I knew the ad takers at the *Times* office had needy relatives, or were being paid off by a few corrupt individuals to give them pertinent telephone numbers even before they were advertised, but aside from those, I could lead the rest of the pack.

So early Sunday morning (not quite six A.M.) I got busy

✳ 85

with the classified section. I was luckier this time. There were three possibilities. After making seventeen phone calls to these three numbers, I finally got one that wasn't busy. This was a lady called Leona Briggs, who sounded jovial and hearty and as though she could do a lot of heavy work without getting tired, so I made an appointment to pick her up at the train station the following morning.

A few hours later I got through to the second number, and after I'd given this girl my references she said haughtily that she'd think it over and call me back, but she never did.

The third number was busy for four days, after which I stopped calling.

In the meantime . . . Leona Briggs. I set off in the car for the train station, hoping against hope.

Well, she was a good three hundred pounds. She was Cockney. She had frizzy orange hair and a great deal of unblended rouge on her cheeks, and when we got back to the house she charged ahead of me like a Sherman tank. She hinted she could use a cup or two of strong tea. Her voice had a timbre that reminded me of those avant-garde concertos some oddball is always composing, like for spoon, saucepan, and screechy blackboard chalk. Bashful, she wasn't. She examined everything, commented on everything, pronounced it all mildly satisfactory, and told me she'd bring her trunk around the following morning by cab from New York, which naturally I'd pay for.

So far I hadn't had a chance to say anything but "Lemon or cream?"

Finally, while her mouth was full of strong tea (and bread and butter and jam, which she'd decided would be a nice accompaniment) I told her, weakly, that I would have to go through the formality of discussing it with my husband. She didn't take him very seriously, and as I drove her back to the train station she kept reassuring me that I wouldn't have to worry about the kids, she could handle any kids that ever lived. She then proceeded to give me the grisly details of how she had managed to discipline a cranky two-year-old, and I must say she was wasting her talents. Idea-men for horror films make good money.

Feeling as though I'd barely escaped from a terrible accident, I made it back to the house just twenty minutes before Sooz's school bus was due, and I used that twenty minutes to call seven employment agencies. Five of them were so bored with me they could barely find the energy to take down my name, saying they'd let me know if anything turned up, in voices that indicated quite clearly I wasn't to hold my breath in the meantime. The sixth one tried to sell me on the idea of waiting six months while they arranged, with my money, to bring over some unknown quantity from Ireland, and when I stuck to my guns about needing somebody right now they got petulant and said they couldn't help me. The seventh was willing and eager to oblige, in fact they said they just happened to have a simply marvelous girl there at the moment and they were sure I'd want to interview her immediately. This was a local agency, and it would only take the girl fifteen minutes to get down to my neighborhood by bus, if I would be good enough to pick her up at the bus stop.

Feeling faintly encouraged, I met Sooz as she got off the school bus, with several Ritz crackers to stay her hunger, bundled her into the car, and off we went to the village bus stop. What got off the bus was Eliza, after three weeks on the ice without shelter or food. She was grayish brown, paper thin, dull eyed, frightened out of her wits. What she needed was not a job but a few years of food, rest, and loving care. This was the agency's "simply marvelous girl."

There was no point to interviewing her, but I knew I'd never sleep again if I didn't at least give her a meal. So I took her home and stuffed her with bacon and eggs, pretending it was just to keep Sooz company, and asked her a few of the usual questions to keep up appearances, and paid her expenses—several times over—to appease my guilt for not giving her free room and board until she recuperated.

After I took her back to the bus stop I called the agency and told them I was going to report them to the police or somebody unless they sent this girl to a welfare organization instead of trying to peddle her, and then I went into the bathroom and cried.

The situation was hopeless. Hopeless. There seemed to be some law of inverse ratio at work in the land whereby the increasing need for adequate domestic help created an increasing obsolescence in the necessary species.

While I was crying into a bath towel the telephone rang and it was Simon, asking why I hadn't called Wingate.

"Why!" I cried, as though it were his fault, "because I can't get a housekeeper, that's why!"

"What's the problem?"

"Everything! There aren't any housekeepers! In the whole world there aren't any! That's all!"

"Did you advertise?" he asked.

There was a pause, and then I said quietly, "Hmm?"

"Did you put an ad in the *Times?* Or in the local paper?"

"Oh," I said meekly, "I didn't think of that."

"What were you doing then? Standing in the street with a hook?"

"Not exactly," I mumbled.

"Well get to work, sweetheart. I have enough problems without Harry calling me to find out what's going on with you."

"Oh, God. I'm sorry, Simon. I didn't know I'd be putting you on the spot. That's the last thing I want to do. Oh, this is terrible."

"Don't be childish. I don't mind it, you know that. I just don't want to see you lose this opportunity, since you seem to want it so badly. Though God knows why you want it. But let's not go into that . . ."

Fear jumped into my throat.

"Lose it? Why? What did he say?"

＊　88

"Nothing. Don't panic. In fact, in a way it was a good thing not to be available right away, because Harry thinks anything that comes easily isn't worth getting. On the other hand don't take longer than necessary because playing hard to get is already stepping on Harry's ego."

It occurred to me it wouldn't take much for me to get fed up with Harry altogether, but I didn't say so.

"I'll put an ad in the paper immediately," I said. "*All* the papers."

Frantically, I spent the rest of the afternoon composing an ad. For an allegedly potential writer it was incredible how long it took me to squeeze out sixteen words. Then I got on the phone and placed it in every paper I could think of except the *St. Louis Post Dispatch*.

The first couple of days after the ad appeared I got as much response as though I'd sent out a call for a trained inchworm.

Advertising! I thought, bitterly. For Madison Avenue it works, not for people.

Then I began to get calls; girls from Brazil and Venezuela whose command of English consisted of "I call job"; girls whose qualifications rested on their experience as carhops, cashiers, attendants in mental institutions, drum majorettes; divorcees looking for a home for their six children, dog, and parakeet. . . .

At the end of the week Alex came home to find frankfurters for dinner and me sprawled on the sofa, my arm across my eyes.

"Posing for a Bufferin commercial?" he asked cheerfully.

"I wish I were dead!"

"Any preference as to method?" He poked my ribs friskily with his pipestem.

"I should have known! Everything you say has a catch to it."

"What did I say recently that was so catchy?"

" 'As long as you can get somebody to take care of things'— you *knew* I'd never get anybody! You *knew* it would be impossible!"

He tried looking sympathetic, but there was a hint of a sly grin pulling at the corners of his mouth.

"Do you mind," he said, "if I go up and wash my face now that you've thrown my words back into it?"

"Go. What difference does it make."

He started up the stairs. "The telephone is ringing."

"I want it disconnected!"

"That's easy." He opened the linen closet, came down with a large pair of scissors, and started for the telephone wire.

I slid by him just in time to save it, and picked up the receiver on the fifth ring. A quiet, patient voice explained that her name was Hannah Bruyer, that she had been housekeeper for a Connecticut family for six years, that she was leaving of her own accord because the children were grown and no longer needed her, that her main interest in any household was the children, but that she naturally did everything else—cooking, cleaning, sewing, marketing. . . .

"Oh yeah?" I thought to myself, having, in light of my experience, become the most thorough skeptic in the world.

I asked her to come up the next day, and then I checked her reference. The lady in Connecticut, who sounded as though she were accustomed to the best of loyal retainers, had nothing but good to say of her. Still, I was wary.

Hannah came to see me the next day. She was quiet, neat, pleasant, mature, sensible, cooperative, gentle, firm, and knew her business. I hired her.

"What are you unhappy about *now*?" Alex asked me that evening.

"Who's unhappy?" I said miserably.

"If you don't like her . . ."

"What's not to like?"

"Then what's eating you?"

"*Nothing*. Absolutely nothing. I think I'm very lucky to get somebody like her.

And inside me a voice was shouting, *I DON'T WANT*

"Very lucky!" I repeated, almost in tears.

What did I have against this Hannah lady? Nothing, except that she was taking over.

Well, but I *wanted* somebody who could take over, didn't I?

Yes, but I wanted somebody who would pretend she wasn't. Somebody strong, but deferential. Like the Jamaican princess.

Of course I should have known the Jamaican princess would never be mine. There's a kind of unwritten housewives' law; if you ever chance upon the one domestic who is perfect for you, it will be at a time when you're too poor to hire her, or when she's working for your best friend, or when she happens to be very pregnant. I had never met a woman whose domestic wasn't a second choice. Like fishermen, they were always talking about the one that got away.

Well, so be it.

The next day I called Wingate and told him I was ready to go to work.

9

SINCE I HAD a handy contract negotiator living in the same house with me, I naturally had to go out and find somebody else to negotiate my contract. Claiming the same emotional involvement that keeps a doctor from treating his own family, Alex austerely refrained from having anything to do with it, and finally Simon arranged for his lawyer to handle the matter. I was to receive a flat fee which seemed enormous until Alex divided it for me by the number of weeks I would probably be working, and the number of expenses—including Hannah—that it would have to cover. It quickly diminished from enormous to adequate. But I was happy. And terrified.

It was Sunday night, I was due to report to Norman Spain's office at ten o'clock the next morning, and I discovered that the fact that Hannah was settled in the spare room with her neat brown suitcase in the closet, her neat brown oxfords under the bed, and a neat, calm, sensible, everything's-under-control attitude pervading the air around her, gave me no sense of security whatever.

True, the kids seemed to like her (she had brought them educational toys). True, she handled them well. True, she was no meanie, no dunce, no crackpot. True, she was a good, dependable, middle-aged lady who knew her way around.

But she was a *stranger*.

She wouldn't know where to look for David if he didn't show up after school. She didn't know you had to make Sooz go to the bathroom the minute she came home. She didn't know we kept a hand-sized fire-extinguisher under the kitchen sink. She wouldn't know you had to check the oven from underneath after lighting it because sometimes it didn't catch.

There were a million things she wouldn't know unless I told her. And if I forgot something important—which is the only kind of thing I ever forget—!

Sunday evening I began making a list: take chicken out of the freezer, stew it with onion but no garlic, call the repair man about the dryer, call Mrs. Button and ask her if she'd mind giving David a lift to Cub Scouts, call Mrs. Jerome and see if Sooz can go with her little girl to dance class, be sure to take in the garbage cans so they don't get full of water (rain predicted), order all groceries before noon or they won't deliver. . . . et cetera, et cetera, et cetera, as Yul Brynner so brilliantly put it.

I made a list instead of just telling her these things because I was afraid if I told them to her that night she might forget by the next day, and I certainly wouldn't be able to remember any of them in the morning, because in the morning I'm lucky if I have enough intelligence not to bump into things.

There were other things I had to do that evening too, before

I could go into New York all spic and span and ready to work. But as luck would have it, Alex decided that night to get playfully affectionate. About ten P.M. he started yawning and stretching and running his fingers up and down my back as I sat hunched over on the sofa tensely trying to put a neat coat of polish on my fingernails. He went around shutting off lights and locking doors and humming "Old Devil Moon" with passion; and I thought to myself what's the use kidding around, this is the call to arms. So I went upstairs.

I was really in no condition for fun and games. I mean how can you play French Courtesan Reclining Seductively Among Satin Cushions, when you feel like Busy Fieldmarshal On The Eve Of D-Day? My mind was like a department store at Christmas time with a hundred customers at the counter and only one salesgirl behind it.

Alex got into his pajamas and brushed his teeth and got into bed and moaned invitingly. I said "Yeah, yeah," and ran into the bathroom and began to put some of my hair up in pin-curls because for some reason it suddenly decided just to hang there as though I'd been caught in a storm without an umbrella.

"Come on, honey," Alex wheedled.

"Yeah, yeah," I panted, "I'm just . . . my hair is . . . why don't you read or something?"

He sighed and reached for William Faulkner, and I finished putting up my hair and ran to make another note on the list on the Don't Forget pad on my dresser. Then I washed out my stockings and made another note, and brushed my teeth and made another note, and patted my face with moisturizer and checked the windows and the hot-air vent and made another note, and started looking for my beige sweater.

I heard the plop of the book as Alex put it away.

"Listen, kid," he said, with the beginning of an edge to his voice, "it's getting late—"

"Okay, okay. I just have to find my beige sweater."

✳ 9 3

"Find it tomorrow."

"I won't have *time* tomorrow!"

I started opening and closing drawers in a hurry.

"I just saw it here yesterday. It was right here. I *know* it was here. Where the hell *is* it?"

"So wear *another* sweater!"

"But I already put out the brown skirt and brown shoes and brown bag that go *with* it! Holy Christ, how does a stupid rotten sweater just *disappear* like that!"

"Look, you've got a million sweaters—"

"Okay, okay." I picked out a green sweater, put the brown skirt back in the closet, took out the green skirt, unearthed my black bag again, dumped out the contents of the brown bag, deposited them in the black bag, put away the brown bag, put back the brown shoes, and started looking for the black shoes.

"Now where the hell are the black *shoes?* I just *wore* them yesterday! What is it, somebody goes around stealing *shoes* for God's sake?"

"So wear the *brown* shoes. What are you dressing up for—a job or a goddamn beauty contest?"

"Brown shoes with a green skirt? What am I, an immigrant?"

Alex groaned and rolled over.

I finally found the black shoes. They were suede and they were filthy, so I started looking for my suede brush, in its little box on a high shelf in the closet. In my haste I knocked down several empty mothball cans left over from the summer.

Alex jumped up and muttered through clenched teeth, "Are —you—coming—to—bed?"

"Yes, yes, I just have to clean my shoes."

"Clean your—!"

Suddenly he reached out an arm like an arrow, switched off his bedside lamp and threw himself violently into a posture of furious sleep.

I let the shoes go, crawled quickly into bed, turned out my light, and reached out tentatively with one finger and poked him gently between the shoulder blades. But it was too late. He was going to punish me no matter what it cost him.

I couldn't blame him. But I couldn't blame me either. How else could I possibly be ready to leave the house first thing in the morning? Then again, how could I possibly face a future entirely devoid of sex? I decided I would just have to give up evenings and start getting ready for bed immediately after dinner.

Since I had to be in good shape the following day—bright, alert, funny and so on—it was important that I get a good night's sleep. So naturally I didn't.

A terrible uneasiness claimed me. It was a feeling very similar to what a bride (or a groom, for that matter) is supposed to feel on the eve of the wedding. "What am I doing? I must be out of my mind! What was so bad about things the way they were? Why should I leave my dear family that loves me, and go consorting with strangers? Strangers don't care about me. I could get *hurt* out there. There's all kinds of *trouble* out there. Who *knows* what's out there. What do I *need* it for?"

The dawn and I were both dull and gray. I showered and dressed and gulped orange juice and coffee, and then I looked at Sooz and she looked as if she had a temperature. So I took her temperature. She didn't have a temperature. But she sounded funny. So I made her get back into bed. Hannah disapproved. She pursed her lips and folded her arms.

"I want her," I quivered defiantly, "to stay in bed today."

Hannah said nothing and looked away. She hates me, I thought wildly.

I grabbed my bag, kissed the children, left the house, ran back for the car keys, left again, ran back for an umbrella, left again, ran back for gloves, left again, ran back for something I couldn't remember once I got there, finally got into the car, drove to the parking lot by the railroad station, left the car in the middle of the parking lot, ran off with the keys, ran back to give them to the garage man, ran to the railroad station, leaped onto the train as it was moving out, collapsed onto a seat, spent twenty minutes trying to catch my breath, and then sat up in horror as the train suddenly jerked to a stop in the middle of nowhere and just stood there not moving for about ten years. I fidgeted, twisted, groaned, ground my teeth, clenched my fists, glared at everybody, got terrible tension pains in my stomach, and then finally the train moved. We got into Grand Central fifteen minutes late, I ran up three flights of stairs, leaned against a newstand to faint, didn't faint after all, ran outside, and hailed a cab. By the time I got to the office I was ready for a long vacation.

I didn't know it then, but I had just set the pattern for all the mornings to come.

And if I'd known it would it have stopped me? Of course not. I was getting out of the house, and any moment of early-morning agony was worth it. I hadn't even thought very much about the kind of work I was going to be doing. The work was secondary. Getting *out* was the big, overwhelming, wonderful thing. Gone the fears and doubts of the night before. I was out! Out in the world, where people were moving and talking and running and driving and yelling and laughing and *alive*. And I had a job that was worth money! I had a place! I was expected!

I sailed down the hallway to Norman Spain's office as if I were the lead float in a parade.

IO

IF NORMAN SPAIN should ever become the possessor of vital, top secret information and were captured by enemy agents, the one sure way they could break him down would be to lock him in a room without a telephone and in which the floor space was completely taken up by furniture. He was a telephoner and a pacer if I ever saw one.

Actually the pacing space in the dinky little room on the fifth floor of an old building on Forty-ninth Street which Norman fondly called his office was not more than three good strides across in any direction, but Norman made the most of it; in fact, he made it seem like a hiking trail in the Black Forest.

In addition to the easy back-and-forth route from the door to the window, he blazed new trails constantly, by swinging left at the window, curving around the corner chair, taking a sharp right between the filing-cabinet and the rickety bookshelf, making a U-turn as he approached the wall, cutting diagonally across to the torn wicker chair in the corner by the door, swinging around that, and then back to the window. Meanwhile I sat in a tottering swivel chair in the fourth corner, behind a typewriter which rested on a heavy brown table covered with imitation leather.

As for the telephone, it was poised on that corner of the table which stuck into the middle of the room, within easy reach in case Norman should get an uncontrollable urge while making his rounds. He got these uncontrollable urges on an average of three times an hour, and when you figure that out mathematically it might seem that we had very little time left for working on the script, but Norman's phone calls, besides being mysterious, garbled and a little hysterical, were also very short. Most of the people he called were never in. He just left messages. He liked leaving messages. I think it gave him a sense of positive identity.

The people he mostly called were his agent, his lawyer, his doctor, his psychiatrist, his dentist, his athletic club, his garage, his tailor, his friend Arnie, a man called Bleckensopp at some advertising agency, a night-club comedian to whom he sold jokes over the phone, and a Miss Walsh who was usually sleeping. The people who mostly called him were his wife.

She would call in the morning to tell him they were having company for dinner and not to forget to come home on time; then she would call at noon to remind him not to forget what she had called him about earlier; then she would call in the middle of the afternoon to say they weren't having company for dinner after all, they were going *out* for dinner, and she hoped he had enough money on him. He never did, and it was always too late to go to the bank, so he just worried himself sick for the next two hours until it was time to leave.

She—Norman's wife—came up to the office the very first day. (To look me over, I guess. She needn't have bothered, Norman and I didn't take much to each other that way.) She was a very nice lady, small, trim, orderly, efficient, and very busy. Over what, I don't know. Norman was devoted to her. Well, that's a little misleading. He *counted* on her, is what it was. I had the feeling that if she disappeared he would react with the same kind of horror as a woman suddenly deprived of a superb and trusted servant who had been with the family for generations. Norman didn't like things to be disrupted. He was meticulous to the point of being a pain in the neck. There always had to be twelve perfectly sharp pencils in the pencil holder. Not eleven. Not thirteen. Not *partly* sharp. If the desk blotter swivelled around during my creative spurts of typing so that the edges were not parallel with the sides of the table, he would stop in the middle of a sentence to jerk it straight. All the books in the bookcase were placed in order of size. A short book between two tall ones could ruin his day.

Of course, all these little patterns emerged only gradually.

When I first arrived at the office the door was standing open and Norman was speaking into the phone, his face, appropriately enough, the color of parchment, his sand-colored hair slicked back, his sad eyes roaming the floor for a sign that all was not lost. He was wearing a very expensive English tweed sport jacket in mixed tones of blue and gray, with blue slacks and navy blue Italian suede shoes without laces, a pretty jazzy outfit for someone who looked as though he were just leaving to attend a funeral. But then Norman always looked that way. He was depressive-depressive.

"Just tell him Mr. Spain called," he was saying into the

phone, "Spain. As in El Greco. Toledo. Madrid. Granada. Hemingway. Never mind." He hung up.

"Hello," I said, tentatively.

He looked around, nodded, waved me in, dolefully. "C'mon in. Man's office is his castle. Used to be his home, now it's his office. Social evolution." He lit a cigar, waved again, and said, "Siddown, siddown."

"The train was late," I said, by way of apology.

"Trains," he grunted, pacing the room, "don't run on time in a democracy. Every man for himself. Bumper to bumper. You get out on that highway on a Friday afternoon in July, you know you're in a democracy, buddy."

He picked up my coat from where I had draped it across the back of the wicker chair and hung it neatly on a hanger suspended from a hook on the back of the door.

"Siddown," he repeated, waving toward the swivel chair behind the typewriter and tramping gloomily over to the window, where he stood looking out at a row of windows across the street. "My son," he said, "is eleven years old. This morning at breakfast he told us he was quitting school and getting his own apartment. On Bleeker Street, yet. I told him!" He paced the room. "My wife is a big help. 'He's just rebelling against parental authority,' she says. Yeah? Well as long as I'm paying his way through life he'll damn well do what *I* think is good for him!" He paced a while. "It so happens I think it's good for him to rebel against parental authority." He paced some more. "He left this morning. Packed a suitcase and walked out. Not only that, he took a taxi. To *Bleeker* Street. You know what that costs, from Central Park West? That was his mother's idea. She doesn't like him to take subways. He can live on Bleeker Street alone, eleven years old, but he can't take the subway. Then she calls the landlord on Bleeker Street—this kid arranged the whole thing by mail, sent a money-order for a month's rent in advance, everything—she calls the landlord and says, 'I understand you have a new tenant arriving momentarily. After you've seen him, would you please send him back to this address . . .' So now he's on his way home, in *another* taxi." He stopped at the window again, closed his eyes, and shook his head. "I've *got* to make more money."

He turned and saw me still standing.

"Sid*down*," he said for the third time.

I sat in the chair he indicated, behind the typewriter. On the table near the typewriter was a copy of my story, with lots of neat red lines underlining various passages, and lots of neat red notes in the margin.

"Okay," he groaned, "let's get down to brass tacks. Though why we should always get down to *them* I don't know. It wouldn't hurt them, once in a while, to come up to *us*." He carefully put out his cigar, and I was just about to stop taking shallow breaths, when he carefully lit a fresh one.

And we began to work.

The story I'd written was based more or less on a girl I'd once known in Brooklyn, named Vilma, who had a very tough time with boyfriends because, without meaning to, she invariably misrepresented her background.

This girl looked every inch Vassar. She was pale blonde, and her hair was soft and straight, and she wore it in that classy casual way, parted on the side and that's all. She had classic bone structure and classic clothes, and she was a good tennis player, and an excellent swimmer, and a fine horsewoman. Altogether she gave the impression of belonging to a set of New England ancestors who had Mayflowered it over here and then set about distinguishing themselves by quietly becoming millionaires.

As a matter of fact Vilma's family was fairly well-to-do, but unfortunately they had caught a later boat, and they were from someplace not very chic, like Poland or Rumania. There were a lot of them—brothers and sisters—and feeling quite naturally a little left out of things in this country, they tended to stick very close together—so much so that they all decided, even after they married, to live together in an enormous three-story house: Vilma's mother and father and her father's unmarried sister on the top floor, Vilma's father's brother and sister-in-law and Vilma's grandmother on the second floor, and Vilma's father's sister and brother-in-law and an unmarried brother on the first floor. In time, with children and all, the total count was eighteen. It was a sort of borough within a borough.

When they first bought it, this house was in a very good neighborhood, but the usual mysterious ethnic and economic changes took place over the years and by the time Vilma was old enough to have men panting after her, the neighborhood she lived in was fast becoming, to say the least, sloppy. The elders, though, saw no reason to leave. This was not only their home, it was their domain, their island, their kingdom. And they were so fond of each other, there was so much warm, deep, unshakeable love and loyalty, and such a tradition among them of total sharing, that every inch of that house was community property. No doors were ever closed, there was a continual flow of traffic up and down the stairs and in and out of all the apartments, and even the telephone (who needs more than one telephone?) was installed, with justice, in the second-floor apartment, equidistant from the other two. All conversations via that instrument were as public as a soapbox speech in Union Square.

Not only that, but Vilma's grandmother, a sweet old lady with a voice like an alcoholic midshipman and an accent that immediately evoked pictures of a steerage full of peasants, always managed, since she was a second-floor tenant, to reach the telephone first.

When Vilma was expecting a call from a current admirer, she would jump a foot off the ground when the telephone rang and race madly down the stairs hoping against hope to beat that frail old lady to the draw, but she never made it, and Grandma's uncompromising midshipman's shout clanged through the house like a death knell.

"Ask not for whom the bell tolls," Vilma used to say, sadly.

✳ 101

CARL A. RUDISILL LIBRARY
LENOIR RHYNE COLLEGE

Every August Vilma would go off with two or three other girls to vacation at some fairly expensive summer resort, where she would inevitably attract a number of young men who saw in her not only a good-looking dish and a gay companion, but also the chance of a lifetime to marry into what was obviously a class family with bundles of money, and to become a junior vice-president the easy way.

So in September the parade would begin. Each Saturday night some long convertible or sleek sports car would pull up, slowly and uncertainly in front of Vilma's family's cooperative, some nattily-dressed young man would step out of the car, look incredulously up and down the decaying street, move in a trance to the front door, ring the bell, and immediately be swallowed up in a sea of humanity.

Not one of the eighteen people living on the premises, no matter what their age, disposition or state of undress, ever refrained from welcoming one of Vilma's dates. They would look him over, ask a lot of uninhibited questions, and then calmly return to their personal squabbles, debates, intimate disclosures and what not, with him standing there helping Vilma on with her coat.

After a first date, none of these young men were ever heard from again. And Vilma, of course, was not the kind of girl who would cater to their prejudice by meeting them in town or anything like that. They had to pick her up. And they had to take her as she was, seventeen relatives and all.

This was the background. In my story the girl's name was Diana, and the plot concerned one of these young men who came—as they say—courting her, but who was *not*, for a change, the least bit affected by her attachment to this shambling commune. These things just didn't mean anything to him, one way or the other; he was in love with this girl and he wanted to marry her, period.

But. By this time Diana was convinced that all men were incapable of loving her for herself alone, and she drove this poor fellow crazy by refusing to believe in his sincerity. She decided that the only reason he kept hanging around was that he had this ulterior motive—he was softening her up for an inevitable night in a motel. The fact that time went on and this didn't happen, did nothing to change her mind. It just made her impatient. Why didn't he play his hand and get it over with? In desperation she decides to trick him into seducing her, just to prove that this was what he was after all along. She was a nut, this Diana. (Vilma never went that far.)

This is the kind of story that somehow, when you begin to tear it apart and reexamine the motives and impulses of the characters and so on, it doesn't take ten minutes before the whole thing is lying there in shreds, and that's what Norman did. By the time he was finished I was convinced there was no story there to begin with.

Then Norman, still tramping around, said, "I'm improvising. This guy Frank . . . He *doesn't* come to the house. . . ." He took three long strides across the room, repeating solemnly, "he *doesn't . . . come* to the . . . *house*," as though this were the solution to all the world's problems. "At the beginning, see? . . . At the beginning she arranges to *meet* him. At—uh—the Plaza fountain. You know, the Zelda Fitzgerald syndrome. Fits in with this image she's projecting. So she arranges . . . what's the matter?"

I cleared my throat and said, respectfully, "She's not projecting any image. The image projects itself. In spite of her. Almost. That's the whole . . . point."

Norman regarded me with profound melancholy. "Didn't you ever hear of the *conscious will?*" he asked pityingly. "One of the fundamentals of dramaturgy?" And he gave me a short lecture proving that Vilma-Diana knew what she was doing all the time.

I didn't believe it, but I didn't talk back.

"So," he said, resuming his improvisation, "she meets him at the Plaza fountain."

✳ 103

I let it go. What the hell, I may have known Vilma, but Norman was a professional writer and professional writers probably know more about your friends than you do.

So Norman went on into a rambling monologue, which I found very difficult to follow, first of all because I was sleepy, secondly because the cigar smoke, in that tiny room, was making me pretty sick, and thirdly because I was worrying about my own problems, like how to conduct a normal sex life on seven minutes a week and what the protocol was on interrupting Norman in order to call home and see if Sooz had developed any temperature.

Suddenly Norman whirled around and said, "Or better yet, she dyes her hair *black!*"

I could only stare at him. Obviously I'd been out of touch for the last half hour.

"How about that?" Norman insisted.

I gazed out the window thoughtfully and said, "Maybe . . ."

I figured if I just kept equivocating long enough, Norman, in trying to convince me, would reveal the sequence of events that were supposed to lead up to this peculiar decision of hers. But he only said, "Okay, what do *you* suggest?"

If I could only get out of this place for five minutes and call home!

"What do *you* suggest?" he repeated.

"Lunch?" I said.

Norman looked resignedly at his watch and decided it could legitimately be considered lunch time. He looked worried, sighed, and began buttoning his jacket.

"I have an appointment at the Oak Room," he moaned, as though he knew that when he got there the tumbrel would be awaiting him. But I realized this was meant to be an apology for abandoning me.

"Oh that's all right," I assured him, "don't mind me."

And he went off to the Oak Room, and I went off to the nearest telephone booth and called home. Sooz was perfectly fine, Hannah informed me, on a subtle note of triumph. So I called Deedee and asked her to have lunch with me. Inside of twenty minutes there we were, across the street from Bloomingdale's with all its tantalizing windows, both talking at once, not even listening to each other because there was so much to catch up on, and having a marvelous time.

After lunch we crossed the street and committed to memory every inch of every Bloomingdale display, happily arguing the merits of silk jersey versus silk crepe, and then we made another lunch date for later in the week and parted, and I walked briskly back to the office.

It's a wonderful thing to have a place to go to after lunch, to know that somebody is waiting impatiently for you, that an important activity has ceased and cannot be resumed until you get there. There is nothing even remotely like it in a housewife's day. I thought of all the lonely tomato sandwiches I'd munched at the kitchen table with only the twelve o'clock news for company, and the knowledge that no matter what I did for the next few hours it wouldn't matter much to anybody.

"I'm so *lucky!*" I sang to myself as I strode up Fifty-seventh Street with its little art galleries and decorator shops, and down Madison Avenue with its windows of chic dresses and expensive sweaters and imported gloves and bags. The street was alive with good-looking people, bright-eyed people, glad-to-be-there people.

There was a strange sensation in my chest, and for a minute I thought it was the first sign of an ulcer, but then it seemed there was something dimly familiar about it, and groping back into the sensations of years ago, I finally recognized it—sheer exhilaration.

I breezed into Norman's office glowing all over with pleasure, vigor, and optimism.

Norman was in a chair, behind a newspaper and a smoke screen, reading a report about a man who had almost been buried alive.

"Interesting dilemma," he said. "Here he is, being buried alive. At the last minute they hear him banging on the coffin lid and let him out. The point is, should he bang on the lid?"

"Wouldn't you?"

"Of course not. People don't like other people coming back to life. They just finished adjusting to your death. They don't have the stamina to go through another emotional upheaval. They end up resenting you. Before you know it you're a social outcast." He shook his head. "Once they bury you, even if they made a mistake, forget it. It's the only way to keep your friends."

I smiled, hung my coat neatly on the hanger in back of the door, and bustled into my chair, feeling much more at home than I had that morning.

It was then that Norman's wife popped in to check on me, and after satisfying herself that my real reason for being there was the same as my ostensible one, and after assuring Norman several times that their son was back in school, she warned him to remember not to forget to come home on time, and left. And we went back to work.

"So what do you think," Norman said, "about dying her hair black?"

I thought quickly, and leaned back in the swivel chair and closed my eyes.

"Tell it to me again," I said, "from the beginning."

I I

I FOUND the solution to the problem of my sex life. It was very simple really, and once I thought of it I was very annoyed with myself for not thinking of it sooner. As it was, I bungled around for a few nights first, trying to work out the arrangement I'd thought of after my initial *faux pas;* namely, getting up from the dinner table and going right to work arranging my clothes, my hair, my instructions for Hannah, and whatever else needed to be ready for the morning.

This arrangement was a fiasco. I'd be in the middle of slipping my hand into the seventh nylon in an effort to find a pair that matched and didn't have runs, and Alex would howl from downstairs.

"Ruth!" in a voice that could only mean I'd done something terrible.

I'd skitter down the stairs, and he'd be sitting at the desk with the balance sheet from the bank on one side and the checking account book on the other, and he'd look up at me with wonder in his eyes and say, "How do you do it? Every month?"

"I *swear* . . ."

"There's thirty dollars missing. Thirty dollars and seventeen *cents.*"

"Not this time! It's not my fault this time. I entered every bloody check I gave out. Every one!"

"Listen. Think. What did you buy for thirty dollars and seventeen cents?"

"Wait a minute. Just a minute. You're not the greatest adder in the world. I've seen you make mistakes . . ."

"Be my guest . . ."

"Seven and eight is fifteen and nine . . ."

And I'd start adding up columns and subtracting the totals from other totals and coming up with even *worse* discrepancies. And then we'd go through the cancelled checks, over and over again. And then he'd make me sit with my eyes closed and think, think, *think* what I'd done with that thirty dollars. And by the time we straightened it out, it was bedtime, and I still didn't have anything ready.

Or, I'd decide that the next day I was going to wear a very smart dress I'd bought a couple of seasons ago and hadn't had much opportunity to wear, and I'd go into the cedar closet and drag it out and discover the skirt was a couple of inches too long,

✳ 107

and I'd be in the middle of turning up the hem, and he'd say, "Honey, what did you do with my stretch sox?"

"What stretch sox?"

"The stretch sox I just bought."

"I didn't know you bought any stretch sox."

"I bought a pair to see if I'd like them. I put them on the hall table. Are you sure you didn't see them?"

"Positive."

"That's funny. I put them right here. Maybe *she* saw them."

"Well, ask her."

He'd look uncomfortable. "*You* ask her."

So I'd go clunking up the stairs to Hannah's room and she wouldn't know anything about stretch sox, and there would be a cellar-to-attic search for the stretch sox, and by bedtime my skirt would still be half up and half down.

Or, my hair, which I kept cut in a style I fondly believed to have a certain gaminlike charm, would be so limp and matted with dirt that I looked a lot more like Medusa than Leslie Caron. I would wash it and be halfway through setting the curls, when I would hear footsteps approaching the bathroom and Alex would appear, a crumpled newspaper in his hand and a wistful look on his face.

"I'm lonely," he'd say.

"I won't be long, honey. Stay here and talk to me."

"I can't. I'm watching the Shakespeare Festival."

"Then how can you be lonely?"

"I like to make comments. Come on. Please? It's no fun alone."

That was when I finally admitted the arrangement was a fiasco. There was no way of getting these things done while Alex was around and awake.

And since he was around and awake from dinner to midnight . . . there was only one possible solution.

Every evening after dinner, I was available for conversation, bank accounts, stretch sox, or anything else. At bedtime I slipped into a piece of nylon and lace, brushed my teeth, slunk into bed with a lazy, provocative smile, and let things take their inevitable course. Then I murmured a sweet goodnight, closed my eyes, and listened for the quiet, regular breathing that told me Alex was sound asleep.

Then I got up, washed my hair, shortened my dresses, ironed my blouses, tweezed my eyebrows, inspected my stockings, polished my shoes, filed my nails, creamed my face, made notes for Hannah . . .

It was the perfect solution. Except, of course, that I didn't get much sleep.

But what's a little wooziness in the mornings, when life is so full and every day is a gift-wrapped package? I felt as though I'd left a nunnery and joined a circus. After years of monotonous ritual, I woke in the morning knowing that any *number* of unpredictable things could happen that day. After years of not particularly looking forward to anything, I looked nowhere *but* forward.

And after years of responding with a shrug or a dirty look to Alex' nightly "Well, what's new?" I finally had an answer. Boy, did I tell him what was new! He couldn't stop me. I bustled into the house every night *bursting* with what was new. After romping with the kiddies (not one harsh word to them, not one shred of impatience, I was a living doll), I slid, breathless, into my seat at the dinner table, bubbling over with information, observation, commentary, and what-have-you. I sparkled, I made jokes, I was a whole floor show.

Alex was a little startled at first, but after a while he settled into an attitude of amused tolerance very similar to the one he used for listening to long involved stories by David or Sooz.

It was a good thing too, that I had so much to say, because the noise helped to mitigate the strangeness of sitting in the dining room and being waited on by somebody in the kitchen. I wasn't used to being served in my own house. I just wasn't, let's

✳ 109

face it, to the purple born. But I was so busy bending Alex' ear that I was only uncomfortable in a subterranean part of me.

Hannah's cooking, I discovered, while frankly it didn't measure up to mine in many respects, had the advantage of not being flavored with the notable lack of appetite I brought to anything I'd had to spend several hours preparing. Consequently I overpraised it.

"Delicious!" I'd say to her, on tasting a mediocre goulash.

"Marvelous!" I'd rave, about the so-so chicken.

And she'd allow herself a small complacent smile.

And Alex would look at me as though I were showing signs of senility.

But I was so giddy with unaccustomed activity and sensation that I couldn't help myself. I just exploded with superlatives every time I opened my mouth. I had no inclination to find fault or to worry. After a few days I didn't even think about the fact that a total stranger had taken over my house and my children. I didn't have *time* to think about it. Every day was new. Every day was amazing. Every day was full of discovery. Huckleberry Finn in high heels.

For instance, I discovered that I could argue with Norman and not only would he not have me court-martialed, he would even, in his own way, give in. I discovered this on the third day, after we'd finally abandoned the dyeing-the-hair-black routine. I had just thought of a possible scene that seemed funny to me. "Uh—here's an idea—maybe—" I said modestly. "Suppose she —uh—she meets him at the Plaza fountain . . . they sit on the edge there . . . he wants to talk to her seriously, about getting married, but he has trouble expressing himself . . . he's shy. . . . He starts the conversation out in left field and has to maneuver his way around to what he wants to say. In the meantime, a kid is walking around the edge of the fountain—you know—the way kids walk on a fence—heel to toe. A real rotten little kid. His mother's walking beside him holding his hand. Around and around and around. Every time he gets to where Frank and the girl are sitting, they have to get up because the kid won't get down and walk around them. Every time, just as Frank gets the conversation around to what he wants to say, this kid shows up, and they both have to stand up, and the mother apologizes, and there's a whole *megilla*, and by the time they get settled again Frank has lost his nerve and has to start the conversation out in left field again. And this rotten kid is *chanting* while he walks. . . . 'One, two, buckle my shoe, three, four, shut the . . .' You can hear him coming twenty feet away. So even before he *gets* there, Frank hears the voice in the distance getting louder, 'One, two, buckle my . . .' What's the matter?"

"That scene goes on the air," he said, "and even Mr. and Mrs. Nine-year-old-mentality out in Broken Elbow Falls are saying to themselves, 'Why don't they just get up and go somewhere else?' "

I hadn't thought of that. I chewed on my pencil for a minute.

"Well," I said, "suppose Frank says 'Let's go somewhere else' and she says 'No, I like it here, this is my favorite spot in the whole world.' "

He puffed on his cigar and made his eyes heavy-lidded like Peter Lorre. "Ex-*cuze* me, lady, I still don' like it."

"Why?"

"First of all kids aren't funny. They only sound funny on paper."

"I've seen some funny kids."

"Never. You never saw a funny kid in your life, except for a few miracles, mostly Italian."

"Maybe we could have a miracle."

"Don't trifle with me. Besides, the whole thing isn't funny. A guy too bashful to ask a girl to marry him. Who's going to believe it, in this century?"

"All right, not bashful. Nervous. Anxious. Anyway, if the character takes it seriously, the audience will too, won't they?"

Norman raised his eyebrows, surprised. "Watch out, Bella

Spewack!" He hiked around the room chewing on his cigar. I wondered if he was getting ready to call Wingate and tell him I wasn't collaborating properly.

"Okay," he said finally. "If you *want* to do that kind of a scene, here's how you do it. They meet in Central Park. They look around for a bench to sit on. All the benches are taken, except one. Frank grabs it. They sit down. He starts talking. He's just beginning to get around to the subject of marriage when a sanitation guy shows up, with a bag and one of those sticks with a point on the end for picking up garbage. Underneath Frank's bench it's loaded with candy wrappers, cigarette butts, broken hypodermic needles—Central Park junk. The sanitation guy takes a look and goes to work. Frank is in the middle of a romantic sentiment and this guy starts poking around between their feet with his stick. 'Excuse me . . . lift up your feet a minute, will yuh? . . . Thanks. . . . Lookit this garbage! . . . How kin people be so doity? I ask you. 'Ja ever see such doit? It's a disgrace, that's what it is.' And he's poking away, and Frank is getting madder and madder. Finally the whole place is cleaned up and the guy goes away, and Frank takes a deep breath and starts again. He's just getting warmed up, there's a gust of wind —the wind blows more crap under the bench, back comes the sanitation guy, 'Excuse me . . . could yuh lift your feet please? . . .'"

I laughed, Norman looked appeased, and I felt good. Obviously we'd use Norman's scene, not mine, but I knew he knew his scene wouldn't exist if I hadn't thought of mine first, and I sensed my stock had gone up a point or two.

That day I went with Norman and his friend Arnie to a Japanese restaurant where we cooked our own lunch right on the table over some Japanese Sterno, and Arnie—a moon-faced bachelor who carried with him at all times a large looseleaf notebook containing the name and telephone number of every showgirl in Greater New York—spoke Japanese to the waiter who couldn't speak Japanese because he was Chinese.

A few days later Simon called, to ask how I was making out, and took me to lunch at an Italian place that was a hangout of his, and all through lunch people he knew stopped by the table on their way in or out; a professor of English at Columbia, an architect, a dress designer, a lawyer who was defending a bunch of terrible gangsters—wonderful people.

The next day Norman introduced me to a Mexican restaurant with bullfighter posters on the walls and waitresses in ruffles, where we met a journalist acquaintance of his called Max who told us how he'd been pulled out of a Cuban fun house in the middle of the night in his underwear and taken to see Castro because Castro suddenly decided he wanted to practice his English for a speech he was going to make, and we had tortillas and enchiladas and God knows what other marvelous poisonous food.

God! I thought. And some people live like this *all the time!*

And in the middle of the second week Wingate called and invited us to lunch with him at *Sardi's*.

I've been around and I know that Sardi's, after all, is just another restaurant, and that anybody at all can have lunch there providing they look as though they have the price of a meal. But I also know, when I go into a department store, that I am a grown woman and that the store is anxious to sell me things, and yet, because in certain situations I still think of myself as ten years old, I keep expecting some stern lady to come over and say to me, "Don't ride the escalators!"

There is a residual intimidation in my blood, with regard to certain institutions, and Sardi's is one of these institutions.

So, while I preceded Norman into the crowded, dimly lit lobby with my head high and an air of cold indifference, I couldn't help feeling I was sneaking in where I didn't belong. While Norman checked his coat I forced myself to glance casually at the famous caricatures on the wall, instead of openly gaping, and then we moved a few steps toward the dining room. A thin, dark, polished, disdainful man stood at the entrance, subtly barring the way. He looked at us with faint contempt and I could almost hear the click as the caste-machine in his mind registered "NOBODY." Then Norman pointed to Wingate at a far table, and the thin man waved us in with a weary hand.

Wingate didn't see us coming, his chair was turned away from the table and he was deep in conversation with three youngish men at the table next to his. They looked vaguely familiar.

"Who are they?" I mumbled to Norman, and Norman mumbled back some names and I remembered who they were. I'd seen an article on them in some magazine; "Playwrights of the Year," the white hopes of Broadway, Off-Broadway, and television. They were considered very gifted, very controversial, very witty, weighty, and profound. I was dying to hear what they were talking about.

We sat down at Wingate's table without his being aware of it—I think—and waited for him to finish his absorbing discussion with the Apostles. I listened as hard as I could.

"The bastard won't *give* you anything. He drills right into the goddamn nerve for half an hour and keeps telling you it doesn't really hurt, it's all in your mind."

"Why can't you ever get a dentist on Sunday?"

"Or in the summer? I had an abscessed tooth last summer."

"What did you finally do about your boat?"

"Would you believe it, I can't *give* it away? When we had that storm in July I kept hoping it would get ripped loose and disappear."

"You know we rented that house for five summers at two thousand a summer and *now* my wife wants to buy it?"

"Julian bought that house at the end of the road. It's ten feet from the ocean. He's building a swimming pool between the house and the ocean."

"Wake up at three A.M. sometime with a toothache and you'll know what tragedy is."

"I heard Janet's teeth cost him four thousand dollars."

"Kids don't have cavities any more. They have orthodontia."

"Well, I thought, you just have to separate the man from the artist.

Wingate finally turned to us.

"Ruth . . ." he smiled, putting out his left hand and touching mine lightly, "Norman—good to see you."

He summoned a waiter, told us what to order, warned the waiter that he expected his shirred eggs just slightly damp, opened his silver cigarette case filled with French cigarettes, passed it around, lit one, and leaned back with the air of an affable monarch about to indulge himself with a couple of court jesters.

"Well," he said, "and how has the muse been treating you?"

"Unemployed writers," said Norman, "have muses. Employed writers just sweat."

Wingate laughed, complaisantly. I noticed out of the corner of my eye that the three playwrights at the next table were looking over at us and mumbling in a speculative fashion. I crossed my legs and puffed on my cigarette, basking in the heady sensation of having three playwrights wondering who I was.

Norman told Wingate in general about our plans for the script, and in particular about the scene on the park bench.

The food came. Wingate forked his shirred eggs fastidiously.

"Mm," he said, thoughtfully, "that scene in the park . . . that's really low comedy, don't you think?"

"Of course. *Supposed* to be."

"Mm. Well. I don't think you can play it on two levels, Norman. Everything else is realistic. That scene . . . I don't know. . . ."

"It works. Believe me. Wait'll we have the whole script, you'll see, it ties in."

"And when," Wingate sipped at his old-fashioned, "do you anticipate having a complete script?"

"This isn't a three-act play, you know," Norman said. "A

three-act play you can toss off in a couple of weeks. These half-hour sunuvabitches take *time*."

"Just a rough draft, Norman. I'm not talking about a completed script. Just a rough draft. I want to set up a taping date for early in January. There's going to be a scramble for studio space, everybody getting out pilots for the spring sales pitch. The sooner we have a property to go with, the sooner I can sign up a studio. And there's another thing, I want to get Mike Garnette to do this, and he'll want to see something before he agrees. . . ."

"Mike Garnett? Directing comedy? He's a great director, but. . . ."

"Wonderful sense of humor. You don't know Mike. How are the Eggs Benedict, dear?"

"Fine," I said.

"You never know. Sometimes they're perfect, and sometimes . . ." He turned back to Norman and they went on talking about Mike Garnett and taping dates, and I sat there eating my Eggs Benedict and wondering how on earth I had come to this. Taping dates! Directors! Studio space! Sardi's, for God's sake! I was lunching at Sardi's! Three playwrights at the table next to me! And who else? I looked around. Celeste Holm! . . . No, it just looked like Celeste Holm. . . . Dana Andrews! . . . Well, no, but it could have been. . . . Ethel Merman? . . . Almost. Yes, that was definitely almost Ethel Merman. A relative, probably.

Finally the coffee came, and then the check. Wingate signed it. (Nothing but signatures at Sardi's. People without signatures eat at Schrafft's.) Then he leaned over to say goodbye to the three playwrights, who were now tensely discussing capital gains, and we made our way to the lobby—Lauren Bacall?—and out.

Outside, we parted company with Wingate and walked back to Norman's office. The sun came out from behind some clouds, a clean tangy breeze billowed the skirts of the girls on Broadway, the city was caught in that churning autumn excitement that only happens in New York, I caught sight of myself in the windows of the Hotel Astor, stepping smartly along in my red suit, and I thought WOW! What a life! And I was convinced that going to work was the smartest thing I had ever, ever done!

I was even more convinced of it the following morning. I opened the front door, stepped into a world of golden sunshine, bounced down the path to the driveway, looked back at my shimmering white house with an absolute riot of lemon-yellow chrysanthemums and tangerine-colored marigolds running around the shrubs and evergreens—nothing makes a city girl feel so filthy rich as owning a nice big hunk of nature—threw my hands to the sky and sang out, "I love you!" Unfortunately Hannah chose that moment to come out with an empty milk bottle, but to hell with her.

I drove to the station through wooded hills of antique gold and scarlet leaves tumbling against a background of royal blue, with WQXR on the car radio playing that crazy Russian ballet music from *Swan Lake*, Tum-tee-DAH-dum, Tum-tee-DAH-dum, ta-da-ta-da-TAH-da . . . arrived at the station, bought my ticket, went skipping out onto the platform to wait for the train, and ran smack into Gloria Betz, who was on her way to an allergist in New York, she said.

I happened to know there was a slight case of mispronunciation here; it was an analyst, not an allergist, but she never discussed it with anyone.

"Well!" she said, in her nasal twang, "what are *you* doing here?" (Hoping, I could tell, that I was going in for the same reason she was.)

"I've got a job," I said.

Her eyebrows went right up into her hairline.

"Really?" she twanged, "I didn't know you were career-minded."

"I'm not. I just got tired of making dinner every night."

"*I love* to cook," she said quickly, and then shrugged, as though she could hardly expect a neurotic like me to understand this. "It takes a while," she went on, smugly, "to realize what true satisfaction there is in being a woman. Just an ordinary woman. Most people don't realize how creative cooking can be. And taking care of a house." She started snapping and unsnapping the catch on her bag. "I really feel sorry for women who run around looking for fulfillment outside of the home. I don't mean *you*." Snap, snap. "I mean those career-minded females. They're fighting their own basic nature is what they're doing. Instead of enjoying it. It's biological, you know. All the big authorities say so. A woman, biologically, *needs* to stay home." Snap, snap. "And the sooner she realizes that she basically *wants* to, the happier she'll be. Thank God *I* found out in time." Snap, snap! Snap, snap! "Well anyway," she said, as we got on the train, "tell me about your job."

So I told her. And I think if she could have poisoned me then and there without having to pay for it, she would have. Putting aside all that malarkey about creative cooking, I had dared, where she had cowered, I had charged where she had retreated, I had won where she had lost. She hated me. I felt twice as successful as I really was. The sun was shining, the chrysanthemums were rioting, somebody else was home doing the cleaning and the ironing, I was out in the world getting looked at by strange men, having lunches in restaurants, active and appreciated—and to top it all here was Gloria, a living example of the fate I'd overcome. Beside her I felt triumph like trumpets blaring all around me.

I didn't even hesitate when she twanged, "And how does Alex feel about all this?"

"He still can't believe it," I said. Which was probably true. Also it was ambiguous enough to be essentially correct and at the same time suggest a picture of a husband overcome with awe and admiration.

At Grand Central we said goodby before turning toward different exits, and as I tripped jauntily up the stairs to Vanderbilt Avenue I could feel Gloria's eyes following me, and I thought to myself that her allergist was certainly going to get an earful today.

I wanted to feel remorse for the feelings she aroused in me, but I couldn't. There's something about somebody else's defeat that makes you feel doubly victorious, and that's that. It's not that you derive pleasure from their pain, in fact you often have such kinship that you suffer right along with them, and yet, at the same time, this other, rotten, thing is going on. I knew so well what Gloria was feeling that it actually hurt me. But at the same time it buoyed me up! Why, I asked myself. Why should I feel enriched by a neighbor's defeat? Is it just one of those human failings people talk about? Is it just a built-in character-istic of us lower-order animals? Is this the lovable little generic mistake that makes us so crazy about the idea of bombing the other guy to pieces? Is this why a king can't be a king unless there are subjects? And a man can't be a man unless . . .

I stopped in the middle of the stairway. A well-dressed cor-poration vice-president thought I was having some kind of attack and paused to assist me. See, I thought, how strong he feels just because he thinks somebody else is sick? Probably a minute ago he was feeling old and tired, now he's a stallion. I said no thanks, I was quite all right and he went on up the stairs, disappointed.

I had stopped because that last thought was a killer.

A man can't be a man unless what? Unless there's always somebody around who is weaker, unhappier, more confused, more frustrated, more trapped, more unfulfilled than he is?

Like for instance his wife?

Was this a fundamental truth? And had I known it all the time? And was this why I'd been frightened at the beginning, and why I'd almost chickened out after the job had been thrown in my lap?

✳ 119

In my mind I rummaged through the past few weeks, scrutinizing Alex' behavior for some clue that he felt unmanned by my independence. . . .

Nooo . . . no, there was nothing, really. . . . Was there?

Why should there be? There was no change in his way of life. Except Hannah. And he never said anything about her. I didn't get the impression he was absolutely mad about her, but then I very seldom got the impression he was absolutely mad about *me*, so that didn't count.

Actually, there was only one discernible change in our life now, and that was the really trivial one of the dinner conversation. There was a change there, no question about it. For years and years the conversation had followed the same pattern:

ALEX: "These guys are incredible. They want a job done, they want it done fast, they want it done well, they want it done cheaply. Then they hamstring the project with a skeleton crew, they waste hours every day with pointless meetings, they don't give anybody enough authority to cut through the red tape, they put the key men on a dozen other projects so they're never available when they're needed. . . ."

ME: "Jeez!"

And now the table talk was more along these lines:

ME: "The thing is the first script is the hardest, because of all the exposition. I mean, you have to introduce all these characters, tell the audience who they are and what their relationships are to each other, and show the background and everything, and you can't just do it straight, it has to be funny while you're doing it, and it all has to happen *while* you're building a story, because you only have a half-hour to do it in, and it has to be the kind of story that begins and develops and ends all in a half-hour so you get a sense of completeness but at the same time you have to leave the audience wanting more so that they'll tune in again next week, so it's impossible."

ALEX: "Uh-huh . . ."

True, every once in a while, between babbling and eating, I

would look up and catch him with a kind of disconcerted look on his face, but that didn't necessarily mean he was upset about anything. . . . Did it?

As I stood on the stairs there at Grand Central, another man paused on his way up. A young executive type. He didn't think I was having an attack. He just liked the idea of me standing there with one foot on the step above, stretching my skirt tight so that all kinds of leg contours were showing. I swallowed a smile and went on up ahead of him. Let him enjoy it.

No, I decided, there was nothing to worry about. Accept it, Ruthie, I said to myself. For once in your life accept good fortune; it really can happen. You made it, kid. You took the plunge and you came out a winner. Alex didn't collapse. The kids didn't collapse. The house didn't collapse. No tensions, no conflicts, they're all wrong, Helen, Vera, Natalie, Simon, all the Cassandras are wrong. Vicki and Shakespeare are right. To thine own self be true. That's all you have to do. It works. It works!

I clicked happily along to Norman's office.

I2   SATURDAY MORNING, as Alex was climbing up to the roof against my better judgment to clean the leaves out of the gutters, and just as I was preparing to drive Hannah to the station for her two days off, the telephone rang.

"Could I speak with Mrs. Bernard please?" said a strange voice.

"Speaking."

"Oh—hello, this is Sarah Spain."

Sarah Spain? I was so used to getting these urgent phone calls from women who wanted me to subscribe to several dozen magazines, or to immediately put up aluminum awnings on all my windows, or to store my nonexistent furs in their vaults, or to go out collecting money for the Westchester Foundation for the veterans of 1812, that it took me a while to realize Sarah Spain was not one of these ladies. Who she was, she was Norman Spain's wife, is who she was. I was astounded.

"Oh! Hi!" I finally managed. And then, because I could think of absolutely no good reason for her to be calling me, I was gripped by an unreasonable fear that something had happened to Norman.

"How are you?" I asked, quickly, "And Norman?"

"Fine, thanks."

So it wasn't that.

"I hear the script is coming along fine. . . ."

"We've only written half a page," I said, wondering what she was getting at.

"Well . . ." she gave it up, "I'm calling you, Ruth, because we'd like very much for you and your husband to come to a small party we're giving tomorrow night. I know it's short notice."

How about that! I found myself grinning.

"Well, thanks, we'd love to," I said, wondering what Alex would say, "What time?"

"Nine-ish. And don't eat too much dinner."

Oh, boy! Food, too!

"I think you'll enjoy the people," she said, and casually mentioned a few names I'd read in the paper from time to time.

"It sounds wonderful," I gushed, "And it's very nice of you to think of us."

She gave me the address and I hung up and looked at Hannah standing by the door, all dressed up and ready to go, and I summoned up my courage and cleared my throat, and said, "That was—uh—a very important invitation on the phone. I mean, we were just invited somewhere . . . for tomorrow night . . . and—uh—it's kind of important . . . uh . . . it's the people I work for. . . ."

(Why couldn't I just rise, graciously, like Joan Fontaine or somebody, and say, in a well-modulated voice, "Hannah dear, we're going out tomorrow night, would you mind terribly getting back at six instead of eleven?")

Hannah raised her eyebrows patiently at me, letting me sweat it out.

"I don't suppose . . . I mean, I hate to ask . . . see, I have to get dressed and all, and the kids . . . dinner and . . . we'd have to leave about eight . . . do you think . . ."

Finally she put me out of my misery.

"What time would you like me to come back?"

And I told her, and she nodded, and I drove her to the station, wondering if there was a course I could take somewhere that would teach me how to feel comfortable in the role of employer.

When I got back to the house I ran upstairs to my bedroom closet to decide which of my fabulous array of one and a half dresses would do for my dazzling entrance into the Spains' living room. I was in a small, happy delirium. Parties, I have always loved. Parties where I am going to meet new people I love even more. And parties where I am going, like Alice, right through the looking glass into a whole new world—I would even trade a dishwasher for one of them.

I settled on the pale blue crepe and ran outside to where Sooz and David were pointing their red noses up at the roof.

"Hey!" I called up to Alex, "guess what!"

"What?" said the kids, immediately.

"We're invited to a party at the Spains' tomorrow night!"

"Oh, boy!" cheered the kids.

"Not you," I said. "Did you hear me, Alex?"

"Hold the ladder, will you?" he said.

I held the ladder, and he came down.

"Did you hear me?" I repeated. "The Spains invited us to a party. . . ."

"Here, David," he said, handing him a brush, "take that into the garage." And he started collapsing the ladder.

"Tomorrow night," I said.

"Oh, yeah?" he said, very offhand. "Who are the Spains?"

"You know—Norman."

"Norman who?"

"Norman *Spain*. The *writer*. The one I *work* with."

"Oh. Yeah?" He started lugging the ladder back to the garage.

"Hannah said she'd come back early tomorrow."

"What for?"

"So we can go to the *party*."

"What party?"

"*Jeesus! The Spains invited us to a party!*"

"Oh . . . Careful, Sooz. Get out of the way." Calmly he set the ladder back on its hooks and went into the house to wash up.

For a moment I had the distinct feeling that his vagueness was deliberate, but I couldn't figure out why he should choose to be deliberately vague, so I decided it was probably just the trauma of having been on the roof, and let it go at that.

But the next day, as evening approached, I noticed he didn't seem to be in any great hurry to get ready. In fact, he hung around in blue jeans, unshaven and unshowered, until about fifteen minutes before we were supposed to leave.

"It's a quarter to *eight!*" I said, standing there in full regalia, powdered and perfumed and practically pawing the ground.

"Okay, okay," he said, mildly, and meandered into the shower.

When he was finally dressed, he started fussing around with his keys and his loose change and his handkerchief and his credit cards and God knows what else, and then, when he couldn't find anything else to put into his pockets, he suddenly decided to call his mother long distance and got into an argument with her that dated back twenty years, and this went on, at forty cents a second, while I stood around with my makeup wilting, remembering how he complained about the telephone bill.

"It's a quarter past eight!" I hissed, and finally he hung up.

I hurried into Sooz's room to kiss her good night, and then into David's, and Alex followed me, and I said "Good night, good night," and scampered down the stairs, but when I reached the front door I realized Alex wasn't with me, and I looked back, and there he was, standing in the doorway of David's room, giving him a lecture on neatness.

"You understand?" he concluded.

"Yes," piped David.

"Okay, let's see if you do. Come on, clean up."

And he stood there, supervising, until David had emptied every last shaving from his pencil sharpener, and put away his forty-two pencils, his sixteen erasers, his sneakers, his Cub Scout manual, his two hundred baseball cards, his Golden Dictionary, his mittens, his Bingo game, his turtle food, his Chinese checkers, his dismantled make-it-yourself cuckoo clock, and about four thousand little piles of assorted stamps.

"It's eight-thirty!" I screeched.

He sauntered downstairs.

"Is this going to be something new?" he said. "You going to announce the time every few minutes for the rest of our lives?"

"Well, if we're going, let's *go!*"

"Relax, relax," he said, and filled his pipe . . . slowly.

I ran out to the car.

Eventually he came strolling out of the house, stopped to examine the weather stripping on the garage door, the tar on the driveway, the fenders, the windshield wipers . . . then he got behind the wheel, got himself comfortable, rearranged the rearview mirror, relit his pipe, unbuttoned his coat, dug in his pockets for some change for the toll booth, buttoned his coat again, got himself comfortable again, started the motor, and finally, at a quarter to nine, we drove off.

Halfway to the city he decided to stop for gas, since we only had seven-eighths of a tank left, and while at the gas station, so it wouldn't be a total loss, he had the man put air in the tires and change the oil and check the battery and generally overhaul the car.

The only reason I didn't scream was that I couldn't unclench my jaw.

Eventually we got to the party. It was quite a party. It was quite an apartment. When a maid in crisp black and white opened the door and we walked in, I thought we'd come to the wrong place. Whatever I'd imagined, it wasn't this. It seemed impossible that Norman Spain, comedy writer, should come home every night from a crummy Forty-ninth Street office to the subdued splendor of this living room; this dull gold rug, this magnificent French-blue sofa, those regal high-backed chairs, the exquisite figurines in the depths of a tall mahogany bookcase, that wall of long narrow windows framed in a series of dull-gold, floor-to-ceiling drapes, delicately ball-fringed and gracefully looped ten inches from the floor. It somehow brought to mind a picture of the Rothschilds quietly coming out of that ghetto and taking over London. There's no question about it, I thought, inside every Jewish boy there's an English Lord struggling to get out.

As the maid took our coats I was aware of the muted sound of Jerry Mulligan music somewhere under the babble of voices, and a crush of heads, arms, faces, and legs that glittered like no heads, arms, faces, and legs I'd ever been in the middle of.

Everything about these people seemed to be just a little bit more so than in real life. The clothes were more than clothes, the bodies were more than bodies, the eyes more than eyes, the hair more than hair, the jewelry wilder, the lips shinier, the lashes longer, the shoes crazier, and the voices like something on a sound track. And the conversation was like what you imagine you'd hear if you could listen in on a group therapy session involving P. T. Barnum, Salvador Dali, Duke Ellington, Max Lerner, Maria Callas, Shirley Temple, Sholem Aleichem, Santha Rama Rau, Ilya Ehrenburg, the crew of the *Kon Tiki*, and Marjorie Morningstar.

✻ 126

Coming from a world of relatively sober, intelligent, and politely inhibited living rooms, I felt like a New England spinster let loose in New Orleans during Mardi Gras. I was thrilled, I was intimidated, I was struck dumb. I went into the guest bathroom to comb my hair. The bathroom was cocoa and black with an antique gold chair in the corner that turned out to be a toilet. Boy, what I had to learn about interior decoration! When I came out Alex was standing alone by the liquor supply with a glass in each hand, and I took a stiff drink of whatever it was he handed me, and then Sarah Spain came over and introduced us around, and then we sort of stood on the fringes of a group (if you can call a collection of insularities a group) and just watched and listened.

There was, for instance, a languid man with a shock of black-and-white striped hair and the most gorgeously dissipated face I'd ever seen, who kept saying, to various females who weren't even looking at him, "Please, honey, don't follow me around, it's embarrassing. I've told you a hundred times you belong to a different facet of my life. You don't belong here. My wife belongs here. My mistress belongs here. But not you. Now will you go back to that alley and wait for me?"

A platinum redhead with a simply fantastic body wearing a thing that started on her shoulders as two thin slivers of black velvet which came down and met somewhere around her navel, widening in the process just barely enough to cover each of her incredible breasts, sat there very straight, all red-headed and big-eyed and baby-faced, saying things like: "You think O'Neill is great, sweetie? You don't think all that torment and anguish sitting on your ass for nine hours till you get hardening of the arteries and on top of that the man writes English like he just got out of sixth grade, you don't think that's a little over-rated, pussycat?"

Somebody's wife, tall, brown, bushy-haired, black-eyed, in some kind of wild print, a real paisan, a regular Anna Magnani, kept saying there were no challenges left in life, and looked like she just couldn't wait for the bomb to go off so she could start from scratch and put the world together *properly,* for godsake!

A slender, dapper little man, in the most elegant custom-tailored suit this side of Noel Coward, with a pleasant twinkle in his eye, sat beside the platinum redhead, his sartorially splendid ankles crossed, leaning back nonchalantly, patting her hand and saying, "You have such a superior intellect, darling, such caustic wit, such a keen sense of the moral issues, such empathy. If only you weren't so dumb."

And a roly-poly comedy writer with receding hair and freckles, who said, "You think it's easy to be in demand? Fer instance, NBC wunts me fer this new show, a prestige show, like 'Omnibus.' But I got this movie cummitmint with Jerry. So I says to the guys at William Morris, Jeez, what did you *submit* me fer? So they said *we* din submit you. They *ast* fer you. They wunt you, and nobody else! They said couldncha over*lap?* I said Jeez, you know workin' fer Jerry is full time, how could I handle an outside projec'? I said whut am I, the only writer aroun'? Let 'em get somebody else. There must be *other* guys could write a adaptation uv Henry James!"

A young man in a blazer with a Van Dyke beard said to the roly-poly comedy writer, "C'mon, Heshy, where are they gonna find another George Bernard Shaw with freckles?"

Another young man, very sad, had managed to capture a bottle of Black and White all for himself, and just sat hunched over in a chair, saying to himself, "I was singing then, and I've been singing ever since."

And an actress, startlingly plain, with a pale face and enormous eyes, clothed in a dun-colored sack and a long scarab necklace, standing like a question mark, clutching nervously at various parts of herself and constantly looking over her shoulder in a frightened way, exuding such modesty, such humility, such painful timidity that it practically amounted to arrogance, was muttering, "No, Zero is a genius, no don't say that, he is, he's a genius."

✳   128

And a well-known actor with a kind of handsome, trampled, sincere-looking face and a blue suede shirt, made his only contribution to the evening by saying to the actress, "Christ, Eleanor, shut up."

It was a twelve-ring circus, all acts performing simultaneously and ignoring all the other acts.

Even Norman seemed to be performing. He wheeled in from some other room with his friend Arnie, and he was drinking and laughing. I'd never seen Norman drink. For that matter I'd never seen Norman laugh. He handed a glass to some girl and she took a sip and said, "What did you *put* in this drink?" And Norman said, "The finest gin money can buy, the best vermouth in the world, and a *little bit* of poison."

After an hour or so, and still another glass of whatever it was, I found that everything was sparkling nicely, and Norman dragged me into a conversation he was having with the people sitting around, about "that rich man's social worker, Harry Wingate," and before I knew it I was talking, and they were listening. Listening to *me*.

And it wasn't until Sarah Spain started herding everybody into the dining room for food that I noticed Alex had removed himself to a far corner where he was sitting all alone looking at a book of reproductions of the French Impressionists. I went over to him.

"Hi," I said. "Let's get some food. There's food. Let's get some. Food."

"Mm-hm," he said, turning a page.

"Well, c'mon then. Let's go. Let's get some food. Let's."

"You go ahead."

"C'mon. C'mon." I tugged at the book, and finally he put it down and came with me to the dining room. But after he got a plateful of food he went back to his corner. I started after him, but Arnie caught my arm and insisted on introducing me to a very tall brunette from a nude show in Las Vegas who said she had come east to join the Peace Corps, and then more people crowded around, and with one thing and another, it was time to go home, Alex said.

We got our coats and said goodbye and the door closed behind us and we got into the elevator, and suddenly it was very quiet. Alex was wearing an expression of gentle melancholy.

"What's the matter?" I said.

He quickly turned up the corners of his mouth. "Matter? Nothing. Why?"

"You look terrible."

"Who—me?"

"You hated the party."

"Nooo, I didn't."

"Why'd you sit in a corner?"

"Corner? Oh. Seemed like a good idea at the time."

"Something's bothering you."

"Bothering? Me?"

"What is it?"

"What is what?"

"That's bothering you?"

"*Nothing!*" He began to whistle, tunelessly.

We left the elevator, went out to the street, found the car, got in, and headed for the highway. There was a lot of silence. I suddenly felt guilty, because I knew that somehow I was responsible for Alex feeling sad. Then I got angry. Why should he make me feel guilty? What right did he have to be sad? Who'd done anything to him?

"Why didn't you talk to anybody?" I demanded.

"I talked to a couple of people."

"What couple? A couple of French Impressionists?"

"Some director . . . some musician. We didn't seem to have much to say to each other."

So that's what it was. That's what the melancholy was all about, and the stalling about getting dressed, and calling his mother and all that stuff. I'd forced him to take part in the ritual ceremonies of a strange tribe to which I was initiate and he wasn't, and thereby I'd put him in an uncomfortable, if not downright humiliating, social position.

How about that.

I remembered a party given by the president of the firm Alex worked for. I remembered being left sitting on a hard chair, surrounded by the strange wives of Alex' colleagues, while Alex drank and laughed and talked shop all night with a bunch of the boys.

Nobody seemed particularly concerned, at that time, with *my* social position. Why was this any different?

Because, Ruthie.

Because certain sexes have more face to lose than others.

I looked at Alex' face. Then I turned down the visor and looked in the mirror at my own. Seemed to me we both had the same amount of face.

Yet here I was feeling unhappy and guilty.

It was then, as I turned back the visor, and watched the approaching Cinderella lights of the George Washington Bridge hanging in fragile loops over the dark river, that the joyous exhilaration of the party, of the past weeks, of my whole new life, first began to show signs of being less than a permanent state of affairs.

13

IT WAS a few days before Halloween that Wingate called and told us he had to have a rough draft of the script within a week because Mike Garnett was back from the coast and he wanted to sign him, fast.

Immediately the atmosphere in the office changed. No more gay little lunches; we called for sandwiches from the delicatessen down the street. No more philosophical discussions about being buried alive. Even Norman's phone calls were cut down by half.

And if he had been morose before, now he was a living dirge. Everything was hopeless. We were doomed to failure. Two minutes after he got an idea, he loathed it. As for my ideas, he didn't even hear them. He was beyond reach of a human voice. Trying to get through to him was like wandering across the moors through impenetrable mists calling "Heathcliffe!"

After a while I began to be afraid we really wouldn't make it. I didn't see, at this rate, how we *could* have a completed script within a week.

And it was Halloween.

If there was one thing I didn't need at that point, it was Halloween.

Usually I'm crazy about holidays, even little ones. Valentine's Day, Election Day, St. Swithin's Day—I don't really care what it is as long as it isn't just Monday or Tuesday or Wednesday. I love Special Occasions. I love the idea of everybody in the whole country getting dressed up and going to Grandma's. I think at some point in my childhood I must have associated a sense of tremendous well-being with something painted by Norman Rockwell, because somewhere underneath all my New York sharpness and skepticism I have this secret, unshakable conviction that the moments of profound happiness in life are the ones you see on the cover of the *Saturday Evening Post*. But Halloween, in the past few years, had become less and less a holiday, and more and more a pain in the neck. And here it was Halloween.

Boy, was it Halloween!

I'd like to see one Halloween—just one—when the temperature didn't suddenly drop twenty degrees overnight and a slashing, icy rain didn't start spewing out of the sky at four P.M. and a heavy fog didn't roll in on top of it, successfully obscuring the vision of masked children and motorists alike, so that every mother in the North Temperate Zone goes rigid with fear for interminable hours waiting for the screech of brakes, the scream, the siren, or at the very least the reappearance, eventually, of several soggy, incipient tuberculars of tender age. If your own kids manage to escape the day without galloping pneumonia, you can rest assured that your neighbors have not been as fortunate and that for the next couple of weeks the school classrooms will closely resemble certain graphic passages in *The Magic Mountain,* so it's only a matter of time before it gets around to *your* house. I could have gladly *killed* Halloween.

But the kids . . . !

"How many days?"

"Three more days!"

"Two! Two! It's only two days! Today's almost over!"

So first there were the costumes. In keeping with my secret devotion to Norman Rockwell, I felt there was something debasing and cynical about going out and buying cheap, ready-made costumes at the five and ten. I always, painfully, and with terrible tenacity, made the kids' costumes myself. Over the years I'd ruined, among other things, one good Mexican sarape, a gorgeous red velvet skirt, an expensive tablecloth, a straw hat, and six sewing-machine needles.

But this year I didn't see any way of producing these miracles of craftsmanship short of working at them between midnight and dawn, and a few hours' sleep at night being one of my incurable vices, I told the children that this year we were going to *buy* the costumes. The jubilant enthusiasm with which they greeted this announcement convinced me once and for all that children have a really crummy sense of values.

For some unfathomable reason Sooz announced that she had decided she wanted to be The Bobbsey Twins. Both of them. And then the big blow fell. David was going to be Walt Disney.

I stared at him.

"Walt Disney?" I said, "Why Walt Disney?"

"Why not?" he said.

Well, the argument was long and fruitless, and finally, the day before Halloween, I came home early, in spite of black, black looks from Norman, and dragged them to the five and ten where, amid the screams and clutching hands of several hundred maniacal dwarfs, they settled, respectively, on a Ben Casey and an Astronaut. I'm still not sure who was which.

And the costumes were only the beginning. Then there was the business of preparing the candy and the money for UNICEF. Used to be you threw the kids an apple and that was that. But Trick or Treat has become one of the major proving grounds of our competitive society. It's Big Business now. Now they come to the door expecting a combination supermarket and Chase Manhattan. There was a five-year-old child down the street who was known to come in after trick-or-treating, go straight to the bathroom, and weigh her shopping bag on the bathroom scale. Anyway, you buy six times as much candy as you need, because God forbid there should be a very large turnout and you're caught short, your name will be mud, not to mention your front door, your windows, your lawn, and anything else that isn't inside the house. But you're never caught short. Au contraire. When the kids start coming around you hand out all this junk sparingly at first to make sure it lasts, and then about eight o'clock you get a little frantic because you still have a three-foot pile of cavity-promoting material to get rid of, and you start hauling large handfuls to the door every time the bell rings, but it's too late. The big crush is over, there are only a few stragglers left, and there you are when it's all over with twenty pounds of lollipops, Tootsie Rolls, Baby Ruths, candy cigarettes, bubble gum, licorice whips . . . and that's *besides* the twenty pounds your own kids bring home from their scavenging. You can't give it away because every other family is in the same predicament. You can't take it back to the store. You can't sell it. You can't melt it down like scrap metal. You can't keep it, because even if the kids only eat one piece a day for the next year they'll be wearing dentures before they're twelve. Even the Salvation Army doesn't want it. There's only one thing to do. Go out in the back yard, in the rain, and dig a big hole.

And that's not all there is to Halloween. There's also pumpkins.

Unfortunately, I was a great one for establishing family traditions, and Halloween without a pumpkin was unthinkable. So I had to go out and buy a goddam pumpkin—and you wouldn't believe the number of lopsided pumpkins they try to sell you, it takes guts, grim determination and about six hours of scouring the countryside before you can find a decent, human-looking pumpkin. And the night before Halloween I had to stay up, bone-tired and worried to death that the rough draft of the script would not be finished in time and cut open this pumpkin and dig out the insides which were—believe me—granite, and carve out two big triangles, one small triangle and a half-moon with teeth. When I was through, I had an orange-colored Chiang Kai-shek. I stuck a candle in it, put it on the table next to the long window by the front door, and knew in my heart that the following afternoon at five P.M. when I was in New York and Hannah lit the candle, the drapes would catch fire and the whole house would go up in flames.

And that's still not all there is to Halloween. There is, for instance, no dinner.

On Halloween night you sit down to dinner and you never get to eat it. You raise your fork and the bell rings and you go hand out the loot to a bunch of wet fairies and Frankenstein monsters and brides and beatniks and ballerinas and gorillas and convicts and rabbits and what-not, and then you close the door and go back to the dining room and lift your fork and the bell rings and you go back to the door and dole the stuff out to a group of dripping bandits and mice and skindivers and Indians, and then you go back and . . .

I would say, roughly, you walk seventeen miles between six and eight P.M. Considering you also don't get any nourishment, you lose quite a few pounds of a Halloween.

Where, you ask, was Alex in all this? Alex who used to cut out the pumpkin and answer the door in a Frankenstein mask? He refused to have anything to do with it. All of a sudden, this year, he disowned Halloween.

✳ 135

"What do they need a pumpkin for?" he said.

And Sooz, incredulous, said, *"Daddy!"*

"Let them wear last year's costumes," he said.

And David looked at me in horror.

"Ignore it," he said, when the doorbell rang for the seventeenth time, and he sat there eating his dinner while I wore out the carpeting.

It was strange behavior for Alex. There was something almost abandoned about his repudiation of Halloween. And there was something suspiciously like gratification on his face when, the morning after Halloween, the alarm went off and I groaned and said, "Not today. I'm not getting up today."

It was the first time in weeks that I didn't roll right out of bed and stagger, bleary but willing, into the shower. This time I wanted desperately to burrow into my warm little hollow and go back to sleep. It took me ten minutes to find the will power to slide my legs out from under the covers, and another ten minutes to follow them.

Finally I made it in and out of the shower and into some clothes, and stumbled down to the kitchen where I swallowed some juice and coffee while hazily arbitrating several disputes between Hannah and Sooz, Sooz and David, David and Hannah, and so on. Alex had already left, whistling cheerily. After the coffee my head cleared a little and I pulled myself together and managed to get out of the house on time to catch the train. I was halfway to the station when I became aware of a strange sensation in my feet, and looked down at the accelerator and saw the toes of my right foot daintily peeping out the front of a bedroom slipper.

I pulled into somebody's driveway, backed out into oncoming traffic, raced back to the house, burst through the front door into cries of, "Mommy!" "What happened?" "Did you break down the car?" "Mom, can I go to Jimmy Portey's after school?" "Mommy, my throat hurts." "Mom, can I take your typewriter for Show and Tell?"—got into my shoes and out the door again, and whizzed back to the station and missed the train by thirty seconds.

"Swell," I thought, "now I'll be a half-hour late. And Norman is already sulking because I left early the other day to buy the costumes."

It was a gray, raw, chilly morning, still damp from the night before. It was even chillier in the station house than it was outside, so I paced the platform trying to work up a little circulation while I waited for the next train.

It was then that the voice of a five-year-old female got through to me.

"Mommy, my throat hurts."

Did she really say it, or did I imagine it? Or did she only say something that sounded like it? Mommy, the goat blurts? Mommy, my coat squirts? It didn't seem likely. I stepped into a phone booth and called home, and confirmed the fact that Sooz considered her throat on the critical list. I told Hannah to keep her home and take her temperature, and I would call again from New York.

I paced the platform again, thinking about the script, and suddenly I got an idea for a whole funny scene, about Diana on a date with Frank, getting home very late, the whole house asleep, and finding she's forgotten her key, and not wanting to ring the bell and wake the entire household she gets Frank to try to open a first-floor kitchen window, not knowing that Grandma, having had a fight with her daughter-in-law, is sleeping there on a cot, and Grandma hearing him and thinking it's a burglar quietly alerts everybody in the family and they all tiptoe into the kitchen armed with baseball bats, tennis racquets, carpet sweepers, and so on, waiting for him to break in. This cheered me considerably. I decided I'd work it out in detail on the train, and surprise Norman with it. Wouldn't that be something, come in with a whole new scene! I scrounged in my bag and found a pencil, the back of a laundry list, and a letter from my mother on pink stationery, of which she'd only used one side. Good enough. I'd write it all down on the train. I had a good forty minutes to work it out.

The train came in and I boarded it with enthusiasm.

I'd forgotten, temporarily, about these trains.

I'd forgotten what had been slowly penetrating my consciousness for the past few weeks.

The New York Central, unfortunately, is not just a railroad. To the casual eye, it might look like an ordinary series of trains, but when it becomes a place where you spend two hours of your time every day, five days a week, then you become aware, slowly and chillingly, that what you are riding on is a mobile hospital ward.

There's probably been more stuff written in the last ten years about suburban commuting trains than about love, death, and Van Gogh's ears, and it amazes me that nowhere in any of this spotty literature has anyone, to my knowledge, mentioned the most phenomenal thing about them. Of course, I have only first-hand knowledge of the one line, but I'd be willing to bet it's typical.

The fact is, that ninety-five per cent of the passengers on any given New York Central train on any day of the week are violently ill.

This phenomenon began to dawn on me toward the end of my first week of traveling. I'd walk into a train car on this New York Central, and I just wouldn't believe it. It looked like some Rotarian's idea of a large-scale practical joke. There would be all these solid citizens—not bums, mind you, not derelicts, not Skid Row characters—but respectable, prosperous bankers, lawyers, merchants, chiefs, and matrons with blue hair emanating the scent of expensive talcum—all good white country-club upper-class Voice of Firestone Americans—proper, successful, Bigelow-carpet, circular-driveway, FAO Schwarz, fifth-row-orchestra-for-*The-Sound-of-Music* Americans—and they'd all be sitting there sneezing and gargling and hacking and coughing up phlegm right into the faces of their fellow passengers.

Not once—not even *half* of once—did I see any of these carefully groomed Abercrombie-and-Fitch, Bronzini-tied, cashmere-coated, Bergdorf-suited, close-shaven, coiffed and manicured gentlefolk ever cover a sneeze or a cough with a handkerchief or a piece of tissue. They wouldn't even reach for one. They wouldn't even turn their heads. They'd just sit there, expansively —and expensively—hands on their big neat thighs or daintily clutching their fifty-dollar-Italian-leather bags—and look you straight in the eye, and let you have it! KA-CHOOOOO! Not one hand would move to cover a mouth. Not one arm would twitch in polite reflex. Not one tentative gesture would be made toward pocket or pocketbook.

And then the coughers would start—the rumblers, the thunderers, the whistlers, the groaners, the chokers—until the whole car was vibrating with pulmonary cacophony. And they'd all just open their mouths and let loose. They'd sit there staring mindlessly ahead or out the window or down at their newspaper or sideways at the person next to them and open those wet pink jaws, and BLAST the air with disease.

Not one sign of diffidence, regret, or even acknowledgement. These affluent, well-bred, *Herald-Tribune,* pure-linen-tablecloth, polished silver, Black, Starr and Gorham, crystal wedding-gift, initialed-thank-you-note, five-dollar-barber, hat-off-in-the-elevator, charity-fund-raising, custom-cleaners, send-me-the-head-waiter-this-fork-is-*dirty* Americans.

Not being really fond of sickness in any form, I wasn't too happy at the thought of being exposed, every single day, to wholesale germ warfare. There was an alternative, of course, namely, driving into New York in my own car, but since I am not so much a good driver as a lucky one, it was the alternative of a quick death rather than a slow. So I had to cope with the New York Central, and I had to find a way to beat it.

By careful observation I began to learn which cars were the least crowded, and I found if I played it right I could sometimes manage to sit in that section of the least crowded car containing the smallest number of germ-spreaders. Then I came up with several other ingenious devices. At first I would quickly grab an empty seat, preferably near the door, on the theory that at each station as people got off and on I would at least get an occasional whiff of fresh air. But I soon realized that the empty-seat tactic was a trap, because even if I spread myself out—bag, coat, umbrella, briefcase or whatever—over the space next to me, and even if there were sixteen other empty seats in the car, sooner or later somebody decided I was the one and only person in the world they wanted to sit next to, and they would stand there looking coldly down at my belongings and say, "*May I?*" So I'd move everything onto my lap and they'd sit down, all two hundred pounds of them, and they would invariably be a person who has been prematurely discharged from a sanatorium.

When I got wise to this I changed my approach. I would wait until everyone else was seated, and then look over the prospects. I would carefully detect and eliminate the more obvious coughers and sneezers, and finally select the healthiest-looking individual and sit down next to him—or her. (Looking down coldly, of course, at their belongings and saying "*May I?*")

But there was a hidden pitfall in this strategy. I could stand at the head of the car for ten minutes, watching one person intently, and this person would sit, serenely composed, sneeze-free, cough-free, no sign of redness around the nose or watering of the eyes, a nice, normal coloring to his cheeks, all the time I stood there. The minute I sat down beside him, his face would suffuse, his eyes water, and he would begin a frenzied series of respiratory convulsions which would continue unremittingly for the whole trip, minus handkerchief, minus Kleenex, minus turning head, minus everything but a self-centered blankness.

I sat there day after day, plotting all kinds of campaigns. When the person beside me started up, I would very deliberately and significantly open my bag, take out several tissues, cover my whole face except for my eyes, turn my head away as far as possible, and sit like that, holding the tissues over my face, until I thought my arm would fall off.

When somebody behind me launched a series of explosions, I would turn around, glare at them with undisguised loathing, and mutter "*My God!*"

But they didn't see me, and they didn't hear me. Zombies, all of them. I would sit there burning, feeling the smoke coming out of the top of my head. I had a recurrent fantasy in which I was a great ventriloquist and when the coughing and sneezing reached a certain peak I would throw my voice to the back of the car and these great, sonorous tones would issue forth, scaring the hell out of everybody.

"Now hear this! All persons coughing or sneezing on this train without the use of handkerchiefs or tissue, will be fined one thousand dollars! *And* promptly executed!"

Then I had another plan. I would write a scathing letter to the Health Commissioner and have it mimeographed and go up and down the train leaving copies on every seat like they do when they explain why they're raising the fares again.

Also posters. I was going to have somebody make me up a large poster showing a small child sitting between a cougher and a sneezer, one male one female, both of whom were turned toward the child, spraying him liberally, while the child cringed pitifully, warding them off with upraised arms. Caption: "Influenza took this child's life!"

Of course it all came to nought. There are all kinds of technicalities about distributing pamphlets on trains, and poster space is prohibitively expensive, and it turned out I have no talent for ventriloquism. So the death cars kept on running up and down the tracks, with me on them, and the commuter rates kept rising.

And this particular morning after Halloween, because it was so raw and chilly, the coughing and sneezing were worse than ever. I tried hard to capture the phantom funnies that had flitted through my mind on the platform and to put them down on the back of the laundry list, but who could concentrate? Between indignation, fear of contagion, and the physical discomfort of sitting at a forty-five degree angle in order to keep as far away from my neighbor as possible, not to mention a recurrent anxiety about Sooz that all these hoarse throats were giving me, I could hardly remember how to spell, let alone how to be funny.

At Grand Central I went into a phone booth and called home, not really expecting any disastrous news, Sooz hadn't looked bad at all, really, and she *was* given to occasional flights of hypochondria.

"Did you take her temperature?" I asked Hannah.

"Yes," she said, with her usual loquacity.

"Well, what is it?"

"One hundred and four."

"One hundred and WHAT?"

"Four."

"FOUR? One-two-three-FOUR?"

"Yes."

The blood drained out of every vein and vessel. My teeth chattered. My hands shook. I stammered into the phone, "R-r-rub her with alcohol. G-g-give her an aspirin, p-p-put on the vaporizer. I'll c-c-call the d-d-d-d-d—"

I hung up and dialed Vicki's number with thick, frozen fingers.

"Vicki!" I suddenly had laryngitis. "She—she—she—she—"

"She who? She what? Where are you? Who is it?"

"Me! New York!"

"Yeah? So? Calm down."

"Soo—Soo—Sooz has a—a—hundred and f-f-four and I—I—I'm in New *York!*"

"There's a connection? I don't get it. She has a hundred and four because you're in New York? What would she have if you were home? Relax, idiot, as soon as I finish with a patient here I'll run over and take a look at her. I'll be there in ten minutes. Did you tell the girl to give her some aspirin?"

I nodded.

"Ha?"

I realized she couldn't see me.

"Yes!"

"All right. Will you take it easy? Give me your number, I'll call you after I've seen her. It's probably this viral thing that's going around. They spike a temp like that for about twenty-four hours. I've got all three of my kids home with it. Take a Miltown for God's sake."

I gave her the office number, quietly, and hung up. Why did she always have to show me up? I had one sick kid, she had to have three. What was she proving, running around so efficiently taking care of other people's children while her own were lying feverish in their beds? So she's strong, mature, courageous and remarkable. Big deal.

I wanted to run home. I wanted to get into a taxi and bribe the driver to head north at a hundred miles an hour. To hell with Norman. To hell with Wingate. To hell with the job. What did any of it matter, if Sooz . . .

If Sooz what? What can happen to Sooz, you jerk? She's sick. She's been sick before. She'll be sick again. If *she's* not sick, David will be sick. Kids are sick every other week until they're seventeen. Are you going to take a taxi home every other week for the next ten years? In the first place, you can't afford it.

This, I thought, is what Helen and Vera and Natalie were afraid of. This is a test. If I can just get through this! And I told myself that come hell or high water, sleet, snow, dark of night or viral infections, if Vicki can do it, so can I. I will learn not to panic. I will learn not to feel like a murderess if my child takes ill and I happen to be thirty miles away. I will learn not to visualize her—or him—being rushed in an ambulance, pale, small, alone, to the nearest oxygen tent, while I coldly, ruthlessly, gluttonously pursue the satisfaction of my ego. I will learn. I will. I must.

And firmly, I picked myself up, left the telephone booth,

found a penny in my change purse, bought myself a paper cup at the water fountain, took a Miltown to dissolve the terrible knot of fear in my stomach, and trotted off to Norman's office, visualizing her—or him—being rushed in an ambulance, pale, small, alone, etc.

When I walked into the office Norman hung up the phone and gave me a frozen glare because I was late, then his expression changed to one of suspicious discomfort.

"You sick?" he said.

"No," I whispered, hoarsely, "I'm . . . fine."

He looked relieved. Norman, I discovered eventually, had such a horror of germs that by comparison my reaction to the New York Central was casual to the point of indifference.

I sat down at the desk making businesslike gestures with the onionskin and carbon paper. I was not going to let my personal problems interfere with my work. I just wasn't.

"I had . . ." I cleared my throat, "I had an idea for a scene. I made some notes." I looked in my bag for the laundry list.

"Good," Norman said, "let's hear."

I looked at the back of the laundry list. "Cms hm lt," it said, "Std frt stp w F. Gr. lns wndw . . ." What did it mean? I couldn't remember a thing about it. Not a thing.

"Uh—well—" I said, "it—suppose she gets sick—uh—she gets a virus—uh—and after all Frank is an intern—and—uh— he disagrees with her doctor's diagnosis and prescribes a different . . ."

Norman stopped pacing and stared at me.

"Forget it," I said, "it's not very good."

Why didn't Vicki call? What was going on? Had Hannah given her an aspirin? Had she bathed her with alcohol? Could I trust Hannah? After all, what was she? A stranger. Sooz wasn't her child. She wouldn't take the trouble . . . she wouldn't take the pains . . . she wouldn't be as careful. . . .

No, I won't think about it. I won't. I'll concentrate on the work.

∗ 144

"Okay," Norman said, like a lament, "let's see if we can crack this thing in the department store."

I stared intently at Norman. My eyes never left his face—or the back of his head, depending on which way he was walking. I listened raptly to every word.

Concentrate, I said to myself. Work. You have a responsibility here. After all, *Norman* doesn't sit here worrying about his family problems. *He* doesn't go to pieces if his kid gets sick.

And a little voice in my inner ear said:

"Of course he doesn't. His wife takes care of all that."

14

s o o z had an infected ear.

For the next few days I got up even earlier than usual so that I could personally check on her temperature (I was convinced Hannah's vision was 70–70), and report to Vicki, and fill the vaporizer, and give Sooz the initial doses of medicine for the day, and keep David away from her until it was time for him to go to the bus stop, and make sure she ate breakfast in her own room and out of her own separate dishes. Where she ate lunch and out of what, God only knows, because Hannah, it turned out, regarded sickness as simply a vulgar weakness which real strength of character could easily repel. She disdained it. It was a kind of Health Through Scorn. I only hoped that some day— when she was no longer working for me—she would get an infected ear that would be so painful they'd hear her screaming in every Christian Science Reading Room around the world.

And every morning, about seven and a half minutes before train time, after piling Sooz's bed with coloring books, crayons, dolls, games, and assorted junk, and promising on my return to bring her everything, including Arpège, I tore myself away and drove, squinting over the wheel through half-shut eyes, to the train station.

I called home four times a day. I just didn't trust Hannah to remember to give Sooz the cough medicine at eleven and three and the antibiotic at twelve and four. I even made secret markings on the bottles in the morning and checked the levels when I got home at night, and when evidence showed that probably two teaspoons had been removed from each bottle I told myself she'd most likely been given all four teaspoons, fast, the minute my car turned into the driveway. I also had visions of David playing in Sooz's room after school, breathing in tons of bacteria hour after hour, while Hannah calmly ironed underwear in the basement.

She was crazy about ironing, this woman. She ironed everything—undershirts, shoelaces, dust rags, sneakers, skipping ropes. Ironing was evidently her idea of the ideal way to spend a life—it was clean, it was quiet, its accomplishment was tangible, and it didn't really demand too much in the way of energy or patience. Personally, I would rather spend a week being tortured in Red China than iron one curtain.

Anyway, Norman didn't like the fact that I called home four times a day. We were only a few days away from the date we'd promised to have the rough draft ready for Wingate. Norman had cut out his own phone calls *entirely*—a sacrifice that has probably never been equaled except maybe by Edward giving up the throne of England.

But I couldn't give up those four phone calls; they were my only badge of motherhood. So I suffered Norman's cold glances and compressed lips, and tried to make up for it by contributing mightily to the work at hand. Unfortunately my major contribution consisted of worrying.

I worried about the department-store scene. I worried about the park scene. I worried about the ending. I worried about spelling things correctly. I worried about the margins. I worried about ordering more carbon paper. . . .

You might think that all this worry was therapeutic—nature's way of giving me a little relief from the strain of worrying about Sooz. It's a classic dodge; people under one kind of pressure find themselves another kind of pressure as a distraction from the first. Well, it didn't work. I managed to worry about both things simultaneously. I didn't lose an anxiety, I just gained a tension.

And it certainly didn't help Norman, or the script. I became acutely aware that Norman thought I was dragging my heels. I could tell from the way he ground his cigars into the ashtrays. I could tell from the way he avoided looking at me. But mostly I could tell from the things he said. Like, "For chrissake stop dragging your heels!" The day before the rough draft was due, Norman announced, first thing in the morning, as soon as I walked in, "We're staying with this thing today until it's finished! I don't care how late it goes!"

It was a Friday. Alex and I had arranged to go out to dinner that evening with the Millers—a colleague of Alex' at the office and his wife. I had a feeling of singular reluctance about telling Alex the glad tidings. I waited until Norman was down the hall visiting the john, and, with obscure misgivings, I called Alex at his office.

"Hi," I said, "how's everything?"

"Fine. What's up?"

"We're still going to have dinner with the Millers tonight?"

"Sure."

"Did you check? I mean . . . they're definitely coming?"

"Of course. Why, what's going on?"

"Oh . . . nothing." I took a deep breath. "I . . . think . . . I have to work late."

"*What?* What do you mean?"

"Work late. You know. Here. At the office."

"Until when?"

"I don't know. Until it's finished. The rough draft. It's due tomorrow."

"Well when do you think you'll be finished?"

"I don't *know*. Could be eight o'clock, nine o'clock. I don't *know*. Norman says I have to stay until it's finished."

Silence.

"I'm sorry," I said, "I know it's . . ."

"Just a minute, honey—" he said, like somebody who's being polite although he has a million things to do, and I heard him tell his secretary something about the files. He came back to me with a slightly preoccupied tone of voice. "Yeah—Ruth? Well, I'll see you later, then. Whenever you get home."

"You're not—upset—?"

"What is it?" he said to his secretary, "Ruth, I have a long-distance call waiting. Take it easy," he said, briskly, pleasantly, "see you later." Click.

I hung up, feeling as though I'd been speaking to a casual acquaintance.

It was ten-fifteen by the old Wells Fargo clock on the wall when I pulled the last sheet out of the typewriter, and Norman attached it to the other pages, glanced through the script disconsolately, shoved it into an envelope and said, "It stinks." He didn't actually mean it—it was just his way of warding off evil spirits; if he damned it nobody else would.

When I got home Alex wasn't there. Hannah said he had come home, changed his shirt, and gone out again, not saying where or when he'd be back. I crawled into bed and couldn't sleep, thinking he'd probably gone out to dinner with the Millers after all, and then thinking that since he'd left at seven and it was now almost twelve, he must have gone to dinner twice. Or maybe they'd all gone to a movie. Except that I remembered Joan Miller saying, when we made the arrangements, that they would have to make it an early evening because she had a teen-age baby-sitter. Maybe he'd gone to their house. Or maybe he was just riding around somewhere, staying out late to get back at me for spoiling his plans.

About one A.M. he came in, not bothering to be very quiet

about it. He clumped around, switched on lights, got undressed with a lot of thumping and clattering. I sat up.

"Oh. Hello," he said, pleasantly, as though he knew the face but couldn't place the name.

"You sound angry about something," I said.

"Who, me?" he said, brightly, and threw a crashing handful of change on the dresser top.

"What are you angry about?"

"Who said I was angry?" he inspected the sole of a shoe.

"Because I worked late? Is that what you're angry about?"

"Boy, these shoes are going," he said, and threw them into a corner.

"If you're not angry what's all the noise?"

"What noise?" He thumped across the room and flung open the closet door. Pling!

"Pretty late dinner you had."

"Oh. Is it late?" he said innocently. "I went to a movie. I figured since you were busy, you wouldn't mind."

"See? You *are* angry."

He put out the light, got into bed. Smash! "Well—good night."

"Plenty of times *you* worked late. Plenty of nights I sat here alone while *you* worked late. I couldn't even go *out*. I didn't even have anybody to stay with the kids. Plenty of times. Once we even had theater tickets!"

"Honey, I'm tired. Let's go to sleep, huh?"

"But that doesn't make any difference, right? It's okay for *you* to disappoint *me*, but not the other way around. Right?"

"Can we go to sleep now?"

"You're boiling mad, right?"

"I'm getting there!"

"Admit it. Admit it. You're mad."

"Yes! *Now* I'm mad!"

"Why?"

"*Because you won't let me go to sleep!*"

∗ 149

The next morning Alex slept late while I got up and took Hannah to the station for her two days off and came back and made breakfast for the three of us, and washed up the dishes, and took the shirts to the laundry, and did the marketing.

Then he got up and had a leisurely breakfast while I took the overdue books to the library and came back and made lunch for the three of us, and washed up the dishes, and drove David over to a friend's house, and played checkers with Sooz, and read her six Dr. Seuss books.

Then he went out for a nice little walk while I prepared the chicken for dinner, and drove over to David's friend's house to bring David back, and argued with David about taking a bath, and argued with Sooz about wearing summer pajamas, and set the table for dinner, and made a salad and a fancy dessert.

Then he sat down and had dinner while I served it.

Then he picked up *Patterns of Culture* and spread himself out on the sofa and started reading it, while I washed up the dishes and put the kids to bed.

Well, I thought, as I tidied up the kitchen, there's no question that a man who works all week needs to relax on the weekend. There's no question about that. There's only a question about this: What about a *woman* who works all week?

I remembered Saturdays when Alex had been part of the family—made pancakes for breakfast, or hamburgers for lunch, went bicycle-riding with the kids, or on rainy days cuddled them around him on the sofa and told them the story of *Aïda* while the music of the opera boomed out of the record player—even helped with some of the chores. How come he suddenly seceded from the union? Was he just tired? Or was it revenge for the night before? No use asking him, I knew the answer by heart. "Me? Angry?" Was it possible he *wasn't* angry? Was it possible he was really just tired?

Finally, about nine o'clock that night I shuffled into the living room and sank gratefully into a chair. I was just about to allow myself the luxury of skimming through *Esquire* magazine, which I understood had recently exchanged the leer for the raised eyebrow—Gore Vidal and everything—when Alex said: "Isn't it about time we had some people over? The Sands, the Bookmans, the Cardells? We never have anybody over any more."

"Okay," I said, and turned a page.

"Next Saturday night, for instance? Why don't you call them and see if they can make it?"

"Why don't *you*?" I wanted to say, but I knew better.

Alex, like most husbands, was officially exempt from making social arrangements. Social arrangements fell into a very large category called "Your Domain."

It was pretty crowded, this domain of mine. Next to my domain a subway car at Times Square in rush hour was the lone prairie.

Making social arrangements was only the beginning. There was also *planning* social arrangements, *preparing* for social arrangements, and *breaking* social arrangements.

Getting shoes repaired was also my domain. Hannah's happiness was my domain. Not to mention Alex's happiness, Sooz's happiness, and David's homework. Also buying mixed nuts, smoked oysters, birthday presents, wedding presents, baby presents, Mother's Day presents, Father's Day presents, mittens, stamps, and extra towels. Finding out about things, like where they have a sale on rubber boots or who has the agency and the parts for an obsolete record player. Getting rid of old clothes and toys, finding lost eyeglass cases, lockets, pipe cleaners, silver polish, nutcrackers, directions on how to get to somebody's house, shoehorns, hair ribbons, birth certificates and old newspaper clippings about lawn care. Replenishing the lunch-money box. Keeping a sharp eye on supplies of ketchup, toothpaste, and toilet paper—all of which Hannah seemed to have an aversion to ordering. Going to school for Parent Orientation nights, talking to the lady from B'nai Brith when she called for a contribution, deciding what movie to see and finding out when it goes on . . .

✳ 151

There's not enough paper in the world to list them all. The final figure is astronomic. Anyway, taking care of all the things in this domain had always been a tall order, but now, what with Norman and the script and catching trains and having to look neat every day, too, it was like trying to bail out the *Titanic* with a Dixie Cup.

I got up out of the chair I had so gratefully—and so recently—sunk into, went to the phone and called Vera. She couldn't make it the coming Saturday but she could make it the following Saturday. I called Helen. She could make it the *coming* Saturday, but not the *following* Saturday. I called Natalie. She couldn't make it any Saturday until the middle of December. So I called Vera back. And I called Helen back. And I called Natalie back. And then I called Vera again. And after about sixteen phone calls we finally set a date, and I crawled back to that nice comfortable chair, opened the magazine, and Alex announced it was time for bed.

"Aw come *on!*" I said, "I'm *tired! I* don't want to go to *bed!*"

Quizzical, I suppose, would describe the look he gave me. But I knew what I was talking about. I needed more than just sleep. I needed a little recreation, a little distraction. I also knew that men, for some cockeyed reason, feel that if you don't want to go to bed when they do—even just to sleep—it's an indication that you don't love them any more. So I closed the magazine and went to bed.

As I lay there in the dark, with that exceptional lucidity that sometimes visits me just before I fall asleep, it occurred to me that heaven does not necessarily protect the working girl. God, I thought, is not necessarily on our side. Whatever gave us the idea He was? After all . . . He *is* male. The more I thought about it, the more obvious it became that God would be out to make it as tough as He could.

And I sensed this was only the beginning. We were still in the realm of minor preliminary skirmishes; small floods and fires, a few unimportant plagues. Armageddon, He still had up His sleeve.

At three o'clock that morning I had a sign. From now on it's going to be pretty hard for me to scoff at eleven-year-old girls in Italy who have visions. At three A.M. I opened my eyes and said to myself—

"Mike Garnett?"

And sank back into oblivion.

15

WHEN I WAS INTRODUCED to Mike Garnett I was busy worrying about my swollen lymph glands. Like most women, I'm an authority in many fields, not the least of which is internal medicine. I immediately diagnosed mononucleosis, or possibly t.b. I saw myself lying, for the rest of my short life, pallid and inert on the living-room sofa, helpless, hopeless, sexless, without even an agonized Bohemian to kneel at my side, singing "Mi—*miiiii!*"

While this interior melodrama was going on, Norman and I were sitting in the control room of a network television studio which had been converted to such from the remains of an old Bundist meeting hall. It was a cold, gray, damp, noisy, steely, smoky, crowded, tense, petulant atmosphere.

Ginger Rogers and Fred Astaire would never have met in a place like that.

Certainly not Nelson Eddy and Jeannette MacDonald.

For Rock Hudson and Doris Day it would have been twice as big, with gleaming white walls and shocking pink cameras and maybe one puff of sky-blue smoke from somebody's cigarette.

Well, that's what you get for not having the sense to be a movie star instead of a person.

The reason we were there, a Wingate production was being

taped, and it was being directed by this man, Mike Garnett, who was going to direct our pilot film. Wingate had called that morning, to say he was taking the rough draft—on which he reserved comment—over to Mike Garnett, and thought it would be a good idea for us to join him so that we could meet Mike and start "communicating."

At least, that was the reason he gave for dragging us into this front-line trench. Personally I suspected he wanted to make a lot of changes in the script and was preparing the groundwork; he figured that if we saw him in action right there on the battlefield, sending out couriers right and left for coffee and paper clips, it would give us a proper respect for a Chief of Staff.

Anyway, there we were, huddled in a corner on our aluminum chairs with our containers, one regular, one black, with sweaty technicians milling around us shouting things into microphones and grabbing desperately at scrunched-up packs of cigarettes, and me surreptitiously feeling the tender glands under my jaw, when Wingate's legs materialized before us and I heard him say—

". . . Spain, and Ruth Bernard . . ."

I raised my head and smiled vaguely at an unshaven chin and a rumpled blue sportshirt, and that was Mike Garnett.

"Jesus, Harry," this husky voice said, "what'd you put 'em in here for? It's murder."

And then there was a little scrambling and we were all walking down a cold stone echoing corridor and into a glaring cafeteria which was at least warm and only half as noisy, and we sat down at one of those blank tables, and after some hot chicken broth had burned its way down to my stomach my eyes began to focus and I saw this man sitting opposite me, Mike Garnett.

He looked like a longshoreman. Well, no. He looked like a method actor playing a longshoreman. He was compact and muscular with strong hands and a great set of teeth. The only remarkable thing about him was that he had magnets instead of eyes. There were hypnotic lights flickering in the depths of those two smoky shadows, with kind of barbed-wire eyebrows over them and webs of little lines at the corners, and after the first quick look I made sure not to meet them head-on again, because . . . well, just because.

Wingate was throwing those sad smiles at the ceiling and making a lot of pronouncements about the production going on in the studio, like when George C. Scott pulled the girl's hair the motivation wasn't clear, and didn't he think that using a gobo for the garden scene was somewhat too traditional, and shouldn't something be done about Barbara's girdle showing through the nightgown, and a lot of top-echelon thinking like that. At some point he said that he wasn't sure the audience would understand that the contents of the glass George was handing her were poisonous, and before I knew it, I butted in.

"Have him say 'drink your milk, dear,'" I said, "And then they'll know."

Mike Garnett roared, and I looked up in surprise. What with Norman's insecurity, it had been a long time since anybody had laughed at something I said. I think that's when I began to like Mike Garnett.

For the next half-hour I kept feeling sparks from Mr. Garnett's eyes coming in my general direction. I knew he couldn't be looking at me, so I kept stealing glances behind me to see what kind of blonde was sitting there. No blonde, just a dirty electrician eating ham on rye. Well, I thought, to each his own. If he has a thing for dirty electricians, who am I to judge? But then the electrician got up and went away and the sparks kept coming. So he *was* looking at me. And immediately I wondered: Why is he looking at me? Is my mascara smudged? Is there a piece of grilled cheese hanging from one cheek? Is he trying to find out if I'm a troublemaker? Is he charming me up for the day when he'll say "This whole page of dialogue has to go"?

I chose the last explanation as the most likely, although I would've given odds my mascara *was* smudged, because it usually is, I usually end up with these ludicrous dark circles under my eyes, and I have yet to figure out how upper eyelashes, which curl *up* (if *I* have anything to do with it), can rub mascara onto the *under*side of a convex semicircle toward which they are pointing in the *opposite* direction of and which, geometrically speaking, they couldn't possibly *reach*.

But, as I say, I chose that last explanation because I was tired and all I really wanted to do was to lie down somewhere warm and soft and quiet, and sleep through the next few troubled periods of world history. So I smiled gamely at Mr. Garnett's unshaven chin and pretended to be letting him charm me, and busied myself with making plans for the care of the children in the event of my death from mononucleosis.

I came out of it only for a brief moment of peculiar shock when I noticed that Mike Garnett was drinking tea, instead of coffee.

Eventually we went back to the front-line trench and they were going to block a scene, and Mike Garnett sat down masterfully in front of a bunch of monitors, at this long counter full of sound men and lighting men and production assistants and telephones and scripts and ear phones and cigarettes and candy wrappers and unfinished sandwiches and soggy coffee containers and memo-pads and Kleenex boxes . . . and began to bark into a microphone.

I watched him, fascinated.

"Re-rack that opening, please—"

"Is Jack tied to him on this P.L.?"

"Try the mat on this, Eddie—"

"Can you truck to them?"

"Don't worry about the boom, the boom'll be out—"

"Wait a minute, camera three has a problem—"

"Try dollying back, Foxie—"

"He's gonna step in, you just pull back—"

"Cheat your left shoulder back just a little, honey—"

"Will somebody get John on his mark? Thank you—"

"Loosen up, Foxie. Good boy—"

"Let me hear you, please—"

"Okay. Stand by. Audio playback coming up—"

I had to keep telling myself that being impressed by mere terminology was juvenile.

Like all that melodrama about operating rooms. Scalpel! Sutures! What's such a big deal about scalpels and sutures? They're tools of the trade. You're doing a job, shut up and do it.

How would it be if a tailor went around saying "Needle! Thread! Scissors!" Or a cook. "Thyme! Oregano! Spatula!"

But I might as well have saved my breath.

"Pre-set six—" Mike Garnett was saying.

"Ride this a little higher, Foxie—"

"There's a cable on camera!—"

"Tighten on her. Tighten!—"

"Goddammit get that cable outa there!—"

"Okay. Tongue left a little—"

"Nice, Eddie. Nice, nice—"

"Cue music—"

"Lose the lamppost—"

"Niiice—"

I was gone. Like a nine-year-old boy in the bleachers at Yankee Stadium. Gone.

After a while Wingate decided we'd had enough of mingling with royalty, and motioned us out of the control room into the corridor.

"Now then," he said, leaning against the wall and smiling wanly over our heads, "Ah . . . Mike has the script . . . ah . . . I have some reservations about it, but . . . ah . . . we'll wait and see what Mike has to say. There will no doubt be substantial revisions . . . but I think we should be able to have a completed script in about . . . two weeks?"

"Sure," said Norman, glumly. "Easy. We could probably do it just working lunch hours and taking the rest of the day off. Anything we can do for you in our spare time? Translate the Dead Sea Scrolls or something?"

"As a matter of fact there is something you can do, while you're waiting for Mike's verdict. . . ."

"Slash our wrists?" suggested Norman.

Wingate smiled feebly. "We'll need outlines," he said, "for at least twelve more shows. . . ."

"This isn't television," said Norman, "it's a pogrom."

"I think the agency has a potential sponsor lined up. In any case there's interest. . . ."

Norman looked less apprehensive, which for him was practically carefree.

"But, as you know," Wingate went on, "these people want insurance. They may go with the pilot alone, but it's better to be prepared. So think along those lines, for the next few days. Think ahead."

And he sent us back to our peasant hut on Forty-ninth Street.

We thought ahead for two days, and on the third day, toward one o'clock of a nice cold, slushy winter afternoon, as Norman and I were beginning to let our motors run down in anticipation of lunch hour, there was a knock at the door, and Norman, who happened to be passing that way, opened it, and Mike Garnett walked in.

Immediately I lost the ravenous appetite I had been building up for the last hour and a half. (I never *did* get mononucleosis, or anything else. The lymph glands just subsided, waiting, I suppose, for a more inconvenient time to break out.)

Mike apologized for interrupting and said Wingate had suggested he drop over and talk to us about the script. He reached in his coat pocket, took out a rolled envelope, removed the script, sat down, frowned, and leafed slowly through the pages. While this was going on, Norman paced very fast back and forth between the desk and the window, moving things, stacking things, pulling things, poking things, brushing things, coughing a lot, and smoking the stub of a cigar until I thought his lips would ignite. I sat perfectly still and calm, tearing an eraser to bits with my teeth.

I didn't know which I was more afraid of, Mike Garnett's verdict or Mike Garnett.

Finally, after several decades had passed and I had suc-cumbed to a series of interesting symptoms like itching all over and pressure on my eardrums and mist in my eyes and loosening of all my teeth—finally he put down the script and grinned at us.

"It's very funny," he said.

Norman's face changed from loden green to its normal grayish-beige.

"But there are a couple of things structurally . . ." he went on, and proceeded to explain to us why we shouldn't do about half the things we'd done, and how we'd omitted a whole bunch of things we should have put in. "And," he concluded, "I'm not sure about the scene in the park. I think maybe it's a little too broad."

"Ah-*ha!*" said Norman, "Wingate works in mysterious ways his wonders to perform."

Mike Garnett kept smiling, but his eyes narrowed.

"*I* said it to Wingate," he said, "before he said anything to me."

"As a matter of fact," Norman said, "we were thinking of junking the park scene and doing something very subtle, like a scene in the hospital where this guy Frank is an intern, with Jack E. Leonard as head of the psychiatric division, and the chief neurosurgeon as kind of a *tummeler,* like Red Skelton. . . ."

Mike smiled, politely.

I knew Norman was more upset than he pretended to be. He was controlling himself because he thought Mike was a big gun.

"Well," Mike said, "let's not worry about the park scene yet. Let's just get the rest of it cleaned up. It's going to be very funny."

He stood, scorching me with a glance on the way up.

✳ 159

"Come on," he said, to both of us, "I'll buy you a hamburger."

Norman fidgeted. I knew he was in agony because he couldn't figure out how to break the lunch date he'd already made and at the same time he couldn't bear the thought of missing out on a chance to consolidate his position with Wingate's favorite director.

"Christ," he said, "I've got to meet this girl . . ." (I happened to know it was his friend Arnie) "Oak Room, the Plaza—maybe I can get away early. Where you gonna be?"

Nervously, I began assembling twenty-eight pages of loose script into a neat pile.

"Oh, don't foul up a good thing just for me," Mike said to Norman, "Ruth and I'll grab a hamburger somewhere—"

Now Ruth is my name. It's always been my name. Over the years millions of people have called me Ruth. It's a thoroughly familiar sound, one I hear every day. When somebody says "Ruth—" I don't jump, I don't panic, I don't break into a cold sweat, I usually just say "Ha?"

But Mike Garnett said "Ruth—" and the twenty-eight loose pages slid right out of my hands off the desk and across the floor in all directions.

As we crawled around the room retrieving them I tried to get out of going with him to grab a hamburger by mumbling something about an errand at Bloomingdale's.

"Bloomingdale's!" he said, with a voice steeped in two thousand years' worth of male scorn for female preoccupations.

So I quickly got my big heavy coat and my rainhat and my gloves and my scarf and my boots, and feeling about as feminine and dainty as a member of the cast of *What Price Glory,* I trudged with him through the raw gray slushy streets to a nearby bar-and-grill.

He talked a lot about Pirandello and the Cuban situation and a movie he wanted to make someday on Long Island Sound, and about boats he wanted to own, and people he got along with

(Otto Preminger, Kenneth Tynan, Geraldine Page), and people he didn't get along with (David Merrick, Jack O'Brian, Geraldine Page)—and once in a while he mentioned his wife and children. Casually.

An hour later I was still trying to swallow my first bite of hamburger, even though it wasn't quite as bad as I had anticipated. Most of the time he looked down at his plate or over at the bar while he talked. There were only two or three dangerous moments when I forgot myself and my eyes barely escaped meeting his.

It's quite impossible, really, to describe the quality of that glance. Obviously it didn't affect everyone the way it did me, because if it had, Mike would be, by now, either in Bellevue or the White House. All I know is it was impossible for me to look directly into those fire-lit shadows without developing a terrifying irregularity of the pulse. Unfortunately when we got back to the door of Norman's office he cleared his throat and before I could remember not to, I looked up at him. And while I was hanging there, impaled, he said, "Next time we'll have to talk about *you*."

If it had been me, I would have answered, "Listen, I don't know what you're building here, but I'm married and you're married, and anyway I don't think it's very healthy for a person to have a constantly irregular pulse beat."

But it wasn't me. It was some lunatic whose bones had turned to water, and she just nodded and quickly went into the office and shut the door in his face.

Luckily Norman hadn't come back yet, and before he did I had time, if not to compose myself, at least to figure out why I was *un*-composed. That last unfortunate meeting of eyes had made one thing sufficiently clear: Mike Garnett wasn't being nice to me the way a director is nice to an author, or the way a co-worker is nice to a co-worker, but more like the way Richard Burton was nice to Elizabeth Taylor. Imagine that!

I walked slowly around the room in a daze of amazement.

✳ 1 6 1

This man was actually looking at me the way boys used to look at me when I was a girl! Little old pot-roast and vacuum-cleaner me. Little old carry-out-the-garbage-and-check-for-holes-in-the-kid's-underwear me. It was incredible!

But then, I told myself, lots of things are incredible. The fact that there are no more Dodgers in Brooklyn. That Princess Margaret couldn't marry anybody she felt like. That rock-and-roll is allowed. That men are climbing into little metal bullets and zipping around the earth in less time than it takes for a crosstown light to change.

No. Even looking at it from that broader perspective and taking into consideration the number of totally unaccountable events in the history of the evolution of man, the idea that this nice, smart, fairly young, perfectly healthy, mentally balanced television director could find me desirable was still incredible.

A fifty-year-old plumber, possibly. An inebriated truck driver, probably. A wounded and slightly delirious soldier in an army hospital—why not? But a perfectly sane, highly successful, well-adjusted thirty-nine-year-old father of four children?

Well, but there it was, so there must be a sound reason for it somewhere. Probably he was married to Edna Mae Oliver's sister. Or on the other hand he had spent the last fifteen years having lunch with Ava Gardner, Rita Hayworth, Gina Lollobrigida, Brigitte Bardot, Julie Newmar, and Melina Mercouri, and he was just sick and tired of all that. He was looking for something completely different.

In any case I had to do something about it. I couldn't let it go on. Obviously. I couldn't. Naturally. Of course not.

16 AS IT HAPPENED, Mike Garnett was called back to the coast for a while and so my only difficulty with regard to him—temporarily—was the pile of notes he left us as a blueprint for revising the script. This revision constituted a fairly staggering amount of work and had to be completed in a relatively short time, and these combined facts sent Norman into a frenzy of self-doubt that was to his former frenizes what *The Guns of Navarone* is to a sorority pillow fight.

A scene he'd been crazy about the day before he would suddenly tear into little pieces. Scene Two—in the basket!

"Crap!" he would wail.

And we'd start all over again.

He would change a single joke sixteen times and then throw it out. He would suddenly dream up a totally new character and try to shift the whole story around so as to fit him in. Then he'd throw him out. Then he'd bring him back. Then in a couple of days he'd say, "What happened to Scene Two?"

"In the basket," I'd say.

He'd howl.

"That was the best scene in the whole friggin' script!"

Luckily I'd kept a copy. I didn't read Thomas Wolfe for nothing.

As the days passed and the deadline grew closer, Norman grew increasingly nervous, and Norman's increasing nervousness made *me* increasingly nervous. The air in the room crackled with such tension that the sensitive delivery boy from the delicatessen had taken to putting the lunch down outside the door, rapping sharply, and running for his life, foregoing his tip and leaving us to work out payment with the delicatessen people. Norman finally had to open a charge account with them.

I couldn't blame Norman for *all* the tension because, although it was primarily a result of his reaction to pressure, I had aggravated that pressure by a thoughtless response. At the beginning, before we began to work on the revision, Norman had summed up the situation as he saw it in a simple, declarative statement. (A *modus loquendi* which in itself indicated the depth of his perturbation.)

"In order to meet the deadline," he had said, "we will have to start earlier and work later."

And I promptly and spunkily said, "Then that's what we'll do!"—a remark that testified beautifully to how little I understood my situation. If I'd understood it I would have said "Impossible!" and saved us both a lot of false hopes and fierce frustrations.

No sooner did we embark on this new schedule than every possible thing that could go wrong, went. It began with a small, obscure interference—the fact that as soon as I began to work late, Alex began to get aloof. He wouldn't say anything, he'd just sort of withdraw, like David's turtle. And I'd go through these hopeless routines:

"What's the matter?" I'd say.

"Nothing. Why?"

"You're so aloof."

"What do you mean, aloof?"

"Like you don't talk to me."

"What do you mean, I don't talk to you?"

I'd stare at him, stumped, not knowing how to make it any clearer. "What do you *mean* what do you mean?"

"What are you talking about?"

"You don't *talk* to me!"

"What am I doing right now?"

"*Answering.*"

"Ruth . . ." with a great show of patient fatigue, he'd rub his eyes with thumb and forefinger, "I don't know what you're talking about."

But it was like Richard III telling those kids they only *imagined* they were in the tower. He couldn't fool me. *Something* was going on.

So even though I got in earlier and worked later we accomplished less, because Alex' aloofness had set me on edge and I was functioning at about one-third of my capacity.

Norman knew it was my fault the work wasn't going well but there wasn't much he could do about it except to tell me "Think *better!*" which *really* paralyzed me. But I tried very hard to get a grip on myself and was almost succeeding when, as I drove home from the station one night the weather report on the car radio predicted snow and I suddenly remembered I had no snow tires. I had no snow tires because Alex always insisted I get snow tires at a special discount place which was about twenty miles away, and nowadays the only day I had time to go there was Saturday and every Saturday they were too busy to put snow tires on my car, and Alex refused to get them at the local place which charged three times as much, so I had no snow tires.

Now that it was an emergency, though, I just naturally assumed we could forget about the discount place just for once.

"It's going to snow," I told Alex that night, "and I still don't have any snow tires. I guess I'd better go down to the gas station in the village first thing in the morning and get some."

He laughed lightly and turned a page of the newspaper he was reading. "Over my dead body," he said.

"But I've *got* to have *snow* tires!" I cried.

"Of course," he said, reasonably. "Just go down to the discount center and get them."

"*When?*"

"Whenever you like."

"They won't take me on Saturdays."

"Then go on Friday or Tuesday. Pick a day and go."

"But I'm *working!*"

"Take a day off."

"I *can't!* There's a *deadline!*"

He lowered the newspaper. "Honey," he said sweetly, "I'm *not* going to get snow tires from that bastard in the village."

"You mean . . . you mean you'd rather have me *risk* my *life* driving without *snow* tires, than pay an extra few *dollars?*"

"No," he said, gently, "but obviously *you'd* rather risk your life than take a day off from work."

Something told me there was no use going on, if I got the snow tires at the local garage he'd just quietly rip them off with his bare hands and take them back. Why? It wasn't the money, I knew that. And I'd seen him overlook many a principle in an emergency, so it wasn't that either. I was on edge all over again. What was bothering him?

Whatever it was, it kept me from getting snow tires, and consequently added the piquant fillip of additional hazard without which I just might have gone along uneventfully getting a job done.

As it was I looked out of Norman's window the next afternoon and saw it beginning to fall out of the sky, soft and innocent, and by that evening when I got off the train at my station there were six nifty little inches of snow on the ground.

Between my house and the station there were several hills which, while you were going up them in snowy weather, you were very sorry you never got around to making out a will. Beginning with petrifying and murderous, there are no adjectives in the world that would not be too innocuous to describe them. With snow tires *and* chains *and* a herd of spike-shoed oxen pulling the car, you could make it, maybe. Even then I had seen cars sliding and slipping and skidding into oncoming cars and getting stuck sideways across the road, and in the morning the hill littered with the corpses of oxen who died from overwork.

I did the only thing there was to do. I hoped fervently that there was an afterlife, and went into a coma. In this coma I inched my way along, consoling myself with the thought that when the spring thaw came and they found my body by the side of the road, Alex would say to himself, "If only I'd been a big enough person to let her get those expensive snow tires at the local garage!"

Somehow, by some miracle, I got home. I came out of the coma and found myself staring at my familiar old battle-scarred garage door.

So far so good. I'd managed to get home. But would I ever get back to the office?

I went into the house ready to tell Alex I was prepared to get expensive snow tires over his dead body, and Sooz and David came flying at me with the information that it was winter outside.

"Yeah," I said. "Inside too. Where's Daddy?"

"Upstairs."

I said good evening to Hannah and marched upstairs to the bedroom.

"Hello there," I said. "Surprised to see me alive?" And then I saw Alex was packing an overnight case. "What—?"

"I have to fly to Denver for a conference."

"Tonight?" I said. "In the snow?"

"The snow is on the ground. I'm going by sky."

It would have been petty, at that point, to mention my harrowing drive from the station, even if I'd remembered to, which I didn't, because the thought of Alex about to go up in a plane crowded everything else out of my mind.

"Call me the minute you get there!" I said as he went out the door, "I don't care what time it is!"

He did. It was five A.M. I could've kicked myself. He would've been just as safe at seven. Anyway, it was patently ridiculous, that morning, to think of making the trip back over those hills to the station in my unequipped car—or, for that matter, to think of taking it out of the garage, considering the state of the driveway, so I called a taxi. The taxi, with snow tires *and* chains, arrived on time, but unfortunately had to pick up seven other people on the way back, and rolled into the station some twenty-five minutes after my train had pulled out.

✳ 167

When I got to the office Norman was standing with his fore-head pressed against the wall, his eyes closed, his arms hanging limply at his sides, a dead cigar in his mouth. He spoke to me without moving.

"What happened? The New York Central ran out of gas? You went to the Library of Congress to do research on comedy? Or it was such a nice day you decided to walk from Westchester?"

"I'm not that late," I said, edgily.

"We have one week left," he said, "Exactly one week. And I am in constant pain. My father was in pain before me, and his father before him. Generically speaking, I've had a headache for two thousand years."

"I don't feel so good myself," I snapped. "Let's not waste any more time."

He turned on me.

"Captiousness?" he cried, "On top of lateness?"

This was a new phase; he'd gone beyond desperation into madness. All day I tried to get him back to desperation, but his mind had taken flight. As the day wore on he got funnier and funnier and we couldn't use any of it. What a life! One man in Denver and one man on his way to a clean white room.

"Well," I thought, going home in the train, "at least I've reached bottom. It can't get any worse."

I walked into the house to find that the washing machine had broken down, the hot-water pressure was mysteriously dying before it reached the upstairs bathrooms, a piece of the ceiling in Hannah's room was threatening momentarily to fall on her head, and David had a bad stomachache.

I stared at Hannah for some time with a dazed and vacant gaze.

"Did you call anybody?" I asked her, finally, in a hollow voice.

"I called the repair man for the washing machine," she said,

* 1 6 8

aggrieved, "but they said leave your name and telephone number. He didn't call back."

"What about the hot water? And the ceiling?"

"I didn't know where to call."

I picked up the local telephone directory and looked up plumbers. I dialed a plumber's number and a service answered and asked me to leave my name and number. Then I looked up carpenters and dialed a carpenter's number and a service answered and asked me to leave my name and number. Then I wrote down the plumber's and carpenter's numbers for Hannah and told her if they didn't call back by noon the next day to call them again, but I had little hope. I knew about repairmen. They never call back. Until you step out of the house for three minutes to take out the garbage or something and there's nobody to answer the phone—*then* they call. And when there's no answer they cross you off the list. And when you call them again they put you on the bottom of the list again. They have very long lists, these repairmen, and you're always on the bottom of them. So I had a pretty good idea of what I was in for.

I went up to David's room where he was lying face down with his stomachache and picked him up and rocked him in my arms for a while, which immediately sent Sooz to bed with a headache, so I went into her room and rocked *her* for a while, and then I went into my own room and rocked myself.

The ceiling falling down I could forgive. The washing machine going on the blink I could live with. Even Alex going off in an airplane I could grit my teeth and bear. But not to be able to take a hot shower!

I washed my face—with lukewarm water, an insult to the skin—and went down to not eat my dinner, after which I huddled in a corner of the sofa, and worried. What would I do if Hannah's ceiling fell down completely? Or if something serious was wrong with the hot-water system and the pipes burst in the middle of the night? It was true, all right, what they said about present-day workmanship. Everything manufactured or put together for current consumption has a built-in obsolescence; guaranteed to collapse the minute your husband goes to Denver.

Not that Alex could fix the washing machine or the hot-water system or the ceiling, but, like a conscientious bystander at an accident, he could at least stick around until the doctor came, if he were here. After all, he did have a much friendlier relationship with machinery and fuses and wiring and beams and two-by-fours, and all that stuff, than I ever had. And appliances and utilities are like horses, they're not likely to act up when somebody's around who knows how to handle them, but leave them alone with an ignoramus like me and they take off! Explode, burst, catch fire, short-circuit, the works!

After I exhausted the household calamities I worried about all the things David's stomachache could develop into, and what the chances were of a plane getting all the way back from Denver without running into a bunch of starlings, or a mountain peak, or a pilot who decided he had nothing to live for. And then I went to bed and spent the night levitated three inches above the mattress waiting for the ceiling to collapse, the hot-water system to explode, and David's stomachache to turn out appendicitis.

Right after breakfast David turned green and threw up and I called Vicki and waited until she came and examined him and said it was a virus and called the drugstore to deliver a prescription, and then I called the taxi again and went off, worried, convinced that "virus" is nothing but a euphemism for some nuclear malady the medical profession has been instructed by the government not to tell us about.

Feeling as though I were trying to walk in knee-high water against the tide, I finally got to the office, two hours late. Norman was sitting at the typewriter, furiously pounding the keys. He was back to desperation. In fact, he was close to apoplexy. I tried to explain but he wouldn't listen. He just kept banging away at the typewriter, the veins standing out on his forehead.

Even the fact that I looked like Judith Anderson in the last act of *Medea* didn't modify his rage.

I sat in a chair for a while, watching him racing violently around the keyboard like some crazy pianist trying to play the "Minute Waltz" on the typewriter in thirty seconds. Finally I said "Norman—" And then, a little louder, "Norman?" And then I yelled, "Norman!" He just kept beating up the keyboard. Suddenly, because I couldn't stand the reek of cigar smoke any more, I went to the window and threw it open. Maybe he thought I was going to jump. Anyway, he stopped.

He sat for a minute with his head in his hands, then ripped the page out of the typewriter, crumpled it into a ball, picked up the phone, dialed a number, asked for Wingate, said into the phone, "Harry?—Catch!" threw the crumpled ball out the window, hung up, and began to pace.

He had a right.

I sat down at the typewriter, shaking a little.

An hour later Norman went down the hall to the john and I grabbed the phone and called home. David was coughing and unhappy, the repairmen had not called back, and Hannah was angry. The dirty laundry was piling up and she had nothing to iron. With visions of Hannah suddenly quitting on me, and wondering if I should call Vicki again about David, and wondering if I should go to the repairman's house in the middle of the night and force him at gunpoint to come over . . . I thought of Alex out in Denver sitting around calmly discussing contracts with a mind totally free of extraneous problems. God, it must be wonderful to have nothing on your mind but the job in front of you! I began to realize what a prodigious thing it was when even one mother, in the whole world, in any given decade, achieved something.

That night Hannah, in a cold fury after moving her bed to the other side of her room so as not to be decapitated in the night by falling debris, washed out a half-dozen things *by hand*, and seemed quite put out that I didn't have a Croix de Guerre handy

✳ 171

to pin on her. So the next morning I got up at six A.M., determined to get hold of a repairman or a plumber or *somebody* before they left for the day. But the plumber was already gone. The washing machine man said he would try to come by "some time during the week." And the carpenter had gone to Puerto Rico on a vacation.

Desperately I turned on the shower, thinking maybe a miracle had happened during the night, but even when I turned it on full force it could barely manage an imitation of a leaky faucet. I tried to fill the bathtub, willing to take a bath in even two inches of water, but it took so long for that little trickle of hot water to cover the bottom of the tub that by the time I got two inches' worth the bottom one and a half inches were cold. I got so mad I ran down to the basement and heaved an empty garbage pail at the hot-water pipe. Strangely enough this seemed to dislodge whatever was choking it; hot water came gushing out of the shower head upstairs. Unfortunately I had left the shower door open and the shower head turned toward the door, and by the time I realized that the rushing sound I heard was water, and got upstairs to turn it off, there was a pretty good flood in the bathroom.

Hannah came up with a pail, a mop, and a cold face.

"Never mind," I said quickly, "I'll do it, I'll do it."

But she wasn't going to be done out of her martyrdom. She had an iron grip on the mop and I couldn't get it away from her. So I ran downstairs and grabbed a pile of rags and ran up again and tried sopping up some of the water, getting in her way, until she said, in a glacial voice, "Which one of us is going to *do* it, Mrs. Bernard?"

I got to the office a half-hour late and without breakfast. I wouldn't have been surprised to find the door locked and a sign on it saying "Keep Out!" But Norman had reached a new crisis. This time he was doing nothing. He was sitting quietly and calmly in a chair, doing nothing. I didn't even bother trying to apologize; I just took off my coat and my scarf and my boots, and sat down at the typewriter, wondering if he would flay me alive if I called the delicatessen for coffee.

"I think," said Norman, in the considered tones of a college professor, "we should have a little talk."

He got up and walked to the window while I sat staring at the empty typewriter, my chin in my hand.

"I'm not looking," he said, "to have things easy. If I wanted an easy life I wouldn't be in television. I wouldn't be married. I wouldn't even be on this planet. I'm used to aggravation. Job had plain sailing compared to me. He was an amateur sufferer! But even *I* have limits! . . ."

"Norman," I said, weakly, "if you want to get somebody else to work on this, it's okay with me—"

"You're walking *out?*" he said, white-faced. "On top of every-thing *else?*"

"I just don't want to hold you back. If you think you can do better with—"

"Four days to go and she walks out!"

"I'm not walking out! I just thought you . . ."

"That's the human race! That's integrity! Am I the only human being left with a sense of responsibility? Is that why I'm so *miserable?*"

"I'm not walk—"

"Jesus! Crazy Jesus! What a profession he picked!"

"I'm not—"

"It's no good, J.C.! Forget it!"

"I'm *not walking out, Norman!*"

"Then let's for chrissake get this motherlovin' script *finished!*"

"All *right.*"

"No more walking in here eleven o'clock!"

"All *right.*"

"And no going home at five o'clock!"

"All—" I thought of Hannah, the Great Stone Face, waiting for me to get home to take the kids off her hands for an hour. I thought of David, lying in bed all day, missing school, missing

✳ 173

his father, waiting for me. I thought of Alex, flying in from Denver, coming home to a silent house, the kids and Hannah asleep and me not there. What was I doing here? How did I get into this?

Oh, well, a few more days and the script would be finished. The script would be finished. The script would be finished.

The TV litany.

By seven o'clock that night it was clear we were both too exhausted to go on.

"Maybe," I said, "we should leave the script on the floor tonight with a saucer of milk, and when we come in in the morning . . ." He didn't even answer.

I got home a little before nine. There was a heavy fog, and no Alex. I turned on the radio and it said the airports were fogbound, the ceiling was minus fifty or something. I called the airport and they said Alex' plane was three hours late. I had visions of it circling around up there, the pilots squinting out the windows wondering where they were and just missing other lost planes by inches, or maybe not missing them, and I kept calling the airport and demanding they find the plane and bring it down, and finally about two o'clock in the morning I began hysterically figuring out the insurance and dividing it by fifteen years to see if it could possibly keep us until David got out of college and thinking, between tears for a wonderful man I would never see again, how lucky it was that I'd had the nerve to go out and work. Lucky for my children, for my creditors . . . and the telephone rang. I fell right out of bed. It was Alex. The plane had finally landed, at the wrong airport, and he was on his way home.

I collapsed.

I was still lying there flung out across the width of the bed where I had fallen after hanging up the phone, when Alex got home. He put me under the covers, crawled in beside me, and in a surge of sleepy affection and gratitude for his safe return, I hugged and kissed him. But I was so sleepy, having had something like four hours of oblivion in the last forty-eight, that I began falling asleep in the middle of a hug. I half-woke again when I realized Alex had taken the hugs and kisses to mean something entirely different, but I just couldn't drag myself out of the stupor. I patted his arm fondly, as in a dream, and mumbled, "I'm . . . too . . . tired. . . ." and fell fast asleep.

The next morning Alex wasn't talking to me.

I woke up and said "Good morning" to his back as he got out of bed, and there was no answer.

"I said 'good morning,' " I said.

"Oh." He smiled abruptly, on and off. Click, click. "I didn't hear you." And he went into the bathroom.

He didn't *hear* me!

I got out of bed and tottered to the bathroom door.

"About last night," I said, "I was what you might call on the verge of collapse."

"Mm. You must have been pretty tired."

"Is that why you're mad?"

"Mad? I'm not mad." He smiled again. Click, click. "Excuse me." And he shut the bathroom door in my face.

He's not mad! What is he then, practicing to be another Judge Bean!

I whispered a mildly nasty word, and tottered back to bed.

Between Norman driving me nuts and Alex driving me nuts, there was a good chance I was going to go nuts.

I heard the shower go on in the bathroom.

Sure, I thought, for him there'll always be hot water.

"Well, God," I said conversationally to the ceiling, "this experience hasn't been a total loss. I know one thing I didn't know before: You—are a dirty fighter."

If Norman should ever tell me again that we had to plan on a rigorous schedule, I would give him the most ambiguous answer possible. In fact, I was slowly becoming convinced that what I was trying to do was altogether impossible. That the way things had been arranged between men and women was an unbeatable setup. That trying to be a person instead of just a

✳ 175

housekeeper had about it some of the lunacy of trying to paddle a canoe from the bottom of Niagara Falls to the top.

Why, then, did I get up, and get dressed, and go right back for more? It might have been what my mother used to call "pure stubberin." It might have been the fact that we were almost finished with the rewrite on the script.

Or it might have been the postcard from California.

17

TWO POSTCARDS from California. From Mike Garnett. They arrived at the office as we were tackling the last page of the rewrite. The one addressed to Norman said, "Back Wednesday, how about lunch Thursday?" The one addressed to me said, "Back Wednesday, how about lunch Friday?"

"If he brings this well-organized mind of his to the directing of the pilot," said Norman, "we're in big trouble. Does he mean Thursday or does he mean Friday?"

I knew what he meant. He meant Thursday for Norman and Friday for me. And Norman's wasn't so much a lunch date as a red herring. Well, I thought, I'm not going to have lunch with Mike Garnett on Friday or any other day. My life is complicated enough. Who needs those eyes of his boring into me. Not that it's such an unpleasant sensation. Not that I couldn't use a little flattery. Not that it hasn't been a long time since a man said something to me in a cheerful tone of voice. Not that . . . no, to hell with it. It's too damn cliché. All these stories you read about suburban ladies having these tremulous little lunches. After all, I'm supposed to be part maverick.

We finished the rewrite that afternoon, and after Norman explained to me in a tragic soliloquy why it was lousy from beginning to end, we started in again on the first of the thirteen outlines Wingate had asked for, and I didn't even glance at the postcard lying in front of me on the desk. At least, not often.

That night I got home and there was a cryptic little message, delivered by Hannah.

"Mr. Bernard is working late."

"Again?" I said. It was the third time in two weeks.

"How late?" I said.

Hannah shrugged.

"Late for dinner?" I suggested.

"He said he would have dinner out."

"Again?" I said. She shrugged again. I nodded, vaguely. Listen, lots of men work late. Of course it was true that in ten years of administrating contracts, come crisis, chaos, cataclysm, catastrophe, Alex had never worked late three times in two weeks. Well . . .

I turned to the kids and discussed the news of the day with them, and settled a few grave question, like whether or not infinity is a number, whether or not it was true that Richard Shapiro's dog died from swallowing a live bee, and to what extent Sooz was obliged to run errands for David, who had taken to calling her "my slave girl, Naomi," which he got from Ali Baba, or Sinbad the Sailor—or maybe from his father.

After they'd gone to bed I had dinner alone, with the latest issue of *Life* magazine, and realized it was becoming more and more difficult to find the magazine in between all that advertising; by the time I found the second half of a picture story, I'd forgotten what the first half was about.

And I wondered why Alex was working late.

After dinner I washed my hair and told myself how nice it was to have an evening all to myself.

And I wondered if Alex *was* working late.

After that I went down to the living room with a couple of things that needed sewing, and turned on the radio and tried to keep my mind busy with figuring out whether what I was listening to was Brahms or Tchaikovsky or César Franck or Sibelius or Berlioz or Debussy, until I ran out of composers.

And I wondered where the hell Alex was.

Was this "working late" supposed to be another punishment, like the snow tires, and the aloofness, and not helping with Halloween, and taking three hours to get ready for the Spains' party, and then sitting in a corner all night?

Or was there some other reason for all these things? Was he sick? Not likely. He ate like a horse. Was he in danger of losing his job? Hardly. They'd just given him a raise. Was he having an affair? Absolutely not. Under those conditions he'd be *friendly*.

Or was there still another explanation? Was I, by some strange alchemy of my own anxiety, turning shadows into bogey-men?

Probably. Very probably. After all, he kept *saying* he wasn't angry. And really, no man as intelligent as Alex would resort to such childish tactics. I must be imagining things. Or exaggerating. It must be me.

So I was a real soap-opera wife when he finally got home, and I said, "Gee, honey, you must be tired, let me get you some tea and cookies." And sure enough the next day he began talking to me again.

He talked at great length. He told me everything that was wrong with the house, with the kids, and with me.

He did it, of course, in an offhand, jovial manner. But he did it.

He smilingly suggested that food was being wasted when some moldy old leftover string beans were thrown out, and when I tried saving some moldy old leftover string beans he smilingly implied that I'd taken up ptomaine poisoning as a hobby. He made airy little remarks about Hannah wasting time dusting the venetian blinds instead of cleaning the soap dishes in the bathroom, and then he made airy little remarks about Hannah cleaning the soap dishes instead of changing the burned-out light bulbs. He pleasantly indicated that we used more paper napkins per year than did the entire state of New York. He cheerfully mentioned that the electric bill was just a little higher than that of a four-acre factory. He noted laughingly that there were never any pomegranates in the house when he wanted one. And as for me —there was no end to the improvements I could stand. My hair hung over my eyes, I had too many pairs of shoes, I ate peanut butter, I forgot to remind him to write to his mother, I brought home lousy books from the library, I didn't cut the kids' toenails every three days, and I deliberately sought out a laundry that tore pillowcases.

"Still sending the pillowcases out? We could get a home shredder, save money in the long run, ha ha."

"Say, did you see the holes in the front of the kids' shoes? Pretty long toenails they've got there!"

This was none of my alchemy. This was just a man looking for a fight the hard way. As though he didn't even *know* he was looking for it. Every so often I stared at him and wondered what had ever become of Alex. Straightforward Alex. Friendly Alex. Alex who used to cradle sick children in his arms and soothe them to sleep. *Nice* Alex. Was he still there, underneath it all? It didn't seem possible. Or had all that sweetness been peripheral and was this the hard-core Alex coming out?

Before I had time to resolve the question, Thursday arrived and Mike Garnett called to confirm his lunch date with Norman. I could hear his voice on the other end, and even distorted by the telephone it made my molecules jump around. He didn't ask to speak to me.

"He said," Norman reported, "he wants to speak to us separately so he can get to know us better. *He's* going to get to know me better. Even *I* can't get to know me better!" And he trotted off to keep his lunch date.

Well, I thought, I'm not going to keep *mine*. Not that it wouldn't be a relief to get away from these terrible delicatessen sandwiches. Not that I couldn't use a change of scene. Not that . . .

∗ 179

No. It's just too damn silly. I'm not going.

So the next morning I put on the best-looking outfit I had, spent an extra fifteen minutes on my makeup, and at the last minute grabbed a bottle of perfume and dabbed a little behind each ear.

I wanted to smell nice for the delivery boy from the delicatessen.

All morning at the office I had great difficulty keeping my mind on the work. Not that my mind was elsewhere. It was nowhere. I had no mind. In fact, the inside of me seemed to be completely empty. I sat there in my good clothes, fancy on the outside, hollow on the inside, like a big silence waiting to be broken.

And then the telephone rang.

Norman, of course, answered it.

"This is the Cabinet," he said, "Dr. Caligari speaking," then he grunted and handed it to me.

"Hello," I said calmly, while the blood pounded in my ears.

"Ruth? I'm kind of hung up here," said Mike Garnett, "so I'm going to be a rat and not pick you up at the office." He gave a soft boyish laugh and my stomach turned over. "Why don't you meet me? There's a French restaurant on—"

I started to tell him I couldn't make it, but something caught in my throat—a small sharp piece of deliberate indisposition I think it was—and I began to choke on it.

"Are you all right?" he asked.

"Not really."

"Good," and he went on, giving me the name and address of the restaurant and telling me to meet him there in half an hour. Then, "They're paging me," he said, "I'll see you soon." And hung up.

I put back the receiver and turned around cautiously, expecting to find Norman's eyes on me with a knowing look in them. But Norman was evidently in a world of his own, standing at the window with his back to me, chewing on a cigar, and without even turning to look at me, he took up the work where he'd left off.

I'll go to the restaurant, I told myself, and tell him I can't have lunch because I'm pregnant and the sight of food makes me nauseous, and I'll leave.

Oh, sure.

When I got there and saw him standing outside the restaurant, looking up and down the street with a kind of contained eagerness, I was all at once flooded with nostalgia; those wonderful years when man after man had stood outside restaurant after restaurant, freezing or broiling according to the season, but waiting for me.

How can you refuse to have lunch with a man who turns the clock back ten years?

He smiled. I smiled. And a minute later we were inside sitting down. There was a lot of lunch put before me, of which very little was eaten. There was also a lot of conversation of which very little was pertinent to the situation. It was the kind of talk two people make when they're trying very hard not to think about something else, like the talk between fellow passengers stuck between floors in an elevator; falsely cheerful, stilted, compulsive, erratic, and pretty dull.

In the meantime, though, there was a *fascinating* dialogue going on that had no words to it at all.

"How's the work going?" said Mike, looking up suddenly from his omelette.

"Oh—pretty good, I guess," said I, looking down quickly at my filet of sole.

"Wingate was asking me about you—" said Mike, shifting his feet under the table and lighting his fourth cigarette.

"About *me?*" said I, jumping as his leg touched mine.

"You and Norman Spain," he said, quickly moving his leg away. "He asked me 'What's your reaction to those two?' "

"And what did you say?" I asked, shakily raising my glass of wine.

✳ 181

"I said 'Two? There are *two?*'" said Mike, pouring more wine, unsteadily.

"What did you really say?" I laughed, crumbling a breadstick to death.

"That I thought you were terrible but I'm just crazy about Norman." He grinned.

He shot me a look, catching my eye, trapping it.

Immediately we both looked at a passing waiter.

"Thanks," I said, tremulously, drinking more wine.

He cleared his throat. "No, really, that's what I said. 'Forget the girl, Harry,' I said, 'I can't work with her. All I can do with her is—uh—take her to lunch.'" He laughed, and shot me another look.

I folded my napkin into sixteenths. "So you have four children," I said.

He ground out his cigarette. "Let's see. Yeah, that's right, four. Two clean ones with dresses, two dirty ones with pants." He looked at me defiantly, "How about you?"

"I have one of each." I reached for my wineglass. He took it away from me, touching my fingers, on purpose.

"I went to the Met last night." He finished my wine. "You like Wagner?"

"I could have a full happy life without him." I arranged some broccoli into a pattern with my fork.

"Oh. You're the *La Bohème* type." He stared at a smudge of my lipstick on the rim of the wineglass.

I fumbled in my bag for a cigarette. "What does your wife do?" I said sweetly, "I mean . . . does she do anything?" I looked up.

He looked at me with an eyebrow raised, smiling faintly. I looked down at my bag.

"She's an actress. A damn good one, too." He leaned back, shifting his legs again, leaving one of them touching mine. "When I first met her she was playing Blanche in *Streetcar* in summer stock. She was good. She's very talented."

I found a cigarette, picked up the matches. He took them from me, lit one, leaned across the table, lit my cigarette, stayed there, watching the smoke. The cigarette trembled. I turned my head, looked casually around the restaurant. "Does she still act?"

He leaned back again, looked down at the matches, turned them over and over. "Well . . . we have four kids. And they're still young. They take up a lot of time."

"That's too bad. I mean . . . not about the kids, but . . ." I watched him turning the matches. He looked up. I looked away. He looked down.

"She'll go back to it." He lit another match and watched it burn. I watched it burn. We both watched it burn.

"You . . . uh . . . you seem to be really proud of her. Your wife—"

"I like talented women. They're quick. They're bright. They're original. Ordinary women bore me. I'm a sucker for the talented ones." He dropped the match in the ashtray, looked me in the eye, and grinned. I grinned back. He kept looking. It was a look like a dropped gauntlet. I sent my eyes around the room again.

"Dessert?" he murmured.

"Just coffee."

Eventually we were out of the restaurant and back on the street.

"I'd walk you back to the office," he said, idly stroking the sleeve of my coat, "but I was due somewhere twenty minutes ago." He took my hand. I found that I wanted very badly to leave it there, so I snatched it back.

"Thanks for the lunch," I said, fiddling with my gloves.

"This is only the beginning."

My eyes and eyebrows went up, simultaneously.

"I mean," he amended quickly, "we have to get to work on the script."

"Oh. That's right. We do."

"I'll call Norman and arrange it."

"Yes," I said, briskly, "That's a good idea. Well—" I looked down the street purposefully, as though I had an imminent appointment with the mayor.

"Ruth—" There was amusement in his voice. What was so damn amusing? I looked at him with dignity.

"Yes?"

"You're . . . very nice."

Very nice. I was about to become indignant when I realized from the expression around his eyes that there were a lot of other adjectives on the tip of his tongue, none of which belonged in the same category with "nice." I tried to look unruffled while blushing furiously.

"Well," I said lightly, "I'm glad to hear it. I always wanted to be very nice. I mean no woman likes to think she's just another Marlene Dietrich."

He laughed, and thinking this was as good an exit line as I was likely to come up with, I made a gesture of farewell, and, with him looking after me, walked, unseeing, down the street, biting my lip to keep from bursting into song.

All the way back to the office I bumped into people. Also I crossed streets against red lights, walked three blocks beyond the office and had to turn around and come back, and, trying this time to be careful about red lights, managed to stand on one corner through four "Walks" and five "Don't Walks" before a kindly old wino from the Bowery snapped me out of it with a long-winded and mostly unintelligible theory about where my money would do the most good.

What exactly was it that was coursing through my singing veins as I stumbled airily around the streets that bright November afternoon? There was no doubt that this man caused a lot of lovely physical shenanigans inside of me, no doubt that my vanity was gratified, no doubt, even, that my heart was somehow touched. But all this, I knew, was incidental. There was something much more glorious going on. Something that usually only children know anything about. Something we all begin to lose, drop, by drop, from about the time we're seven years old, give or take a year. It was a sense of the miraculous possibilities of life. The pure joy of being alive.

I was alive. I was new. I was proud. I was full of infinite unrealized wonders. I was America at that history-making moment when Columbus stepped out of the boat and said, "Hey, look what I found!" By the curious light in Mike Garnett's eyes I had been re-endowed with the magic and mystery of a live, growing being. In his eyes I saw that my potential was incalculable. I might become anything. Anything.

And as soon as I saw this, I saw the other. I saw very clearly, as I walked down the cigar-haunted corridor to Norman's office, that with Alex I had no potential at all. With Alex I had been defined for all time. To him I was thus and so, for ever and ever. It had to be that way for his sense of security. I had to have certain prescribed dimensions, for him to be content. As I stopped with my hand on the knob of Norman's door, I suddenly saw Alex as a busy little Japanese gardener, stunting and pruning me and making sure to snip off any new little shoots that threatened to spoil the pattern.

Mike Garnett didn't want to prune me. He was crazy about my shoots.

18 FOR THE NEXT WEEK or so I

saw a good deal of Mike Garnett because he came to the office for a few hours every day to go over the rewritten script. Of course, Norman was there too, but he kept constantly fading into a kind of background music. We argued about characterizations, we shifted lines around, we laughed, we joked, we argued some more, but all this somehow had the offhand quality of the activity that goes on in a candy store which is fronting for a bookie joint. The *real* business is going on in the back room.

Of course, the only real business going on between Mike and me was the same old business that had gone on in the restaurant —looking up, looking down, looking sideways—but I was so busy worrying about whether or not Norman noticed this, that I was almost unaware of the crisis that was developing between Norman and Mike.

It was that park scene again. That miserable funny park scene. Mike still wanted it changed, and Norman still said he would learn English and go to work for the B.B.C. before he would change the park scene.

When Mike would leave the office after a conference, Norman would say to me, "I told Harry! I told him this guy doesn't have a sense of humor!'"

"Oh, I wouldn't say that," I would protest mildly, unwilling to think badly of any man who made me feel as good as Mike did.

"How can he have a sense of humor?" Norman would persist. "Not only is he not Jewish, he's not Italian! He's not even Irish! How can you belong to a majority and be funny?"

"Like for instance James Thurber?"

"I'll *bet* you," Norman would shout, "that somewhere along the line Thurber was Jewish, Italian, *and* Irish!"

Then it would be Mike's turn. Norman would go down the hall for a few minutes, and Mike would scowl and say to me, "He writes very funny lines but he doesn't know a goddam thing about structure."

"Oh, I wouldn't say that," I'd say, because after all this script was *our* baby—Norman's and mine.

"He doesn't understand that you can't jump from comedy into farce and back again without throwing the performances off kilter!"

"It doesn't *have* to be farce, does it? It depends how they play it."

"In the beginning," he'd say, solemnly, "was the word."

So they kept shooting at each other, and there I was in the middle, five-feet-two of no-man's-land. I didn't really know whose side I was on because frankly the issues were clouded with personal feelings in both directions.

Finally, after a few days of this, Mike stood up in the middle of a session and said crisply, "I don't think we're getting anywhere. We'd better speak to Harry."

"*Okay!*" said Norman, with malice toward all, "Fine! Let's by all means speak to Harry, the greatest humorist since Mark Twain!"

"He's putting up the money," said Mike flatly, and left.

For fifteen minutes Norman strode around the room announcing the end of the world.

"Finished! The end of the line! No director, no pilot, no show, no job, no money, no residuals, no sense, no guts, no*where*, no*how*, no*body*. . . !"

And then Wingate called. Norman snatched up the phone.

"Debtors' Prison!" he yelled, "If this is a collect call I will not accept the charges! . . . That's right, Mr. Wingate. Yes, sir, Mr. Wingate . . . That just about sums it up, Mr. Wingate. . . . Critical is the word for it, sir. . . . Yes, sir, I think we *should* put it to a vote. I believe the General Assembly is in session. . . . *Okay*, Mr. Wingate, sir . . . Right!" He slammed down the receiver. "Mr. Wingate will see us the day after tomorrow at three o'clock in his office. He would see us sooner, but he is busy casting a Petroleum special, starring Tony Perkins. He wanted Olivier, but Olivier was busy, so he got Tony Perkins. For a while he was thinking of using Shirley Booth, in drag, but he was afraid of the sponsor. So he has Tony Perkins. Now he has to find a leading lady who will not look too old for Tony Perkins. He is on his way to the School For The Performing Arts to find a teen-ager who can play the role of a widow with three children."

"Day after tomorrow?" I said.

"At three o'clock. Mr. Wingate's sumptuous office overlooking the Radio City Rockettes, the East River, and parts of New Hampshire and Vermont."

Norman was livid. I had heard the word "livid" almost all my life and never really seen an example of it, but looking at Norman's face at that moment I knew, without anybody telling me. That was livid.

Oh, God, I thought, going home on the train with the coughers and sneezers, this is a real crisis. It could mean the end of the whole thing. After all that work! After all those delicatessen sandwiches and all these rides on the New York Central!

I couldn't let it happen. I'd invested too much of my time and energy and digestive tract. And for putting up with the coughers and sneezers *alone* I deserved at least one royalty. I had to save the project. I had to find a solution to the deadlock. I had to go to that meeting and . . . and . . . and . . . and . . .

Well, maybe something would come to me between now and three o'clock the day after tomorrow.

I came home to announcements from David and Sooz that they had both, that day, embarked on theatrical careers. David had been given a leading role in the school Thanksgiving presentation, and Sooz was going to be a snowflake in the Christmas play. My first impulse on hearing this news was to call the principal and say, "Never mind the fancy stuff, how about teaching them to read and write!" But then my ego took over. I knew David would make a great actor, because first of all he could project his voice farther than any kid in the neighborhood, and did, constantly. As for Sooz—well, what mother in her right mind doesn't want her daughter to be a snowflake?

I read over David's script (with more than a little condescension) and realized he had seventeen improbable speeches to memorize, and then Sooz gave me a note which told me to call her class mother, so I did, and the class mother told me there were six other snowflake mothers and each mother was making her own child's costume, and there would be a meeting at the school to

✳ 188

discuss the costumes, *the day after tomorrow, at three-forty-five*
P.M.

What else?

I looked up in the general direction of the dirty fighter and
murmured, "Nice going."

"Can I be a snowflake, Mom? Can I? Huh? Can I?"

I looked at Sooz. Her face was a sun, her eyes were stars. She
wanted to be a snowflake more than even Romeo wanted Juliet.

"Can you make me a costume, Mom? Can you? Can you go
to the meeting?"

"Certainly," I said. "Of course. Why not? Are you kidding?
You'll be such a great snowflake the others'll look like rain!"

"Will you help me rememorize my lines, Mom?" said David.

"Memorize, not rememorize. You remember and you memorize. I think."

"Will you?"

"Sure."

And Alex came in and said, "You know there are six library
books overdue?"

And my head began to hurt.

I tried to figure out how a person could be at a very important meeting in Manhattan and a very important meeting at a
school thirty miles away, at one and the same time.

Next morning I called the school and spoke to the teacher
in charge of the Christmas play. She had a querulous, taut, high-
pitched voice that conveyed the impression she was just barely
restraining herself from murdering everybody in sight. I explained that I had a business meeting which conflicted with the
costume meeting and asked if could I possibly come to the school
later in the week and get the necessary information.

"What? Later? What do you mean? I'm sorry. I don't know
what you people expect. It's difficult enough. I must have co-
operation. We must stick to a schedule. I can't have chaos. If you
can't spare half an hour we'll just have to count your daughter
out of it. We can't make individual arrangements for each per-

son. It's unwieldy. The whole thing's unwieldy. I don't even know where I'm going to get the plasterboard for the scenery!"

It's things like that give rise to the philosophy that wars are inevitable.

Well, I'd just have to get Wingate to change the other meeting. Somehow, I'd have to get him to change his meeting. I could just imagine Norman's reaction. "You have to go to school for *what?*"

"You think," I asked Norman timidly the next day as he bit into a club sandwich without leaving even a shred of lettuce or bacon trailing, which is a pretty neat trick, "You think we could ask Wingate to make the meeting a day later?"

"No!" said Norman, and took a small hike around the room.

We had ordered sandwiches instead of going out to lunch because out there it was hailing and sleeting and snowing and raining and a few other strange elemental things, and this had evidently prompted all the office personnel within a five-mile radius to order sandwiches from our delicatessen, because we had ordered the sandwiches at twelve o'clock, and it was now two thirty-five, and the drippy delivery boy from the delicatessen, which was a fast fifty yards down the street, had just departed, leaving our lunch and a big puddle outside the door. The fact that two and a half hours and seven vicious phone calls to the delicatessen had passed between our initial hunger and its satisfaction had made Norman even more serene and affable than usual, so naturally I picked that moment to ask him.

"Why not?" I persisted, biting into my chopped-egg sandwich and scattering chopped egg all over the desk and trying to scoop it up fast before he saw it and fainted.

Norman picked up a container.

"The friggin' coffee is *cold!*" he exploded.

There are times when Norman can be very charming. I'm sure there are.

"Take mine," I said, bribing him, "It's still warm."

He ignored my offer.

"Why the hell should we postpone the meeting?" he threw at me as he hiked, "You got something more important to do tomorrow?"

"As a matter of fact," I said, glad to see the old talent had not deserted me, "my mother's having a rather serious operation . . ." I trailed off, assuming he couldn't possibly know my mother was now living with my brother Arthur in Tampa.

"For Christ's sake, *everybody's* mother has a serious operation at least once a week! Is she having it exactly at three o'clock in the afternoon?"

"Well, no," I admitted, figuring that fiction, unlike life, can milk coincidence only so far. "No, it's scheduled for noon. But—" Norman waved a hand, dismissing the whole problem.

"By three o'clock she'll be making chicken soup. I know mothers."

I kept a dignified, mournful silence, nibbling halfheartedly at my sandwich. After a while Norman said, "Jesus Christ!" and went to the telephone and called Wingate, and the upshot was that Wingate changed it from three o'clock to five o'clock on the same day.

So now my only problem was how to get all six unknown snowflake mothers to arrive at the elementary school precisely on the dot of three forty-five and force them to make a unanimous decision about the costumes in eight minutes flat so that I could make the three-mile dash to the station in fifty-six seconds in order to catch the three-fifty-four which would get me into New York in time to be only ten minutes late for the five o'clock meeting with Wingate.

I don't know much about mathematics, but I know a lot about my kind of luck, and the chances of several snowflake mothers getting lost and wandering into the wrong rooms, and not being able to decide between organdy and tulle, were, in my case, better than average. I saw, with the cold, clear vision of a born loser, that there was only one way to do it. I would simply have to cut the traveling time in half by driving my own car into New York.

Driving my own car into New York!

"I'd be better off," I wailed to Alex that night, "roller skating around the track at Hialeah during the fifth race."

"Just stay in the right lane," he said, as he crouched on the living-room floor replacing the cords on a dismantled venetian blind, "and you'll be all right."

"Oh, yeah? And what about those hidden accesses with the ivory-tower drivers sailing calmly out in front of your nose giving you exactly one second to switch to the next lane only you can't, because in the next lane they're bumper to bumper and screaming by a hundred miles an hour? And what about those rotten toll booths that you always find yourself in the exact-change lane of when you haven't got the exact change and if you slow down and wait for a chance to get into the *inexact* change lane the guy behind you who's doing *two* hundred miles an hour is going to keep coming, right through your trunk and your back seat and out through your windshield? And what about Manhattan, where the streets now run westbound for two blocks and then eastbound for two blocks and then north and south the rest of the way, and if you want to make a left turn you have to go down to Canal Street and up the East River Drive to the Bronx and then take the subway back, and if you want to make a right turn you have to go out to La Guardia and fly in? . . . They don't tell you about those things when you take your driving test. No. They just make sure you can park upside down on an icy hill and they give you a license and say go kill yourself."

Alex kept measuring and threading cord and clattering around.

"I hate cars!" I said miserably, wandering back and forth in front of the blindless window, arms folded across my chest, "I hate airplanes! I hate speedboats!"

"Hold this," said Alex, handing me one end of the blind.

✳ 192

"There's something wrong with this century," I muttered, holding the blind, "You take Proust. People used to ride out in carriages. Carriages, you hear? Clip, clop, clip, clop. Graceful, elegant, leisurely. The quiet sky above, the gentle breeze, the budding trees along the Bois or whatever it was. In those days even in *winter* it was spring. And the people always looked gorgeous. They spent two hours in the bath and three hours dressing, and they clip-clopped along that Bois, pearl-buttoned gloves, dove-gray hats a mile wide, with veils. *That's* the way to live. People were interested in *meeting* other people, not passing them. They'd see friends coming along in another carriage and they'd stop to chat. . . . Can't you see a Corvair and a Chrysler Imperial stopping for a chat in the middle of the Thruway? There's something wrong with us!"

"No, dear," said Alex, hanging up the venetian blind, "it's just that everybody hears the sound of a different drummer except you." And he cast his eye about the room for something else to dismantle.

My anxiety over driving into New York to save the script took up so much time that by bedtime I still hadn't figured out a way to save the script. I went to bed, but not to sleep. I had very few hours left. I had to think of *something*.

From midnight to four A.M. I thought, furiously. I thought about David needing a new pair of shoes. I thought about sending my mother some pictures of the kids like she kept asking me to. I thought about getting one of those new cameras that develops its own negatives. I thought about the noodle pudding my grandmother used to make. I thought about the way my brother Walter used to pull out my loose baby teeth. I thought about snowflake costumes. I figured out how many days it was to spring. . . .

The next day I was in no condition to drive a tricycle across the street, let alone a car into New York. Besides, the slush of yesterday had frozen in ridges all over the roads. And I had a terrible headache. I decided I had no alternative but to squander ten dollars on a cab to New York. This change of plans supplanted one series of apprehensions with another. What if the cab were late? What if it never showed up at all? (This had been known to happen.) What if I got one of those *old* cabs—the ones that were always breaking down?

I called the taxi man and informed him that I had to be in New York by five P.M., but that I couldn't leave before four-thirty, that the roads were terrible and he must send me a suitable vehicle, preferably an armored tank, and have it pick me up at the school *no later than four-thirty*. Luckily Gloria Betz had to be at the school meeting too, she was a cranberry mother, so I arranged to get a lift to the school with her.

Now, I thought, *now* I will just take a headache pill and spend a few hours lying quietly in bed figuring out how to save the script. The pill eventually took care of the headache, and when my head stopped thumping I got an idea. The thing about the park scene that Mike and Wingate both objected to, was the sanitation man with the stick poking around under the bench. I remembered the scene I had first suggested, the one Norman didn't like, the one at the Plaza fountain, with the little kid walking around and around. I had an idea that Mike would settle for anything that wasn't the sanitation man, that Wingate would go for anything with a kid in it, and that Norman could be persuaded to accept the compromise rather than risk scuttling the whole project by refusing to rewrite the park-bench scene according to Mike's specifications.

I was about to call Norman and tell him what I was planning when I realized I barely had enough time to get dressed before Gloria came to pick me up. I showered and dried and was hooking myself into a bra when something happened that was at the same time unprecedented and inevitable; both a carpenter and a washing-machine repairman arrived simultaneously. I could hear Hannah twittering at them crossly, irked all to hell because they'd interrupted her ironing. Hannah in a bad mood was all I needed.

"I'm coming right down!" I yelled, grabbing stockings out of the drawer.

"Whatseemstabeatroubleawasherma'am?" called the repairman."

"It doesn't—" Zoom! A run, right up the front of the stocking! "—spin!"

"Whatsat?"

Hannah twittered.

"Spin!" Another stocking from the drawer. "You can do your ironing, Hannah; I'll take care of it!"

Hannah clumping down to playroom. Carpenter, from downstairs. "You want the roof fixed, lady?"

"The ceiling! The ceiling! Just a minute!" I pulled on a stocking.

"You say 'spin'?" Repairman again.

"I'll be right down!" I pulled on another stocking. Sounds of repairman clumping downstairs to laundry room. I grabbed a slip from the drawer.

Suddenly, outside the window, a ladder!

I tore my robe off the hook on the bathroom door. Carpenter's face at the window! "No!" I cried, clutching the robe to my chest, shaking my head at the transfixed face, "Not the roof! Not the roof!" The face disappeared. I dropped the robe. Into the slip. A shout from the laundry room.

"That machine spins all right, ma'am."

"No, it doesn't!" Into a skirt.

Carpenter coming in the front door, "Lady, does your roof need fixing or not?"

"Hannah—I'm sorry—would you show the carpenter your *ceiling? Please?*" Into a sweater. Hannah clumping upstairs. Oh, hell, she's mad. Repairman coming up from laundry room.

"Machine seems to spin all right, ma'am." Sound of repairman leaving.

✳ 195

"Wait a minute! Wait a minute!" Into shoes, out of the bedroom.

Carpenter stops on way up to Hannah's room with Hannah. "What's the matter now?"

"Not you! *Repairman,* wait a minute!" Down the stairs. Carpenter needn't take that tone just because he almost saw me in a bra! Out the front door. "Come back! Come back!"

Repairman coming back. Sounds of Hannah's ceiling being demolished. Hannah clumping down the stairs, mumbling about a dirty mess.

"Machine's spinning all right, ma'am."

"Did you try it with *clothes* in it?"

"Well, no . . ."

"It only spins without *clothes* in it!" Sound of school bus stopping. Repairman down to laundry room. Wild sounds of kids alighting from school bus. Back to bedroom for makeup. Bang! The front door. David singing "On Top of Old Smoky": "On top of spaghetti, all covered with sauce, a lonely old meatball . . ." Grinding sounds from the laundry room, metal against metal. Bang! The front door. Sooz complaining that David ran ahead and didn't wait for her. Hannah twittering. Lipstick on crooked. What else, with a trembling hand? Crash! Hannah's ceiling. Beep-beep! Gloria's horn outside. My headache was back, with bells on. Down the stairs. The kids all over me. Into my coat, head thumping, kiss the kids, and out the door.

The steps were icy.

Hanging onto the edge of equilibrium like Pearl White to the edge of a cliff, I pigeon-toed my way down the icy steps to Gloria's station wagon, and got in.

"You look terrible," said Gloria, who looked great.

"How's your allergy?" I countered.

"Fine," she said. (Whatever *that* meant.) She started up the engine. "I hear the Cardells are going to Mexico for the holidays."

"Oh?" I felt obscurely betrayed that Gloria should know this before I did.

"The Sands might go away too."

"The Sands?" I suddenly felt very weak and tired.

"Stanley and I were thinking of taking a cruise in February."

"That's nice." A cruise. That's what I needed.

"Vera and I went to De Pinna's on the Post Road the other day. I picked up this coat—on sale—"

"Pretty color."

"We had lunch at that new place with the antiques."

"Sounds like fun." I felt distinctly underprivileged.

"How's your show?"

"Oh. Fine." I perked up a little. "Matter of fact I hope this snowflake business doesn't take too long, I have to run in for a meeting at five o'clock."

"You're lucky you have a snowflake. White stuff is easy to get. With the cranberries I have a feeling we're going to be up to our necks in red Tintex."

I waited for her to ask more questions about my important meeting, but she didn't. She was all wrapped up in her cranberries and going on a cruise and buying resort clothes and getting tickets for the kids to see the "Nutcracker Suite" at the City Center and whether her mother-in-law would sit for her on New Year's Eve and how soon the pond on Acorn Road would be frozen enough for skating, and by that time we were at the school. I thought it was pretty lousy of her to be so self-absorbed. I thought longingly of that far-off day on the train to New York when I was a celebrity and Gloria was sick. Whatever happened to that arrangement?

We walked into the school cafeteria where we were supposed to report, and there were about twenty-five female Gullivers wandering confusedly among the Lilliputian chairs and tables, dressed in a colorful assortment of things; ski-pants with fake fur jackets and salmon-colored sneakers, striped, dotted and flowered stretch-slacks with car coats and chiffon scarves wound around hairdos, plaid wool skirts with ski jackets and lined boots, cloth coats, seal coats, old persian-lamb coats cut off at the hips—the melting-pot of the fashion world.

Eventually we found that snowflake mothers had been assigned to Table I (so designated by a large piece of cardboard which kept falling face down on its roman numeral), cranberry mothers to Table II, nursery-rhyme-character mothers to Table III, and other, miscellaneous mothers to Table IV. We were instructed to have our paper and pencil at the ready and to wait for the arrival of the teacher in charge of our particular contribution to the American Theater.

We waited, time passed, my stomach churned. I wondered what Madame Teacher was doing the while; drinking coffee, powdering her nose, counting her fingers? Finally, she arrived, took the roll call, and discovered that two snowflake mothers were missing. Everybody looked distractedly at everybody else and the teacher said perhaps we should wait a few minutes more. I bit my lip and watched the second hand move jauntily around the face of the clock on the wall. Four-twenty and not a word had been uttered about snowflakes. My head was really pounding away now. A rasping sound issued from my throat.

"I—" I cleared my throat—"have to leave soon. Could we please get on with the discussion of these"—I had a tremendous compulsion to use Norman's favorite adjective, but I fought it— "costumes?"

And the debate was on.

White organdy by the yard or ready-made nylon petticoats? Tinsel or no tinsel? Tinsel all the way up or tinsel only around the bottom? Tinsel on the shoulders or no tinsel on the shoulders? Crowns or no crowns? Combs to hold on the crowns, or bobby-pins to hold on the crowns or elastic to hold on the crowns?

Maybe I'll die young, I thought, hopefully.

At four twenty-five a figure burst into the cafeteria; wind-

✳ 198

blown, red-cheeked, breathless, with a streaming mane of chestnut hair.

"Where am I?" Vicki grinned at the nearest person, "I'm a miscellaneous mother. Where do I go?" She saw me. "Hi, sweetie! I got a postoperative kid at the hospital, I gotta get right back. Table IV? Four—four—four" She ran off and before I could gather my notes together and put on my coat, she'd been to Table IV, collected her information, shouted goodbye to me, and scrammed.

I stared after her. "Maybe she's not an earthling," I thought.

The pounding in my head was worse than ever. I would have to take another headache pill. God knows what would happen, they were powerful pills, barbiturates or something, I'd never before taken two in one day. But I'd never make it to the meeting without another pill. I'd have to chance it.

I found a water fountain, took the pill, and after waiting outside the school in an icy wind for only five minutes, the taxi showed up and we headed south, fish-tailing down the glassy highway for forty minutes like an imitation of an old silent-movie chase, the taxi driver spitting out Armenian curses all the way. This is not my idea of a whole lot of fun even when I'm feeling vigorous, and I was very glad I'd taken that second pill, because it—or it on top of the other pill on top of three hours' sleep—had numbed my nerves and woozied up my brain so that I bounced quite passively around the back seat as we swerved, sidled and veered, and finally slid into the streets of Manhattan.

It was twenty past five when I walked drunkenly into Wingate's office and slithered into a chair in the middle of a tensely dramatic scene. Mike was seated to my left, bent over staring at the carpet, his forearms on his knees and his fingers interlaced, crying out, "Burlesque!" Norman was pacing to my right, howling "Sense of humor!" And Wingate was sitting at his desk, his mouth pursed, making a pattern of little circles all over his blotter with the end of a silver cigarette holder.

My eyelids were feeling very heavy.

Mike stood, suddenly, picked up the script from Wingate's desk and dropped it again with a crisp motion of impatience.

"I read Ruth's original story," he said. "There was a quality in the original material that just isn't here! It gave you a sense of the poignancy of the situation, even while it was being funny. There was a *female* quality. The girl was a real *girl*."

In spite of my wooziness and in spite of Mike's toneless, impersonal delivery, the implicit compliment trickled into the cockles of my heart like warm syrup. Obviously it trickled into the cockles of Norman's heart like poison.

He spluttered.

"You think you're gonna sell those guys with a goddam sensitive little script?" He turned to me with a gruff apology, "You know what I mean—"

"Sure," I said, and batted my eyes to keep them open.

"A series," he went on, "has to have laughs! It has to have jokes!"

"I think," said Wingate, getting up and looking pointedly out his executive-type window with its lordly view, "I think you've hit on the exact dichotomy I'm talking about. Laughs are one thing. Jokes are another."

Dichotomy! Norman and I exchanged glances like raised eyebrows.

"I don't see," Wingate continued, "why we can't dispense with the sanitation man and make the scene on the park bench even—ah—" he scanned the ceiling, "even . . . tender . . . romantic. I think it would be a nice change of pace."

Even Mike winced at that. And I realized, by my own reaction, that I'd learned enough from Norman to know why Wingate, empire-builder though he was, was an ass when it came to comedy. I knew that sticking a romantic scene into the middle of this script would be like sticking a pin into the middle of a balloon. Phhhht. The whole show would lie down and die. This was the point in the story where low-key humor had to explode into comedy. Norman was right. In a vague, detached way the knowledge that I'd acquired knowledge passed me.

Now words were flying back and forth between the two of them, Wingate's insistently high-flown and polysyllabic, Norman's defiantly low-flown and, to put it nicely, succinct. This, too, was like a scene out of an old movie; snotty little Jackie Searle standing in front of his big rich house insulting tattered little rough-and-tumble Jackie Coogan. Searle has Wealth and Power on his side. Coogan has Truth and Beauty on his. Which comes out on top? Wealth and Power, what else?

Well, the time had come to interrupt this nonsense and give them the solution.

"Listen!" I said loudly. I *think* I said loudly. It *seemed* loudly to me. But nobody paid any attention. Norman ranted, and Wingate was looking at the ceiling with his sad little smile, preparing to cast another pearl before swine.

"If you remember, Norman," he said, "I took exception to that scene from the beginning. Not only because it's farcical, but because, candidly . . . it's jejune!"

Jejune! Bro-*ther!* I slowly swiveled my head in Norman's direction, but he was sunk in a chair with his eyes closed like a man whose life is ebbing. And no wonder. Dichotomy was bad enough, but *jejune!*

"Listen!" I bellowed. I'm *sure* I bellowed. But Wingate kept on talking. I looked hazily around for Mike. He was still studying the carpet, but when I turned he looked up quickly and I was transfixed, with my mouth partly open, hung up again on that hot, solemn gaze. I blinked my eyes to break the spell but all I could manage was half a blink; the eyelids went down, but they didn't come up.

The next thing I knew they were all standing around with their coats on.

✳   2 0 1

"We'd better wake her," Mike was saying.

"I'm fine," I mumbled. "Who . . .?

"How's your mother?" said Norman.

"Who? . . . Oh. She's fine. What? . . . I'm *awfully* sorry. I . . ."

"Are you all right?" said Wingate, looking at his watch.

It was then I realized they were getting ready to leave.

"Is it all over?" I said fearfully, "What happened?"

"Nothing," said Norman. "Where did you go? To a story conference. What did you do? Nothing."

"I really have to run," said Wingate, "I'm late." He started toward the door. Something told me the pilot film was going down the drain.

"Wait!" I bellowed, tottering to my feet and flinging an arm skyward, commandingly. "*Just one minute! Just hold on!*" Suddenly I was very angry. Mostly at myself, but how were they to know? Wingate stopped and looked at me with the startled and slightly incredulous look of a pedigreed wolfhound being barked at by a terrier. But I was impervious, in my barbiturate fog. I went on. "I tried to say this before but nobody would listen! So I'd like to say it now! Can I say it now?"

I think for a moment it was a toss-up whether Wingate was going to fire me or sit down. He sat down. And I rattled off an explanation of the Plaza fountain scene, of how it could be substituted for the park-bench scene, and why it was the solution to all our problems.

"Hm-mm," said Wingate when I finished, and looked at Mike, who was staring at me from under his eyebrows, and Norman, who was staring at me almost as though we were friends.

"I like it," said Mike.

I sank into a chair, embarrassed, now that I'd succeeded.

"Yes," said Wingate, having gotten his cue, "it has possibilities. I think perhaps we should discuss it again."

"In detail," said Mike, "before you start writing it."

So another appointment was made, for Tuesday at three o'clock, in Wingate's office, and Wingate rushed off, and Mike helped me into my coat and guided me out to the elevator, while Norman said to me, "Got any other little aces up your sleeve that I should know about?"

"I'm sorry, Norman," I said, "I was going to tell you, but the carpenters came."

"Of course," he said. "It's always the carpenters. 'I'm sorry, Mr. Roosevelt, I was *going* to tell you they were planning to attack Pearl Harbor, but the carpenters came.'"

But I could see he didn't really mind what I'd done. In fact, he was in a pretty good mood, for Norman. I was in a pretty good mood myself. What with winning a merit badge, and the headache gone, and Mike squeezing my hand goodbye as I got into a cab. I was feeling so good I didn't even mind, when I got home, finding that Alex was working late again. I cheerfully spread some chopped liver on a sesame-seed cracker and settled comfortably into a corner of the sofa with several pieces of dog-eared paper to help David rememorize his lines.

" 'That's enough of that!' " he chirped, pointing a finger at an unseen host, " 'From now on' . . . uh . . ."

" 'From now on all you turkeys' . . ."

" 'From now on all you turkeys better behave yourself!' . . . Uh . . ."

" 'Come on . . .' "

" 'Come on, children'—uh—'we're going to'—uh—'make'—uh—"

" 'Make this a real . . .' "

" 'A real Thanksgiving!' Oh, baloney, I'll never do it."

"Sure you will. You're doing it already. You're going to be great. I can hardly wait to see you on the stage. You'll be the best one."

"Can Daddy come and see it too?"

"Listen, David, you know Daddy has to work."

"Well *you're* coming, and *you* work."

"It's easier for me to take time off."

"Couldn't he just take one little Tuesday afternoon?"

"No, he . . . one WHAT?"

"Tuesday . . ."

"THIS Tuesday?"

"Yeah. Two o'clock. When we do the play . . ."

Oh Jesus God Christ Murder Hell Damn PHOOEY!

19

ON TUESDAY MORNING I drove the car into New York. Yes, drove the car into New York. No snow tires? Tough. So I'd get killed. I was tired of worrying about trivialities. I was tired of tensions, tired of conflicts, tired most of all of the knowledge that nobody could care less about my tensions and conflicts. The minutiae of motherhood—such an ignominious way to be torn limb from limb. To hell with everything! I drove into New York. Let the pedestrians fall where they may.

I looked neither to right nor to left. I followed no signs, made allowance for no other traffic, asked not if a toll booth were exact change or inexact, I just went.

Barreled into Manhattan, put the car in a parking lot, went to the office, and sat at the typewriter exchanging vetoes with Norman on ideas for one of the thirteen outlines, while he removed the dust from the bookshelves with paper towels and a bottle of Mr. Clean until lunchtime. When he went to lunch I went back to the parking lot, climbed into the car, did some more reckless driving, northbound, and marched into the school auditorium with all the other mothers.

Looking around at all those other mothers, I knew I'd done the only possible thing. If I hadn't come I would have spent the rest of my life waiting for David to end up lying on a couch, saying, "I remember I was in a play . . . all the mothers of the kids in the play came to see it . . . after the play was over all the mothers came over and told the kids how good they were . . . but my mother wasn't there . . . she was too busy."

My eyes began to water and my throat felt peculiar. Unshed tears? Or bacteria?

Then David came out on the stage and began trumpeting his lines like a pint-sized Falstaff, and I was suddenly shocked. He was so *small!* In the tumult of day-to-day living I'd forgotten he was a little boy. In our house he was just one of the family, a person who measured up to here by the TV set and up to there by the refrigerator. But out here in the world, in a big auditorium, on that big stage, in front of a mob of mothers . . . he was little! Striding around up there, being an actor! I was seized with a strange mixture of giggles and tears. Then the curtain came down, there was wild applause, I rushed out to the hall, found David, hugged him, told him he was the loudest, clearest, best-looking off-Broadway star I'd ever seen, and made for the highway again, my hands clammy on the wheel, my neck rigid with fear, my scalp tingling, but my soul at peace.

As I turned, finally, into the Danse Macabre of Fifty-seventh Street, it began to snow. I put the car in the nearest parking lot, hailed a cab, and got to Wingate's office at two minutes past three, shaking.

It took three hours to go over the Plaza fountain scene in detail, and a good deal of the time was consumed in waiting while Wingate stared at the ceiling trying to find just the right words in which to couch the wrong suggestion. Wingate's affinity for humor was about on a par with the Marquis de Sade's affinity for outdoor sports. However, he was the boss, so we waited politely, and during these intermissions I watched the snow falling, heavily, beyond the window, and wondered how the hell I was going to get the car home.

By the time we broke up, the snow had turned into a blizzard and I knew I couldn't possibly drive the car home. I'd have to leave it in New York. The garage bill would be unheard of. Alex would incinerate me. Oh, how I wished the day were over. Especially the part where I would have to stand there while Alex said "You LEFT the CAR in NEW YORK?"

Downstairs, just before we left the building, Mike held me back a few paces behind Norman and murmured to me to try to get more of that "female" quality into the new scene. Then he hesitated and looked down at the glove he was holding which had my hand in it, and said, "Can I buy you a drink?" The words immediately conjured up the tempting image of a stolen hour in a warm, dim bar, sipping old-fashioneds and eating olives with a man who made me feel irresistible. It was the best suggestion I'd heard all day. There was only one thing wrong with it; I was sick as a dog. My throat was sore, my knees were buckling, my eyes were watering, and little chills were running up and down my arms.

But a true courtesan doesn't discuss her illnesses with an admirer, nor does she let him know that having to refuse him is killing her. So I just smiled, shook my head, and said—my voice already husky with laryngitis—"I'd love to, but I can't drink during a blizzard. I'm on the snow-removal committee."

He laughed and insisted. "One drink?"

The fact that I shook my head again was adequate proof to me that I was not at all well.

He squeezed my hand in resignation and propelled me to the curb where Norman was flailing his arms at cabs going by with Off-Duty signs on them and yelling, "Stop, you goddam middle-class bastards, stop!"

After about ten minutes of flailing, running around, and cursing, they beat a rich old matron to the draw and got me a cab. At that moment I loved them both profoundly.

The cab bumped me along and ultimately spilled me out at the entrance to Grand Central. The blizzard raged. Throngs of people were pushing through the doors of Grand Central and down the divided stairway, all but trampling each other into the ground. Because of the blizzard the normal rush-hour frenzy had swollen into a full-fledged dementia. They ran, tumbled, shoved, shouldered, strained forward; men with hard, fearful eyes and outthrust jaws, women like nervous birds, clutching sophisticated Christmas-motif shopping bags from Saks and Tailored Woman. There was a blizzard! They might be snowbound between here and home! A nasal voice boomed from the loudspeaker. There was something wrong with the trains. The New Haven had broken down again without first having the decency to get off the New York Central tracks. The six thirty-two was doomed. Forget it. Make for the seven-ten.

The wild horde turned as one and charged Gate 24, heads lowered, hoofs thundering. The seven-ten was already loaded with the unfortunates from two earlier abandoned trains filling every seat. There was standing room only, but the buffalo stampede surged forward, crushing through the doorway into the cars, and stopping, pressed together, in the entrances, front and rear, squeezing in on top of each other until there was no room even for the doors to close.

I squeezed myself onto the train and got trapped between a heaving ocean of a woman holding sixteen splitting packages, and a craggy old man with bad breath and elbows all over his body.

The train pulled slowly out of the long tunnel and into the night and the blizzard. It took two hours to make the forty-five-minute run, and then I was dumped out at my station, wind and snow slashing at me from all directions, the cold biting viciously at all my extremities. There were no taxis. The man in charge of the taxi stand was screaming into his two-way radio. Apparently half his taxis were stranded on various impassable hills or had simply vanished into the storm never to be heard from again. The other half had thrown in the towel and were heading for Florida.

A group of miserable, blue-lipped, red-nosed would-be passengers were huddled together in the shelter of the taxi stand; orphans of the storm, abandoned by their kith and kin. Not me.

I crawled stiffly into a phone-booth and dialed my number with an icicle that used to be my index finger. Hannah's voice floated into my ear, warm and full of nice comfortable kitchen smells. I asked for Alex. He sounded warm and comfortable too. I told him there were no taxis, come and get me. He said, in a puzzled voice, "I thought you took the car." I said I would explain when I got home, come and get me. He explained that his chains had broken three times on the way home, he would never make it to the station, and I'd better wait for a taxi.

"Okay," I said, trying to sound threatening while my teeth chattered, and hung up and said to myself, "But if I'm not there by midnight, you can get yourself another woman."

I joined the rest of the orphans.

A good frozen half-hour later a taxi showed up. I was one of twenty-seven people who climbed into it. My house, naturally, was the one most remote from the taxi station, so I took a grand tour of the entire state while the driver tortuously guided the screeching, spluttering, gasping vehicle up one rutted mountain pass and down another, conveying my fellow passengers to their various incredible eyries. Several times we reached an impasse, the wheels went round but the taxi stood still, so we all climbed out in the whipping blizzard and pushed, uphill, inch by punishing inch.

It was some time after eleven when we finally chugged up to the entrance of my driveway, hip-high in snow, and I got out and staggered through it and up to my front door, thinking to myself, "You are demented, my girl, you are desperately sick in the head. To go through all this—*voluntarily!* You don't even have the justification, like Florence Nightingale, that you're saving lives. Or like Madame Curie, that you're making history. Or like Maria Callas, that you're too *tall* to be a housewife. What makes you *do* it?"

I went into the house. Alex was in the big chair smoking his pipe and reading a manual on Armed Services Procurement Regulations. He looked up.

✳ 2 0 8

"Well," he said, "you sure picked a great day to take the car to the station."

I just stood there dripping and looked at him. His eyebrows went up a little.

"Or *didn't* you take it to the station?"

I told him where I'd taken it. He stood up, slowly.

"You LEFT the CAR in NEW YORK?"

I sometimes think the worst thing about marriage is being able to predict exactly what the other one is going to say. There's such an end-of-the-line feeling about it. No more surprises, ever.

Maybe that's the answer, I thought, as I tottered unsteadily up the stairs to bed, too tired and queasy to want even a warm drink. Maybe that's why I do it—because a person needs a few surprises now and then, to live. At the moment, though, it didn't really seem like a good enough reason.

20   THE NEXT MORNING there was practically nothing right with me. My throat hurt. My head hurt. My stomach hurt. My toenails hurt. My earlobes hurt. And my eyelashes didn't feel so good either.

I tried getting out of bed, but there didn't seem to be any floor on the room. And I thought it was pretty strange weather for November—ninety-eight in the shade. However. If I didn't show up at the office today to work on the fountain scene after making such a production of convincing everybody it was the only way out . . . ! I tried walking again, but it was just plain foolish. I couldn't even find the bathroom door. I sat down on the rug and waited for Alex to come up from breakfast to get his jacket.

He didn't seem very surprised to see me sitting on the rug. He just nodded, cynically.

✳ 209

"You're sick," he said, implying that this was just another in a long line of irresponsible acts.

He led me to the bathroom, put me back into bed, gave me some aspirin, said "Happy Thanksgiving," and left for work.

Oh, God, tomorrow was Thanksgiving. Deedee was supposed to come, with her husband and children. I'd have to cancel it. It would take us weeks to finish a ten-pound turkey. And how could I have Thanksgiving dinner with the kids anyway, in this condition? I'd have to eat through a surgical mask so as not to infect them!

And the car was in that New York garage, piling up debts, with nobody to bring it home! Why couldn't Alex work in Manhattan for a change?

I stared out the window at the cold, colorless sky. The events of the past few weeks swam around in my head like the ghosts that came to Scrooge. And out of it all a moral floated to the surface; Gloria Betz sits on her behind and gets taken on a cruise, I knock myself out and get taken to a hospital.

Maybe that was the only smart way to play it, Gloria's way. Pretend you like being a housewife and go to an analyst on the side.

Maybe James Barrie was right and it was superfluous for a woman to try to establish herself in a profession. She was born into one. The catering business.

Maybe I should give up.

I wondered if I only felt this way because I was sick. Or if I was sick only because I felt this way. Did I want to quit? Did I want *not* to quit? What did I want? There was only one way to find out. I picked up the phone and managed to focus my eyes long enough to dial Vicki's number.

"Hello, Doctor?" I wheezed. "I have an important question to ask you. Yes, I'm home. Well I'm not in the pink of condition. Listen, are you going to be giving out pills anywhere in the neighborhood? Gee, would you? When? Oh, good."

I hung up, spent several minutes trying to remember how to

dial Information, dialed it, got the Spain's phone number, and with great concentration succeeded in dialing all its ten digits. A very young male voice came over the wire. "This is the Hilton C.P.W.," it said. (Heredity? I wondered weakly, or environment?)

"Is your father there?" I croaked. Norman came to the phone. "I have this ridiculous fever . . ." I said.

There was a silence. Then he said, "As of today I'm closing the office. I'm going to get myself a nice, clean, orderly job as a mercenary in the Belgian Congo."

After apologizing for a while I put away the phone, and Hannah appeared in the bedroom doorway holding a tray of coffee and juice and toast, which she deposited near me, with Olympian contempt. Even with contempt, it was nice to have breakfast in bed.

I sipped coffee and nibbled toast while the life of the house went on around me. The kids were home, the Board of Education, as usual, beginning their Thanksgiving twenty-four hours before the rest of the country. Sooz was in her room creating priceless works of abstract art, and David was down in the playroom practicing pitching, and, I gathered from Hannah's threats, using the ironing board as home plate, while she was ironing.

Loud conversations went on between David downstairs and Sooz upstairs.

"SOOZ!" he would yell.

"WHAT?"

"If apples cost six cents each and you want to buy three apples, how much money do you have to pay?"

There would be a long silence from the kindergartener up in her room to whom a nickel was still only one-fifth as good as five pennies, and then she, whose hearing is exceptionally good, would yell down, "WHAT DID YOU SAY?"

That would go on for a while until he finally flabbergasted her with the right answer.

Then he'd yell, "SOOZ! You know why they don't allow

flowers in a sick person's room at night while they're sleeping?"

A pause, and she'd yell back uncertainly, "Because they make too much NOISE?"

He'd set her right about that, and then he'd shout up a gratuitous piece of information.

"YOU KNOW WHAT, SOOZ?"

"WHAT?"

"All the planets are named after gods!"

Another silence and Sooz would shout back.

"After God's *what*?"

Ha!, I thought, even Norman couldn't top that. And with a faint smile on my virus-racked face, I dozed.

I woke to Vicki standing beside my bed.

"You look terrible," she said, "What happened?"

"I was always like this," I said through a stuffed nose, "the other one was the disguise."

She took out a tongue-depressor. "Open up."

"I'm not your patient."

"It's on the house." She depressed my tongue, poked around here and there, said "Hmmm," took out her prescription pad and wrote on it.

"Don't bother," I said, "I'm not sure I want to get well."

"Don't start talking like that," she said, lighting a cigarette, "I didn't have to come over here to get depressed. I was doing that beautifully all by myself."

"You?" I said, with a ghost of a laugh, "Depressed?"

"Suicidal."

I stared at her, incredulous. I could see her being harassed. I could see her having hysterics. But suicidal? The leader of the wagon train suicidal?

"You're crazy," I said.

"What then, suicide is an indication of sanity?"

"But how? Why? What for?"

"Oh, who knows." She sat down on the far end of my bed and I realized that for the first time since I'd known her she really did look spiritless. "I just got out of bed three days ago. I had the flu or some damn thing. Is that ridiculous? You'd think I'd be immune to everything by now. Ugh! I hate being sick. I'm a lousy patient. Anyway, life stinks, right?"

"Oh, my God," I moaned, and sank into my pillow, "the blind leading the halt, or the halt leading the . . . whatever it is. I thought you had the secret of perpetual health."

"Me? I assure you, madame, if I had it, the whole world would get it. Especially people who have to spend their lives trying to be in two places at the same time, like you and me." She got up and tinkered with an assortment of junk on my dresser top. "Both of us would probably be jumping around like teen-agers if we didn't have to split ourselves down the middle all the time. Men have plenty of problems, but there's one problem they never have. When a man goes to work, he goes to work, period. He has one job. Not a hundred and twenty-three. He doesn't have to run home when the children are sick. He doesn't have to concern himself with their playmates, their social obligations, their fights, their costumes, their dancing lessons, their dentist appointments, their birthday parties, their notes for the teacher. He takes care of them when he has time. And when he feels like it. But nobody *expects* him to. It's not his responsibility. Neither is the house. He doesn't have to worry about the housekeeper's day off, the housekeeper's asking for more money, the housekeeper's threatening to quit. Or the dry cleaning, or the kids' new clothes, or having people over for dinner. Not only that. He doesn't have to worry about getting new bras and girdles, about runs in his stockings, about setting his hair or tweezing his eyebrows or moisturizing his wrinkles. . . . You know what a man has to do? He has to get up, shave, and get out. Once he's out that door he has only one responsibility—to make money. I grant you, that's not easy. But at least it's singular."

"Yeah," I mused, "no wonder they look younger longer."

"Mind you," she said, sitting on the bed again, "there are plenty of men who do their best to pitch in and help. My husband, for instance, a charming, sensitive human being. But even when they do their best to share the responsibility, it's not the same for them. The onus isn't on them. Society doesn't expect it. And they know it. That's what makes the difference."

"Some distribution of labor," I said, dabbing at my watery eyes with Kleenex, "How did it all start? Who made these arrangements? I'll bet, way back there, some smart aleck in a loincloth got a bunch of the boys together in a cave one night and said, 'Listen, fellas, I think we got a good thing here. Last night I dragged a girl in here by the hair and she didn't even holler. See what I mean? We can get away with *anything*.'"

Vicki laughed. I went on, encouraged.

"And then they made up all these rules. The fun things, like hunting and fishing and fighting, would be for the men, and the rest of the stuff, which is a drag, like cleaning the cave and cooking the dinosaur and sitting by the sandbox with a bunch of little kids, that would be for the females."

"But listen," Vicki said, grinning, "there must have been one man there who raised his voice in the cause of justice."

"Oh, sure. There was one decent guy who said, 'Say, this isn't really fair, is it?' And they clubbed him to death."

Vicki squealed and doubled over.

"What I want to know," I said, "is who was that first fink girl who let herself be dragged around by the hair?"

"Aah!" Vicki put out her cigarette. "Her descendants are all over the place. I could show you finks by the mile."

"What is it, some kind of perversion?"

"No. Just chronic infancy. 'Hold me, carry me, feed me, tell me what to do.'"

"Huh!" I snorted, "Immaturity!"

"You said it."

"Cases of arrested development."

"Bull's-eye."

"No guts!"

"No guts," she agreed.

"So we have a hundred and twenty-three jobs to do instead of just one," I said. "So we have anxieties and tensions and conflicts that pile up on us until we break down and get sick. So what? Is that any reason to give up and say 'Go ahead, drag me around by the hair?' "

"Of course not."

"So how come I feel like giving up and saying 'Go ahead, drag me around by the hair'?"

Vicki stood up. "It's a temporary aberration. When the sore throat goes away the aberration disappears. Happens to me all the time."

"All the *time*? You didn't *tell* me this when you said go out and get a job!"

"You wouldn't have believed me. Besides, it wouldn't have stopped you."

"How do you know?"

"Is it going to stop you now?"

I blew my nose and thought about it.

"No!" I said.

Vicki picked up her little black bag. "Oh—what was that important question you had to ask me?"

"You just answered it," I said.

And after Vicki left I lay there convincing myself that I could lick a hundred and twenty-three problems a day with one hand tied behind my back. But I'd forgotten about the hundred and twenty-fourth problem. It had a name, this hundred and twenty-fourth problem. In fact it had three names, a closet full of blue suits, an honorable discharge from the army, a law degree, and two cars, one of which was stranded in a New York garage.

While I was recuperating, Alex entertained me nightly by giving me the latest figures on the New York garage bill, and when that began losing its sting, he looked around, with this strange new personality of his, and found still another target.

It began the following Monday morning, which was very

wet. In fact, the last time it was that wet somebody started gathering the animals two by two. A few weeks previous we'd had a rainy morning almost as bad, and Alex had driven the kids to school so they wouldn't have to stand at the bus stop getting soaked. So this morning I said, "Don't dawdle over your breakfast, kids; Daddy's going to drive you to school."

And Daddy said, "What the hell for?"

I stared at him. He stared back.

"There's no reason they can't go to the bus stop like everybody else!" he said, and then turned on the kids and pointed the finger of authority at them. "You go to the bus stop like everybody else. You're not going to melt!"

They gawked at him, mystified, like who was he threatening, because as far as they were concerned they'd *rather* go to the bus stop and get soaked. They *loved* getting soaked.

Then that night as Sooz was going to bed she asked if she could wear her party dress to school the next day because it was somebody's birthday and they were going to have lollypops and everything, and I said sure, like a nice mommy. Then Daddy came in to say good night and she told him the good news, and Daddy, who had never before paid the slightest attention to what they wore, they could have gone to school in black lace underwear for all he knew, said: "No party dresses! You're not wearing party dresses to school! School is not a party! No party dress! Is that clear?"

"Why not?" asked Sooz, through trembling lips.

"Because I *said so!*"

Her first lesson in logic.

Then it happened again with David going to Stanley Rump's house to play. I didn't like him playing with Stanley Rump, because Stanley Rump was constantly eating snow and sitting on David's chest against David's will and watching horror movies on television. So I said he couldn't go. No sooner did Alex hear this than he decided David should go to Stanley Rump's house the very next day after school.

Then a dictum was handed down about afternoon snacks, which they'd been having ever since they were old enough to mangle an Arrowroot biscuit. Suddenly, no more snacks.

And suddenly there were new rules about brushing teeth every hour on the hour, and polishing their own shoes, which created a black-and-brown tile floor in the bathroom where once had been pure gleaming white, and learning six new words from the dictionary every night, and no more ice cream in the wintertime, and no television until they learned to play a decent game of chess. That tore it.

I could no longer delude myself as to the reason for all this behavior. It hadn't been fatigue that bothered him when I worked late. It hadn't been a principle with the snow tires. It was no accident that he hadn't helped on Halloween. He'd never been worried about David needing glasses. None of it was my imagination. From the moment I told him I was going to work, he'd been boiling, seething, raging, roaring mad!

"My God!" I said to him, "Are you really going to make a little girl still in kindergarten learn ten ways to checkmate an opponent just to prove you're still master in your own home?"

" 'Master'?" he said, "What do you mean, 'master'? You sound like a real parlor psychiatrist. 'Prove'! Who's proving? I'm *teaching*, that's all. I'm *disciplining*."

It was no use, he wasn't going to admit it. He was just going to go on, like an iceberg, one bland eighth above water, seven hostile eighths below. How long could I take it?

While I was wondering, Norman called, in terrible conflict. He wanted me desperately to come back to work, and at the same time he wanted me desperately not to come back until I had rid myself of every lingering germ. I knew without a doubt that he'd been spraying the office with disinfectant and handling the script with gloves on. But even his fear of germs retreated before his fear that the whole project would fall through if we didn't get the Plaza fountain scene written in a hurry, so he asked me if I could stand up without support and when I said yes, he said come back.

I went back with a feeling that my days were numbered.

I also went with a shopping bag full of a small nylon petticoat and sixteen yards of tinsel, which I sewed at, defiantly, on the train, while people stared at me.

I also wrote out a check for a lot of money and took the car out of the garage in New York and drove it home, surviving a dozen near accidents, and Alex saw the notation in the checkbook and said, "Do you know what we could have done with this money?" and from then until bedtime he enumerated the things we could have done with it. I was about to come back at him with a list of several things *he'd* done in his day that had cost us quite a few dollars, like leaving the air-conditioner running for two weeks while we were on a summer vacation, when I remembered there was no point to it. He wasn't really talking about the money. He wasn't really talking about the car. He was talking about something he refused to admit he was really talking about.

How far can this go, I wondered?

And that weekend I found out.

21 IT WAS the night the Bookmans and Sands and Cardells came over.

I had a fairly set routine for entertaining. Over the years I'd organized the whole business of ashtrays, coasters, cigarettes, matches, nuts, mints, candles, flowers, sofa cushions, drapes, lighting, music, and so on, so that now, with efficiency and concentration and about thirty-five minutes, I could have everything exactly the way I wanted it, almost without thinking. Alex had never bothered interfering in this ritual. He'd always figured his was not to reason why, his was but to take care of the ice cubes.

So this particular Saturday night I began to do what I'd been doing with very little deviation since time immemorial. I took down the silver dish and filled it with mints. I took down the Mexican bowl and filled it with nuts. I took down the divided crystal platter and put an assortment of crackers on one side and an assortment of little cubes of cheese speared by colored toothpicks on the other.

And then it began.

Alex walked into the kitchen, all showered and shaved and talcumy, with a fresh white shirt still open at the throat and an elegant blue tie thrown carelessly over one shoulder, and I was just beginning to think how really attractive he was, when he gave the platter a narrow-eyed look and said, "What's all *that* for?"

I stared at him. He might as well have walked into Mrs. Ben-Gurion's house on Passover night and said, "How come all this unleavened bread?"

"Hmmm?" I said.

"It's a little ridiculous, isn't it, putting out a spread like this every time somebody comes over? These people just had dinner. In a couple of hours you'll be giving them coffee and cake. Is that all they come here for, to *eat*?"

"But we always . . ."

" 'We always.' Exactly. 'We always.' It's a pretty sad comment, if you feel people can't enjoy our company unless they're continually stuffing themselves. I, personally, feel they can." And he actually began taking all the little colored toothpicks out of the cheese and putting the crackers back in the box.

This is the end, I thought, I can feel it coming, this is the end.

I went into the living room, removed some old magazines from the coffee table, and put out fresh cigarettes, little matchboxes, and a small arrangement of flowers. Then I put the bowl of nuts on one end table and the dish of mints on another, and went back into the kitchen.

And Alex went into the living room and put the old magazines back on the coffee table, moved the cigarettes and matches to one end table, moved the mints from that end table to the other, moved the bowl of nuts onto the television set, and put the flowers in the dining room.

I came back into the living room, saw this, bit my lip and said nothing. I lit the tall candles in my old Spanish candlesticks, opened the blinds, drew the drapes, and went out again.

Alex put out the candles, shut the blinds, and drew back the drapes.

I put Andrés Segovia on the record player.

He took off Segovia and put on the *New World Symphony*.

All this without a word. I felt as though I'd been trapped in one of those old Marx Brothers routines where one of them keeps taking clothes from a drawer and filling a suitcase and each time he turns his back the other one takes the clothes from the suitcase and puts them back in the drawer. Only, that made *sense*, compared to this.

"The end!" I told myself, and went upstairs to finish disguising my face.

The company arrived.

I sensed a slight air of tension, like there used to be in the days when we were first getting to know each other. At first I couldn't pin down the cause of it, and then slowly it came to me. It was *me* that was different. Or rather, their attitude toward me. Especially the men.

These three men, Don Bookman, Charlie Sands, and Victor Cardell had regarded me for years as a community fixture, like the supermarket, comfortably familiar, with a predictable layout, all the items in their usual places, vegetables to the left, canned goods to the right, meat counter straight ahead, all very handy and pleasant, nothing to get excited about but a nice place to visit once in a while when you want to get out of the house.

Now suddenly it was as though I'd come under new management and had been turned into a Gourmet Shoppe. They entered warily, a little suspicious and on guard, but curious, respectful, even intrigued.

With Vera, Helen, and Natalie it was a little different. It was as though we'd all been campers together, sharing the same routine, the same inside jokes, the same resentment against those in authority, and suddenly I'd been promoted from camper to counselor, and it wasn't the same any more. There was still an attachment, because after all I'd only just come up from the ranks, but what I gained in prestige, I lost in intimacy.

This was quite a state of affairs to find myself in, suddenly, in the middle of my own living room. I got very nervous and started splashing the wrong liquor into the wrong people's glasses, and they all started asking me about the show and about television and about Wingate, and because I was so nervous and so self-conscious and uncomfortable in this new relationship they'd foisted on me, I was afraid to stop talking. I don't know what I thought would happen to everybody if I stopped talking, but I just couldn't stop. I talked and talked and talked, until there seemed to be no sound in the world but the sound of my voice. Everybody's eyes were on me, nobody interrupted, so I just had to go on and on and on. Oh, God, I prayed, let somebody stop me! But no. There was this ridiculous voice babbling away, making terrible jokes and unforgivable pronouncements, and I could no more stop it than I could press a button and become invisible.

Then Alex' voice cut across the room from the corner where he had been sitting and glaring and quietly lowering the level of a bottle of scotch.

"Conversation, anyone?" inquired this voice etched in acid.

I reeled a little from the blow, and there were a few embarrassed murmurs from the others, but at least that put an end to it. Slowly the conversation began—leaky basements, incompetent school principals, the validity of an analysis in a magazine article on the situation in South America, theories on the motives of various political figures, the uncalled-for behavior of a certain neighbor in the matter of a community snowplow, etc.

At first Alex, although he had initiated the conversation, just sat back in his corner biting hard on his pipe and getting stoned. But by the time we were at the table having coffee, he had joined in. And when he joined, he joined. Like the Americans joining a World War. He came in to *finish* it.

It went something like this.

VERA: "But I don't think Joan of Arc had any real understanding of politics. I think she was motivated *emotionally*."

VICTOR: "But Vera, in order to take sides she had to be aware of the issues."

NATALIE: "I think Vera means that the issues were incidental. Emotion must have been the strongest factor. *Why else would a woman lead an army into battle?*"

ALEX: *"The usual reason—to get out of the house."*

Then, a little later.

DON: "In that case, I don't see what makes De Gaulle different from any other dictator."

HELEN: "Oh, there's a world of difference!"

VERA: "The very temperament of the French people—"

CHARLIE: "I don't think he is one, and I don't think he can become one."

NATALIE: *"Alex, do you think De Gaulle will ever become the dictator of France?"*

ALEX: *"Not so long as there's a MADAME de Gaulle."*

And still later—

VERA: "I thought it was a terrible play. What was the point of that man-eating plant?"

DON: "The reviews said it was supposed to be a symbolic picture of suburbia."

HELEN: "Suburbia? How could it be suburbia? *There wasn't a single female in the cast.*"

ALEX: "Sure there was. *What about that man-eating plant?*"

And on and on. He got snider and snider, and I kept going into the kitchen to make more and more coffee long after everybody stopped drinking it.

✳ 222

So at last it was out in the open. It took half a bottle of Scotch but finally it was out. He hated me. He hated me because I was trying to be something more than just his wife. He absolutely, unquestionably, no-kidding-around hated me. That was the truth. Everything else was a lie. All that stuff about believing women were people—malarkey! The last honest words he'd said to me were "Well, well, so you're going to work!" Since then he hadn't spoken one word of truth.

He hated me.

"And I'm supposed to live with this?" I said in my mind to Vicki, "I'm sorry. The other hundred and twenty-three problems, okay. But this? Forget it. I know when I'm outmaneuvered. I give up."

Let him pull me around by the hair. He had me licked. The contemporary caveman, I thought to myself, standing there in the kitchen. Same Neanderthal fella, hasn't really changed much over the years. Only the weapon gets more subtle as the centuries go by. First the club. (Wham!) Then convention. (Go to your room, Daisy, this is not for a woman's ears!) Now psychology. (See what you're doing to me? You're destroying my masculinity and making me hate you!)

I looked up at the ceiling and whispered, "Listen, God. Here it comes. . . . 'Uncle!' "

Finally everybody went home, with Alex waving cheerily from the doorway. I waited for him in the living room, an ashtray full of butts in one hand, a dirty coffeepot in the other.

"That was nice," I said, bitterly.

"Yeah," he said blithely, "Wasn't a bad evening."

"Especially the conversation," I said, "I was crazy about that. Man-eating plant. Madame de Gaulle. All that witty stuff."

"Yeah," he said, "I thought it was pretty funny."

Trying to focus his fuzzy eyes he carried some dirty dishes into the kitchen, singing, "Younger than SPRINGtime . . ."

Now that he'd gotten some of the bile out of his system he

was feeling pretty good. I followed him into the kitchen, quivering.

"So now we know where we stand!" I said, putting the dirty coffeepot into the oven, instead of the sink.

"Stand? Who?"

"You could have saved me a lot of trouble, you know that? A lot of trouble! All you had to do when this whole thing started was say: 'No! You're not going to work for somebody else! You work for *me!* That's why I hired—oh—pardon me—*married* you!' Actually you shouldn't have said married *or* hired. You should have said bought! That's what I was—*bought!*"

And I put the ashtray full of cigarette butts into the refrigerator and slammed the door.

"What are you talking about?" he said. "Do you know what you're talking about?"

"You couldn't say that, could you! No. Men don't say that kind of thing any more. They're too enlightened. So they just make nasty little jokes about women in general. Or they don't talk to you for days at a time. Or they start working late. Or they yell at the kids. Or they don't let you get snow tires. Go! they say. Go on out! And then they tie a hungry lion to the front stoop!"

And I scraped some leftover cake into the sink and deposited the English china in the garbage pail.

"Lion?" he said, "*Lion?*"

"Well, you'll be happy to know it's all over! I give up! You win! I'll quit! I won't go to work any more! Okay? You happy now? You satisfied?"

He took the English china out of the garbage pail with great dignity and put it in the cookie bin.

"You shouldn't drink," he said. "You really shouldn't drink."

"That's what you wanted all along, isn't it? Isn't it?"

He looked pained. "You're babbling, dear."

I grabbed his lapels.

"Please," I said hoarsely, "just admit it. Just once. I don't care about anything else. I just want to hear you say it. Please. Please. Say it!"

"It."

"*Alex!*"

"*Ruthie!*"

"Be honest for *one minute!* Admit it! You want me to quit! You want me back in the house! You don't want me to have a job of my own! Or a mind of my own! Or money of my own! You want me dependent! You want me to be *less!* So *you* can be *more!* Just *admit* it!"

He looked at me haughtily, terribly offended.

"That's a rotten thing to say," he said. "And stop smashing my lapels."

He disengaged my hands and stalked out of the kitchen.

"*Admit it!*"I wailed after him.

But I knew he never would.

22　　　THE NEXT DAY I opened the door to Norman's office, and walked in, and closed it behind me, and leaned against it, and stared at Norman like those dramatic actresses in the movies used to stare at the man they really loved when they came to tell him they'd just decided, for financial reasons, to marry Ralph Bellamy.

It flashed through my mind that I was feeling much more loyalty toward this comparative stranger than I was toward my own husband. And then I realized that Norman only represented something that was part of me. It was the commitment to myself that hurt so much in the breaking. To thine own self . . . Well, so long, mine own self. Better luck in the next incarnation. From now on I was just going to be what all those idiots in sociology said was supposed to make me happy . . . a receptacle. Let somebody else carry the torch. Let somebody else fight twenty centuries of conditioning. So what if I felt alive for the first time in years? What's the good of being alive if it's killing you?

So I stood there looking at Norman with "The End" written all over my face. He got the message immediately. Well, not *the* message, but *a* message. He clenched his jaw and gripped the back of a chair.

"The bomb's coming!" he whispered hoarsely.

"No. But I'm going."

He stared at me, his jaw unclenched. Hanging, in fact.

"I . . . I have to quit," I said, "I'm . . . I'm quitting."

"No," he said, white as a sheet, "No, don't tell me that. Tell me it's just the bomb coming."

"I . . . I have personal problems," I muttered.

"Personal problems! What the hell is that? Do what everybody else does, get a legal separation until the script is finished!"

I shook my head, went to the desk, opened the drawer and took out my soap dish, my cologne stick, and my suede brush. The Fig Newtons and the Anacin I left for Norman.

"Oh, crap!" he said, feebly, and fell into a chair. "Oh, they find me. They really find me. Every Judas in the whole world spends his life looking for Norman Spain. What kind of job can I get where I won't have to depend on anybody? I'll be a piano tuner. . . ."

I dabbed at my eyes with a tissue.

"Cry!" he said. "Bawl your eyes out! If there's one thing in the world that doesn't bother me it's the sight of a woman crying!"

"I'll call Harry," I sniffled, and went out.

That afternoon I was hanging around the kitchen trying to figure out some dignified way of giving Hannah her two weeks' notice, when the telephone rang, and I picked it up and Simon's warm, familiar, Fifty-seventh Street voice came over the wire and into my ear.

"How are you doing, sexy?"

For a minute I felt good again.

"I heard you were sick," he said.

"Oh . . . that was a long time ago. I'm fine."

"You don't drink enough tea. With lemon and honey, a quart a day, you'll never catch cold."

I promised to do that.

"I spoke to Harry last week," he said. (Last week. So he didn't know about the resignation.) "He's pretty impressed with you."

"He's *what?*"

"He thinks you did a nice job on the script."

"He *does?* You'd never know it. He must be a great poker player."

"He's a businessman. Like me. It's his job to keep a writer's price down."

"Oh," I said, feeling a small glow at the word "writer." Then I remembered that it didn't apply to me any more. And what Harrison Wingate thought about me was academic. I cleared my throat for the dramatic announcement. "By the way . . . Simon . . . I . . . I'm not working on the script any more. . . ."

"No?"

"No. I . . . well, it was just too much . . . the whole thing. I mean . . . I didn't have any snow tires . . . and those trains . . . and the kids were sick . . . and I had to sew six yards of tinsel on a nylon petticoat . . . and those trains . . . and Norman gets so nervous when the coffee's cold . . . and Alex isn't . . . well, mostly it's those goddam trains!"

"So you quit?"

"Yeah. I . . . uh . . . I told Harry, and . . . well, he was pretty upset. But I explained to him . . . that it was just . . . I just couldn't go on. You know . . . Uh . . . I mean it's just impossible. I know it's a rotten thing to do. I didn't want to do it . . . believe

✳ 227

me . . . I was going to call you just as soon as . . . well, anyway, now you know. They're going to work out some kind of arrangement about the royalties, but . . . I . . . won't have any more to do with it. I'm . . . I'm not going to work any more."

There was a pause, and then Simon's voice came through, clear as a bell.

"I'm glad to hear it!" he said.

I nearly dropped the phone. Glad to hear it! What kind of reaction was that, glad to hear it? Didn't he care that I was letting a promising career slip through my fingers? Didn't he think it was a damn shame that I should give up now, on the brink of success, after so much backbreaking work? What was the matter with him, anyway?

"Why?" I barked. "What makes you so glad?"

"You're not cut out for it, Ruthie. I told you that in the beginning. You're a nice young married woman."

"Meaning what?" I snapped.

"Meaning you're not one of these sharp neurotic broads with a big drive. And thank your lucky stars for that. Basically you have the right instinct—to be a wife. But you've been fighting it, God knows why. I'm glad to see you finally came to your senses. Take my word for it, I've been married seventeen years . . ."

And he was off again, about how there's nothing so beautiful as a woman who takes pride in spending her life keeping her Dispos-all free of household germs.

"Simon," I interrupted, "are you telling me there are only two choices for me in this world? Neurotic broad or Dispos-all? Are you serious?"

"What are you mad about?" He sounded puzzled. "You said you quit, didn't you?"

"You could've at least told me to reconsider!"

"You just finished giving me a long story about snow tires and cold coffee. What was that all about?"

"Okay," I said, "never mind. You're right."

✳ 228

"I take people at their word—"

"You're right. You're right."

"Unless you didn't mean it—"

"I said you're right."

"It's not a question of being right—"

"Of course not. You're right."

I heard his phone ring on the other line.

"Hold it a minute," he said, and disappeared, and then came back again. "Ruthie? I'll tell you what, when you get into town give me a call, I'll take you to lunch."

Sure, I could see myself running into New York for lunch once Hannah was gone.

"I'll do that, Simon. Thanks for calling."

I put back the receiver, picked up a pencil, and broke it in two. Then I broke each of the halves in two. It didn't help. "Nice young married woman!" It was like being a nice piece of pie, or a nice armchair, or a nice doggie. What was he saying, underneath all that baloney, under all that corny pseudo-psychology? The same old song. "You wait with the ladies down in second-class, honey, while we go up to first class, and live."

I thought of that traitor way back there, who let herself be pulled around by the hair. And here I was, her twentieth-century counterpart, doing the very same thing, letting Alex take away my hunting and fishing license and send me back to the cave.

Wasn't it the worst kind of moral crime, to perpetuate something I *knew* was wrong? Wasn't it unforgivable cowardice, to surrender to what I believed was a life-stifling prejudice? Did I want some dame in 2160 saying to herself, "If it wasn't for that fink Ruthie back in the twentieth century, I wouldn't be stuck up here on Mars while Jack goes out in the universe every day and has lunch on all those different satellites"?

Then a great weariness overcame me.

To hell with that lady in 2160, I told myself. What does she know about my problems? Helen and Vera and Natalie were

✳ 229

right. They were right to be scared. They were right to chicken out. Where you've got children you've got to have a husband. Where you've got a husband you've got to have male vanity. Where you've got male vanity, cowardice is the better part of wisdom.

I started back for the kitchen to tell Hannah she would have to make other plans, and the phone rang again.

It was *that voice.*

"Ruth—!" It said.

"Mike—"

"I just spoke to Wingate. You're not serious about this?"

"Oh—listen—I don't want to think about it any more."

"It's not going to work without you."

"Oh, don't be . . . what do you mean?"

"I won't be able to do it with Norman alone."

"Oh, that's ri*dic*—"

"Norman doesn't know how to make that girl *female.*"

"But it's practically finished . . ."

"It's finished when it's on tape, and not before. What happened, anyway? What's the matter?"

"Oh, I . . . it's too complicated."

"Well . . . I need you. Badly. If that means anything."

There was a loud, fast thumping in my ears as of a heart beating like crazy.

"Oh, don't say that. I'm in pieces here."

"So am I," he said.

That did it.

"Oh, Jesus. I can't. I—it's impossible. You don't know. I made up my . . . it's impossible. Really. There are too many . . . no, I can't. I really can't." I took a deep breath, "Okay, I'll think about it."

"Have lunch with me tomorrow."

"Well, I . . . I'll let you know."

"I meant it. What I said before. I can't do this without you."

"Uh—okay, Mike . . ." The racket in my ears was deafening.

"Call me back."

"Yes . . . yes . . . I will . . . sure." I hung up, quickly.

He needs me. He wants me. He respects me. He can't do the job without me. The whole project depends on me. Thousands of dollars. Big business. Waiting for me. I'm somebody. They can't finish it without me. I'm important!

I didn't go back to the kitchen to tell Hannah she would have to leave.

Alex came home. He was in good spirits. He'd been feeling unusually fine lately . . . ever since I'd quit the job, in fact. Strange coincidence. Lighthearted as a boy he was, for the first time in months, laughing, joking, tousling my hair, letting the kids jump all over him.

"David!" I said, sternly, "I told you twenty minutes ago to take your shower. Now you go up this minute and—"

"Oh, let him play for a while," said Alex expansively, magnanimously, "The kid's having a little fun. What's the big hurry?" He picked up Sooz and kissed her on the nose. Harmony emanated from him like Bach from an organ.

What price harmony?

If I could *enjoy* it. But it was like enjoying a wooden leg when you've lost your own. Sure, it's a good thing to have. It makes life easier, it lets you get around and *function*. But it's not your own leg!

And it wasn't my own harmony. It was *Alex'* harmony. You can only enjoy somebody else's harmony up to a point, once in a while you have to have some of your own!

If Alex' harmony came from getting what he wanted, and getting what he wanted meant my not getting what I wanted . . . what about *my* harmony? Had I not eyes? Had I not hands, organs, dimensions, senses, affections, passions? If you prick me, do I not bleed? If you poison me, do I not die? If you take away my harmony do I not get all shriveled up with discord, same as you?

He *needs* me! *They* need me. *I* need me!

* 2 3 1

"Well," said Alex pleasantly, as we ate dinner, "did you tell her?" With a nod of his head toward the kitchen.

I cleared my throat. "It seems," I said, "that they're not going to let me quit."

"Oh?" The fork paused for just a fraction of a second on its way to his mouth.

"They're holding me to the contract."

"How come?"

I shrugged. "They've got some crazy idea that what I do there can't be done by anybody else."

"Mmm." He turned in his chair and bellowed. "David! Get out of that playroom and take your shower! *Now!*"

"What happened to your good spirits?"

"I *want* him to *take a shower*. That's all. It has nothing to do with my *spirits*."

"Uh-huh."

So I went back to work. Not without fear and dread for my home life, but with something that was evidently stronger than that; a feeling that somewhere, if not from Alex, I could get respect and admiration for the person I was—for all of me—not just the part that said "Yes, sir."

23

IF YOU live long enough, you stop being amazed that people somehow survive being trapped in mines, or floating for days on a piece of wood in the middle of the ocean . . . because somewhere along the line you're bound to live through a period in your own life that matches it, not in the physical details, but in the certainty that nobody could go through this and come out alive. And when you finally face such a situation, you find that nature provides you with a sort of general anesthesia so that you can get through it. Anyway, that's the way it was in my relationship, those days, with Alex. When I was with him I walked around novocained from head to foot, and from the way he walked around, I gathered he was in more or less the same condition.

It was a stalemate as fundamental as the one between Russia and the U.S. The ideologies were polarized, and peaceful co-existence was only a word. Like the cold war, there were alternate periods of tension and of deceptive calm, and the outcome was something nobody wanted to think about. Me least of all. I ran to work the way other women run to the beauty parlor—to change temporarily what I couldn't really change, in the long run.

Mike made much of me, with his warm glances. It was the only heat in a cold winter. The Plaza fountain scene was written, and received with gratifying enthusiasm, and one late December afternoon we all had a meeting in Wingate's office and Mike told him he was satisfied we finally had a rehearsal script. Wingate, either because he was relieved to hear it or because the festive atmosphere of the Lord and Taylor Christmas windows had penetrated his dissociated heart, took us all downstairs to one of his favorite bars and bought us drinks.

He raised his glass and toasted our project, and we all drank to it, and then he turned to Mike.

"When do you expect to get back from the coast?" he asked.

And Mike said, "Right after New Year's."

And Norman said, "When are you leaving?"

And Mike said, "Tomorrow."

It was the first I'd heard of it. I caught sight of myself in the mirrored wall opposite, and realized I looked just like Sooz when Alex told her there'd be no more ice cream until summertime. Feeling suddenly deserted and forlorn, I stood up from the table, said I had to catch a train, and told Mike to have a good trip.

"Wait," he said, gulping his drink, "I'll give you a lift to the station."

There was a flicker of an eyebrow from Wingate and a brief

* 233

gagging sound as Norman choked a little on his cigar. Good God, I thought, they're thinking terrible things and I haven't even had the pleasure of doing them.

"Going that direction anyway," Mike said, which only made it worse.

And then we were sitting side by side in a cab with absolutely nothing to say to each other. Outside a feathery snow falling out of a purple-black sky, Christmas lights and tinsel, gold and silver, red and green and icy blue lights winking and blinking, that interminable chorus carrying on over Saks Fifth Avenue, sidewalk Santa Clauses ringing their tinny bells, furry little people scurrying by, and there we sat, each of us looking glumly out our own window, and couldn't think of a thing to say.

In the middle of my glumness I found time to be glad of *his* glumness. No other reason being apparent, he was obviously unhappy because he was leaving me, which was pretty nice, and I felt a little less forlorn.

At Grand Central he paid the driver, got out of the cab and held out his hand to help me out.

Now where is he going, I wondered. Is he coming *home* with me?

"I'll walk you down to the train," he said, still glum, and we marched silently down the stairway side by side, like a couple of M.P.'s on duty. At the train gate he stopped, looked up at the time of departure, glanced at his watch, thrust his hands into the pockets of his Burberry, stared down at the floor, and said nothing. I began to feel ridiculous. I cleared my throat.

"What are you going to be doing on the coast?" I asked.

"Going home. For Christmas," he answered, still examining the floor.

"Oh!" Somehow it hadn't occurred to me that people *lived* out there. So that's where they were, the talented actress and the four kids, two clean, two dirty.

"Oh," I repeated, and it was my turn to look at the floor. But as I lowered my head he brought his up with such a snap I barely straightened up in time to avoid a collision.

"Ruth—" he said, and searched my eyes with his, "I'm going to miss you—"

"Are you?" I managed, through parched lips.

"Don't look for any answers," he said (which would have started me immediately looking for them except I wasn't quite sure what kind of answers not to look for), "I'm not going to pretend this isn't some kind of enormous self-indulgence . . ." he paused, waiting for me to agree, or contradict, or look intelligent, or just anything, but my pulse was hammering away at such an abnormal rate that it was all I could do to stand upright.

He must have sensed an imminent collapse too, because he took my hand, led me to the wall, plastered me against it and stood with his palms against the wall, one on either side of my head, and his face about two inches from mine. I felt more secure. Even if I began to sag, he could pin me to the wall with one move.

I was working on a brave little smile and trying to think of something witty to say about California that hadn't been said before, when he kissed me. I dissolved.

That kiss was a masterpiece. A genuine masterpiece. It was the kind of achievement that could not possibly be the result of talent alone, or even genius. It had to be the product of years of training, of experimenting, of refining and mellowing. A kiss like that could never come from an inexperienced young man, any more than his greatest works of art could have been created by an adolescent Michelangelo. This was the Sistine Chapel of kisses.

Naturally I didn't struggle, or pull away, or pound on his chest. I just did what any art lover would do. I stood still and experienced it. All through me I experienced it.

When he finally drew his face away from mine he didn't wait for my reaction, which was a pity, as I might have come up with a testimonial he could have used to warm the entire wintry span of his old age. Instead he shoved one hand into his pocket and brought out a small flat box, Christmas wrapped. He handed it to me.

"Oh," I whined, "I can't . . . you . . . it . . ."

He kissed me again, but briefly this time (another sign of genius), and walked away. I just stood there shaking from head to foot, the small package rattling in my hand, and watched him cross the width of Grand Central and disappear into the arcade. Then, very carefully, I went through the gate and down to the train, one step at a time, holding onto the rail for dear life.

This was probably the one and only time I didn't mind that long ride on the New York Central. In fact I was hoping it would just go on until I'd figured out who I was and what was really happening and just how I was supposed to go home and sit at the same table with Alex and eat dinner.

"You're not in love with this Mike," I told myself. "You're just in love with yourself because he's making passes at you." And I answered myself, "Yeah. Sure. I know all that. *But.*"

I opened the package. It was a gold cigarette case. The only inscription—shrewd—was the date. I wondered what on earth I was going to do with it. I put it in my bag. Then I thought what if Alex goes looking for some change or a book of matches or the gas bill or something? So I took it out of my bag and put it in my coat pocket.

Then I thought what if there aren't enough coat hangers and Alex hangs his coat over mine and then in the morning he accidentally takes them both off the hanger and my coat swings against him and this thing goes *clunk?* So I took it out of my coat pocket and just held it, and thought of giving it to the conductor for Christmas, and then finally sneaked it down the front of my dress until it lodged just above my belt. It was very cold.

After this I sat back and thought about the last twenty minutes, and then about the last three weeks, encounter by encounter, minute by minute, look by look. I hadn't had occasion for such a revery for . . . too many years. I gave myself up to the delicious ego-balm of it all. I spun it out in my mind, hung on certain spectacular moments, going over them again and again, elaborating, rewriting a little, restaging a few key scenes.

Then after a while I began to feel that I'd been riding an awfully long time. I looked out the window, and even though it was dark I could tell I'd never passed this way before. None of this landscape was familiar. Strange formations rose in the distance and flashed by, unrecognized. Odd-looking houses. Trackless wastes where trackless wastes had never been before. I began to panic. I looked at my watch. Sure enough, I'd been due at my station half an hour before! I peered desperately out the window. Where the hell was I?

The train slowed down and came into a station. It was some milk-run stop twenty miles north of where I was supposed to be.

I rushed off the train and it chugged away, leaving me in total blackness. Alone. Nobody lived here! There wasn't even a light on the rotten platform! There seemed to be nothing for miles but the dark, the cold, the emptiness, the wind. No people, no taxis, no nothing!

Again panic flooded me. This was no accident. It was meant to happen. This was the inevitable, monumental, thundering retribution! I heard the eleventh commandment booming across the sky: Thou shalt not kiss a strange man in Grand Central Station!

Then I heard the faint sound of a car, and I ran towards the noise, yelling "Help! Help!" like an idiot. The lights of the car suddenly appeared, from a totally different direction, and before I could change course it had swept out of sight. But as it swept, the lights had hit a pole not far from me, to which was attached a telephone. I started for it, then stopped cold. A horrible certainty froze my blood. I was in for a demonstration of the divine sense of humor. I would get to the phone, reach in my bag . . . open my change purse . . . no change! I was sure of it. I refused even to look. I would play it out to the bitter end. I had too much respect for the profession now to spoil the Grand Guignol.

✳ 237

Slowly I walked to the phone. Slowly I slipped my hand into my bag. But even as my cold fingers curled around my empty change-purse, my brain registered the sign above the phone. It was a direct line to the taxi company! Through my relief I thought "Does this only prove you can't even count on things to go *wrong?*"

Five minutes later I was speeding back to that dear little spot on the map where my very own car was slowly disappearing under a pile of feathery snowflakes. A half-hour later and a ten-dollar bill lighter, I exchanged cab for car and started for home. As I nosed up the first wet hill, a bubble of hilarity burst in me and I giggled. It was one of those rare moments of sanity when I saw life for what it really is: a Mack Sennett original. Then I sobered up, being, after all, just as stupid as anybody else, and began to worry again, about how I was going to walk into the innocent, trusting bosom of my family with my guilty secret clunking away between belt and bra.

I couldn't recall exactly what went on between Madame and Doctor Bovary when she came trotting back from her first rendezvous. Was she remorseful, frightened, or so far gone she didn't care? Scarlett, of course, just blazed defiantly at Rhett after making melting eyes at that anemic fellow of hers. I had been terribly impressed by the beautifully understated tension of that nice lady in *Brief Encounter,* and the basic decency of her attitude before, during, and after. Phaedra—well. If her insides were torn to pieces she deserved it. Anybody who would throw over a full-grown tiger for a skinny little cub!

Anyway, none of my literary references prepared me for the way it would happen to me. If I had any sense, I'd have figured it out. Some people are accident-prone. I am anticlimax-prone.

When I pulled up in my driveway I took a deep breath, got out of the car, walked bravely up the path, opened the front door, walked in . . . and Alex wasn't even home. He was working late again.

Even when he finally arrived, and even in the days and

nights that followed, nothing worked out like it was supposed to. There was no drama, no moment when, in a sudden intuitive flash he looked at me and *knew*. In fact it was pretty difficult even getting him to *look* at me. And as for the tumult in my own treacherous breast—shame, fear, remorse, defiance, disgust, despair—I felt none of those things. I felt just great.

I felt marvelous. I felt tall. I felt beautiful and sexy and elegant and chic and witty and delectable and gorgeous and wealthy and pampered and privileged and royal and indestructible and blonde.

In fact, I lorded it around the house like I'd just come into a private fortune of several millions. I felt kindly toward Alex—I could afford to. I felt indulgent toward the children, and thought how lucky they were to have Du Barry for a mother. I affected a languid walk and began to take my showers with scented soap, and sang to my reflection in the mirror. At one point I even found myself thinking of buying a chaise longue for me to lie around on, in seductive negligees. Except the only place we had room for a chaise longue was in the basement. And anyway, there wouldn't have been much point, lying around like that just for the edification of two kids and a housekeeper, since I couldn't get Alex to look at me.

Every so often I was surprised that my heart kept soaring and that the rest of me seemed to be going right along with it. It didn't seem right to be so completely un-conscience stricken, in the light of all I'd been led to believe. But there it was. Evidently one can live very comfortably on the wages of sin.

The only real problem I had was with that damn gold cigarette case. Every day I hid it in another place. Under the mattress. Then in a box of old Halloween costumes. Then in the bottom of a garment bag in the cedar closet. Then on a dirty little high shelf in back of the hot-water heater. Then between the wall and a loose board at the back of a kitchen cabinet. Then at the bottom of a box of Brillo Soap Pads. In desperation I even thought of renting a safe-deposit box at the bank, or maybe a whole vault, but that would involve documents and signatures and what not. Finally, on the theory that a tree is least conspicuous in a forest, I simply put it in among a lot of junk jewelry in an old jewelry box and said to hell with it, if Alex finds it I'll just say it's a token of love from an ardent admirer and he'll say come on, what's the real story, and I'll finally let him worm it out of me that Wingate gave them to his employees for Christmas.

24

CHRISTMAS! Facing the stairway at Grand Central was a Cinemascopic Kodacolor enlargement, three hundred feet high by nine hundred feet wide, showing the happiest, prettiest, wholesomest American family you ever saw, dog and all, in red bathrobes, including the dog, on a white rug by a green Christmas tree in front of a yellow fire in a brick fireplace. Go live up to that.

The only part of Christmas that was any fun was going to school to see Sooz be a snowflake. When she came out on the stage with the other five snowflakes on tippy-toe and flapping her arms, I almost strangled with pride. No question, she was the best.

After that, Christmas was all downhill. Of course it's an old story, about the ill-will that's invariably generated by occasions of good will. There's nothing like the public proclamation that this will be a day of peace, harmony and love of fellow man, to let loose the dogs of war. It has long been established that all across the country on Christmas morning, just exactly five minutes before that magic moment when everybody's supposed to open their presents with Ohs and Ahs and hugs and kisses, all the husbands and wives begin to foam and fume with furious anger. It also happens, of course, on birthdays, anniversaries,

Mother's Day, Father's Day, any day of sanctified sentimentality. The mere *suggestion* that we should be happy or love each other is enough to trigger a battle.

And maybe we're right to react this way. Maybe this is the individual's last faint squeak of rebellion against the ultimate automation. Or maybe we just feel it's a terrible insult, implying that we all hate each other so much we'll never be nice to each other unless somebody schedules it.

In any case, we were no exception to the rule. We always hated each other on Christmas morning and went ice skating in the afternoon. This ice-skating routine was something I really looked forward to, because it was such torture for me that it constituted penance for a whole year's worth of misdeeds, and when it was over I felt cleansed and purified.

As with everything else, my idea of what ice skating should be, and the actual flesh-and-blood reality, were poles apart.

I had this foolish picture in my mind of a clear glassy pond, several miles wide, empty save for the four of us gliding, like a Currier and Ives print, over its smooth, brilliant surface, four graceful, rhythmic dots of color against a blue, blue sky.

What it always turned out to be was a lumpy, uneven, grayish mess, not more than a hundred feet in circumference, covered with screaming adolescent bullies zigzagging across the ice at breakneck speed in every possible direction, knocking down small children and slow-witted grownups to fast loud corny music from a speaker in the hot-dog stand at the entrance. Your life wasn't worth two cents, not to mention the lives of your children, whose stability on skates, which were always too big or too small or too tight or too loose, had to improve a great deal even to be *poor*. Also, of course, it didn't take two minutes for toes and fingers to go numb with cold, noses to start running, and Alex to start yelling at the three of us as we staggered around on our ankles that we just *weren't trying!*

But we never gave up. Winter after winter, Christmas after Christmas, we drove out to this dump, sat in a freezing car grappling icy-fingered with the laces on the too-big, too-small, too-tight, too-loose skates, and clumped out onto that so-called rink, four dedicated, red-nosed Kamikazes.

Fortunately, like all good things, Christmas Day does come to an end. And then all you have to worry about is being in a good mood for New Year's Eve. Sometimes, if you're lucky, you can't get a sitter for New Year's Eve, and you can just sit at home and be tired and depressed if you feel like it without having to chalk it up as a failure.

But of course I'm talking about *ordinary* years. This year was not ordinary. The tension this year had a different quality, it lacked the comfortable certainty that it would only last until January first. It was just one more eruption of the subterranean hostility that reached back into the recent past and forward into a dim future. The long Christmas weekend only aggravated everything by forcing togetherness on people for whom, at this point, apartness was the only answer.

And aggravated it to such a point that what happened was as close to inevitable as you can get.

When you have a mountain—whether of rock or resentment —you can't be too surprised if you have an avalanche. And there is usually one little pebble that starts it. One stupid pebble gets dislodged and down comes the whole crashing roaring mess.

My pebble was cheese. Alex was a cheese fiend. He looked in the refrigerator on Friday night and there was no cheese for breakfast on Saturday morning. Luckily Hannah had gone to visit her sister for Christmas, because he raised his voice and called her things that would have turned her hair green. So the next morning, while Alex was in the shower, thinking to avert a disastrous weekend, I pulled on ski pants, a sweater, and a ski jacket over my pajamas, and high-tailed it to the shopping center where I bought cottage cheese, blue cheese, Swiss, Gorgonzola, Edam, Muenster, Cheddar, American, Port Salud, and Bel Paese. I zoomed back to the house and had them all spread out on the table by the time he came into the kitchen. Instead of laughing, which he would have done six months before, he said "Hm!" took some bagels and lox from the refrigerator, went back to the table, scanned the purchases, threw down the bagels, and roared, *"No cream cheese?"*

There is a tide in the affairs of men which taken at the flood leads on to drowning. I took that tide, or let it take me, and it swept me right up to the bedroom and out of my clothes and into the shower, where I stood, quivering and sobbing with anger, soaping myself with a soap that was guaranteed to be ninety-nine per cent cold cream, and telling myself this was the beginning of the end for Alex and me. Nobody was meant to live like this. It was hopeless. We could not live with each other any more! The kids . . . (Broken home! Broken home!)

I turned the hot water hotter, to see if maybe I couldn't just scald myself to a quick death, but I realized immediately that there must be easier ways to die, so I turned off all the hot water and turned up the cold. That stopped my tears in a hurry. Gasping, I shut it off, scurried out of the shower stall, wrapped myself in three bath towels and stood trembling in front of the full-length mirror. Between my yellow shower cap and the top of an orange towel my red eyes looked out at me. I was a picture. By Jackson Pollock. I tore off the cap and brushed my hair. The flooding tide was carrying me to California. Mike. That no-good rat had gone home to his wife. . . . What was I *thinking?* But I needed him. I needed somebody around who *liked* me! And he wouldn't be back until after the first of January.

I went to the phone and called Vicki.

"I have to talk to you. Can we have a cup of coffee somewhere? The drugstore?"

"What's the matter now, nutty?"

"I'm soaking wet with towels around me. Can we?"

"Oi! Well, let's see, I have about six house calls, I have to be at the hospital by two-thirty . . . oh listen, do you happen to own a long rope of decent pearls? I'm going to a formal thing next week, can you believe it? I got this slinky black dress with the long white gloves, you'll die! So I need pearls, but all I have is a choker and that's no good for this dress, and you know me, I hate to spring for fifteen dollars for pearls just for one night. . . ."

(My life is falling apart and she's worrying about pearls.) I said I'd bring whatever I had to the drugstore, and she said okay, one o'clock.

When I got there she was already at the counter, her little black bag on the seat beside her, saving it for me, and she was going through her standard two-minute flirtation with the counterman while deciding between a bacon-burger and a cheese-burger. I hoped she wouldn't get cheese. She did. I sat down and ordered coffee. Ordinarily I could never sit at this counter without eating something—the combined aromas of sizzling hamburger, fresh rolls, strong coffee and big dishes of pickles and Bermuda onions on the counter would drive me crazy. Today they only made me ill.

"Coffee *seul?*" Vicki said. "Have a little nourishment."

I shook my head, took the assorted pearls from my bag and plunked them down on the counter.

"Ah!" she said, as though they were real, "magnifique!" And she tried them on, one after another, asking the counterman, the waitress, the pharmacist, the delivery boy, two old ladies eating English muffins, and an itinerant truck driver, which did they think would look better with a slinky black formal.

While I became increasingly depressed, the counterman put her food and my coffee in front of us, she decided to take the pearls home and try them on with her dress, wrapped them carefully in a paper napkin and put them in her doctor bag, and abruptly turned her attention to me.

"So, crazy?" she said, piling mustard, ketchup, pickles and onion on her hamburger, "what's bothering you now?"

I stared tensely into my coffee cup.

"I think," I murmured, "I'm going to leave Alex."

"Ohforgodsake!" she said. "What happened?"

I spent the next ten minutes unfolding the story of the awful metamorphosis, the fairy tale in reverse, the prince who changed into a beast.

She put on her calm face.

"Most men," she said, "don't like being married to competitive women."

"Competitive!" I choked.

"Well, let's face it, we do compete," she said. "We're right in there doing everything they're doing."

"But . . . but . . ." I looked at her helplessly, beseeching logic, justice, all those things that were just not pertinent, "But why is it *us* who are competitive? Why not *them*? I mean if you were like from Mars or something and you didn't know the rules down here, you could just as easily say women don't like being married to competitive *men*. Couldn't you? I mean who's competing with whom? I mean shouldn't everybody have a fair shake, regardless of how long their hair is? And besides, what *difference* does it make to them? What are we taking *away* from them? What . . ." I looked wildly around the drugstore as though maybe they might have the answer for sale somewhere.

"It's only natural," she said, "for a guy to get upset when he's used to one way of life and he suddenly has to adjust to another. Men aren't very adaptable. Have a little patience."

"Ah, Vicki, don't feed me sugar pills. The truth is . . . the truth is *he doesn't care if I'm happy or not, as long as he is!*"

"Sarah Bernhardt! Please!"

"It's the truth!"

"Have you talked this over with him?"

"Talk—!" I laughed bitterly, "Oh, boy! Ooooh, boy! You don't understand. He . . . I can't even . . ." I threw up my hands. How could I tell her? If anybody told *me* a man could consistently look at a red flag and call it a white handkerchief, I'd start thinking a lot of peculiar things too.

"Talk to him," Vicki insisted.

"I have."

"Talk to him again."

"I have."

She lit a cigarette and looked at me over the flame. "Is there somebody else?"

Immediately I thought of Mike.

"Of course not!"

"That's too bad. It might be a good idea if you got close to somebody else for a while. That sometimes clears up a lot of things."

"How could a thing like *that* clear up a thing like *this*?"

"You wouldn't believe me if I told you. Anyway—don't leave Alex until you've tried it."

"That's some prescription!"

"I'm unorthodox."

The counterman came over to collect and she went into her usual routine.

"How much for this measly little hamburger, my friend? *What*? Scandalous! My congressman will hear about this. There will be legislation passed. A price ceiling on hamburgers . . ."

And so, to the accompaniment of high-pitched giggles and drugstore badinage, we left, Vicki to ride off to the hospital, me to sit moodily in my car and stare with unseeing eyes at a sign in the window of the real-estate office announcing the availability of "Happy Homes."

Get close to somebody else for a while!

Was she kidding?

It didn't occur to me then, that from the very beginning, each time I had consulted Vicki, it was with an unacknowledged sense that she would tell me exactly what I wanted to hear.

It *did* occur to me, though—*had* occurred to me for some time—that a brief public embrace in Grand Central station was not Mike Garnett's idea of the high point of a relationship. And it didn't seem to me that a man of his virility would give a lady a gold cigarette case as an indication he was content merely to look upon her. And I wasn't at all sure that if, as, and when the moment of truth arrived, I would find that truth incompatible with my ideas of right and wrong.

Especially since my ideas of right and wrong—and truth—were changing every day.

It had also occurred to me that Mike Garnett didn't seem to resent being married to a "competitive woman." He respected his woman. He admired her talent. He was proud of her. *He* obviously had no need to prop up his faltering ego with a subservient female. He was above the convenient little social conventions that gave each man one roost to rule. His roost was the world, and there were no rulers in it, only other people. He made no obeisance and demanded none. He was willing to stand or fall on the strength of what he was. *He* asked no unfair advantage!

I wondered briefly how it would be to be married to Mike Garnett. Somehow I couldn't imagine it. When I tried to visualize a domestic atmosphere and put him into it, the atmosphere immediately began to shift and change, and in two seconds would dissolve from a back yard at high noon to a mountain lodge at midnight, from a hot kitchen smelling of roast beef to a hot strip of sand smelling of passionflowers. Also, whenever I put myself into these visions with him, I kept losing all my clothes.

Finally I turned the key and started the car for home, opening the window to the cold air, which I seemed to need.

Very soon it would be the first of January.

25

ADULTERY IS, of course, something that happens to *other* people. Like earthquakes, floods, forest fires, or finding yourself with a smoking gun in your hand and a corpse on the floor. To other people, not to you.

Not that you don't *toy* with the idea from time to time. (And let her throw the first stone who hasn't paused while trying to fit a new dust bag into the vacuum cleaner, and closed her eyes, and wished herself out of those dungarees and into a Traina Norell, with nocturnal blue on her eyelids, Je Reviens on her ear lobes, moving—barely moving—on some dimly lit dance floor, glued to the chest of some muscular stranger who murmurs against her burning cheek, "Let's get out of here . . . *now*.")

If this kind of day dreaming seldom gets translated into action it's because we all suspect there is a great big difference between vacuum-cleaner fantasies and the real thing. Fantasies, after all, have one big advantage—they can make lightning transitions: zoom! you're on the dance floor, zoom! you're on the hotel bed. No going out in the rain, no putting on your plastic boots, and getting your hair messed up in the wind, and not being able to get a cab, and wondering who, if anybody, is going to deprive the next generation of a possibly interesting mixture of genes. All that messy stuff is taken care of off-camera.

I sometimes think the main trouble with life is that there's no off-camera.

Anyway, there'd never been any question in my mind that fantasies definitely have the edge, and that anybody with half a brain would stick to fantasies.

Somewhere in the course of the next few weeks I lost that half a brain. Everything that happened in those weeks seemed deliberately designed to make me lose it.

In the first place, when Mike got back from California there was a hint of thunder in his voice, a glint of lightning in his eye, storm signals radiated from an ominously still and brooding center within him, and when I asked him what was wrong, he said, quietly, "It's Jean," and would say no more. For some crazy reason a man who broods about his wife has always held a fatal fascination for me.

In the second place he got very busy, first with casting, and then with rehearsals, and I didn't get to see very much of him, which made me want to see more of him.

In the third place there was this blond actress he got to play the part of Diana.

The minute I saw her, one of the great hatreds of all time was born.

It was in Wingate's office, whence Norman and I had been summoned to hear her read the part. She was sitting on Wingate's desk (on *Wingate's desk!*), leaning over it and laughing into Wingate's face, and Wingate was giggling and blushing like something out of Booth Tarkington. She was one of those pastel girls, the kind who look so sleek, tidy, and unmarked it's hard to believe they've been alive for more than two hours. She was the kind who could come in out of a tornado with every hair in place, who could crawl out of a mine shaft without a smudge on her, who could cross a desert on foot and not perspire enough to wrinkle her dress, who could go through six divorces and twenty children and never have a mark to show for it.

She had so many eyelashes she could have opened an eyelash store, and she was wearing some kind of Wedgwood-blue thing that managed to combine the wholesome outdoorsy American look of a Winston cigarette ad with the suggestion that for anybody with enough influence the Wedgwood blue would come off in a trice. But it was all very classy, like she was vulgar by appointment only.

And Mike Garnett was standing there grinning and casually flicking his eyes, from time to time, at her carefully crossed legs.

Now, if ever, was the time to quit.

But masochism is not a habit you can kick whenever you feel like it, so I just sat down in a corner with a murderous little smile while worms gnawed at my vitals.

She read the part. I thought she was dreadful. Norman was so busy with the eyelashes, I don't think he heard her. The other two were wrapped up before she even began. So she was in.

As we were leaving she took a step toward me, script in a

＊ 249

long white hand that had obviously never held anything grimier than the stem of a wineglass.

"I think it's marvelous," she said, all pearly white teeth and wispy ersatz friendliness.

"Drop dead!" I said (to myself).

"Mmm," I said to her, and smiled while maliciously grinding out my cigarette as though it were her head, and marched stiffly to the door. The last thing I heard, as Norman followed me out, was Mike's husky voice.

"What's the story with that musical?" he was murmuring at her. "Is Logan really sewed up?"

"Oh, you know Josh." She laughed, softly, as one initiate to another, and I thought to myself, "There's your answer, Brooks Atkinson, *that's* what happened to the American theater!"

Her name was Betsi Rawlins.

Norman and I went back to our hole in the wall. We were still working on those thirteen outlines. I felt rotten. I stared at the typewriter and all I saw were Betsi Rawlins' turquoise eyes making tracks all over Mike Garnett. While I was thus constructively employed, Norman paced briskly around the room working out loud on the outline and privately, I thought, planning sixteen ways of getting those turquoise eyes into some motel.

But I underestimated Norman.

"Listen, that broad—" he said, from behind his cigar smoke, "you think she's really okay? I know she's beautiful and all that crap, but does she understand comedy? What do you think?"

I smiled at Norman. I smiled at him with all my heart.

"Don't ask me," I said, "I rule myself out on grounds I want to murder her."

"Jealousy!" he groaned, "the American way of life! I'm worried about our future, you're worried about her phony boobs."

"Do you think they *are*?" I said, ecstatic.

"Psychologically they're phony. But what isn't? Well—we'll see what happens. Call the delicatessen. You want a coke or something? Get me a cream soda. Christ almighty, in Paris

∗ 250

people are sitting by the Georges Cinq sipping *apéritifs*. In Rome they're lounging in front of Doney's, guzzling vermouth. What did I do wrong?"

I called the delicatessen and felt a little better. But a few days later we took an hour off and went to the studio to watch a rehearsal, and my blood turned to vinegar all over again.

There she was in pale yellow cashmere slacks and a loose white cashmere shirt, the price of which could have fed and housed an average family for a couple of years, and she was cutely spread-eagled in a chair, her head tilted girlishly to one side, gazing up seriously into Mike's face as he hung over her, one hand on each arm of her chair.

That seems to be his favorite position, I thought to myself, pinning down females.

Wingate was there, and he came over to us and began some annoying conversation with Norman while I strained like mad to hear what Mike was saying to Butterball three feet away. I caught disconnected phrases.

"... Not Chekhov, you know. ... Lift it up. ... Get an image of ... or maybe Jean Arthur ... but pace yourself ... want you ... between silk sheets. ..."

Want you ... between silk sheets? What silk sheets? There were no silk sheets in the script! What did silk sheets have to do with anything? What was going to happen between silk sheets? With whom? Where? When?

Ice began to form in my veins, freezing the vinegar in my blood and turning me into a living bucket of sour ice cubes.

Then Mike turned around, saw us, and came over with a perfectly innocent grin of welcome.

"I think the fountain scene is playing better now," Wingate told him.

"*I* don't," said Norman.

"It's all timing," Mike said. "It'll take a while."

Suddenly I felt his hand slip into mine, and squeeze it.

"My *God!*" I said, and everybody turned to look at me.

"I'll be right back," I choked, and made for the door.

What was going on with this man? What was going on with me? Who was he, anyway? What did he want? *Whom* did he want? *Did* he want? What did *I* care? *Why* did I care? *Did* I care?

I raced down the hall. When in doubt, go to the ladies' room.

I went through a door into a whiteness smelling partly antiseptic, partly Revlon Hair Spray. I stood looking down into a washstand, quivering. The door opened again and a girl entered, moving carefully so as not to disturb the two acres of hair piled on top of her head. Another girl followed her in. She had the same two acres, but sideways.

"Sooo," the second girl said to the first girl, and I had a feeling she was continuing a conversation that had been going on between them, from one ladies' room to another, for years and years.

"Yeah?" prompted the first girl, gingerly touching her mountain of hair with a comb.

"So the true fact is, it happens to be a four-carat diamond."

"So did you tell her?"

"So I told her," said the second girl, examining herself in the mirror through half-closed eyes, "I said, 'Not that appearances make any difference to me, after all I'm marrying the man, not the diamond. . . .'"

"Good for you."

"But it hurts, you know, to have a person go around behind your back and make remarks about your ring like that. . . ."

"She always had a small character."

"You can say that again. Soo . . ." she bent forward into the mirror, applying another layer of mascara to the seven or eight already on her lashes, "I said to her . . ." Now the other eye. Slowly, carefully. I waited with bated breath to find out what she'd said to her. She stepped back and surveyed the effect. "I said to her, 'Mona, I only hope you get a ring *half* as valuable when your turn comes. *If* it ever does!'"

The first girl broke into a high, shrill sound meant to be laughter and they both shambled out, leaving me feeling that I had somehow stumbled into a foreign country.

I looked at my face in the mirror. It looked like a nice, basically sensible face. Decent. Honorable. Fairly intelligent.

How could I be such a nut? How could I, wife of one, mother of two, have come to this pretty pass? How could I, ordinary, average, run-of-the-mill Ruthie, luncher at Schrafft's, weeper at weddings, high-credit-rater at Bloomingdale's, signer of petitions for state aid to education, standard middle-class home-owner with two dogwood trees—how could I be standing here shaking with wanton desire and jealousy over a man who not only squeezed my hand while simultaneously making a pitch for a blonde but was also married to a third party and on top of everything lived in California?

"What are you, crazy?" I asked myself, "There are about seventeen triangles here!"

I washed my face and put on fresh makeup.

To hell with him, I thought. If there's anything I can't stand it's an indiscriminate man. I can understand him being attracted to a lot of different women, but my God, where's his *taste*? If he only sees in me what he sees in her, then what is he? A goat? What do I need with a goat?

I went back into the studio and there she was, both arms around his neck, laughing and whimpering about some mistake she'd made, and I immediately looked around for a weapon with which to kill her. Then I remembered I was above it all, and sat down.

"She's no good," said Norman.

"That's a nice understatement," I said.

He looked worried. "You mean it? I don't trust my own judgment any more. I think she's blowing the whole thing. If you think so too, we'd better do something about it."

"Oh," I said, realizing he was talking about her *acting*, "I don't know. Maybe it's too early to tell." I was suddenly afraid

✳ 253

to say any more. How did I know if her acting was good or bad? All I saw when I watched her was red. I sat through the rest of the rehearsal trying very hard to be objective and professional, but it was tough going.

If Betsi Rawlins had been a deliberate tactic in a complex strategy of seduction, Mike Garnett could not have hit on a better one. Just as the stiletto edge of my jealousy was beginning to blunt and my wantonness beginning to flag, under the suspicion that I was just one in a herd of female goats, Mike did an about-face. Presto! He stopped being nice to her.

He spoke to her sharply, called her by her last name, lost patience when she fluffed a line. I couldn't believe it.

"What's going on?" I said to Norman.

"Manipulation," he said. "You know—director's technique. First he's nice, then he's mean. Like you train animals."

My heart jumped. Technique? Is that all it was? It had nothing to do with *her*? I looked desperately for confirmation, and the next day I got it.

Mike was ready to block the show for the cameras. The sets were finished, and as Norman and I walked in they were hauling pieces of wall and a staircase around, and making marks on the floor with chalk where a couch or a table would stand. Mike was striding around snapping out orders in a tense voice, and Betsi walked in, looking sulky, and said something to him, and he hollered at her and she ran off, crying.

Norman got nervous and trotted up to Mike.

"What happened? What's the matter?"

I ran after him in time to hear Mike saying, matter-of-factly: "Oh, these goddam actresses. She can't have her own hairdresser. Wouldn't you think they'd develop one brain by the time they reach her age? Don't worry, she'll be over it in five minutes. She's too stupid to remember anything longer than that." And he disappeared into the control room.

I left the earth. I soared, weightless, into a summer sky, like little Pascal in *The Red Balloon,* floating high above the rooftops in the wake of multicolored helium.

And at that very moment Mike threw the switch in the control room and snarled "Take five," and came out of the control room and without even looking at me, grabbed my hand and started down the corridor to the cafeteria. The master stroke.

If ever I doubted it, this convinced me; philanderers are born, not made. The swift, sure impulse that prompted this move came with equal instinctiveness, I'm certain, to Don Juan and Casanova. They also knew just when to cut out the gallantry and treat 'em rough.

He dropped me at a table, went to the counter, got two coffees, brought them to the table, sat down, leaned wearily back against the wall, and said quietly, "Stay in town and have dinner with me tonight."

Everything went dead. Like when a radio blows a tube. There's been all kinds of noise, music, news, voices, droning, a little static, and then, suddenly—nothing. That's what happened to me. Blankness. I'd blown a tube. I sat there, a dead radio. Finally he opened his eyes to see what was going on and when he saw me with my tube blown he leaned over the table, harpooned me with his eyes, and said, urgently, "Please." There was no mistaking the nature of the request.

Now everything came rushing back, too loud and too fast. I was unendurably excited, and frightened to death.

"Don't be silly I couldn't do that and anyway what would I tell them at home I wouldn't know what to say I mean how could I what do you mean dinner I'm not even dressed but I mean it's nice of you to ask me I'd love to but I can't but thanks anyway I mean you know what I mean oh Mike I wish you hadn't for God's sake listen to me I can't stop it's like a disease or something and I'm shaking all over I don't even know why it's ridiculous ha-ha-ha . . ."

And then I made the mistake of trying to lift my coffee cup.

✳ 255

It was quite a mess. By the time we finished mopping it up the "take five" was over and we had to go back to the studio.

On the way back he didn't drag me by the hand, but as we passed an empty telephone booth he suddenly stopped, grabbed my arm, and drew me into it. Have you ever been in a telephone booth with a man you were afraid you wanted to go to bed with? People have had strokes from less.

With every inch of him touching every inch of me, he held up a dime for me to see and said, "Call home."

I stared at the dime. I stared and I stared. Finally I looked at him and whispered, "It's a twenty-cent call."

For a few seconds he didn't move. Then he threw back his head and guffawed. Then he stopped laughing. Then he kissed me. It was nothing like that earth-shattering kiss at Grand Central. It was worse. Much, much worse.

He put another dime in my hand.

"Call," he said, and left me there.

I looked at the two dimes in my hand.

There was liberty, with wings on its head. In God We Trust. Nineteen forty-four. What did it all mean? Liberty . . . God . . . Nineteen forty-four?

"What am I *doing!*" I said. I skittered out of the phone booth. And stood there. And went in again. And out again. And in again. Finally I stood inside the telephone booth gazing at the little round disc in the middle of the dial while my whole life passed before my eyes.

Norman came out to find me.

"What are you doing?" he asked.

"Drowning."

Norman was in no mood for obscure personal references. He lit a fresh cigar from the end of another fresh cigar and said: "Come on, they're blocking that stinking fountain scene. We oughta watch it." And went away.

Slowly I followed him back to the studio and into the control room, and sat beside him watching the monitors. I could see absolutely nothing on those monitors. I know there must have been something going on because everybody else was watching them, but I couldn't see a thing. I couldn't even see Norman, who was right beside me, or the A.D. or the production assistant, or the sound man. There was only one body in that control room. One head, one face, one voice.

Suddenly I got up and stumbled out of the control room. The Life Force was calling. Something was calling. Maybe it was Tarzan. Who cared? I headed for the phone booth, digging nervously in my bag for the two dimes. I shut my mind to all qualms and questions, enough of that. There was nothing to fear but fear itself. And maybe detection. I'd simply call home and say I was staying in town for dinner. What was so wrong with that? *Men* did it every day. I was simply going to eat a meal in New York instead of at home. So what? Why should anyone narrow their eyes at that? What's so terrible about having dinner? So it *happens* to come from room service!

I stepped firmly into the booth, shut the door, deposited the money, pointed my finger at the dial, and stood transfixed.

What the hell was my phone number?

Oh, my God! Let's see . . . 2038? 3802? 0328? 7567? They *all* sounded right.

I dialed information and asked her for my number. She said I didn't have any.

"*What?*" I screamed. "Listen, this is me! I live there! I'm a mother! I have two children out there! There *has* to be a number!"

Hostile now, she asked me my name again, my street and number, my village, and the date of my last vaccination. Finally she admitted I might just possibly exist.

"I have a B-e-r-n-*A*-r-d," she said, as though I'd been spelling it with a Z.

I wrote the number in my book. You never know when amnesia will strike again. I dialed the number. There was a busy signal. I waited a few minutes, pacing the corridor in short,

* 2 5 7

nervous, jerky steps. Then I called again. Still busy. So *that's* how Hannah spent her afternoons! I marched back to the control room, tried to sit still for five minutes, then bolted for the phone booth again.

Somebody was in it! Smoking like a fiend, too. The door was open a crack. "I won't do it," I heard him say. "No I won't. Well, it's not in my contract. Well, you just ask the Guild about that. Yes, I went down to Brooks and they didn't have a thing. Not a thing, sweetie. Yes, in the whole goddam place. Well I can be just as bitchy as he can. Yes, well that's too bad. No, I won't. No. . . ."

Finally, just as I was about to throttle him, he came out.

The phone booth was solid cigarette smoke. I tried not to breathe, and dialed. *Busy!* For the next twenty minutes it continued to be busy. My nerves were slowly being shredded to bits. Something must be wrong. Hannah was probably on the phone with the doctor, the hospital, Alex, the fire department! The police! This was my punishment for even *thinking* of . . . then I remembered something. I remembered once walking into my bedroom just as Sooz was leaving, and discovering the receiver of the upstairs phone lying casually on the floor.

I dialed the operator, she checked, I was right. Nobody was talking on that line. I called Gloria Betz. (*Her* number I remembered.) I asked Gloria to tell Hannah the phone was off the hook. I waited another few minutes. By this time I could hardly remember why I was calling. But I called again.

At last. The phone was ringing!

And ringing . . . and ringing . . . and ringing . . . and nobody answered! Impossible! Where were they? I let it ring. Again. Again. Again.

My *God!* I raged. You can't even commit *adultery* in peace!

Then just as I was about to hang up, the phone was lifted at the other end and Hannah's cool, calm voice came over the wire.

"Yes? This is Bernard residence."

"Hannah! Where've you *been?*"

✳ 258

"Oh, we took a little walk."

I breathed deeply.

"The—uh—the phone was off the hook."

"Yes. Mrs. Betz told me."

"Uh-huh. Well. Uh. Is everything all right?"

"Yes. Fine."

"Good . . . Uh . . . Did that package come from Blooming-dale's?"

"No. No package."

"Oh. Well . . . uh . . . there's some . . . uh . . . some trouble here . . . uh . . . at the rehearsal. We . . . uh . . . we have to change the script and . . . uh . . . so I'll be working late and . . . uh . . . I won't be home for dinner so . . . uh . . . tell Mr. Bernard and . . ." I ran out of words.

"Yes? Tell Mr. Bernard—?"

"That's all."

"And you will be home what time?"

None of your business, nosey.

"I don't know, Hannah. It depends. I mean . . . well . . . I don't know."

"I see."

Oh, you do, do you?

"So . . . uh . . . tell the children I'll see them in the morning. I have to go now. Goodbye."

I hung up, feeling depressed. The whole tone of the conversation had been wrong. It just hadn't struck the proper note of sophisticated abandon. Somehow the whole thing seemed so . . . *pedestrian*. I slunk back to the control room and avoided looking at Mike. Suddenly I didn't want to see him. I didn't even want to be near him. I concentrated on the monitors. The show looked terrible. I felt the beginning of a headache. My stomach wasn't exactly in tip-top condition either. And my throat was a little sore. Maybe if I worked on it, by six o'clock I'd be sick and *have* to go home. But it didn't work out that way.

At six o'clock Mike called it a day and Norman stood up,

adjusted his jacket, his tie, and his handkerchief, said, "Come on," to me, and started out of the control room.

Good God, I'd forgotten about Norman! We always left to-gether so that he could tell me how lousy the show was and how it would never be sold.

"Norman—" I called after him, "you—you go on ahead. I want to comb my hair and—uh—"

"Well, hurry up. I'll wait at the front door."

"Well—it might take a while. I . . . I have to make a phone call too."

I felt my face growing hot. Was it really *worth* all this?

"Okay, make it fast. I'll be in the cafeteria."

"Norman—!"

Norman what? Norman, please don't wait for me, I have an assignation? Anyway he was gone. I had visions of him sitting in that cafeteria hour after hour, the lights in the building going out one by one, a weary attendant behind the counter finally saying, "Hey, Mac, it's one A.M., we're closing up now," and Norman objecting, "You can't close this building! There's a woman in here somewhere!"

Through the glass panel I could see Mike out on the floor talking to one of the technicians. I left the control room and crossed the floor to him, and when the technicians walked away I told him about Norman. He laughed and called over the graphic-arts boy and told him to find Norman in the cafeteria and tell him I'd had to leave in a hurry. Then he took my hand and we ran out of the building and down the street.

At the corner, waiting for the light to change, he gave me a quick, uncertain smile, then looked up at a billboard and said, casually, "I'm dirty as hell. I've got to wash up and change my shirt. Let's grab a cab over to my hotel."

Why is it that when you get involved in something like this, everything that happens is a cliché? I crossed the cliché hotel lobby in a cliché nightmare, Mike went to the cliché desk and collected his cliché mail which included a cliché letter from his cliché wife. There was the cliché silence in the cliché elevator, the cliché door, the cliché key. . . .

And there it was, the supreme cliché. That big square bed.

Not being a stolid, phlegmatic type in any case, it was all I could do to keep my teeth from chattering.

Mike, however, proving once again that there's no substitute for experience, immediately got two glasses from the bathroom, poured a little good scotch into each of them from a bottle on the dresser, made me drink mine straight, and in a few minutes the machinery began to slow down.

He stripped off his shirt and went into the bathroom to wash, while I perched on the edge of a chair by the window (with an eye to what?).

"Where would you like to eat?" he called, still playing the game.

"Oh," I croaked, "anywhere."

"Twenty-One?"

I laughed, a little hysterically.

"Why not?" he said, coming into the room rubbing himself with a towel.

"Oh, please," I quavered, "Me? Like this?"

"Yes, you. Like that."

He draped the towel around his neck, sat on the edge of the bed, leaning forward, his forearms on his thighs, sending terrible messages with his eyes across the few feet of air that separated us.

Brace yourself, lady, I thought, here it comes. If Vicki was right, this should clear up a lot of things.

"You," he said, softly, and gestured with his head for me to come to him.

I tried to move but I seemed to be rooted. A great big oak from a little acorn had grown, and was taking root in that chair. And I knew why. The situation was suddenly too significant, I suddenly felt there was a very important answer waiting for me on that bed, and I wasn't sure I wanted to hear it.

"Ruth—" he said, and reached out his hand.

✳ 261

It was a strong hand, an honest hand. It was, after all, I reminded myself, the hand of a man who thought of me as a person. Limply I put my hand in his and let him pull me to the bed. He kissed me and I began to tremble, and felt weak and faint, and then, still kissing me, he pushed me gently backward onto the bed, and I felt weaker and fainter. . . .

And then something crackled under me.

I looked. There on the green chintz bedspread was a white envelope. The letter from his wife. Gingerly I picked it up and handed it to him. The storm clouds gathered in his eyes—the same thunder and lightning he'd come back with from California. He threw the letter to the floor and slowly pressed me down again.

"Hey, wait a minute," I said, pushing myself up. "Don't throw it on the floor."

"This is no time to be neat," he murmured, kissing my neck and pressing me down again.

I sat up.

"But it's your *wife*."

"You want me to read it right now?" he mumbled, nibbling my ear and pushing me down.

I sat up again.

"But not on the *floor!*" I protested.

He pulled me down. "Stay put, will you?" he said, and his hands began to travel, spreading fire. But I pushed myself up.

"*Please* pick it up."

"Ruth! I'm making love to you!"

"It *bothers* me on the floor!"

He swooped down, picked it up, threw it onto the dresser top and pinned me down again.

I sat up.

"Why do you *treat* it like that?"

"For Chrissake—!"

"*Why?*"

"It's just a *letter*. It's not even a *nice* letter. Believe me. I know." He began looking surreptitiously for a zipper.

"*How* do you know?"

"I know her letters."

"What do you mean?"

"Sweetheart, will you please shut up?"

I sat up, looking hurt.

Gently he trailed his fingers up my arm and began pushing me back down.

"I'm sorry," he murmured, and he kept trailing his fingers, hither and yon.

"I'm sorry too," I said, breathing unevenly, "I just . . . I just can't . . . I just can't understand your attitude!" I sat up again.

He sat up slowly, pushing his hand through his hair.

"What attitude?" he said, wearily.

"Toward that letter," I said, pointing.

"Okay," he said, patiently, "I'll explain my attitude. You see, I don't have to read that letter to know what's in it. Over the years I've had about two hundred letters just like that one. All her letters say the same thing. When I'm home she says it to me in person. When I'm away, she writes it. Over and over. 'I've got to get out of here,' she says. 'I can't stand being with little kids and dirty dishes twenty-four hours a day. It's driving me batty. I can't stand it in this house another minute, I'm going out of my mind. It's like being in prison. I want to get *out*. I want to *work*. I want to *act!*' . . . That's what I've been listening to for six years. That's what's in the letter. Okay?"

He reached for me but didn't quite make it

"Uh—what do you answer her?" I said.

"I say, 'Tell your troubles to the analyst, baby. I've got my own problems.'"

He reached for me again but I moved again.

"You mean . . . you don't care . . . that she's miserable?"

"She makes herself miserable."

"Could she go out and work, if she wanted to?"

✳ 2 6 3

"Honey, she's *got* a job. She's a wife. She's a mother. It's her job to stay home and take care of my house and my kids! *That's* her job. Until they're grown up, anyway."

"Oh," I said, and got off the bed.

"Hey," he said, softly, where you going?"

I didn't answer. He got off the bed.

"What are you doing?"

"Pulling up my zipper!"

"*Why?*"

"*Take your hands off me.*"

"Ruth . . . what happened? . . . What's the matter?"

I tugged at my zipper.

"You're not upset about . . .? Ruth, my marital problems have nothing to do with you and me."

Wrong, mister. One hundred per cent wrong.

The zipper was stuck!

"Ruth—"

"What did you *do* to it!" I wailed. "How can I go home with my *zipper* open!"

"You're not going home . . .?"

"*Fix* it!" I cried, "*Fix* it!"

He began tugging at the zipper.

Five minutes later I was on my way down in the elevator, alone, wearing my coat, underneath which the zipper of my dress was still open. It was completely broken now. So was everything else. My heart. My spirit. My faith.

I crossed the lobby with my head high, trying to look like a legitimate hotel guest, preferably a visiting horticulturist in British tweeds, under whose coat all zippers were tidily fastened.

When I reached the street I suddenly realized I had nowhere to go. Home was out. The way I was feeling it was beyond my powers of fabrication to explain why I was arriving for dinner when I'd just finished concocting a business crisis that was so urgent I couldn't possibly be home for dinner.

What to do? I could take a crosstown bus to the East River

and drown myself. Or wait . . . why a bus? For my last ride I could certainly splurge and take a taxi. But then, how did I know I'd drown? Maybe that treacherous primitive urge to survive would take over at the last minute and make me swim, and maybe even yell for help, and some couple necking on the shore would hear me, and I'd be pulled out, and how would I explain that? About the only good being hauled out of the East River would do, would be to overshadow the broken zipper and avoid the necessity of explaining *that*.

I could call Deedee. She'd invite me to dinner. And I could pin myself together at her place.

But no. For the rest of my life I'd have to worry every time we saw them that she would make some inadvertent remark about the night I'd come to her house for dinner with my zipper open. I could think of a million topics that might lead to such a revelation.

Veal parmigiana.

"I wish I could make decent veal parmigiana. With me it always comes out like a big piece of leather with a little piece of leather on top. Oh, *you* remember, Ruthie—I made it the night you came over with the broken zip—"

Winter.

"God, how I hate winter. It takes two hours to get those kids dressed before you can get out the front door. Those snowsuits! And the zippers always get stuck. God how I hate zippers. Remember, Ruthie, when your—"

Huntley and Brinkley.

"We used to watch them religiously and then one night the TV set went kaflooie and somehow we never got around to fixing it, and you know something, it was a big relief not to have to watch them any more. Of course, I was sorry we didn't have the set when Ruthie's show finally went on, especially after all the trouble she had. Remember, Ruthie, when you were working on the pilot and one night you came over and your zipper—"

No. No Deedee.

By this time I had walked six blocks and I found myself standing in front of a coffee shop. There was nobody in it, but it looked clean enough. I walked in, sat down in a booth, and ordered myself an elegant dinner of griddle cakes and bacon. The waitress was solicitous, smiling at me gently, indicating that she too knew what it was to live alone, facing endless solitary dinners. I wished she'd go flip her griddle cakes or something.

Well, Vicki, I thought, this has certainly cleared things up. One thing, anyway. Yes indeed. One thing is very clear. There is no fair play and probably never has been. They all live by the same credo, from Kubla Khan to Ali Khan: there's only one kind of wife who has any human rights—somebody else's.

I felt very tired. Not tired as in having put in a long day's work. Not tired as after shoveling snow off the driveway or mowing the lawn or having six people for dinner. I was tired in my spirit, in my brain, in my eyes and ears and nose. I didn't want to think any more, see any more, hear any more, smell or taste or feel any more. I'd had it with all the innumerable sensitive parts of me. A clod, I wanted to be. A vegetable. A potato, with its head in the ground.

Why bother trying to be a person? I'd given up once before, and I'd only gone back to work—I realized now—because of Mike. Because as long as there was a man somewhere who thought of me as a person, I had hope that Alex might get around to it too. Now I knew that Mike and Alex were one and the same—they both put on a good show until you were married to them. Neither of them wanted women to be people. Nobody wanted women to be people. Even some women didn't want it. A wife mustn't grow, mustn't change. It upsets the applecart. A wife has to be the constant—solid, earthbound—the launching pad from which the husband can take off and go into orbit.

And what happens to the launching pad that wants to be a rocket?

Tough luck, little launching pad. That's all. Tough luck.

Eventually I took the train home.

✳ 266

When I walked into the house Alex was at the dining-room table working away on some contract.

"What happened?" he asked, preoccupied.

"I'll tell you as soon as I come down," I said. "I have a wild headache, let me get some aspirin."

I went upstairs without taking off my coat, slipped out of my mangled clothes and into a bathrobe, and went back down. I looked at Alex bent over the table, puffing away on his pipe, and beyond him, stretching into the distance, I saw a million Alexes, a million Mikes, like a long parade of overgrown Boy Scouts, all, manfully and with patronizing smiles, helping old ladies across the street in the opposite direction from where they wanted to go.

Unaccountably, I felt a surge of deep affection for all of them; for Alex, for Mike, for Boy Scouts everywhere. They were, finally, so helpless, thrashing around in their inherited cages. Like me. Like everyone. I walked up behind Alex, put my hands on his shoulders and my cheek on his head.

"So what happened?" he said, looking up from his papers.

"Well," I said, "this actor collapsed in the middle of re-hearsal. Peritonitis. So they took him to the hospital, and Wingate called up an agent who sent us another actor, only this one is very tall and the other one was very short, and there were a lot of jokes in the script that weren't appropriate, so we had to sit down on the spot and figure out a whole new batch of . . ."

26 THE NEXT MORNING as I was dressing Norman called.

"You know what they're doing to us, don't you? They're mur-dering us," he said. "That girl is murdering us. The scene at the fountain is like something from Eva Le Gallienne. Don't come to the office. I'll meet you at the studio."

When I walked into the studio they were already huddled in a corner, Norman, Wingate, and Mike, with stubborn red faces. It was like another Geneva. I walked over, not feeling very self-conscious about the night before, feeling, in fact, very empty and indifferent.

"What do you *expect* her to do with those lines?" Mike was saying. "There's nothing *there*. She can't give it something it hasn't got!"

"Crap!" Norman said. "She's *acting*. She's acting all over the goddam place! Who the hell wants her to act? Let her be funny!"

"Are you aware," said Wingate, "that we only have this studio until four o'clock? That there are technicians standing around here at hundreds of dollars an hour?"

"Oh, let's not keep the goddam *technicians* waiting," said Norman. "Hell, no. Let's put any old crap on tape. . . ."

"I think we've had enough of your solecism, Norman . . ."

Solecism, for chrissake!

"All right," said Mike, "I'll run the scene and *you* tell me what's wrong. *You* show me how to make it funny!"

He ran the scene. I watched it, literally, for the first time. I had never seen it before; all I'd ever seen was a sexy blond louse. Now I could see much more than that. I could see a sexy blond lousy actress, with absolutely no sense of humor.

"She's ruining the scene," I said, when the four of us reconvened in the corner. "I think maybe she's wrong for the part."

"*Now* she says it!" Norman growled. "Where were you last week?"

Mike turned away. Wingate went white and cracked his knuckles.

"Technicians . . ." he murmured.

"You saw it, Harry. We gotta get another girl. Somebody like Ellen Carl."

Mike laughed nastily. "Now there's a beauty."

"She's *funny*," said Norman.

"Are you absolutely certain?" said Wingate to me. I was his last hope; he was appealing to me to save the project. I didn't really care one way or the other, but I owed it to Norman to tell the truth.

"She's all wrong," I said flatly. "She's so wrong it's unbelievable."

Mike walked away. Let him walk. Let them all walk. Who cared, anyway? Suddenly the whole thing seemed trivial to the point of foolishness. All this fuss about a stupid television show. All this money. All these people standing around. Networks, offices, vice-presidents, studios, cameras . . . for what? Twenty-seven minutes of escapist humor. I lit a cigarette, profoundly disinterested in everything but the state of my nails.

Within half an hour the whole house of cards came tumbling down. The company was dismissed. The technicians disappeared. Mike had stomped out. Norman had told Wingate we not only needed a new girl, we needed a new director. Wingate, looking like polysyllabic death, said we could consider the project suspended until further notice, and rushed back to his office to do whatever producers do when they suspend projects. Norman said the next time I saw him he would be working for the government, as a mailman. And that afternoon there was a paragraph in the television section of the *Herald Tribune* saying that Harrison Wingate was producing the pilot film of a wildly funny situation comedy series called "Diana's House," starring Betsi Rawlins, written by Norman Spain and Ruth Bernard, and directed by Mike Garnett.

I cut it out of the paper and kept it, for a souvenir.

I couldn't help wondering how much of what happened that day was the result of what happened the night before. If I hadn't seen what I'd seen in Mike's hotel room, would I have had the objectivity to see what I saw in the studio the next day? When you begin to strip away veils isn't it self-perpetuating or something? Or wouldn't I, in another mood, have been more inclined

✳ 269

to preserve the project rather than destroy it? Didn't my feeling that my struggle to be a person was hopeless, have something to do with my uncompromising "no" on Betsi Rawlins?

Anyway, a week later, when it was definite that the project was on the shelf for a good long time, I gave Hannah a letter of recommendation which she packed into her suitcase with her sensible clothes, and she left, and I was back home, and I didn't care. Even if Wingate revived the project eventually, it would have to get along without me. I was through fighting.

It was strange to be back at home, with no trains to catch, no tight schedule to keep, no running around, no noise, no motion, no typewriter, no Norman. For the first few days after Hannah left, I wandered around the quiet house like a stranger, not knowing exactly what to do next. All those things that had been so automatic I now had to recall with effort. But soon enough it came back, and, naturally, I enjoyed it. There's nothing like novelty for making something essentially awful seem like a lot of fun.

It wasn't so bad, eating a decent roast chicken for a change. It was pretty nice, being able to hang the potholders where *I* wanted them. It was a pleasant change, to talk to Alex at night without worrying what the lady in the kitchen thought of our politics and our four-letter words. I mean domestic help is a great idea in a forty-room house where you just shut off a wing and all you hear is the distant discreet clinking of silver being polished.

Alex didn't say much about the change in the situation. He murmured a few conventional sympathetic words when I told him what had happened, but that was all. *Verbally* that was all. But mentally, emotionally, and physically he reacted like a rosebud to sunlight.

Peace, it's wonderful.

March seemed to blow in and out in a couple of hours, and suddenly it was April. April turns up regularly every year, but it always catches me off guard because I just have no faith in miracles. April again. And in the middle of it we had a hot spell and the whole world changed. It didn't take more than a week. The ground was suddenly covered with lush, new, moist green grass. The big, thick, matriarchal fruit trees burst into masses of delicate white blossoms. The huge graceful willows dripped with pale misty yellow-green lace. The mountain pinks quivered in the rock gardens. And everywhere along the roads, springing up beyond the hedges and bursting over the whitewashed split-rail fences, great wild clumps of forsythia exploded in a zillion golden flowers.

The birds came back. The robins and the bluejays and the cardinals. And in a couple of weeks the streets were lined with the pastel pinks of dogwoods and magnolias and the wine-colored flowering crab trees, and the lilacs, and then there was an azalea riot; bushes of pomegranate-red and apricot and watermelon pink. . . .

Who needs New York?

I drove to the supermarket every day, whether I needed to or not. It was only a mile and a half away, but it took me an hour to get there because I went by way of three different villages. I drove through the hills with the car windows open, breathing in the smells of warm earth and buds and grass, with the sun shining on my left elbow and the peaceful sounds of lawn mowers floating on the air, and the bright shapes of houses and trees and church spires clear-cut against an innocent blue sky. I went sailing blissfully along through red lights, swinging dreamily around corners without remembering to signal, singing . . .

"Oh, your daddy's rich . . . and your mommy's good-lookin' . . ."

And people came out of their houses. All that solitary cowering in the individual caves was over. Neighbors emerged onto their porches and patios and lawns, tilting thier faces to the sun, and smiling. When I took out the garbage cans in the morning, there would be Natalie walking down the road toward me with her youngest child, and she'd stop and tell me all about how her washing machine broke down. When I kneeled at my flower border rooting out the weeds, a horn would honk and there would be Vera in her beige-colored Chevy on her way to the village, and she'd tell me about the local real-estate man who ran off to Mexico with the wife of some guy he'd just sold a house to. As I wandered out to the road in midafternoon to watch for the school bus, I'd see Helen down the street crawling around on her lawn planting new bulbs and I'd go over and we'd discuss the latest rumors about the new school tax. It wasn't exactly the heady intellectual life of Big Sur, but it was warm, it was pastoral, it was companionship.

And one day when I was pruning the evergreens, Vicki's station wagon pulled into my driveway, the entire inside of it, except for the few inches where Vicki was hunched over the wheel, filled with an enormous apple tree, branches sticking out of the windows, roots dragging out of the open back, and it seemed that one of her patients had dug it up out of his own yard and dumped it on her lawn in an excess of gratitude, and she already had so many fruit trees she had to spend most of the summer spraying.

"All summer I spray fruit trees, all winter I spray sore throats. I've got spray fatigue," she said. "Please take this goddam—motherless apple tree and put it in the ground. If somebody doesn't plant it soon it'll die."

And we lugged the tree around to the back of the house, and then I baked some frozen pizza and we sat out on the porch and ate it and drank Welch's grape juice on the rocks.

And I said to Vicki, gesturing languidly at the green branches of trees bowing to us in the breeze, "What's so bad? I mean, really. It's nice country. It's a nice house. It's a nice porch. Nobody's bothering me. . . ."

"Everybody needs a vacation," said Vicki.

"This is not a vacation," I said, "this is it. No more rat race. I'm going to enjoy the little things. Every bloody little thing I'm going to enjoy. A leaf, a chair, a glass of grape juice. Life is too short. I'm not going to spend the rest of it fighting. I'm just going to sit back and relax and enjoy it."

"Good," she said.

I didn't like the way she said it. It was like when you were a kid and you told a grownup you had decided to become a great opera singer when you grew up, and the grownup said "Good." It had that same profound insincerity.

Big shot! I thought, as she drove off. Like she knows something I don't know!

And then it was time for Alex' two-week vacation, and we took a trip through New England with the kids and a Triple-A map. The kids hit each other a lot, and it rained most of the time, and we never found Klean-Kut Kottages where we had the reservations, but who cared? As long as somebody carted me around and didn't yell at me, I wasn't going to complain.

And then it was August. Ninety-five in the shade with the humidity two hundred per cent. If you sat still you dripped, if you moved you were a human waterfall. The Cardells were gone on vacation. And the Bookmans. And the Sands. Vicki vanished for the whole month. The place was a ghost town, deserted except for David and Sooz and three strange dirty little boys they picked up who kept trooping into the house every twenty minutes demanding ice water. I spent most of August stretched out by the air conditioner, reading and dozing, and getting up occasionally to serve ice water, and spending long hours with the children, annoying them with well-meaning stories and games. They played with me out of a sense of duty and wished I'd find somebody my own age. Day dragged after sodden day, and what difference did it make. Relax, be comfortable. Be passive and receptive and pleasant and the wheels will turn smoothly, and that's all that matters.

Gloria Betz had a nervous breakdown and was said to be in a hospital somewhere. I wondered about this for a while, but not really in depth.

The Sands and Cardells came back and we had a barbecue,

✳ 273

and Vera announced that she was going back to work in September, something to do with advertising for a trade paper. And I looked at her husband who was busy protesting that he firmly believed a woman should have some interest outside the home, and I wondered how long it would take *him* to find out what a stupendous liar he was.

I wandered through the days with a dustcloth in my hand. Occasionally I put some clothes in the washing machine. With an absolute minimum of interest I ordered groceries and made meals. I yawned a lot; that killed some time. And I slept. As the nights went by I went to bed earlier and earlier. It got so that I could barely make it through dinner.

One Saturday morning I went to the library to get some new books—easier to get than heroin—and when I got back Alex and the kids were washing the other car. I got out of my car with the books and some groceries I'd picked up.

"Hi!" I said, cheerfully.

There was a mad rush to ignore me. Nobody even said hello. But as I reached the front door Alex called out, "How about some lunch?" And David yelled, "I want frankfurters!" And "Me too!" yelled Me-too. And I went into the kitchen and immediately there was a scream from outside, and Sooz came staggering in. "My knee! My knee!" like Camille. And I took her up to the bathroom and washed and painted and Band-Aided her knee, and started back to the kitchen when David barged in, sopping wet. "I ran into Daddy's hose." And I yanked him into the bathroom and took off his clothes and dried his hair, and started back to the kitchen and Alex came in, starving. "Where's lunch?" And I sliced bread, tomatoes, cucumbers, carrots, opened a can of baked beans, tested the frankfurters, poured the milk, and in a few minutes they were all sitting around the table eating like maniacs.

"Mustard—" Alex said, between bites.

I got the mustard.

"More butter—"

✳ 274

I got the butter.

Nobody seemed to notice I had not joined the festive board. Nobody seemed to notice me, period. I had seen waitresses in restaurants get more personal attention than I got. Ugly ones, yet.

I leaned against the refrigerator and watched them, and, although classical literary allusions seldom, if ever, leap unbidden to my mind, one did then. Congreve. *The Way of the World.*

"I may by degrees dwindle into a wife."

I felt very sleepy. I went upstairs and took a nap.

And one evening just before Labor Day weekend I was carrying dessert from the kitchen to the dining room when the telephone rang and it was Norman, all the way from Westhampton. He'd spent the summer there with his family, with his friend Arnie as a house guest, and they had been working on an idea for another television show. He was full of jokes, his own, other people's. He'd seen just about everybody on the beach there, friends of his I'd met at his party, at lunches, Max the journalist, the A.D. who'd worked on the pilot, one of the actors, too, even Betsi Rawlins, who had asked about me (!).

(For a few minutes I was suddenly wide awake. Little tingling sensations galloped through my veins. What do you know, there was still a world going on out there!)

He'd run into Wingate the other day, on the beach. Wingate had a new girl and a new director in mind for the pilot. He wanted to talk to us about it, some time next week.

Just then Alex, waiting impatiently for his coffee, got up, annoyed, and went to get it himself.

"No," I said to Norman, and felt sleepy again. "No, I decided not to bang on the lid."

He didn't know what I was talking about.

"You said it yourself," I reminded him. "If they make a mistake and bury you alive, forget it. Stay dead. It's the only way to keep your friends."

✳ 275

Norman protested, but I told him no a few more times and finally we said goodbye.

"I'm sorry about the coffee," I said to Alex, stifling a yawn. "Is it hot enough? Let me get you some hot."

"It's hot enough. What do you want to do this weekend?"

"Oh, I don't know. Do we have to do something?" I stifled another yawn.

"No," said Alex, with an edge to his voice, "we don't *have* to do something. But it's a four-day weekend. . . ."

"Well . . ." I made an effort and took a sip of coffee. "I thought maybe we'd just laze around. . . ."

"I don't *want* to laze around. . . ."

"Oh. Okay, honey, whatever you like."

"What do you mean, whatever *I* like? You doing me a *favor?*" I blinked my eyes.

"No," I said, vaguely, "I just meant . . . sure . . . if you want to go somewhere, let's go somewhere." I made another effort, picked up the coffee cups, took them into the kitchen and started washing them.

"Where, for instance?" said Alex, from the dining room.

"Gee, I don't know. Anywhere is okay with me. Where do *you* want to go?"

"How about the lake?"

"That's a good idea." I yawned a big yawn.

"Thanks for the wild enthusiasm."

"Sorry . . . So sleepy these days."

"So I noticed." He strode into the living room and began filling his pipe, fiercely.

I followed him. "What should I pack? Sweaters, I guess. It could be cold at night."

"Never mind," he said, like a knife. "Forget it."

I blinked at him. What the hell was *this* all about?

"Forget what?"

"We won't go anywhere. We'll stay home and *laze around*."

✳ 276

He puffed furiously on his pipe. "You can sleep the whole god-dam weekend!"

"What did I do *now?*"

"Nothing! You do nothing! You're not even half-alive. You don't talk about anything, you don't think about anything, you don't react to anything, you don't have opinions about anything —you're nothing!"

He slammed out of the house and didn't come back for an hour, and when he did he wasn't speaking to me. He wasn't speaking to me the next day either, or the next.

Oh, *boy,* I thought, nuts to *this!*

I burst into Vicki's house. She was making linguine with clam sauce.

"What does he want from me *now,*" I yelled, "—blood? When is he going to be *satisfied?*"

"Taste this—" she said.

"*I'll* tell you when he'll be satisfied—never! That's when! It needs more garlic."

"Nobody's ever satisfied," she said, "until they've been dead a good week."

"Well that's just too goddam bad! Just too goddam bad! What am I supposed to do now? You can't win. You just can't win. You try to be a person and they hate you because you're not a cow. You try to be a cow and they hate you because you're not a person. How can you be a gay, charming, intellectual cow? How?"

"Taste it now."

"Better. Goddamit, what am I gonna do? This is just as bad as when I was working! He was mad then and he's mad now! I might as well be working! One way or the other he's going to be mad! Goddamit I might as well go back to work!"

"Why don't you?"

I looked at her, timidly.

"You think I should?"

"Nutty!" she said. "You *came* here so I should tell you to!"

It was October. The sky was cornflower-blue. I walked up and down the station platform waiting for the train, thinking how much sexier Alex had been lately. And how good he looked in those blue jeans when we were raking up the leaves. And how often we laughed, these days.

Of course it was only a matter of time. By next week, or next month, he'd be hating me again. Integration isn't easily won. But one thing is sure. By cows it's *never* won. Only by people.

I lifted my face to the sun. I felt very young and healthy. Things were going to happen today. And tomorrow. And the next day. Work, and people, and plans. I was full of energy. Back at the house David and Sooz, recently fretful under my bland, amiable listlessness, were sparkling again in response to my own sparkle, and Adelaide's cousin, the Jamaican princess, was installed in the kitchen, unpregnant. The baby girl was living nearby with her grandma.

I took a deep breath of October.

Suddenly Vera was there, on the platform, on her way to work.

"Guess what," she said, "we got a new editor yesterday and she says she knows you. Rita Marsh. She says you used to work for her husband, Simon."

I was still smiling when the train pulled in.